Books by Sabrina Jeffries:

Project Duchess
The Bachelor
Who Wants to Marry a Duke
Undercover Duke

Published by Kensington Publishing Corp.

Undercover
DUKE

SABRINA JEFFRIES

ZEBRA BOOKS
KENSINGTON PUBLISHING CORP.
www.kensingtonbooks.com

ZEBRA BOOKS are published by

Kensington Publishing Corp.
119 West 40th Street
New York, NY 10018

All Kensington titles, imprints, and distributed lines are available at special quantity discounts for bulk purchases for sales promotion, premiums, fund-raising, educational, or institutional use.

Special book excerpts or customized printings can also be created to fit specific needs. For details, write or phone the office of the Kensington Sales Manager: Attn.: Sales Department. Kensington Publishing Corp., 119 West 40th Street, New York, NY 10018. Phone: 1-800-221-2647.

Zebra and the Z logo Reg. U.S. Pat. & TM Off.

First Printing: June 2021
ISBN-13: 978-1-4201-4858-9
ISBN-10: 1-4201-4858-3

ISBN-13: 978-1-4201-4862-6 (eBook)
ISBN-10: 1-4201-4862-1 (eBook)

10 9 8 7 6 5 4 3 2 1

Printed in the United States of America

*To my late mom, I miss you
and wish you hadn't gone so soon.
Thanks for all the years of looking out for us and Dad.*

Lydia's Husbands

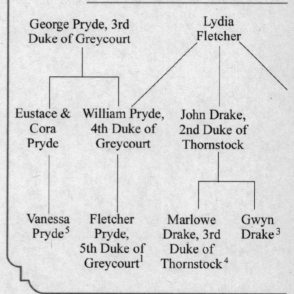

George Pryde, 3rd Duke of Greycourt — Lydia Fletcher

Eustace & Cora Pryde

William Pryde, 4th Duke of Greycourt

John Drake, 2nd Duke of Thornstock

Vanessa Pryde[5]

Fletcher Pryde, 5th Duke of Greycourt[1]

Marlowe Drake, 3rd Duke of Thornstock[4]

Gwyn Drake[3]

1 *Project Duchess*
2 *Seduction on a Snowy Night,*
   "A Perfect Match", w/ Cassandra
3 *The Bachelor*
4 *Who Wants to Marry a Duke,*
   w/ Olivia Norley
5 *Undercover Duke*

and Children

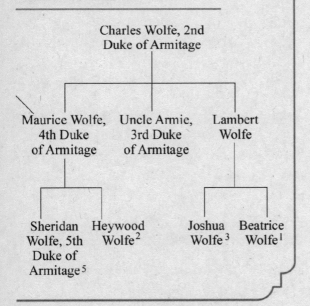

Charles Wolfe, 2nd
Duke of Armitage

Maurice Wolfe,
4th Duke
of Armitage

Uncle Armie,
3rd Duke
of Armitage

Lambert
Wolfe

Sheridan
Wolfe, 5th
Duke of
Armitage [5]

Heywood
Wolfe [2]

Joshua
Wolfe [3]

Beatrice
Wolfe [1]

LONDON SOCIETY TIMES

THE LAST DUKE STANDING

Dear readers,

I, your esteemed correspondent, cannot believe it. Not only has that randy devil, the Duke of Thornstock, actually married, but he chose Miss Olivia Norley as his bride! And this, after she refused him most soundly years ago. He must have reformed because Yours Truly knows full well Miss Norley would never have married him otherwise.

This means that his half brother, Sheridan Wolfe, the Duke of Armitage, is the only one of the dowager duchess's offspring not yet married. What a coup it will be for the young lady who snags him! Although the usual wagging tongues claim he must needs marry a fortune to shore up his estate, that will not matter to anyone with an eligible daughter. He's a duke, after all, and a young, handsome one at that, which is particularly rare. I daresay he will not be left unwed for long.

How delicious it will be to watch him hunt for his bride. Armitage is discreet where Thornstock was not, and he's more reclusive even than his other half brother, the Duke of Greycourt. So it will have to be a most intriguing lady to pierce his armor and seize the rare heart that surely beats beneath. We await the result with bated breath.

Chapter One

Armitage House, London
November 1809

"The Duke of Greycourt is here to see you, Your Grace."

Sheridan Wolfe, the Duke of Armitage, looked up from the list of horses in the stables of his family seat, Armitage Hall, to find his butler in the doorway. "Show him in."

Grey, his half brother, was supposed to be in Suffolk. Thank God that wasn't the case. Grey would be a welcome distraction from trying to decide which horses should be auctioned off. Sheridan didn't want to get rid of any of the truly superior mounts or prime goers. But the Armitage dukedom was being crushed by a mountain of debt, thanks to his late uncle's overspending and the fact that Sheridan's father . . .

A lump stuck in his throat. The fact that his father—Grey's stepfather—had died much too soon.

Sheridan shoved the list aside. Damn it, it had been a year already. Why did Father's death still haunt him so? Even Mother seemed to be handling it better than he was.

If not for Grey's arrival, he could take Juno out for a run in Hyde Park to get his mind off of it.

Perhaps later. The Thoroughbred mare had a knack for—

With a groan, he remembered that Juno no longer belonged to him. She'd been the first he'd had to sell to keep the estate afloat. He'd hated to do so—she was the best saddle mare in his late uncle's stables—but it was either sell her or one of the racing Thoroughbreds, and he could still get money out of those in stud fees and racing prizes, even if they didn't make good saddle horses.

What a depressing thought. He rose and walked over to the brandy decanter. He supposed midafternoon was early for spirits, but if he couldn't ride, then he needed a brandy and a pleasant chat with Grey. He poured himself a glass and was about to pour one for his half brother when the butler showed Grey in, and Sheridan's idea of a pleasant chat evaporated.

His brother looked as if he'd drunk one too many brandies already and was now about to cast up his accounts. Pale and agitated, Grey scanned the study of Sheridan's London manor as if expecting a footpad to leap out from behind a bookcase at any moment.

"Do you want anything?" Sheridan asked his brother, motioning to the butler to wait a moment. "Tea? Coffee?" He lifted the glass in his hand. "Brandy?"

"I've no time for that, I'm afraid."

Sheridan waved the butler off. As soon as the door closed, he asked, "What has happened? Is it Beatrice? Surely you're not in town for the play, not under the circumstances."

In a few hours the rest of the family would be attending

a charitable production of Konrad Juncker's *The Wild Adventures of a Foreign Gentleman Loose in London* at the Parthenon Theater. Although Sheridan barely knew the playwright, his other half brother, Thorn, had asked him to go because the charity was a cause near and dear to his wife's heart: Half Moon House, which helped women of all situations and stations get back on their feet.

Grey shook his head. "No, I came to fetch an accoucheur to attend Beatrice. Our local midwife says my wife may give birth sooner rather than later, and she is worried about complications. So I've rushed to London to find a physician to examine Beatrice, in case the midwife is right. The man awaits me in my carriage even as we speak."

Lifting an eyebrow, Sheridan said, "I would suspect you of having taken Beatrice to bed 'sooner rather than later,' but you've been married ten months, so this is hardly an early babe."

"No, indeed. And the midwife might be wrong, but I can't count on that. That's why I stopped here on my way out. I need a favor."

Sheridan cocked his head. "Sadly I have no skills in the area of bringing babies into this world, so—"

"Do you remember how we decided I should be the one to question Aunt Cora about those two house parties we suspected were attended by my father's killer?"

"I do indeed."

Their mother's five children had finally concluded that her thrice-widowed status had not been just a tragic confluence of events. Someone had murdered her husbands, including Maurice Wolfe, the father of Sheridan and his brother Heywood, and the previous holder of the title

Duke of Armitage. They suspected the person behind the murders was one of three women, all of whom had been at the house parties underway when the first two husbands had died. So Sheridan and his siblings were now engaged in a covert investigation, and had each taken assignments. Grey's was to question his aunt Cora, otherwise known as Lady Eustace, who was no relation to any of the rest of them.

Sheridan suddenly realized what the "favor" must be. "No. God, no. I am not doing that." Damn.

"You don't know what I'm going to ask," Grey said.

"I can guess. You want me to be the one to question Lady Eustace."

Grey sighed. "Yes, given the situation."

"You'll be back in town soon enough. It can wait until then, can't it?"

"I don't know. I honestly have no idea how long I shall have to be in the country."

Sheridan dragged in a heavy breath. "Yes, but why ask *me* to do it? I barely know her."

"The others don't know her at all," Grey pointed out. "But you at least are friendly with Vanessa, and that gives you an excuse."

Which was precisely why Sheridan didn't want to do it. Because questioning Lady Eustace meant being around her daughter, Miss Vanessa Pryde, who was too attractive for his sanity, with her raven curls and lush figure and vivacious smile.

"I've chatted with Vanessa a handful of times," Sheridan said. "That hardly makes me ideal for this."

"Ah, but my aunt and I hate each other. That hardly makes *me* ideal, since it's unlikely she'd tell me the truth."

It was a poorly kept secret in their family that Grey's uncle Eustace had badly mistreated Grey as a boy, hoping to force him to sign over several properties. That Grey's aunt Eustace had looked the other way while her husband had done so.

Sheridan sipped some of his brandy. "And why should your aunt tell *me* the truth?"

"Because you're an eligible duke. And her daughter is an eligible young lady. Not that I'm suggesting you should even pretend to court Vanessa, but her mother will certainly see the opportunity, and be more likely to let her guard down."

"I'm not so sure. Your aunt has always been cold to me, probably because I'm a *poor* eligible duke. She's looking for a wealthy man for Vanessa. And Vanessa will need one, to be honest. The chit is spoiled and impudent, a dangerous combination for a man who can't afford expensive gowns and furs and jewelry for his wife. I'm already barely treading water. A wife like Vanessa would drown me."

Grey narrowed his gaze. "Vanessa isn't so much spoiled as determined to get her own way."

"How is that different?"

"A spoiled girl has had everything handed to her, so she expects that to continue once she's married. Trust me, while Vanessa has been given certain advantages, she's also had to grow up in a turbulent household. Hence her determination not to let anyone ride roughshod over her."

"Still, marrying such a woman means having constant strife in one's marriage."

"Gwyn and Beatrice are both of that ilk, and so far Joshua and I are quite content. Indeed, I rather like being married to a spirited woman who knows what she wants."

"Good for you," Sheridan clipped out. "But you have pots of money to indulge her if you wish, and I don't. Nor does *your* wife have an absurd fixation on that damned poet Juncker."

"Ah, yes, Juncker." Grey stroked his chin. "I doubt that's anything more than a girlish infatuation."

"Trust me, I've heard her babble on about Juncker's 'brilliant' plays plenty of times. She once told me some nonsense about how Juncker wrote with the ferocity of a 'dark angel,' whatever that means. Frivolous chit has no idea about what sort of man she should marry."

"But *you* know, I take it," Grey said with an odd glint in his eye.

"I do, indeed. She needs a fellow who will curb her worst excesses, who will help her channel her youthful enthusiasm into more practical activities. Sadly, she has romantic notions that will only serve her ill, and those are leading her into wanting a man she thinks she can keep under her thumb, so she can spend her dowry as she pleases."

"You mean Juncker," Grey said.

"Who else? You know perfectly well she's been mooning after him for a couple of years at least."

"And that bothers you?"

The query caught Sheridan off guard. "Certainly not." When Grey smirked at him, Sheridan added with ill grace, "Juncker is welcome to her. She could do better perhaps, but she could also do a hell of a lot worse."

"You've convinced me," Grey said blandly. "Unless . . ."

"Unless what?"

"You're merely chafing at the fact that she thinks dukes

are arrogant and unfeeling, or some such rot. So she would never agree to marry *you*."

"Yes, you told me." More than once. Often enough to irritate him. "And I'm not looking for her to marry me."

"I suppose it's possible you could coax her into *liking* you, but beyond that . . ."

When Grey left the thought dangling, Sheridan gritted his teeth. "You've made your point."

Not that Sheridan had any intention of making Vanessa "like" him. She was not the right woman for him. He'd decided that long ago.

"Didn't you agree to fund Vanessa's dowry?" Sheridan added and swallowed more brandy. "You could just bully Lady Eustace into revealing her secrets by threatening to withhold the dowry unless your aunt comes clean."

"First of all, that only hurts Vanessa. Second, if my aunt is cornered, she'll just lie. Besides, all of this depends upon our pursuing our investigation while the killer still thinks she got away with it. That's why I haven't told Aunt Cora *or* Vanessa that we've determined my father died of arsenic. Which is another reason you should question my aunt. She won't suspect you."

"What about Sanforth?" Sheridan asked. "Originally we decided I was to ask questions in the town. What happened to *that* part of our plan to find the killer—or killers—of our fathers?"

"Heywood can manage the Sanforth investigation perfectly well."

That was probably true. Sheridan's younger brother, a retired Army colonel, had already made significant improvements to his own modest estate. Compared to that, asking questions of Sanforth's tiny populace would be an afternoon's entertainment.

"So you see," Grey went on, "there's no reason for you to even return to the country. As long as you're in town for the play this afternoon, you might as well pop into the box my aunt's brother has at the theater and see what you can find out. You can pretend you're there to chat with Vanessa."

"That's assuming they even attend the play," Sheridan said. "Charitable productions don't sound like things Lady Eustace would enjoy."

"Oh, they'll be there," Grey said. "Vanessa will make sure of it. It's Juncker's play, remember?"

"Right." He stared down into the shimmering liquor and bit back an oath. "Very well. I will endure Lady Eustace's suspicions to learn what I can." Which meant he'd also be enduring Vanessa's foolish gushing over Juncker.

His throat tightened. He didn't care. He *wouldn't* care.

"Thank you," Grey said. "Now if you don't mind . . ."

"I know. Beatrice is waiting for you at the estate, and you've got quite a long journey." He met his brother's anxious gaze and softened his tone. "Everything will be fine. The Wolfes come from hardy stock. Not to mention our mother. If she can bear five children to three husbands before the age of twenty-five, I'm sure my cousin can give you an heir without too much trouble."

"Or give me a girl. I don't care which. As long as Beatrice survives it, and the child is healthy . . ."

"Go." Sheridan could tell from Grey's distracted expression that the man's mind was already leaping forward to the moment he would reach his wife. "Go be with her. I won't disappoint you."

Sheridan knew firsthand the anguish love could cause, how deep it ran, how painful the knot it tied around one's throat. Helene hadn't meant to, but she'd made him wary of love.

That was precisely why he never intended to be in such a situation again. Just seeing Grey's agitation was more than enough to caution him. Love could chew a man up and spit him out faster than his Thoroughbreds could run. Sheridan already had plenty of things to worry about. He didn't intend to add a wife to that number.

Chapter Two

"Wait, girl," Vanessa's mother said as she stopped her daughter from entering the Pryde family box. "Your headpiece is crooked." She shoved a hat pin into Vanessa's fancy turban, skimming her scalp.

"Mama! That hurt!"

"It's not *my* fault it won't stay put. Bridget must have put on the trim unevenly. Serves you right for not buying a new turban."

Her mother always wanted her to buy new instead of remaking something. Unfortunately, the estate of Vanessa's late father didn't produce enough income—and the widow's portion for her mother never stretched far enough—for Vanessa to spend money recklessly. So Vanessa and her lady's maid, Bridget, were always practicing small economies to ensure she and Mama lived within their means.

Mama didn't see the point of that. First, she was incessantly trying to impress someone with how lofty they were. Second, she was pinning her hopes on Vanessa marrying well.

"It's not the trim, Mama," Vanessa grumbled. "The whole thing is lopsided from your fooling with it."

"I'm merely trying to fix it. You must look nice for the gentlemen."

Vanessa really only wanted to look nice for *one* gentleman, but he would probably ignore her as usual. If he did, she would have to give up hope of ever gaining his attention. So far, nothing seemed to have worked in that regard.

Uncle Noah Rayner, her favorite relation next to her cousin Grey, patted Vanessa's arm reassuringly. "You know your mother—always thinking about your suitors."

"And with good reason," her mother said. "The girl doesn't have the sense God gave her when it comes to men. She *should* be married to Greycourt, but instead she dragged her feet, and now he's married to that low chit Miss Wolfe."

"That 'low' chit," Vanessa bit out, "is the granddaughter of a duke just as I am. So if she's low, then so am I. Besides, I like her." Beatrice had proved a fitting match for Grey when Vanessa had despaired of ever seeing him wed.

"Of course you do." Mama fussed a bit more over the turban. "You always prefer the wrong sort of people."

"I find they're generally more interesting than the right sort," Vanessa grumbled.

"Like that playwright you're enamored of?" Her mother shook her head. "Sometimes I think you want to marry the poorest fellow you can find just to vex me."

"Mr. Juncker is very talented," Vanessa pointed out, for the very reason her mother had given—to vex her. Despite his very German name, Konrad Juncker had been raised in London, having been born to German immigrants. He was handsome, too, with a winning smile, teasing eyes, and good teeth, but Vanessa didn't care about any of that.

Her uncle huffed out a breath. "Are we going to enter the box sometime before the end of the century, Sister?"

"Oh, stubble it, Noah. The orchestra is still tuning its instruments."

"That sounds like an overture to me," he said. "Which is why the corridor is empty except for us."

"Almost done." Her mother *finally* left off adjusting Vanessa's turban, only to give Vanessa's bodice a tug downward.

Vanessa groaned. "It will just creep back up. Honestly, Mama, do you *want* me looking like a strumpet?"

"If it will catch you a good husband? Absolutely. You're not getting any younger, you know."

Her mother pinched Vanessa's cheeks. Hard.

Vanessa winced. "I fail to see how pinching rolls back the years."

"You must trust your mother on this," Mama said. "I swear, someday I hope you have a child as recalcitrant as you. 'Twould serve you right." When Uncle Noah cleared his throat, Mama scowled at him and opened the door. "Very well, *now* we shall go in."

Thank heaven. Navigating Mama's machinations and attempts to wed her to "the right sort" was as perilous as sailing a ship on the deepest ocean. One moment a light breeze carried it along on wings of silk, and the next moment stormy seas threatened to engulf it. She never knew which to expect of her mother—bad temper or cool disdain or syrupy kindness as false as it was cloying. Mama had kept her off-kilter her entire life.

"Are you expecting someone in particular tonight?"

Vanessa asked as they entered the box. Her mother usually primped her, but this went beyond the pale.

Mama lowered her voice as she scanned the boxes. "I heard that the Marquess of Lisbourne might attend."

An involuntary shudder passed through Vanessa.

Her mother went on without noticing. "They say he owns more property than even your cousin. And if he does come to the play—"

"He will magically decide to marry me because my cheeks are rosy and my bosom is half-bare?"

"Men do that, you know," her mother said. "Anything to make him notice you is good."

Heaven help Vanessa if Lord Lisbourne noticed her. She would have to join a convent.

"Lisbourne is sixty if he's a day, Cora," Uncle Noah said.

"A robust sixty," Mama said.

And a notorious debauchee to boot.

Uncle Noah shook his head. "Personally, I think my niece should set her cap for Armitage. He's closer to her age, very eligible, and related to your nephew."

"But according to the gossips, Armitage has pockets to let," her mother said.

"He's a duke," Uncle Noah said. "As long as he's not a gambler, he can get money."

Her mother's voice turned steely. "Then let him get it from Greycourt and not my daughter's dowry."

"My dowry is provided by Grey, Mama. So Armitage would be getting the money from Grey either way."

"Yes, but if Armitage uses your dowry to pay his debts, then Greycourt has kept the money in *his* family and hasn't had to lay out both a dowry *and* financial help for his brother. I don't need to fatten his family's coffers, do I?"

Uncle Noah blinked. "That makes no sense. And what do you have against Greycourt, anyway?"

"He's Mama's nemesis," Vanessa explained with a sigh. "I don't know which she considers worse—that Grey resisted her attempts to marry him off to me, or that I think of him as the big brother I never had."

Mama snorted. "If you'd had a big brother, there would be no problem. Your brother would already have inherited your father's estate, and we wouldn't need to rely on my pitiful widow's portion to live. But since you didn't have an actual big brother, you should have married Greycourt."

"Mama! I didn't want to marry him, nor did he wish to marry me. Besides, he has been more than kind to us." Especially considering how her parents had treated him when Vanessa was in her infancy. "Aside from my large dowry, he has paid the rent on our town house so we can remain in London, which is more than generous." And he'd done it so Vanessa could find a husband. Very kind of him indeed.

"All the same," her mother said, "I mean to make sure you don't marry Armitage. If you marry Lisbourne, who by all reports is rich, you'll have pin money to spare."

Which Mama was undoubtedly hoping to get her hands on through Vanessa.

"But if you marry Armitage," her mother went on, "and your dowry goes to the man's debts, which it will, you won't have any pin money at all. Indeed, Grey undoubtedly doubled your dowry because he knew he could get it back into his family by arranging for his penniless half brother to marry you."

"That's ridiculous," Vanessa said. "Sheridan—I mean, Armitage—isn't penniless. Besides, he has no interest in marrying me." More was the pity.

Her uncle nudged her. "I thought you were friendly with him."

"Not exactly. We know each other, and we've shared a few dances, but—"

Someone nearby shushed them, and they took their seats.

From the moment of her first dance with Saint Sheridan—she would never get used to calling him Armitage—the dratted fellow had relegated her to the position of pesky little sister, even though he was only twenty-nine years old to her twenty-five. By their third dance, Vanessa had realized she didn't want to be his pesky little sister. She wanted to be his *wife*. It was most annoying.

Why him? He wasn't her sort at all. Her firmest requirement was that the man have no secrets and be incapable of subterfuge—in other words, be as opposite to her late father as possible. So whom did she fancy? Sheridan, of all people, with his well of quiet that hinted at nothing *but* secrets. Worse yet, all she ached to do was uncover them, drat him.

Why was he the only man who made her blood roar and her pulse falter? Was her body that stupid? Because somehow, despite his aloof manner and a typically duke-like reticence she fought to ignore, he gave her goose bumps . . . and then goose bumps on her goose bumps.

She'd think he was playing some game to catch her, but

he didn't seem to play any games. He certainly didn't seem to notice her in *that* way. Or care if she was drawn to him. It maddened her.

If she could just figure him out, she could prove whether he'd make a reliable husband. It was all she could hope for these days, with Mama going to increasingly desperate lengths to catch her a rich fellow. Vanessa lived in daily fear that her mother might trick her into being caught in a compromising position with the likes of Lord Lisbourne.

Fortunately, Sheridan wasn't known to be a debauchee. *Unfortunately,* after their initial three dances, Sheridan had avoided her. At first, she'd chalked it up to his being in mourning. But mourning had ended for him at the beginning of last season, and still he'd kept her at a distance. Meanwhile, Mama had nearly thrown Vanessa into Lisbourne's arms half a dozen times. One day she would succeed . . . if Vanessa didn't find a husband herself before that.

Her uncle leaned forward to whisper in her ear, "If it's not Armitage you have your eye on, who is it? Juncker, perhaps, as your mother claims?"

Oh, dear, this was a dicey conversation. "Mama doesn't know what she's talking about."

"No? She's not the first person to say you're enamored of him."

That was her own fault. She cursed the day she'd told Grey she had a tendre for some unnamed poet. She'd said it just to tease him . . . and to keep him from guessing she really had a tendre for Sheridan. Because if he were to tell Sheridan and Sheridan were to disdain her for it, she would die of mortification.

After that, at Grey's wedding, Sheridan had asked her, rather condescendingly, about the identity of the poet she was romantically interested in. First, she'd wanted to brain Grey for telling him about her "poet" at all. Then, desperate to think of a poet she might know, and having just read a book of Mr. Juncker's poetry, she'd told Sheridan it was Mr. Juncker.

From there, her white lie had run amok with her life. Mr. Juncker had discovered it and had started flirting with her. Grey had learned of it and started teasing her regularly about it, while Thornstock had taken her aside to warn her about Mr. Juncker's raffish ways. Even Mama had heard and now lectured her frequently about not being taken in by people of Mr. Juncker's "sort," whatever that was.

Out of that, however, had come one distinct advantage. Sheridan had seemed jealous. She couldn't be certain, since he was mostly as inscrutable as ever. But having him regard her as a grown woman—no matter how infrequently—was better than not having him regard her at all.

Which prompted the question: Was Sheridan even here tonight? Leaning forward enough to see if he sat in the Armitage family's box would give Vanessa's interest away. Then a thought occurred to her. "Mama," she whispered, "do you have your polemoscope with you?"

With a nod, her mother drew it from her reticule. But before Vanessa could seize it, her mother asked, "Whom are you using it to observe?"

After her mother's diatribe against Sheridan, she dared not say it was him. "The marquess, of course."

"Don't toy with me, girl." Funny how Mama always assumed other people lied as much as she did. "I know you have your heart set on that playwright, and he is far beneath you."

"Yes, Mama."

Taking the polemoscope from her mother, she put it to her eye and leaned forward. Mama had purchased the curiosity after Papa's death, but Vanessa had never used it.

Until now. The polemoscope looked exactly like an opera glass or spyglass, which was ironic because it literally allowed one to spy on the people in the boxes to one's right or left without anyone knowing. She could easily see everyone in the Armitage box.

Thornstock and Sheridan sat behind their sister, Lady Gwyn, and their mother. The two ladies were clearly chatting, but although his brother chimed in from time to time, Sheridan seemed disengaged from them, cloaked in his usual stoic manner. Like a saint.

Or a sphinx. A sphinx fit him better, given his impenetrable character. Suddenly he looked over at her, and she started, unnerved by his attention, though she knew he couldn't tell she was watching him.

She dropped the polemoscope into her lap.

"Is he there?" Mama asked.

"Who?"

"Your Mr. Juncker."

Good Lord, she hadn't even checked. "Yes," she said, praying he was. She lifted the polemoscope and scanned the other boxes. And there he was, Mr. Konrad Juncker, the supposed object of her affections. Plenty of women worshipped him for his wild golden hair and his Nordic blue eyes, though he wasn't really accepted in good society. He dressed like a poet and talked like a playwright. Indeed, at the moment, he was clearly flirting with some lady Vanessa didn't even know. That was why she would never be enamored of him. He was rumored to be quite the rakehell, resembling her late father too well to suit her.

Still, she wished she'd never blurted out the words that had set her on the path to pretending to care for him. Because if she seemed to switch her affections to Sheridan at this juncture, Sheridan would think her fickle. Or worse, playing some deep game. Which she hadn't been initially. But as Sir Walter Scott had written, "Oh, what a tangled web we weave / When first we practice to deceive." Her web grew more tangled by the day.

She set the polemoscope down. Vanessa had prayed she'd get a chance to speak to Sheridan, but she despaired of that happening. Especially as the play reached the end of the first act, and a quick glance at the Armitage box showed he'd disappeared. No doubt he was flirting with some other—

"Good evening," said a smooth-as-brandy voice. "I trust you're all enjoying the performance?"

Vanessa's pulse jumped as Sheridan came around the chairs to lean against the balustrade, facing her and Mama. Sheridan was in her uncle's box? How unexpected.

How delicious.

"We're liking it as much as one can, given that it's not new," Uncle Noah said from his seat behind Mama. "Still, I'll take an old play by Juncker over a new one by just about any other playwright. He knows how to entertain, I'll give you that."

Only the slight furrowing of Sheridan's brow told her he wasn't pleased by the praise of Mr. Juncker. She only wished she could be sure why.

"Armitage," Mama said coldly. "I don't believe you've met my brother, Sir Noah Rayner."

Given the rude familiarity of Mama's greeting, Vanessa wouldn't have blamed Sheridan one whit if he'd left. Fortunately, Uncle Noah glossed over it by rising and coming around Mama's seat to thrust out his hand. "It's a pleasure to meet you, Duke." His gray eyes twinkled a bit. "I've heard so much about you from my sister."

"Don't be silly, Noah," her mother snapped. "Ignore my brother, if you please, Your Grace. I am not a gossip."

What a lie. Mama was both a gossip *and* a manipulator.

Her uncle gestured to the seat beside his, the one directly behind Vanessa. "Do join us. My niece was just saying she would love your opinion on the performance."

Clearly Mama wasn't the only one who could turn a situation to her advantage. But at least Uncle Noah was pushing Vanessa toward Sheridan and not toward Lord Lisbourne.

When Sheridan focused his gorgeous green eyes on Vanessa, she pasted a flirtatious smile to her face. "Nonsense, Uncle. I already know his opinion."

Sheridan's expression didn't change one whit. It exhibited a perfect blend of boredom and nonchalance. "Oh? And what might that be?"

"That the shenanigans of Felix and his friends are ridiculous. That you don't consider such frivolity entertaining in the least."

"If you say so." He shrugged. "Honestly, I have no opinion whatsoever."

It was the sort of thing he always said. "Ah, but you must admit that when you do, it's contrary to everyone else's. Why, I once heard you tell the Secretary of War that Napoleon was a masterful strategist who would win against us if we didn't recognize it and act accordingly."

"That wasn't an opinion; it was the truth." He stared her down. "Just because the man is our enemy doesn't mean we should assume he's stupid. Greater men than our Secretary of War have made that mistake, to their detriment."

The words piqued her uncle's curiosity. "Forgive me, Duke, but are you familiar with military strategy?"

"My father trained me from an early age to follow in his footsteps in Britain's diplomatic service, a profession which requires knowing strategies of all kinds. So yes, Sir Noah, I do know quite a bit."

Mama turned up her nose at the very idea. "I'm sure your late father was relieved when you became his heir to the dukedom instead. What a fortuitous event that was."

Sheridan shifted his attention to Vanessa's mother. "I doubt Father would have called the death of his brother fortuitous." As if realizing Mama might take offense at his blunt speech, he softened his words. "Personally, I'd have preferred a post abroad over inheriting the dukedom, but that wasn't meant to be."

Vanessa wasn't sure she believed him. He didn't sound convincing. Perhaps he was trying to convince himself? Then again, watching his every word and bowing to the needs of England over his own would probably come naturally to him, given his reticence.

As if Mama wondered about it herself, she lifted an eyebrow. "You would have been happy to live outside of England as some low envoy all of your life?"

"I wasn't born in England, Lady Eustace. So if I'd had

the chance to live the remainder of my days in Prussia, for example, I would have been perfectly content."

"With all your family here?" Vanessa asked, genuinely curious now. "Wouldn't you miss them?"

His gaze swung to her. "Of course. But if I were still in the diplomatic service, it would be because my uncle was still alive and my parents and Gwyn were still in Prussia."

"Still, wouldn't you miss your brothers?" Vanessa said. She would miss Grey terribly if he were abroad, and he was merely her cousin.

"Until the past year, I hadn't been around them for a very long time." A small frown knit his brow. "I was used to that. I was only a child when Grey left, Heywood got his commission when I was seventeen, and Thorn departed when I was nineteen. I spent nine years without them all." His fraught tone belied the nonchalant words.

"But surely you would have missed entertainments like this or hunting house parties or our glittering balls," Mama said.

Uncle Noah shook his head. "They have those in Prussia, too, eh, Duke?"

"But not peopled by Englishmen," her mother persisted. "And those Prussians are not to be trusted."

Vanessa stifled a groan. "Do forgive my mother. She finds all foreigners suspect."

Sheridan ignored Vanessa's commentary. "I will confess, Lady Eustace, that the house parties in Berlin paled to those my mother always describes from her youth in England. Prussian house parties were orderly events, with every activity scheduled. Whereas my mother says that her first husband's parties at Carymont were madcap and not the least scheduled. Everyone had differing plans for activities, and no one consulted with anyone else concerning those plans."

"Exactly," Mama said, brightening. "That's how they were indeed. We did as we pleased in those days. None of this 'Oh, the young gentlemen must be appeased' nonsense. We enjoyed ourselves however we could."

"I suppose that left time for guests to roam Carymont and explore," Sheridan said.

"And have assignations," Uncle Noah added, slyly.

Mama swatted her brother with her reticule. "No one was having assignations, Noah. I was newly married and not about to risk my marriage for any man. And my husband wasn't even there." She glanced at Vanessa and colored. "Not that he would have done such a thing either."

It was all Vanessa could do not to roll her eyes. How could Mama think Vanessa hadn't noticed Papa's many payments to ladies through the years? Vanessa had done the books for him from the time she was old enough to know what an account ledger was. Papa had been woefully bad at managing money. "The gathering at Carymont," Vanessa mused aloud. "What was the occasion or was it just a typical house party?"

Her mother sighed. "We were supposed to be there to celebrate Grey's christening. Instead—"

"Grey's father died," Sheridan said bluntly.

Vanessa groaned. She'd had no idea or she would never have brought it up. But her parents hadn't revealed any details about the death of Grey's father except to mention that Grey had been a mere infant at the time.

Uncle Noah's gaze shot to Mama. "*That* was when it happened?"

"It was indeed." Sheridan focused on Mama. "I wonder

how the guests felt about that, Lady Eustace. It must have lowered their spirits dramatically."

Mama waved her hand in the air. "Oh, let's not talk about it. It's . . . too awful and sad. Besides, the next act is about to begin."

Sure enough, the orchestra began to play a more dramatic piece. Uncle Noah took his seat but Sheridan continued to lounge against the balustrade.

"Would you like a lemon drop, Your Grace?" Vanessa asked as she drew one out of her reticule, hoping to keep him there.

"Thank you, but no," Sheridan drawled, flashing her the faintest of smiles. "I gave up sweets for Lent."

When she and Uncle Noah chuckled, Vanessa's mother frowned. "Lent was several months ago."

Mama had never had much of a sense of humor.

"Exactly, Sister." Uncle Noah smiled at Vanessa. "But I'll take one of those lemon drops." He snatched the comfit right out of Vanessa's hand.

Then a boy took the stage and began a comic introduction to the second act, which effectively ended all conversation.

Looking frustrated—for no reason that Vanessa could tell—Sheridan pushed away from the balustrade, unwittingly drawing her attention to his fine physique. The man had the best-crafted calves she'd ever seen, not to mention a chest as broad as a pugilist's and clearly capable of any test of strength. As if that weren't enough to tempt a young lady, his hair . . . Oh, she must not even think of those glorious ash-brown curls. It made her want to run her fingers through them, a possibility that clearly escaped him, since he ignored Vanessa completely while twice more bending to whisper something to her mother, as if to renew their conversation.

Like a balloon deflating, she felt the air go out of her happiness. He was here to visit—to talk with—Mama, given that even after he took his seat behind her mother, he leaned forward to exchange remarks with her. Vanessa couldn't understand why, but the point was he wasn't here to be with *her*.

What must she do to get him to converse with her? Or notice her? If she couldn't think of anything to pry him from Mama, she'd have to give up the foolish dream of marrying him and instead find some other safe, reliable, and preferably young man to wed.

Using Mama's polemoscope, Vanessa surveyed the boxes nearby, racking her brain for something to say to Sheridan that might get his attention. Then she spotted Mr. Juncker.

Her mother and Sheridan were still murmuring, so she shushed them. "My favorite part is coming up," she said sotto voce. "And I shall miss it for all your whispering."

Sheridan and Mama fell silent. Vanessa waited, wondering if Sheridan would take the bait.

"You have a favorite part?" Sheridan finally asked, under his breath.

Her heart pounded. It was working, although she dearly wished she didn't need the goad of Mr. Juncker to get Sheridan to speak to her. "Not just one, of course." She turned in her seat so she could talk to Sheridan. "Mr. Juncker is such a brilliant writer that I have three or four favorite scenes in each play. That's to be expected."

"I would have thought you enjoyed the costumes most,"

he said in a brittle undertone, "given your passion for fashion."

To keep from losing her temper at him more visibly, she returned to watching the stage. Her "passion for fashion" indeed. Once again, he saw her as only a frivolous ninny. "And I would have thought you enjoyed the wit most," she said archly. "But perhaps you need someone to explain it to you."

Sheridan gave a low laugh that rumbled around in her body for a bit, making her feel all soft and mushy inside.

Then he whispered, "Is that your polite way of saying you think me witless, Miss Pryde?"

"Oh, was I polite? That was unintentional."

Perhaps she should just face the fact that Sheridan had no romantic interest in her. No matter what she did, she would always be someone for him to tease and then ignore. He would clearly never see her as a woman capable of being his wife. Why, even when he'd danced with her at balls, it had been out of a sense of duty to his oldest half brother. If dancing hadn't changed his perception of her, what else was there?

On the stage, a young man was trying to steal a kiss from the lady destined to be his true love, and that sparked a wild notion. A kiss. That was it! Vanessa's pulse began to race. She had to get Sheridan to kiss her. Kisses could be magical. Well, none that she'd ever experienced had been so, but clearly she just hadn't found the right person to kiss. Why else would kisses punctuate the crowning moments in comedies, the lovely parts of ballads, and even the thrilling verses of poetry?

But how on earth could she get Sheridan to kiss her

when he didn't see her as the enticing enchantress she wanted to be to him?

Idly she picked up the polemoscope. As if to add insult to injury, Mr. Juncker appeared in the aperture. Even as she watched, Mr. Juncker rose, clearly meaning to leave his box.

That gave her an idea. Sheridan already thought her enamored of Mr. Juncker. She could still use that. But first she had to convince Sheridan to leave the box with her. And her view of another box gave her the perfect excuse.

Vanessa leaned back to whisper in his ear, "I've spotted a friend of mine in a box down the way. I simply must go speak to her. Will you accompany me?"

He eyed her askance. "What about your favorite scene?"

"It just finished," she said hastily. "Besides, it looks as if my friend might be leaving, and I haven't seen her in months."

"Why don't you ask your uncle to go with you?"

"You mean the uncle who is presently emitting a loud snore?"

Sheridan looked at Uncle Noah and grimaced.

"You can remain here," she added. "I'll just go by myself." She rose, praying that Mama didn't try to stop her, and that the overprotective Saint Sheridan followed her. When he did, she released a long breath.

Once they were in the now-empty corridor, Sheridan muttered, "Who is this special friend of yours, anyway?"

She kept slightly ahead of him. "Miss Younger."

"Never heard of her," he said, clearly skeptical.

"That means nothing. First of all, you rarely go into society unless your family forces you to. Second, you avoid me whenever possible, so you wouldn't necessarily have encountered her. Third—"

"Wait, wait, stop." He grabbed her by the arm to stay her. "What do you mean, I avoid you? That implies an active dislike."

"Call it what you will, but you must admit you go out of your way to keep from chancing upon me." She stared at him, daring him to deny it.

"I don't— I haven't—" For a moment, he looked flustered. It was encouraging to think she could fluster him. Then he smoothed his features into the usual stern expression he used only with her. "We'll have to agree to disagree on that one."

"Hmm." She continued down the corridor. "In any case, you would never have met her because she hasn't even had a coming out."

"So how did she get to be friends with *you?* You had your coming out a while ago. If your friend is of an age to come out, then she must be aptly named indeed, since she'd have to be a good six or seven years *younger* than you."

"How clever of you to make such an obvious play on words with my friend's name." She peered down the corridor and slowed her steps. Where in blazes was Mr. Juncker?

"I'm clever enough to know that a name like Younger is clearly fictitious."

"Why would I create a fictitious—" She halted so suddenly, he tread on her train. Not that she cared. Now was her chance. Pivoting toward him, she said, "Quick. Kiss me."

"What?"

"*Kiss* me!" When he merely arched one eyebrow, she

muttered, "Oh, never mind. I'll do it myself." And gripping his shoulders, she pulled herself up on tiptoe to press her lips to his.

He jerked back and glanced down the corridor to see what she'd seen—Mr. Juncker headed toward them. Then with a frown Sheridan pushed her against the wall and kissed her back.

Except that his kiss was perfunctory, the kiss of a man forced to do something he ought, not something he wanted. He let it go on in a most unsatisfying manner until Mr. Juncker had slid past them with a murmured, "Beg your pardon."

Only then did Sheridan release her. That's when it dawned on her what he'd been doing: once again protecting her, treating her like a . . . a silly schoolgirl. Making sure that Mr. Juncker didn't see her being kissed, while at the same time not really kissing her at all.

Anger took over, and she shoved him. Hard.

He stumbled back a step. "What the hell was that for?"

"For . . . For . . ." Well, she could hardly tell him the truth, or he'd guess how she felt about *him*. "You know precisely what it was for."

"Kissing you?"

"If you can call it that." No, she couldn't complain of that to him, or he'd guess he was the real target of her affections. So her only choice was to continue mooning after Mr. Juncker, no matter how much she hated that. She peered in the direction the playwright had gone. "You didn't let him see me kissing you."

He pinned her with a hard look. "Are you trying to destroy your reputation, Vanessa?"

"No, indeed." He'd missed the point. She lifted her

chin and lied for all she was worth, "I'm *trying* to make Mr. Juncker jealous. But if he doesn't know I was the one being kissed—"

"Hardly the one being kissed," Sheridan grumbled. "You were the one kissing *me*."

"He wouldn't have realized that." She tilted her head. "And if you had let him witness the incident, I might have secured him."

"*Secured* him?" Sheridan glared at her. "That man will never marry you. So do you really want to sacrifice your reputation to a fellow who has no interest in establishing a respectable connection with you?"

She gazed down the corridor after Mr. Juncker. "How do you *know* he wouldn't establish a respectable connection? Or do you simply think me too silly to attract an eligible suitor?"

Sheridan blinked. "It has nothing to do with you. He's a rogue, and rogues don't marry."

"Thorn did."

"My half brother had other reasons for doing so." Sheridan's face clouded over. "But Juncker has no such reasons—no heir he must sire and no estate requiring a rich dowry. He also has any number of unsavory females eager to share his bed, so why would he marry?"

"I have no idea, and neither do you. What would you know about rogues? You aren't one in the least. So you can't possibly understa—"

Sheridan kissed her again. Only this time it wasn't perfunctory or false. This time he gave her the sort of kiss a man would give a woman he truly desired.

Vanessa's head spun as his mouth seduced and supped, by turns rough and tender, making her knees wobbly. He braced his hands on either side of her shoulders and leaned into her, his hard body covering her soft one as if trying to subdue her. Except that she was more than happy to be subdued by him.

Heavens, but he certainly knew how to kiss.

She caught him by the waist, needing to hang on as he catapulted her far beyond their surroundings and into the clouds. In the chilly theater, his body shed warmth like a sun heating a meadow, and he smelled of sun, too, and leather, and some spicy cologne.

Then he parted her lips and delved inside her mouth with his tongue. Good Lord in paradise, what was he doing? What an exquisite sensation, one she'd never experienced. Her arms crept around his waist—she wanted him even closer.

And when his response was to groan and press into her, she exulted in it. The very weight of him turned her to jelly as the kiss went on and on. . . .

He *did* care. At last.

Chapter Three

Sheridan knew he was making a mistake. He shouldn't be touching her, let alone kissing her. But their first two pecks on the lips had whetted his appetite for a real kiss. To make her think twice about Juncker and his damned roguish ways. To show her that every man had needs and that trying to tempt a fellow like Juncker into expressing them was asking for trouble.

Kissing *her* was asking for trouble. God save him, he was sailing in uncharted waters, an adventurer heading for foreign climes. Her lips were soft and her body warm, yielding to his. She tasted like lemon drops and sunshine, and the more he thrust his tongue inside her mouth, the more he ached to have it inside other places. Sheer insanity. Especially since she wasn't exactly stopping him. And why?

Because she was a flirt. He could possibly steal her away from Juncker if he so desired. But of course he didn't want that. Should not want that.

He definitely shouldn't keep standing here kissing her in a corridor where anyone might easily see them! Regretfully he broke off the kiss and stepped back to give her room to move.

There was no shove this time. She merely stared up at him with her crystalline blue eyes as if seeing him in a new light. That wouldn't do either. It tempted him to let her in, and he'd already vowed never to do so, even though she looked fetching in her fashionable turban and her costly gown, with its décolletage that showed far too much of her breasts for his peace of mind.

Why, Vanessa wasn't even the sort of woman he usually desired. Helene had been precisely that sort—tall and willowy and elegant. Vanessa was a short, voluptuous vixen, the sort of fresh-faced, flirtatious female any man wanted to tumble in a haymow somewhere.

He drove that observation ruthlessly from his thoughts. She would break his heart—this he already knew. And one heart-breaking was more than enough for him.

Besides, his life was too complicated right now. The last thing he needed was a woman like Vanessa muddying the waters even more.

He drew in a deep breath. "Now you know how easy it is for a man to play the rogue. Even me."

"I do indeed," she said, her tone wary. "I confess I'm surprised. You don't seem the sort."

"The sort to do what?"

"Kiss a woman passionately."

That stung. But he mustn't let it. Instead he forced coldness into his tone. "That's because I'm not. I merely thought you could use the lesson. It might save you from ruin one day down the line."

"So your kiss was a lesson?" she said skeptically. "If so, it was certainly a convincing one."

"What good is a lesson if it's not convincing?"

"True." Her gaze turned frosty before she dropped it to her gloves, which had slipped down her forearms, exposing her elbows.

As she pulled them up, he felt a stab of disappointment. She actually had very pretty elbows. Why hadn't he noticed that before?

"In any case, it doesn't change a thing," she added. "I still mean to catch Mr. Juncker if I can."

The sudden roaring in his ears caught him off guard. *Over my dead body.* Only with an effort did he not say the words aloud. She might not be the woman for him, but Juncker would never be the man for her. Somehow he had to keep her out of that scoundrel's arms.

Besides, he did have to spend more time with her mother. Lady Eustace hadn't yet told him what he needed to know. "Well, if you're determined on that score," Sheridan said, "I can help you with that."

She looked up at him and raised one silky black eyebrow. "Why on earth would you? You went to great lengths to hide me during our first kiss, when I tried to make him jealous."

"Because I thought that would be the end of it. You've made it clear I was wrong. So if you still mean to pursue him, I will help you, if only to demonstrate he's not the man you think."

"But why do you even care about that? For that matter, why care if he ruins me? Or I marry him and he gains my dowry? Or whatever you think will happen if I keep going after him?"

Her expectant gaze sent him scrambling for a convincing answer. He could hardly say it was because he needed to interrogate her mother. "I consider us friends." Yes, that was the way to go. "Don't you?"

She laughed hollowly. "You barely talk to me at balls. You avoid me when you encounter me with Grey and Beatrice. You certainly don't seek me out in public. What exactly makes us friends?"

"Our connection to Grey, for one thing. Think of me as an older brother."

"Yes," she snapped, "I could tell how brotherly you were when you were kissing me."

He gritted his teeth. "I told you—"

"You were looking out for me. Teaching me a lesson. Right."

She sounded angry. Why should she be angry? That made no sense. But when he searched her face, whatever anger had been in her tone did not match her nonchalant expression, making him wonder if he'd imagined it.

"And in any case," she went on, "I don't need another older brother. Grey is more than enough, trust me."

"Ah, but he's preoccupied these days. And I am not."

"I see." She tucked a wayward curl up in her turban. "Very well. Tell me how you intend to go about helping me snag Mr. Juncker."

"You might have failed in making him jealous tonight, but I can give you plenty more chances to do so." He quickly amended that. "Chances that *won't* mean your ruin." He stared her down. "I'll court you publicly. But as a gentleman. If that doesn't wring an offer of marriage from him, then nothing will, and I will be proved right about his character."

Sheridan could practically see Vanessa's clever mind

weighing the proposition, turning it this way and that in the light to figure out if it had any dark side.

To his surprise, as he awaited her response his breath quickened and his pulse raced. He told himself it was only because he needed to get more information from her mother. So far, he'd learned practically nothing about that period of Lady Eustace's life and Mother's, except that his mother had been considered a diamond of the first water in her youth, which he already knew. According to Lady Eustace, men had done extraordinary things to get Mother's attention. One fellow supposedly even killed himself when she refused him.

That was the most absurd thing Sheridan could imagine—killing oneself over a woman, even a woman as widely admired as his mother. He would never allow himself to get into such a state over anyone again. Aside from the scandal and the financial burden of it, it didn't make sense in terms of one's family. His had been through enough grief. He would never add to it.

"You're willing to pretend to court me," Vanessa asked, "and risk being branded a fool once I marry Juncker just on the chance you'll be proved right about his character?"

If it helps find my father's killer, I am. He shrugged. "I *like* being right. That's not unusual in a duke, you know."

"Oh, trust me, I know. Grey has that particular vice himself." Vanessa stared down the corridor in the direction Juncker had gone. "And if your plan *doesn't* wring an offer from Mr. Juncker? Aren't you worried you'll be irretrievably linked to me? That people will expect *us* to marry?"

"They can expect whatever they wish," Sheridan drawled. "Men court women all the time without success. All you need do is say the word, and I shall suddenly lose interest in you. Or, if you're worried such behavior will hurt your future with other suitors, you can jilt me. Either way, we'll be done with each other."

He would have to arrange it, however, so that it only happened *after* he'd gained from her mother what he needed for their investigation.

She tipped up her chin. "All right then. I agree to your proposal. With one caveat. That if Mr. Juncker does show an interest in marrying me, you will bow out gracefully."

"Of course." But Sheridan would wager any amount of money that Juncker would never do so. Sheridan knew his type. They didn't marry—not for love or money.

The sound of applause came to his ears, signaling the end of the second act.

"Oh, dear," Vanessa said. "We must hurry if I'm to catch Miss Younger before she and Lady Whitmarsh leave the box."

She started off in the direction she'd been heading before, and Sheridan hurried to follow. "Wait," he said. "Do you mean there really *is* a Miss Younger?"

"Certainly. What kind of ninny do you take me for? I could hardly invent a friend when it would be very easy to check if such a person existed."

He had to admit there was no escaping her logic. Did that mean she *hadn't* been heading off to search for Juncker? That they'd really only encountered the man by chance?

Somehow he doubted that.

Vanessa watched uneasily as Sheridan went out of his way to charm her friend Flora Younger. Not that Vanessa was surprised. Flora wasn't pretty so much as she was arresting. Unlike most tall women Vanessa knew, she didn't try to play down her height. Then there was Flora's dark blond hair, which lay in elegant waves in her coiffure, and Flora's eyes, an unusual amber color that shone golden in candlelight.

Vanessa fought not to be jealous of her, but it was difficult since Sheridan had never shown *her* such warm congeniality. He was certainly capable of it. Vanessa had seen glimpses of it in his behavior toward his half sister and his cousin Beatrice. But after having been kissed by him so thoroughly and then dismissed like a . . . a maidservant, Vanessa couldn't bear that he still couldn't show *her* such warmth.

The only thing that kept her from resenting her friend was Flora's complete lack of guile. Flora knew that the Duke of Armitage was as unlikely to marry her as the king himself.

"Don't you think so, Vanessa?" Flora said.

Vanessa blinked. "Um . . ."

"Pay her no mind," Sheridan told Flora, nodding to Vanessa. "Your friend there has a tendency to woolgather."

"How would you know?" Vanessa asked. "Why, you've seen me in society only a handful of times—scarcely enough to form an opinion of my character."

"On the contrary, I think I know your character very well," he quipped, eyes gleaming. "You love fashion, frolics, and folderol."

Vanessa scowled, but Flora burst into laughter. "Clearly, you don't know her at all, Your Grace."

"And you know her better, I suppose," he teased Flora.

"I should hope so. I've been attending the same balls

as Vanessa since her debut. Her mother is related to my employer."

Sheridan raised an eyebrow at Vanessa. "Employer?"

"You didn't give me a chance to explain earlier," Vanessa said. "Flora is the companion of Lady Whitmarsh." Who presently sat chatting with a friend in the corner. "Flora is also two years older than I."

That seemed to stymie Sheridan. But only for a moment. "So her post as companion is why she hasn't had a debut," Sheridan said smoothly. "Ah. That makes sense."

To Vanessa's pleasure, Sheridan in no way showed what he had to have surmised—that Flora had little money and no rank in society. Only the kindness of Lady Whitmarsh allowed Flora to do such things as attend plays and go to balls. Vanessa could have kissed him for not changing his manner one jot now that he knew.

Vanessa cast her friend a smug smile. "His Grace assumed you to be much younger than I. He thought you some blushing schoolgirl. Didn't you, Sheridan?"

"Pray do not drag me into such a conversation. A man speculating on women's ages can never get out of it without scars."

Flora and Vanessa laughed together.

Then Flora winked at Vanessa. "Your Grace has not yet allowed me to correct your impressions about my friend's character. The fashion part, I'll grant you. Vanessa's attire is always flattering and in good taste—she works hard to make it so."

"By her judicious shopping, you mean," he said, with annoying condescension.

"No, indeed. Vanessa spends quite some time reworking her gowns and retrimming her bonnets and hats. That sparkling net overdress on her present gown? She took it off of one of her mother's old dresses and put it onto her plainest claret evening gown from last season. And that trim on her white satin turban? She embroidered it of gold silk thread. Once she added the dyed claret feathers, her suit of clothing was complete, with only the cost of some thread and a couple of feathers."

Vanessa blushed at being thus unmasked. So to speak. "Heavens, Flora, don't give away all my secrets."

"He's a man," Flora said. "He probably doesn't understand half of what I just said."

"I beg to differ," he put in, leveling his intent gaze on Vanessa. "My sister used to do such things. Probably still does."

"My point is," Flora went on, "while I will admit that Vanessa enjoys frolics and folderol as much as the next young lady, she also has hidden depths."

"Don't waste your breath, Flora," Vanessa said. "He thinks me merely a frivolous fribble, and nothing you say will alter that impression."

"I never called you a fribble," he pointed out.

"Perhaps not, but admit it—you think me foolish, frittering my days away in featherbrained fun."

At Vanessa's unconscious alliteration, Flora cocked her head. "Have you ever noticed how many words there are that begin with an *F* and mean something silly or useless? Especially things often attributed to ladies. Why, we've already mentioned frolic, frivolous, fribble, foolish, fritter, featherbrained, fun, and folderol. Then there's flibbertigibbet and—"

"Fashion," Vanessa said. "Men think fashion is the

utmost in silly. Unless, of course, they're talking to their tailors, at which point they all wish to be fashionable."

Flora nodded. "Meanwhile, women are criticized for that very thing. There's flashy and fancy and fast, fudge and fustian—"

"And 'fuss,'" Vanessa said. "Women are always accused of making a fuss out of nothing. Except that it's only 'nothing' to the men."

"Which is why the most obvious word is 'female,'" Sheridan drawled.

Both women gasped. When they drew themselves up to give him an earful, he held his hands up. "I'm *joking,* for God's sake. There are *F* words meaning inconsequential used specifically for men, too, you know. Fop. Foxed. Um . . ."

Vanessa tipped up her chin. "You can't think of any more, can you?"

"No," he admitted. "But there are numerous words meaning 'fool' or 'nonsense' for every letter in the alphabet. *A* for arse, *B* for buffoon and blockhead and balderdash, *C* for clodpate and clown, *D* for dolt and dunderhead— all of those are generally reserved for men, by the way—and dunce—"

"Not to mention dimwit," Flora said helpfully.

"Every letter, hmm? What about *Z?*" asked Vanessa.

"Zany," Sheridan said.

"*Q?*"

"Questionable," he said.

"I'll accept that, although it's a bit questionable."

Sheridan rolled his eyes. "You are the soul of wit."

Vanessa laughed. "What about *P?*"

"Poppycock." He smirked at her. "I can do this all day, you know."

A voice came from the door to the box. "Please don't." Mr. Juncker flicked some lint from his coat sleeve. "It's best to leave wordplay to the writers."

Sheridan eyed him askance. "Let a man pen a few farces and suddenly he's an expert."

"They're not farces," Vanessa said. Thanks to her bargain with Sheridan, she was forced into the position of defending Mr. Juncker. "They're comedies, and excellent ones, too."

"That's a matter of opinion," Sheridan drawled. "What do you think, Miss Younger?"

Belatedly, Vanessa realized she hadn't yet introduced Mr. Juncker to Flora. But as Vanessa turned to her friend, words left her entirely. Flora's face was the pallor of paper and her eyes were haunted.

When Vanessa looked back at Mr. Juncker, she saw *him* staring at Flora as if she'd risen from a grave.

"*Miss* Younger?" he asked in a clipped tone. "Still?"

"Yes, still." Flora looked as if she wished to sink into the floor. "And you, sir? Are you still a bachelor?"

"I am," Mr. Juncker said. "I'm just . . . I did not expect . . . How long have you been in London?"

"Not long." Flora clearly wished she could be anywhere *but* London at the moment.

Sheridan looked at Vanessa as if seeking an explanation of this stilted interaction. She had none to give. Flora hadn't once mentioned Mr. Juncker. Then again Vanessa had never encountered her friend at one of his plays, either.

"The two of you know each other?" Vanessa asked.

Flora merely nodded, but Mr. Juncker said, "We met in Bath. Years ago."

Lady Whitmarsh rose, having just then noticed the new arrival in her box. "Haven't you done enough to my dear Flora, Mr. Juncker?" She made a motion as if she were shooing a hen. "Go on now. The next act is about to begin, and you don't want to miss your chance to glory in it."

Apparently Lady Whitmarsh knew what had happened "years ago," too. Now Vanessa was desperate to know it herself, although she would have to put off finding out until she could get Flora to herself.

Mr. Juncker bowed to Lady Whitmarsh and started to leave, but Sheridan called out, "Juncker, hold up! I need to speak to you."

Vanessa tensed. What was Sheridan up to now? She didn't trust him to keep quiet about their supposed plan to make Mr. Juncker jealous, so she followed him into the corridor just in time to hear him say, "Thorn told me to remind you that you're invited to Thorncliff after the play." Sheridan saw her and added, "You're invited to Thorn's supper as well, Miss Pryde. You and your mother."

Mr. Juncker glanced past them through the doorway into the box, to where Flora had already turned to face the stage and Lady Whitmarsh still stood glaring at him. "Tell your half brother I had already fully meant to attend. But I may be a bit late."

"As may we," Sheridan said, tucking Vanessa's hand into the crook of his elbow in a wonderfully proprietary manner.

Mr. Juncker appeared too distracted to notice. They could hear voices on the stage, signaling the beginning of the third act, but even that didn't make him stir from contemplating the back of Flora's head.

Then he shook himself, as if to free his body from a spider's silken web. "I shall see you both then." He walked back to his box, obviously deep in contemplation.

"What was that all about?" Sheridan asked.

"I have no idea," Vanessa said.

Sheridan's gaze bored into her. "Why not? Surely she's heard you speak of Mr. Juncker frequently and would have commented on it. God knows you speak of him often enough around *me*."

"She never gave any indication that she knew him." And Vanessa certainly hadn't, given that she didn't care two figs for the man.

"Doesn't it worry you that Flora may prove a rival for his affections?" Sheridan persisted.

The whole thing had so rattled Vanessa that she nearly said, "Whose affections?" But she caught herself in time. "I doubt Flora would wish to be my rival. Clearly, he did something unforgivable to her."

Sheridan started walking her back to her uncle's box. "That should tell you all you need to know about his character."

It did, unfortunately. And now she had to stand up for Mr. Juncker yet again. "They said it was years ago. Surely he has matured in that time. He did look stricken by guilt at the sight of her."

Sheridan shot her a veiled look. "No matter what I say, you defend the man."

"And no matter what *I* say, you attack the man. Perhaps you're worried he will be *your* rival for Flora's affections.

Or for mine." She'd said that last bit offhandedly, hoping it would slide in under his walls.

"That's absurd. I'm not interested in having anyone's affections." The sudden stiffness in his arm said otherwise.

How very interesting.

"But you will come to Thorncliff this evening, won't you?" he went on. "You and your mother?"

She let him change the subject. "Surely you didn't really mean to invite us. You merely found yourself trapped when I overheard your invitation to Mr. Juncker."

"Not in the least. Thorn was quite clear on the subject. I was to invite you both. Besides, it would be remiss of me if I didn't invite the woman I'm supposedly courting." He leaned close. "And it will give you plenty of chances to make Juncker jealous."

Sheridan's bargain with her—if she could call it that—still made no sense. Why did he care whether she snagged Juncker? Until now, Sheridan had barely wished to spend one dance with her, so why engineer a faux engagement where they were forced to be together? She couldn't quite believe his assertion that he would do it just to be proved right about Mr. Juncker's character. Yet she couldn't imagine any other reason, unless he wanted to court her in truth, perhaps for her dowry, assuming that the gossip was correct. But if so, why not just come out with it? For all he knew, Grey already could have told her of Sheridan's need to marry for money.

Then again, Sheridan was a proud and taciturn sort.

"I would certainly love to attend the affair," she said, "if only to have the opportunity to see Thornstock's mansion. I've heard that Thorncliff is magnificent." She gazed down the corridor at the open door to Uncle Noah's box. "But I can't go without a chaperone, and Mama and I together can't go without Uncle Noah."

"Bring Sir Noah along. Truly, it will be very informal, only a few close friends and family. There might be dancing, and you can try to finagle Juncker into dancing with you."

She eyed him closely. "I'm surprised Thornstock would allow any of my family into his home. Mama isn't exactly . . . welcome at any of Grey's houses, and Thornstock is not only bound to know that but be well aware of why. As is your mother."

Sheridan sobered. "To be honest, we're all aware that your mother is persona non grata to Grey, although he won't tell us the full reason for his dislike of her. Do you happen to know?"

Bother it all. She did know. But if Grey hadn't revealed the secret, she certainly wouldn't.

As if guessing why she was reluctant, Sheridan added, "I do know it has naught to do with you."

"I should hope not. I was only eleven when he left our home. I didn't see him again until I was the age to have my coming out."

"Grey had something to do with your debut?"

"He was more than happy to help with it and to indulge my occasional visits to his London town house through the years, for which I shall always be grateful. Because of that, I'm loath to bring Mama to an affair which he no doubt will also attend, along with his mother, *your* mother. I know Mama and your mother knew each other well once, but their paths have definitely diverged."

"That's true," Sheridan said. "But Grey is still in the

country, and Mother is helping Olivia with the supper, so she'll be too busy to care. Thus Thorn won't mind one bit if the three of you come."

"You're certain? I don't want our presence to cause trouble in the family."

"It won't, I promise. I daresay he won't even notice you're all there. He's got stars in his eyes now that he's married to Olivia."

The sudden tightness in his voice gave her pause. "Do you not approve of her?"

He blinked. "No, no, nothing like that. Olivia's wonderful. It's just that . . . well, I thought Thorn and I would be bachelors together, unless I was forced into matrimony. He never seemed like the marrying sort. God knows I'm not."

"Why?" she asked, her stomach sinking. "You're perfectly personable and aren't a carouser like him. I've never even heard of you associating with a . . . demi-rep. And aside from your woeful tendency to tell women what to do at all times, you—"

"I don't tell women what to do," Sheridan bit out. "Ask Gwyn. Hell, ask any woman I know. I believe women should have their due, and I encourage them to decide what that is."

"So it's just *me* you make assumptions about, me whom you consider incapable of deciding who is the right man to marry."

"I'm only trying to advise you."

Releasing his arm, she narrowed her gaze on him. "You're *trying* to get me off the subject of why you're not the marrying sort. And why would you ever find yourself 'forced into matrimony,' anyway? Men rarely are—

even when they've ruined a woman—and dukes almost never. So unless you're planning to deflower a princess, you could ride roughshod over anyone seeking to force you into marriage. From what I understand, that's what all dukes do."

He eyed her askance. "I have no intention of riding 'roughshod' over any woman, princess or peasant. Good God, you don't know me at all."

"What do you expect? We've already established that you don't know *me*. It only follows that all that lack of knowing means I have no idea why you would end up forced into marriage. So enlighten me."

He scowled. "It's not something I wish to discuss."

"Then why mention it in the first place?"

"Because you asked—" He muttered an oath under his breath. "Forget it. I spoke out of turn, all right? Suffice it to say, I most likely won't be able to avoid taking a wife, but if I could, I would prefer not to marry. And that's all I intend to say on the subject."

Might Sheridan be a secret debauchee, more like Thornstock than she realized? Might he want only to have mistresses or scandalous encounters with married women? That gossip rag had implied he was discreet, so perhaps he was more discreet about his dalliances than either of his brothers.

No, she had trouble believing that of him. It didn't seem in his character, although Lord knows she could be wrong, given how he'd shocked her with his passionate kiss.

And he'd just made it fairly clear he wasn't interested in marrying for any reason, money or affection, which meant he probably wasn't interested in courting her in truth.

"Suit yourself," she said with a sniff, tired of trying to

unravel his secrets. "But don't blame me if you end up alone and miserable at the end of your days."

"With a family like mine always hovering about?" he said dryly. "That's unlikely. Even if I outlive my brother and half siblings, they're busily trying to fill up their nurseries even as we speak. I'm sure there will be little Greys and Gwyns and Thorns and Heywoods running about wreaking havoc for generations to come."

She halted to fix him with an earnest look. "Having nieces and nephews isn't the same as having your own children."

"How would you know? You have none."

"True. But I hope to one day."

"Little Junckers, I suppose?"

"Who else?" she said lightly.

The edge in his voice mitigated some of her distress at hearing him so set against marriage. Somehow she would bring him around. Whatever reasons he had for being determined not to marry could be dismissed if she could make him care for her enough. Because when he went to marry *her,* she didn't want him to be forced into it. Her parents had possessed such a marriage, and it hadn't gone well.

So that would not do at all.

Chapter Four

When Sheridan arrived at the supper, the Thorncliff ballroom was already abuzz with spirited discussions, coming mostly from members of his family. He could only imagine what the place would be like once all the guests arrived.

Thorn's new wife, Olivia, approached him with a worried expression. "It's my first affair as Thorn's hostess. Please tell me I'm not out of my depth."

"If you are, I'm sure Thorn or Mother would have told you already," he said as he pressed her hand.

"Your mother is too kind to ever say a bad word about me. And Thorn's not here yet. He's still at the Parthenon, trading stories about theater life with Mr. Juncker. Oh, and taking apart tonight's performance."

"Yes, my brother is nothing if not critical of theatrical productions."

"You can hardly blame him for caring what is done to his plays," she said absently as she scanned the ballroom entrance for approaching guests.

"*His* plays?"

Olivia's gaze shot to him. "Oh! Oh, no. I-I meant Mr.

Juncker's plays . . . Of course I meant that. Mr. *Juncker's* plays."

"Olivia?" he said in that tone one used in trying to elicit the truth.

"What?" She smiled brightly.

He wasn't fooled. Thorn might be able to talk his way out of hell itself, but his wife was very bad at dissembling, something Sheridan had learned almost upon meeting her. "Tell the truth now. Is it possible . . . Are you trying to say that *Thorn* wrote the Felix plays?"

She crumpled before his very eyes. "I thought you knew. I-I just assumed, since you're his brother and you were talking about it as if—" She seized his hand. "You can't tell my husband I told you. You mustn't. No one knows."

"No one? Seriously?"

"Not a soul!" She paused. "Well, Gwyn knows and Mr. Juncker, of course. Oh, and my mother—I told her when I first found out."

"Yet not a soul knows," he said, trying not to laugh.

"Don't tease me." She tapped her chin. "Actually, Mama doesn't know. I told her that Mr. Juncker had written about . . . um . . . stories Thorn had told him. So there are really only three people who know, counting me."

"And Thorn. And me."

"Well, of course Thorn knows. As for you, that was accidental. But no one else in your family, not even your mother, is aware of it. The theater owner himself still believes they're Mr. Juncker's plays."

Sheridan was having a hard time not grinning. Juncker wasn't so *brilliant* after all. Ha! So much for Vanessa's infatuation. She was mooning over the wrong man. He couldn't wait to tell her that her precious Juncker was a fraud.

Well, not entirely a fraud. When Grey had first mentioned Vanessa's interest in Juncker, Grey had said the man was a poet. What if her primary reason for liking Juncker was his poetry? If so, then telling her the truth about the playwriting might not alter her interest in the man one whit. Unless . . .

"What about Juncker's poems?" he asked. "Did my brother write those, too?"

"Good Lord, no." Olivia eyed him askance. "Thorn isn't the least bit keen on poetry. Don't you know that?"

He sighed. "I suppose I should. We had the same tutors in Prussia. But I didn't much pay attention to what Thorn was reading."

Because Father had given Sheridan other things to read—books about diplomacy and strategy and the art of conversation. Sadly, Father hadn't thought to give Sheridan any tomes on accounting, which was mostly what Sheridan seemed to be doing these days. And not as well as he'd like, either. He hated arithmetic. The numbers never seemed to come out right for him, a fact that Father had never let him forget once they'd returned to England and Sheridan had become the heir presumptive.

Father. God, why must his grief over the man he'd spent his whole life trying to understand hit him at such odd moments? It reminded him he had more important things to do than worry about the ducal estate. All of them did. "I don't suppose you've had the chance to question your mother about the house parties she attended."

"No." With a wry expression, she added, "Thorn had said *he* must do it, but Mama has taken quite a liking to him, and he's reluctant to do anything that might change that." Olivia moved closer and lowered her voice. "Speaking of Thorn, please promise me you won't tell anyone else about his playwriting. And especially not any of our guests here tonight."

Damn. He'd already been looking forward to gloating the next time he saw Vanessa.

"Sheridan, are you listening?" Olivia cried in a tone of pure desperation. "You must promise you won't let Thorn's secret get out."

The last thing he wanted was to injure Olivia's relationship with Thorn. Or, for that matter, risk hurting his brother. "I promise I won't say a word. Cross my heart and hope to die."

Relief suffused her face. "Thank you, *thank* you."

"But in exchange, you must swear not to tell Miss Pryde—or anyone else for that matter—that my sole interest in her lies in finding out what her mother knows about those same two house parties."

Olivia looked skeptical. "Are we speaking of Grey's cousin?"

"The very one."

"Then I shan't say a word."

"Purposely or otherwise," he stressed. "I can't have you blurting out to Miss Pryde or her mother things about our investigation."

She drew herself up. "I beg your pardon. I would never—"

"You just told me a secret of Thorn's that he's never even hinted at," he said.

A blush stained her cheeks. "Yes, but . . . well, I wouldn't . . ." She fixed him with a sullen stare. "That's different. You're his brother, and I thought you knew. Besides, even if I did say something untoward to Miss Pryde about your *dis*-honorable intentions, I doubt she would care. Not if she is as enamored of Mr. Juncker as everyone says."

He fought the urge to deny that even as he acknowledged he couldn't.

Fortunately, just then Olivia gazed across the room to where the footmen had brought in more chairs. "Oh, dear. Pray do excuse me. I have to direct the servants as to where I want those."

"Of course. I understand."

As he watched Olivia cross the room, it occurred to him that her revelation about Thorn's playwriting explained so many things, like the close friendship between Thorn and Juncker. Granted, until Olivia had come along, both men had been rogues, eager to blaze a path through London's gaming hells and brothels. So Sheridan had assumed it was merely their activities in the stews that they had in common.

But although Thorn had inherited substantial wealth, Juncker could never have afforded such a way of living, given that his father had been some sort of tradesman, according to the rumor mill. It wasn't as if playwrights made much money, either. So if Thorn had been paying Juncker for his name on the plays, not to mention his silence . . .

Well, that made more sense. On top of that, Thorn had always shown a decided interest in the plays themselves—reading reviews of them, attending a number of productions, and even setting up this charitable production tonight. That went beyond what a friend would do for another friend. Sheridan had chalked it up to Thorn wanting to be a patron because of his love of the theater, but Thorn had never supported any other playwrights or artists or musicians. Just Juncker. It was rather surprising they'd even kept it quiet until now.

Damn it all. Sheridan scowled at nobody in particular. He really wished he could tell Vanessa she'd put her eggs in the wrong basket. But he couldn't, simple as that. For one thing, Olivia would never forgive him for revealing the truth to someone outside the family. Best not to rock that boat.

For another, he couldn't be sure *why* Vanessa had set her cap for the blackguard. She could just as easily want Juncker for his skill at writing poetry or his dancing ability or even his ostentatious good looks. Blasted fellow probably spent as much money on his tailor as Vanessa spent on her gowns.

Except that Miss Younger had said Sheridan was wrong about that. Did Grey know? And if so, why hadn't he said anything?

It didn't matter. If anything, it made it more imperative that Sheridan keep to his plan to show Vanessa how bad Juncker's character was. She simply could not end up with that fellow, or all the fashion frugality in the world wouldn't save her from poverty.

So he needed to play her suitor a bit longer, at least until he was sure he'd disabused Vanessa of her fanciful ideas regarding the man. Besides, Sheridan hadn't even begun to find out all he needed to know from Lady Eustace.

A sudden commotion in the hall outside the ballroom made him groan. Thorn had arrived. And from the sounds of it, he'd brought half the theater with him. This was going to be a long, noisy night, the kind that generally had

Sheridan fleeing. But much as he'd prefer to spend the rest of the evening by his cozy fire with a glass of perry from his estate's own pear trees, he couldn't leave.

Moments later, his half brother entered with Juncker at his side. "Olivia!" Thorn shouted. "Olivia!"

His wife hurried toward him. "I'm right here. What is it?"

"We raised a thousand pounds for Half Moon House," he told her, loudly enough that the entire room could hear him.

"Excellent news." Olivia seemed to be fighting a smile. "And it appears that you've invited plenty of friends to celebrate it."

As people filled the ballroom, chattering and looking about, Sheridan shook his head. Thorn seemed a bit foxed . . . or perhaps just carried on by the excitement of having raised so much money for his wife's pet cause. Juncker, on the other hand, looked sober as a church. In fact, he seemed rather angry, if Sheridan was to judge from his scowl.

Was it because of that woman Flora's rebuff at the theater? Or because Vanessa had been hanging on Sheridan's arm earlier?

Sheridan found himself disturbingly interested in finding out which it was. Especially since Vanessa and her uncle entered right behind Thorn and Juncker. But what had happened to Lady Eustace? She was the only reason Sheridan was enduring this crowd.

Well, she and her impudent daughter.

Muttering a curse under his breath, Sheridan stalked over to Vanessa. "Where's your mother?"

Vanessa arched one eyebrow. "It's lovely to see you here, too."

Her uncle started to laugh until Sheridan glared at him, and Sir Noah sobered at once.

"If you're worried about my lack of a chaperone," Vanessa went on, "I can assure you Uncle Noah is prepared to perform that service." She smiled up at the man. "Aren't you, Uncle?"

"Certainly." He surreptitiously surveyed the grandeur of Thorn's ballroom. "As long as you don't get lost in this cavernous place."

"She won't," Sheridan said smoothly. "I'll make sure of it."

Now her uncle fixed a baleful gaze on Sheridan. "Forgive me, Duke, but *I'll* make sure of it."

Wonderful. Just what Sheridan needed—a suspicious baronet on his arse, no Lady Eustace to question, and Vanessa up in arms. This was precisely why Sheridan had wanted someone else to do the questioning—because he could never be easy around Vanessa. It was either keep his distance or kiss her senseless.

"I don't understand why a woman of my advanced years needs a chaperone, anyway," Vanessa said.

"Advanced years?" Sheridan snorted. "You're twenty-five, Vanessa, not fifty."

She pointed her chin at him in that odd way she had of examining people. Like a raven. Or a magpie who enjoyed stealing away whatever glittered. "I'm surprised you noticed. You treat me as if I'm twelve."

"If you wouldn't act as if you're twelve, I wouldn't treat you that way."

Sir Noah muttered something about needing punch

and hurried off, but Sheridan was already regretting his too-swift response. He could swear the temperature around him had dropped ten degrees.

Her eyes certainly resembled ice. "If you wouldn't act as if you're fifty, I'd refrain from pointing out that even my aged uncle knows how to enjoy himself at a party, especially one with good music, excellent food, and plenty of punch."

The lady did know how to wield her tongue, didn't she? "Pax," he said with a rueful smile. "I admit my remark was uncalled for."

"And rude, too." She gazed across the ballroom as if looking for any companion but him.

That goaded him into saying, "Now it's your turn to apologize."

"For what? I only spoke the truth."

He groaned. His plan to cozy up to Vanessa in order to get to her mother wasn't exactly going swimmingly. "So I take it your mother is not in attendance then?" he asked, just to be sure.

"No. She was feeling poorly after the play." Vanessa searched his face. "But that's all for the best, don't you think? It makes matters easier with your family, since I dare say none of them like her."

"Did you ask her not to come?"

"No, indeed. She decided that all by herself once she heard it was to be an 'informal' affair with 'only a few close friends and family.' How could she possibly know that your 'close friends' number in the hundreds?"

He chuckled. "I'm afraid I was a bit misinformed myself about the nature of the event."

"Clearly." She relaxed a bit. "But it's of no matter. I always enjoy myself better when Mama is not around."

Before he could comment on that, Thorn called out to the orchestra, "Play music, sirs! 'Come, come . . . Let's have a dance ere we are married, that we may lighten our own hearts and our wives' heels.'"

The quote from Shakespeare startled a laugh out of Sheridan. All this time, he'd been attributing Thorn's theatrical flourishes to their family's general love of the theater. How strange Sheridan had never guessed before that Thorn was a playwright.

Sheridan scanned the room for his sister-in-law, to see *her* reaction to Thorn's quote, but although some other newly minted duchess might be embarrassed at such lavish language, Olivia beamed at the man she obviously adored.

Vanessa leaned up to whisper, "You have to admit they're perfect for each other."

"Only time will tell." Sheridan knew she was alluding to their earlier conversation about marriage. "They're still in the honeymoon stage."

"I swear, for a man who's only ever been a bachelor, you certainly seem to think you know a great deal about marriage."

Despite never having entered the wedded state, he knew enough about it to be cautious, though few realized it. He wasn't the sort to blather his personal affairs to all and sundry.

The musicians had taken Thorn at his word and had already struck up a lively reel. The guests were moving aside to allow room for dancing couples to take the floor.

So Sheridan laid his hand in the small of Vanessa's back and murmured, "We'd best get out of the way."

She tipped her head up at him. "You're not going to ask me to dance? And here I thought you were my suitor."

Damn, she was right. But before he could respond, Juncker approached them. "Miss Pryde, would you do me the honor of dancing this set with me?"

Sheridan answered for her. "She can't. She has already promised it to me."

Vanessa looked startled by his response but didn't gainsay it. "As His Grace said, I am otherwise engaged."

"Then I shall request the next," Juncker said.

"In that case, thank you." She flashed him a broad smile. "I'd be delighted."

She didn't have to be quite *so* delighted, blast it. As Juncker walked away, Sheridan scowled after him. What was the fellow up to now? Sheridan didn't trust him one whit.

At least Sheridan had Vanessa for the present. And he meant to take advantage of it. His hand still lay in the curve of her back, and he marveled at how supple it felt, even through her gown.

"Well, our plan seems to be working," Vanessa said, obviously oblivious to the intimate position of his hand. "And better than I hoped, too. Did you know Mr. Juncker has never before asked me to dance?"

"Then he's more fool than I realized," Sheridan said, and took her to the floor. When he caught Vanessa eyeing him as if he'd made a damning admission, he added, "You're an excellent dancer. You make it easy for a partner to lead you, which is more than I can say for most of the ladies in society."

"Why, Your Grace, I do believe you paid me a compliment. A rather surprising one, too, considering you've only danced with me thrice."

"Once would be enough to recognize your ability, but thrice certainly is. I'd be a dimwitted fellow indeed if I hadn't noticed it after *that*."

She flipped her fan open and fluttered it over her bosom. "Your extravagant flatteries have left me all atwitter."

Sheridan fought a smile even as her motion drew his gaze to the upper swells of her lovely breasts, which was undoubtedly her intention. "Do not tease me, you insolent chit," he said, jerking his eyes back up, "or I will tread on your toes in the dance."

"You would never." With a minxish gleam in her eyes, she dropped her fan to dangle from her wrist. "I have yet to see you falter on the floor. You obviously had an excellent dancing instructor."

"My parents made sure I was well prepared for my role in diplomacy. And now it's all for naught."

"Hardly. As duke you'll be expected to impress everyone with your lightness of foot. After all, you don't want to ruin your reputation as Saint Sheridan."

Groaning, he took her gloved hands in his. "I don't know how I got that damned nickname, but I hate it."

"As I recall, it came from your family." They circled as they were supposed to. "Because any time the rest of us are being merry and kicking up our heels, you're the one going off to sequester yourself in some back study to heed your duke-ish responsibilities. Lord only knows what you're doing in there."

"Trust me," he said dryly, "it's nothing whatsoever that would interest you." He faced the other lady with a dip of his head, did the requisite steps, and then once more found himself opposite Vanessa. "This is much more to your taste, I would imagine."

Her sparkling smile faltered, and it was as if white, fluffy clouds suddenly showed their dark undersides. He wanted the fluffy clouds back. What had he said? How could he fix it?

Damn, why did he care if he fixed it? Vanessa had her eyes on another man, and he *didn't care.* Best to remember that.

She remained silent for a while, doing the steps, sliding here, sliding there, and in short being the perfect dance partner he'd characterized her as. But her enjoyment of the dance had clearly dimmed.

When they halted opposite each other at the bottom of the set, waiting for the other couples to come down the center one by one, he had to say *something.* She was breaking his bloody heart with her clear disappointment. "I'm usually going over the books."

She blinked. "I beg your pardon?"

"In 'some back study.' While I'm sequestered. I'm going over the books for the estate."

"Oh." She fanned herself again, but this time undoubtedly because it was damned hot in the ballroom, especially for November. Unfortunately, the fanning wafted her floral scent to him—although he couldn't place the flower it came from. Perhaps it wasn't a flower at all, but some exotic perfume she'd bought at Floris on Jermyn Street.

He was still breathing it in when she added, "I would have thought you'd have . . . people to do that for you."

To do what for me? he nearly asked. Right. Go over his ledgers. He didn't dare say he couldn't afford to have people do that for him, not entirely anyway, and certainly not if he wanted to save the dukedom for future generations. "Regardless, it's important to gain a sense of how one's money is being spent. If you know what I mean."

God, what was he doing, blurting out this sort of information in the midst of a ballroom?

But the darkness had faded from her face. "I know exactly what you mean."

He got the distinct impression that she actually did. Which was absurd. What could she possibly know about running an estate? According to Grey, her father's holdings had been modest, and in any case, wouldn't have been managed by *her*.

They found themselves at the top of the set again, forced to perform certain steps and then join hands to dance back down. She had a firm grip for a woman. He liked that about her. No limp hands for Vanessa, oh, no. And suddenly he wished they were alone together in a room somewhere. . . .

Nonsense. What was he thinking? He and Vanessa would not suit. Even she must know it.

Then they reached the bottom of the set and she took her spot across from him and he noticed that her gloves were slipping down her arms as before. He found himself wondering if . . . waiting to see if she would let them fall below her elbows as before, too.

Her gloves were on the verge of doing so when she absently pulled both up, one after the other. He stifled a sigh. One day very soon, he was going to get her alone somewhere and draw down one of those curst gloves just to see her bare elbows. And then he would press his lips to the inside bend so he could find out once and for all if her pulse would beat for *him* during such an intimate moment.

Not because he truly meant to court her, and not because he wanted anything further. Just so he would know. Because if one intended to forego sweets for Lent, it was only a sacrifice if one had tasted those sweets often enough to know how much one would miss them.

Chapter Five

Vanessa couldn't stop smiling. Her dance with Sheridan had gone better than she'd hoped. She wished etiquette didn't require that she dance with a variety of partners, because she could easily have floated through every set with Sheridan. But she still owed Mr. Juncker a dance, and she would have to pretend to be happy about it.

As the poet took her to the floor, she swept her gaze about the ballroom to see whom Sheridan was dancing with. Her pleasure faltered when she spotted him with her friend Flora. It wasn't that she didn't want Flora to enjoy herself and have plenty of partners. Vanessa would merely prefer that none of them be Sheridan. And that they not make such a handsome couple.

She tore her gaze from them to focus on Mr. Juncker. "How long have you known Miss Younger?"

The question seemed to annoy her present partner. "A few years. Since we met in Bath."

But why had Flora never mentioned him? As soon as Vanessa had the chance, she would ask her.

He released Vanessa in the dance, and by the time they came back together, didn't seem to wish to enlighten her any further. "And you? How long have you been friends with Miss Younger?"

"Ever since my coming out." She bowed and twirled. "We met when I was riding in Hyde Park with some fellow Mama had foisted on me as punishment for me not trying to snag my cousin Grey as a husband."

"Let me guess," Mr. Juncker said. "Your mother's punishment was an elderly sort with a noble title who leered at you every chance he got."

She laughed. "No, that's just who she's forcing on me these days. This fellow was young but vain as a peacock. And with no good reason, either, since he routinely wore baggy pantaloons and an awful powdered wig that he thought made him look sophisticated."

They separated for a few minutes in the dance. When they came back together, she continued her tale. "It was March and a fierce wind blew up out of nowhere, sending his wig flying right beneath the brim of Miss Younger's hat to get caught in her bow. She screamed because she thought it was a bird, and only after Lady Whitmarsh had the foresight to yank off her bonnet did my friend realize she wasn't under attack." She smiled at Mr. Juncker. "That sounds like something from one of your plays, doesn't it?"

"Except that in my play, the wig would have knocked off her hat and hit a horse, which would have spooked and galloped off, dragging its rider with it."

Vanessa cocked her head. "How would you show that on the stage?"

With a dismissive wave, he said, "That's for the stage manager to decide. I do not concern myself with such minor matters." Then he grinned at her, negating her impression that he was a rather pompous fellow. "Although the stage manager would grumble and groan about it."

"No doubt," she said dryly.

He laughed, and that made her like him. Why must things be so easy with Mr. Juncker, whom she didn't want, and so difficult with Sheridan, whom she did? It simply wasn't fair.

They went through the steps in silence for a bit. They sometimes found themselves weaving between Flora and Sheridan as part of the dance, and Vanessa would strain to hear the other couple's conversation. But she never heard them speak at all. She didn't know if that was good or bad. Sheridan was a quiet gentleman in general. Perhaps he would prefer a silent dance partner to a chattering one like her. That would make him Silent Sheridan. Nay, Studious Sheridan, to judge by what he'd said about spending his time going over the books.

As if Mr. Juncker had read her mind, he asked, "How long have you known Armitage?"

"Since he arrived in England."

"So, not long."

"Long enough," Vanessa said as Mr. Juncker turned her in the dance. "Over a year."

Mr. Juncker was a good dancer, light on his feet and adept at leading, but still not nearly as good as Sheridan. Or perhaps she was biased. She sneaked a glance at Sheridan and Flora. They looked perfect together, both of them tall and elegant, gliding along the floor in harmony.

Vanessa considered herself well-dressed, but elegant she was not and never had been. She was too short. Too fidgety. Too talkative. Too prone to laugh heartily. Mama had always said so, anyway. *A lady mustn't do anything heartily, girl. It smacks of low breeding.*

That bit of dubious advice had become fixed in Vanessa's head years ago, though she rarely followed it.

"Do you fancy Armitage?" Mr. Juncker asked as he gazed at the other couple.

"Do you fancy Miss Younger?"

"I know better."

"I'm afraid I don't," she admitted. "Not yet, anyway." She stole a look at Sheridan. "And if you ever say a word of how I feel to Sheridan, I will ruin matters between you and Miss Younger forever."

"You can't ruin what I've already done a bang-up job of ruining myself."

Vanessa took a deep breath. "It's never too late for mending fences."

Mr. Juncker smiled ruefully at her. "I only wish that were true."

"Will you promise to keep my secret anyway?"

"Absolutely. I happen to enjoy annoying Saint Sheridan, who has always seemed to feel an active dislike toward me, for no reason I can see."

Dare she hope it was out of jealousy over her supposed infatuation with Mr. Juncker? It certainly lightened her heart to think it.

To her surprise, their dance ended just then. It had proved more pleasurable than expected.

"Tell me something," she said as he led her to where her uncle stood chatting with some people. "Why did you ask me to dance?"

"I'm turning over a new leaf." He patted her hand where

it lay on his forearm. "Your cousin Grey no longer joins me on my adventures, and neither does my friend Thornstock. So I'm shifting my priorities to a more respectable realm. I've even begun a novel, with Thorn's encouragement. If I succeed in gaining a publisher for it, not to mention an audience, I may actually settle down and get married."

"Not to me, I hope."

He laughed heartily. Apparently *men* could laugh heartily without reproach. "Surely your mother would never approve of me as a suitor."

"True."

"But I must start somewhere, and you seem as good a place as any to begin practicing how to please a respectable lady."

"You probably shouldn't use me as an example of respectability. Mama claims I voice my opinion far too readily to be called that."

"Well, I wouldn't want to marry *too* respectable a lady," he said, smirking at her. "I may be settling down, but I still prefer a bit of pepper in my fare, if you know what I mean."

"I do, indeed. I like pepper myself."

"I fear you won't find much of that in Armitage."

"You'd be surprised," she muttered as she saw Sheridan take his leave of Flora.

Vanessa and Mr. Juncker had now reached her uncle. With a bow, Mr. Juncker headed off to find some other female for his foray into respectability.

She had scarcely joined the small group when someone came up behind her with all the stealth of a wolf on the hunt.

"Save the supper dance for me, will you?" the man whispered in her ear.

She jumped and turned to find Sheridan there. "Are you *trying* to give me heart failure?"

"Merely trying to secure you for supper."

"I will see what I can do. If Mr. Juncker wants it—"

"You will damned well turn him down," Sheridan muttered.

It took all her will to hide her delight. "And why would I do that? He *is* the man I'm pursuing, after all."

Sheridan's lips tightened. "Be that as it may, you don't want to tip your hand too early or you'll lose him."

"That does make sense," she said. "Very well, I'll save the supper dance for you."

"Good. Thank you." He walked off.

My, my, but this party was going well so far. Two dances with Sheridan, a demonstration of his jealousy, and the gain of an unexpected ally in Mr. Juncker. What more could a woman ask for?

Uncle Noah noticed her standing on the outskirts of the small group. "There you are, my dear. Why are you not dancing?"

"I was, Uncle, but now I need punch. I'm parched, I swear."

Her uncle laughed. "I'll fetch you punch, but first I'd like to introduce the Duchess of Armitage." He winked at Vanessa. "Your friend Sheridan's mother."

Vanessa had only met the famous Lydia Pryde Drake Wolfe once, at Grey's wedding, and she'd barely had time to curtsy and smile at the duchess, much less converse. The woman had still been in mourning, after all. Meanwhile, Vanessa had spent most of the wedding breakfast dancing with Sheridan's half brothers or chatting with him and his brother Heywood, since they couldn't dance because they had also been in mourning.

But the mourning period had clearly ended even for the duchess, given that she was splendidly dressed in a white silk robe and petticoat, with a drapery of celestial blue organza fastened on one shoulder with a gold brooch. Even the woman's fashionable turban was of the same shimmering organza, with two jaunty feathers to accentuate the ensemble. The duchess had come out of mourning with a vengeance.

"Actually, we've met," Sheridan's mother said, favoring Vanessa with a smile.

"Better and better," Uncle Noah said. "That means the two of you can renew your acquaintance while I fetch you both some punch."

Her uncle headed off on his mission. Before Vanessa could even speak, the rest of the small group melted away, some to go dance, some to find the card room, and a few to circle the ballroom in search of friends or acquaintances. That left Vanessa and the duchess entirely alone together.

"I'm honored that you remember me," Vanessa said, not sure what else to say, and painfully conscious that she hoped to have this woman for a mother-in-law one day.

"Of course I remember you." The duchess's vibrant blue eyes searched Vanessa's face. "How could I forget the young lady who was nearly engaged to my son Grey?"

Vanessa blushed, remembering how Mama had tried forcing Grey into marrying her. "That was a mistake in the newspaper, Duchess. It should have listed Beatrice."

"So I'm told," the duchess said with a wry smile. "And thankfully it was quickly corrected."

"Thankfully indeed," Vanessa said, a bit too heartily. "Otherwise I'd be married to a fellow who is more like a brother to me than a cousin. We both would have been miserable."

The duchess regarded her most intently. "So you truly had no interest in Grey."

"Not as a husband, no."

"But perhaps my other bachelor son interests you? I saw Sheridan whisper in your ear." The duchess fluttered her fan. "He thinks I don't notice these things, but I do. Not for nothing have I spent the past year in mourning. When a woman isn't allowed to indulge in lively social activities, she learns to pay more attention to the people around her. And to notice when her son is dancing with a particularly fetching female."

Vanessa was at a loss as to what to say. "Forgive me, Duchess, but are you asking if my intentions toward Sheridan are honorable?"

Her tart reply made the duchess chuckle. "It's hard to believe you are Cora's daughter. She would never have posed such an entertaining question." Her gaze sharpened on Vanessa. "If I *were* asking that, what would be your answer?"

"That you would have to see what happens. I can hardly know what my intentions are without knowing how the courtship will progress."

"So it's a courtship, is it?" the duchess asked.

With that pointed question still hanging in the air, Uncle Noah approached bearing two glasses of punch and handed them to the two ladies. Thank heaven. Vanessa had the feeling she'd just escaped a dissection by duchess. Next time she'd have to be better prepared.

If there was a next time. Vanessa drank deeply of her punch. The duchess appeared to have a vested interest in choosing Sheridan's mate. And Vanessa couldn't tell if the duchess approved of her or not.

At least Sheridan would support Vanessa's claim that they'd been courting. After all, the courtship intended to make Juncker jealous had been *his* idea, not hers.

Her uncle looked from Vanessa's face to the duchess's. "Am I interrupting something?"

"Not in the least," the duchess said, to Vanessa's relief. The woman sipped her punch. "I should like to know, Sir Noah, how it is we've never met until tonight. You seem like just the sort of jovial gentleman whose company I enjoy."

"My wife wasn't fond of town," he said. "Only recently did I begin making forays here again."

"Because she changed her mind about town?"

Uncle Noah stared down into his glass. "Because she passed away . . . early last year."

"I'm so sorry," the duchess said softly. "I didn't know."

He cast her a rueful smile. "I fell out of the habit of coming to London." His gaze sharpened on her. "But I mean to remedy that." When the duchess pinkened, he looked a bit triumphant. "Besides, we couldn't have met anyway. You only returned to England a short while ago, correct?"

"Actually a year and a half ago," Vanessa said. "I remember because . . ." Because that was the first time she'd danced with Sheridan. Indeed, she'd danced with him twice during his family's first week in London, before they'd headed to the country.

The duchess and her uncle both regarded her with eyebrows raised, and she stammered, "It doesn't matter why." She gazed at the duchess. "You did arrive in May of last year, did you not?"

The duchess smiled. "We did. Maurice and I were still in mourning for his brother, although our children were able to go out and about. Then just as that period ended for me and Maurice . . ."

When she trailed off and sadness stole over her face, sympathy for the duchess welled in Vanessa's throat. "You had to go into mourning again."

The woman nodded. "My mourning only ended last month." She paled a bit. "I swear, I have never been so sick of wearing black in all my life."

"I can only imagine," Uncle Noah murmured. "We gentlemen barely change our clothes while in mourning, but you ladies have a more drastic alteration to endure." A devilish look crossed his face. "And while I'm sure you look lovely in black, Duchess, you look even more beautiful in that shade of blue."

"Careful, Sir Noah," the duchess said with mischief in her voice. "Flattery is the devil's plaything."

Vanessa frowned. "I thought it was 'idle hands.'"

"Those, too," the duchess quipped.

Uncle Noah laughed. "It's not flattery if it's true."

"And that, sir, is but another flattery," the duchess said.

"Then perhaps I should demonstrate my admiration in some way other than words." He leaned close. "Will you give me the honor of dancing this next with me, Duchess?"

"It's the supper dance," the duchess said. "Are you sure you want to be forced to share my company for supper as well?"

"I can think of nothing I'd like better," he said, "although a lowly fellow like myself can only dream of having a dowager duchess's company."

"You are . . . are . . ."

"Handsome? Well-groomed?" He winked at her. "Witty?"

"Attempting a dalliance," the duchess answered. "Though I don't mind that a bit."

When he offered his arm and she took it, Vanessa shook her head. She'd never seen her uncle flirt before. It was decidedly unsettling. And very unlike him, too. So to watch him flirting with a veritable stranger—

"Is that my *mother* dancing with your uncle?" Sheridan asked as he came up beside Vanessa.

"Oh, yes. And she seemed quite eager to accept his invitation."

Sheridan gazed out over the floor at the pair. "I hope he's not assuming she's a wealthy woman. My father left her with only a minimal widow's portion."

Vanessa rolled her eyes. "My goodness, you're such a cynic. He's not dancing with her for her money. He has plenty of money and property of his own."

"In that case, I find their interest in each other intriguing."

"How so?"

"I wouldn't think they'd be well-suited as a couple. Unless . . ." He grimaced.

"Unless what?"

"Nothing. I'll ask her later what she sees in him."

Vanessa chuckled. "I think she sees a good-looking fellow to partner her for a dance."

"And supper. If we were anywhere else and if this were anything more formal, they wouldn't be paired to go in to supper together."

She stared at him. "You are amazingly stuffy sometimes, do you know that?"

He shrugged. "I was brought up with the idea that my future lay in helping hostile countries negotiate agreements satisfactory to all. I learned proper protocol at my father's knee."

"Then I should point out, Your Grace, that I most certainly would not be the one you'd take in to supper 'anywhere else . . . more formal.' So tell me, why are you willing to break protocol to dance with a lowly miss like *me?*"

He shook off whatever he was thinking and smiled at her. "Because, my dear, sometimes I like to live dangerously."

She caught her breath. So did she.

Offering her his arm, he said, "Shall we?"

"Of course," she responded.

As they headed to join the others on the floor, he muttered, "Poor William Bonham."

"Who is that?" she asked.

"Just a fellow who will be very disappointed that your uncle is flirting with my mother, and that my mother is flirting back."

"And are *you* disappointed?"

"Not disappointed so much as . . . concerned."

She laughed. "It's only one dance, Sheridan. I doubt it will lead to anything serious."

"You may be right." He seemed deep in thought as he led her to the end of the line of dancers. When he caught her staring at him, he broke into a decidedly false smile. "Never forget, my mother has had three husbands. I wouldn't put it past her to try for a fourth."

But despite his attempt at joviality, she sensed something else going on beneath his smooth exterior. He was back to being a sphinx. And that worried her.

Chapter Six

Sheridan spent half of his and Vanessa's dance watching his mother. Surely it was no coincidence that the only man Mother had danced with this evening was Lady Eustace's brother. Mother had said she would help their investigative efforts, and they'd all insisted she not do so. What if this was her helping? She wasn't good at subterfuge; not *their* mother. She could very well destroy Sheridan's own efforts.

By the time the dance was over and they were headed toward the supper room, Sheridan was already imagining all sorts of scenarios where Mother blurted out something that gave Sir Noah pause.

"He's not going to hurt her, you know," Vanessa murmured. "He *is* a gentleman, after all."

"Who?" Sheridan asked, playing dumb.

"My uncle, of course. You look as if you want to take him aside and give him a stern warning. Or a good thrashing."

He forced his attention back to Vanessa, who wore her worry on her sleeve. "That's absurd. For one thing, you're right—he *is* a gentleman. For another, my mother is perfectly capable of taking care of herself."

"Oh, good. Then we agree."

Sheridan chuckled. "We probably agree on a great many things, if you will only admit it."

"Really? Like what?" Her sparkling eyes entranced him as she and he stood in the line forming at the entrance to the supper room.

"That you look lovely in that gown."

She didn't appear as flattered as he'd expected. "Thank you," she said thinly. "Although it would be rather vain of me to agree with you on that."

"True." He cocked his head. "Then we can both agree that *I* look dashing in my theater attire. I don't mind being considered vain in the least."

She clearly fought a smile. "But I mind your assumption that I will agree."

"How could you not agree?" He grinned. "I'll have you know my valet worked very hard to make me a man of fashion for this evening."

"He can work as hard as he likes, but you will never be a man of fashion."

He blinked. "Why not?"

"You're too . . . too obviously unconcerned about your appearance. You're the very opposite of vain." She reached up with both hands to fool with his cravat. "For example, our dancing seems to have set this askew. A man of fashion would already have noticed that in a mirror and straightened it."

His heart thundered to have her so close. And God, but her hair smelled delicious, like lilies. Yes! That was the exotic scent he hadn't been able to place. Leave it to Vanessa to choose a scent that smelled exotic but was as

English as plum pudding. He barely resisted the urge to lean forward and sniff to make sure.

Clearly he had lost his mind. He must make this less personal at once, before he fell under her spell and did or said something he regretted. "What were we talking about?"

She smirked at him. "Things we agree on. So far, there has been only the one."

"Ah. Then I would point out that we both like polemoscopes."

A deep blush spread from her bosom up to her face, which only increased her spell over him, damn it. "I don't . . . know what you mean."

"Of course you do. You used one while I was in your uncle's box." He lowered his voice. "Probably to spy on Juncker."

She glanced away. "Right. Who else would I spy on?"

"Speaking of Juncker, what do you think of his poetry?" It still bothered him he couldn't reveal to her the true author of Juncker's plays. "I'm assuming you've read some of it."

"Of course," she said, a bit too hastily. "It's very moving."

How curious. Could she *not* have read his poetry? Wasn't she mad for the fellow?

They passed through the doorway, and he led her to a spot at the largest table, where his family seemed to be congregating. Juncker was at an adjoining table, so Sheridan made sure to offer Vanessa a seat with her back to the man before taking the one beside her. Sheridan had *not* enjoyed watching that fraudulent arse dance with Vanessa and be so charming and theatrical, playing a part in a farce of Juncker's own making, where Vanessa was the heroine and Juncker was the hero.

But even if Sheridan couldn't tell her Juncker hadn't written the plays that had made the man famous, Sheridan fully intended to, at the very least, expose Juncker's true character as a roué.

The food was laid out in an adjoining room, which was normally Thorncliff's breakfast room, so after placing napkins on the table to save their spots, they went to gather their provisions. As they wended their way around the room, he noticed she took an extra buttered crab, which was one less than he'd taken.

While they headed back to their seats, he said, "I see you like crab as much as I do."

"How ungentlemanly of you to notice." Her teasing smile belied her words. "A lady isn't supposed to partake so blatantly of food."

"Surely even ladies must eat."

She cast her gaze about the room. "Yes. But most ladies I know pretend that they mustn't. It's a peculiar game they play—in which they aren't supposed to eat heartily even though they do so at home."

"I take it that theirs isn't a game you enjoy."

A faint smile crept across her face. "You take it correctly. I fear I have quite a lusty appetite and no desire to hide it."

Just the word *lusty* stoked his imagination with flashes of her removing each piece of her clothing one at a time until she wore nothing but a come-hither look.

He gripped his plate as if it held the key to a wanton lady's boudoir. She was talking about food, damn it all. *Food.*

"Good," he said. "And I think no less of you for your . . .

er . . . appetite. So we will leave those other ladies to starve, if that's their preference, but in the meantime, we will eat our fill. Agreed?"

This time her smile was broader. "Agreed."

God, how he loved that rare smile, as if he had hung the moon. How he wished he *had* hung the moon for her, and not merely criticized a societal more.

They headed back to their seats. Thorn sat across from them, with Olivia on one side and Mother on the other. Next to Mother was Sir Noah. Sheridan hated to admit it, but he much preferred that his mother spend time with Sir Noah rather than William Bonham.

Thorn disliked Bonham because he thought the man too far beneath Mother for marriage. But that wasn't Sheridan's issue. He'd be happy to see Mother find companionship with someone if Bonham didn't already have a tendency to treat Sheridan like a son who needed instruction in running an estate.

Granted, Bonham had been working for the dukes of Armitage for decades, so if anyone had the right to act paternal, it was him. Still, while it was probably petty of Sheridan, as far as he was concerned no one could fill the position of mentor, advisor . . . friend except his actual father. So he didn't appreciate Bonham sniffing around his mother, trying to take his late father's place.

Mother wouldn't care how Sheridan felt about Bonham, of course. Her marriage to Sheridan's father, while amiable, hadn't exactly been a love match. And besides, she'd always behaved as she pleased.

Apparently, so had Vanessa, judging from what foods she'd put on her plate. To his surprise, most of it was the same as his. He couldn't believe anyone else liked

Brussels sprouts. Other than Thorn, that is, who had the same fondness for them as Sheridan, probably because of their upbringing in Prussia. The Prussians did love their Brussels sprouts.

"So, Sheridan," Thorn said, seeming to dissect his roast beef most deliberately, "what did you think of the play?"

Olivia paled and kept shaking her head, obviously begging Sheridan to keep silent.

Mischief seized Sheridan. "Don't tell your friend Juncker, but I thought it a bit silly."

Beside him, Vanessa let out a huff. "Isn't that exactly what I *said* you thought of it when you came to Uncle Noah's box? You don't like such 'frivolity.' You said you had no opinion, but clearly you lied."

He looked at his brother, whose brow was darkening. "You're right," Sheridan said. "I actually thought it an inane tale of events that made no sense."

Olivia cast her gaze heavenward as Thorn glowered at Sheridan. "What didn't make sense about it? And what right do you even have to judge?" Thorn sat back, having apparently given up on eating. "You're hardly a connoisseur of dramatic literature."

"Perhaps not, but I recognize good writing when I see it."

Thorn looked as if he'd swallowed a chunk of ice, shocked and annoyed all at the same time. "There's nothing wrong with Juncker's writing."

"He's your friend, so of course you would say that. But I'm not blinded by friendship."

Now Olivia, too, was shooting daggers at him. It roused his guilt. But only a bit. Thorn would have tormented him just as mercilessly if their situations had been reversed. That was what brothers did, after all.

"Surely you will at least admit the play was amusing," Thorn remarked.

"I suppose my sense of humor differs from yours," Sheridan said, now truly enjoying himself. "Clearly you like farcical situations. Whereas I prefer more subtle humor."

"That is an untruth, and you know it, Sheridan," Vanessa said. "I heard you laughing at certain scenes during the play. Do you deny it?"

Leave it to Vanessa to make a liar out of him. "I suppose there were a few droll moments." He shot Thorn a furtive glance. "A very few."

Thorn's gaze narrowed on him. Then he called out to the other table. "Juncker! Sheridan claims there were only a few droll moments in the play. What do you say to that?"

Juncker chuckled. "Your brother is simply jealous of my success—with writing as well as women."

Sheridan twisted around in his chair to face his nemesis. "The hell you say."

"How many plays have *you* written and had performed, Duke?" Juncker asked. "I daresay not a one."

"True," Sheridan shot back, "but then I've never considered playwriting my particular talent."

"Exactly." Juncker smirked at him. "It's easy to criticize something you've never attempted yourself."

"I have never attempted to play the violin, either, but surely you will grant me and everyone else here the ability to tell when it's being played off-key."

A gasp sounded from everyone overhearing the conversation, followed by tittering here and there.

Juncker did not look pleased. Good. Perhaps it would keep him from being so full of himself.

"For a man who was trained as a diplomat," Vanessa said under her breath, "you are being awfully undiplomatic to Mr. Juncker, not to mention downright rude."

"He'll survive," Sheridan murmured. "He has the skin of an elephant. Besides, Thorn is the one who involved him in our private conversation in the first place, not me."

"And what do *you* think, Miss Pryde?" Juncker called out to her. "Was my play amusing? Or, as His Grace puts it, 'played off-key.' No pun intended."

Vanessa shifted in her seat to look at Juncker. "I thought the play was witty and entertaining and not the least bit farcical. As usual."

"Traitor," Sheridan said under his breath.

"Thank you, Miss Pryde," Juncker said, clearly gloating. "I'm glad to see that *someone* here appreciates good theater."

Voices were raised around him, reassuring the man that his plays were *very* appreciated, at least by the crowd.

"I, too, appreciate good theater," Sheridan put in. "When I see it, that is."

At the mix of protests and laughter from the other guests, Juncker stared hard at Sheridan. "I wouldn't expect a duke to know much about that. Especially one who spends all his time trying to keep his ailing dukedom afloat."

The room went utterly silent. It was one thing to attack a man's talent or taste. It was quite another to bring finances into it.

"Now see here, Juncker," Thorn cried behind Sheridan. "That's my brother you're insulting."

"I can fight my own battles," Sheridan told Thorn, loudly enough to be heard by Juncker. Then he pasted a dismissive smile to his lips. "Especially when the man I'd be fighting gets his only exercise from wielding a comb."

"And a pen," Juncker said, practically daring Sheridan to announce the truth. And if not for the fact that Thorn and Olivia would never forgive him for it, Sheridan would have obliged. Even after Juncker added, "At least I don't get it from chasing heiresses."

"Not that the heiresses are complaining." Sheridan turned to Vanessa, who looked as if she found the entire exchange entertaining. But she would, wouldn't she, since she was trying to make Juncker jealous. "Are you, my dear?"

"I haven't uttered a word of complaint, but only because this discussion is ridiculous." That brought a general rumble of laughter from the others. "I refuse to get in the way of two gentlemen engaging in verbal fisticuffs."

Juncker gazed at her. "Would you prefer physical fisticuffs?"

Alarm crossed her face. "No, indeed. It would be vulgar for a woman to encourage such a thing." The crowd murmured their approval. "Besides," she went on, "I suspect neither of you knows *how* to engage in physical fisticuffs."

At the shout of laughter from the onlookers, Juncker clutched his chest. "You wound me deeply, dear lady."

"I doubt that," Vanessa said with a smile. "His Grace claims you have the skin of an elephant."

More laughter ensued.

"And the heart of a lion," Juncker shot back.

"More like the heart of a mouse," Sheridan said dryly,

"or a minor insult from a lady wouldn't have you clasping your chest."

Juncker leaned forward. "I can still use fisticuffs to prove my lion heart, if you prefer."

"I'm game for it," Sheridan bit out.

"Enough," his mother said as she rose. "There will be no fisticuffs of any kind from you two or I shall ban you both from attending any future social affairs I'm involved in."

"You'd ban your own son," Sheridan said skeptically.

"Absolutely, if he acts like a brute rather than the gentleman I taught him to be," she said in that steely voice he remembered from his childhood.

Sheridan struck his chest theatrically. "Now *I* am wounded deeply."

"I'll lend you my elephant skin if you like, Armitage," Juncker called out.

"No need," Sheridan answered. "When Mother sees fit to enter the fray, it's time to stand down." He fixed Juncker with a dark gaze. "Agreed, sir?"

Juncker hesitated only briefly. "Of course. God forbid I be regarded as a brute by the duchess."

That was considered the final word, thank God, since Sheridan definitely didn't want to cause more pain to his mother. She'd suffered enough of it in her lifetime.

And that was an end to the skirmish between him and Juncker, if it could even be called a skirmish. Although Sheridan suspected that the entire mess might have been avoided entirely if. . . .

If what? Vanessa had come down squarely on his side? If she had put herself in his corner in the first place?

She would never do that. Snagging Juncker was her

aim. And though that rankled, Sheridan was willing to help her, even if it annoyed him. Even if he disapproved. Even if all he could think of was Vanessa coming to him the way one came to a lover. . . .

Damn it all, that wasn't acceptable.

He forced a smile for Vanessa's benefit. "Shall I fetch you another buttered crab, sweetheart?"

Sweetheart? What the hell was he doing?

Wooing Vanessa, apparently, for she gave him the tenderest look she'd ever given him. "I'm fine, thank you," she said softly.

Good. Excellent. Now, what was he to do with that? It was impossible to know.

They finished their meal, making the politest of conversation with his family. The guests drifted back into the ballroom, and a gentleman snagged Vanessa for a dance.

Sheridan was about to head to the card room when Thorn pulled him aside, looking annoyed. "Olivia told me she blurted out my secret earlier. So your needling me merely served to reinforce the public impression that Juncker writes my plays."

"Well, now that you know I know, I assume it's all right if I tell Vanessa."

"It certainly is not."

Sheridan scowled. "Why?"

"Because you so obviously want to." Thorn flashed him a thoroughly devious smile. "I suppose that's enough comeuppance for your remarks earlier about my writing ability."

"You know I didn't mean any of that."

"I'm sure my guests assumed you did."

That stymied Sheridan. "Since when do you care what other people think?"

"I don't." Thorn laughed. "I merely get the same amount of pleasure from tormenting you as you did from tormenting me."

He did have a point. Sheridan stared him down. "I don't need your permission to tell Vanessa, you realize."

Thorn shrugged. "But if you do, you'll be breaking your promise to Olivia. Are you a man of your word or not?"

Sheridan released a frustrated breath, then started to walk away.

"It really bothers you that Miss Pryde has a tendre for Juncker, doesn't it?" Thorn said.

Halting to face his brother once more, Sheridan said, "Don't be absurd. I don't care about that. She and I are merely friends." Perhaps if he kept telling himself that, it would eventually become true. Because he couldn't afford to have her as anything but a friend.

"No man who is merely a friend to a woman looks at her the way you do."

Sheridan bit back an oath. "And how is that?"

"As if you aren't likely to see her kind again. As if she's the answer to your unhappiness."

"What makes you think I'm unhappy?"

"Come now, Sheridan, you've been unhappy since before Father died. Admit it—you hated how he pushed you to learn estate management when all you wanted was to serve England in the diplomatic services."

Sheridan tamped down the pain that knifed through him. "Clearly you don't know me at all." It wasn't estate management he disliked. It was his own inability to grasp the nuances of double-entry accounting so he could get a good grasp on what the property needed and where all the money had gone. "But I guess nine years apart does change things a bit."

Thorn eyed him askance. "What do you mean?"

"Never mind. You wouldn't understand." And he wasn't about to explain. It angered him that he couldn't handle the numbers. It was apparently a necessary part of over-seeing his role.

At least Father had thought it was. He'd relied on his man of affairs out of necessity, since Bonham had been attached to the Duke of Armitage for years, but Father had insisted on Sheridan learning how to make sure things were done right, too. Sadly, Father had died without ever being certain his son could handle that aspect of the burden put on him as duke.

"Very well. You can keep your secrets to yourself." Thorn moved closer. "But just so you know, Grey told me he was having you question his aunt Cora. Any luck?"

"Not yet. At the play, she was decidedly uncommunicative on the subject. I do wonder, however, if she stayed away from your party precisely because she doesn't want to discuss what happened."

"Or she wanted to give you and Vanessa time together."

Sheridan gritted his teeth. "I told you, Vanessa and I—"

"I know, I know. You're just friends." He shook his head. "You might be able to find out something from Vanessa, you know."

"Vanessa wasn't even born until after both your father and Grey's were dead."

"I don't mean about those murders. I mean about *your*

father's murder. My true father's murder. Because you know I consider him my only father."

"Of course." Sheridan had no doubt of it. All three of his half-siblings had grown up as his Father's children, with only Grey leaving home as a boy. Thorn and Gwyn hadn't even been born when their own father died. "But I don't see how Vanessa would know anything about either of the two later murders. Surely you're not suggesting that Lady Eustace actually went out to meet Father in the country and shoved him off a bridge. Why, she's older than Mother!"

Thorn shot him a rueful smile. "And you think our mother too old to push someone off a bridge?"

"I guess she could, but—"

"You're right." Thorn sighed. "I don't believe any of our suspects could do that, either."

"Or pull Uncle Armie off of his horse a few months earlier."

"Precisely." Thorn cocked his head. "But if one of them—Lady Eustace, for example—hired someone like Elias to do it, Vanessa might have seen the fellow. Or heard her mother talk about him or to him."

Sheridan nodded absently. A young criminal they'd uncovered during their investigation, Elias had been murdered before revealing who'd hired him. "I suppose. I'll see if I can learn anything from either of them." Remembering what Olivia had said, Sheridan stared at his brother. "And how is it going with the questioning of Lady Norley?"

"Oh, God," Thorn muttered. "I can't do that myself. She's my mother-in-law, for pity's sake. She'll hate me."

A laugh escaped Sheridan. Olivia had been serious about that. "So? Have your wife do it."

"She will. But we just got married, and frankly, I don't think Lady Norley's capable of it."

Sheridan smirked at his brother. "I see. Don't want to rock the boat."

"You have no idea. Just wait until *you're* married, and then you'll understand."

Not if I have anything to say about it. Sheridan saw their mother approaching.

"Olivia is looking for you," she told Thorn, blessedly keeping Sheridan from having to answer his brother. "She's in the ballroom."

"We'll talk about this more later," Thorn told Sheridan before walking off to find his wife.

"What were you discussing?" Mother asked.

Sheridan forced a smile. "Nothing important."

Mother stared hard at him for a moment, but she'd always had an uncanny ability to recognize when her sons shouldn't be probed for more information. "If you say so."

"I thought you were going to dance with Sir Noah again."

She shrugged. "Later. Although I suspect the dancing is dying down. With this small a crowd—"

"Small! There must be thirty people in there at least."

"That's barely enough to get a good cotillion going."

"Is that such a necessity?"

"Of course." She tapped his arm with her fan. "I should hope you would be part of it."

Propriety dictated he couldn't dance with Vanessa again, and he wasn't in the mood to dance with any other woman.

"Some of the gentlemen are playing cards. I mean to join them."

"Oh, very well." She paused, then added, "I like your young lady."

That put Sheridan instantly on alert. "What young lady?"

"You know very well whom I mean. Miss Pryde. Cora's daughter."

"She is hardly *my* young lady."

"Oh? She as much as told me you were courting."

"Did she?" Why should that surprise him? It was exactly what they were supposed to be doing—pretending to court. "I suppose the cat is out of the bag now."

"You were trying to keep it secret?" Mother asked in a deceptively neutral tone.

No wonder she hadn't probed him about Thorn's remark. She'd been saving her ammunition for this.

Then he wouldn't disappoint her. "Secret from you? Absolutely. I know how you get when you're trying to determine if someone is good enough for one of your children."

She looked insulted. "And how is that?"

He hid a smile. "Nosy, intrusive, frighteningly direct."

"For your information, I was none of those things." She sniffed. "I merely wanted to make sure you weren't taking advantage of her."

Sheridan tensed. "Now why would I do such a thing?"

"So you can get close to her mother and find out what Cora knows about my first husband's murder."

Damn. His mother was far too intuitive. It was how she'd survived all the deaths—the murders, possibly—of her husbands. "It's not as bad as it sounds."

"Isn't it? You're playing with the heart of a lovely young woman. I'd rather see none of you solve Maurice's murder than have you harm an innocent like Miss Pryde."

He drew himself up. "Do you really think me capable of that, Mother?"

"I think you capable of . . . doing what you must to get what you want."

"Thanks for the vote of confidence," he said sarcastically. "But Miss Pryde isn't remotely interested in me."

His mother cocked her head to one side. "No?"

"No. She has her heart set on Juncker. And I promised to help her get him by courting her so she could make him jealous."

"Juncker? The *playwright?*"

"What other Juncker is there?" he said irritably.

Mother burst into laughter. "Oh! Oh, dear . . . that's rich."

"What's so funny?"

She shook her head. "You poor deluded fools."

He crossed his arms over his chest. "To whom are you referring?"

"You and Miss Pryde, of course." She patted his shoulder. "I withdraw my concern. Clearly the two of you have everything quite well in hand." She walked away. "Juncker! What a lark."

All he could do was stand there staring after her. It appeared that losing his father had unhinged his mother at last.

Vanessa couldn't find her uncle anywhere. Where could he have gone? It was long past midnight, and after a play, several dances, and a supper, she was ready to go home.

She wandered down a hall and heard chatter coming

from behind closed doors. When she peeked inside, she found not only her uncle and Mr. Juncker playing cards as partners but Sheridan cheering them on.

He had practically come to blows with Mr. Juncker earlier, and now they were jovially ribbing each other about the cards? Discussing the quality of the champagne they were drinking, and Lord knows what else?

She would never understand men. Only a man could go from sworn enemy to congenial comrade in the space of a few hours. Although she'd never actually been in a situation where her female friends turned on her, if they ever did, she sure as the devil wouldn't be playing cards with them a short while later as if nothing had happened!

Meanwhile, Thornstock and some gray-haired fellow with his back to her were apparently losing and none too happy about it. Indeed, Mr. Juncker and Sheridan were taking turns tormenting them, punctuated by the occasional jibe from Uncle Noah.

But Uncle Noah mostly seemed too busy flirting with the dowager duchess to bother with the other fellows. How very interesting.

And who was Thornstock's partner? She had no idea until the man made some sullen remark to Uncle Noah. As she recognized the voice, she let out a silent oath. Lord Lisbourne. Oh, dear. She hadn't realized the marquess was even here! He must have been in the card room the entire time. Thank goodness Mama had chosen not to attend the party, too, or she would already have tried to throw Vanessa and Lord Lisbourne together.

Now Vanessa was in a quandary. Go join her uncle despite the presence of the marquess? Or sneak away and find Lady Thornstock to ask Uncle Noah how much longer his game would go?

"Miss Pryde!" Lord Lisbourne called out.

Too late. The dratted fellow had spotted her.

Pasting a false smile to her lips, Vanessa entered the card room. "So this is where all my dance partners have disappeared to."

"Oh?" Lord Lisbourne said, a frown beetling his pale brow. "Is the dancing over already?"

"Already!" She laughed. "It's nearly two A.M., sir."

He shrugged. "That is nothing to the usual fashionable balls."

And he should know, since he went to plenty of them. Despite his age, the marquess was considered by all the mothers—and even some of the young ladies—as quite a catch. He was attractive enough, Vanessa supposed, with his trim figure and his ready smile. But he had a penchant for dressing oddly, like tonight in his lavish coat and waistcoat of bright green velvet worn with brown silk breeches. His attire seemed hopelessly old-fashioned next to the more subdued colors, wool coats, and trousers of Thornstock, Sheridan, and even her uncle.

And now Thornstock was frowning at him. "This wasn't a ball, Lisbourne, but a very informal entertainment after the play. Besides, the hour *is* growing late."

"Nonsense. The night is still young." Lord Lisbourne patted the chair next to him. "Do come and sit by me, Miss Pryde, to observe the game. We're playing quadrille, and I'm in dire need of the kind of good luck only a damsel as pretty as you can provide."

She wouldn't take that chair for all the world. Lord Lisbourne had a tendency to lean too close to a lady, especially if he thought he could get a glimpse down the front of her gown. "Forgive me, sir, but duty dictates that I give my store of luck, meager as it is, to my uncle."

"You had *better* do so, Niece," Uncle Noah said. "Because if I lose, I'll be forced to keep you here another two hours to win my money back." He darted a glance at her. "And I can see from the droop of your shoulders that you're ready to leave."

"Not a bit," she lied, loath to ruin her uncle's fun. Not since before the long illness of her aunt had she seen him this cheerful. "But I will expect a percentage of your winnings in exchange."

Uncle Noah gave a hearty laugh. "I can provide that quite soon. Juncker and I are trouncing Lisbourne and Thornstock. Let us win this hand and perhaps the next, and I will meet your price." He gazed up at Sheridan's mother. "Besides, I daresay the duchess is as weary as you but simply better at hiding it. And since she is the one regulating our various quadrille payments, we cannot do without her."

"Do not underestimate my stamina, sir," the duchess said in a lilting voice. "It's not yet that time of the morning when the guests are having too much fun to leave but know they should do so before they keel over from exhaustion."

"No one is keeling over on my watch, Mother," Sheridan said, his eyes twinkling. "Come, Miss Pryde. Stand by me so you can see Juncker's cards and signal your uncle about what our friend has in his hand."

Thornstock scowled at Sheridan. "That is *not* amusing."

"Don't worry, Thornstock." Vanessa approached

Sheridan. "Contrary to what your brother seems to think, *I* am not a cheat."

"And you couldn't cheat anyway," Uncle Noah said, "since you don't know how to play quadrille."

"Uncle! Must you reveal all my secrets?"

"Don't get yourself in a huff," he said. "I only recently learned the game myself."

"I don't know how to play it either," Sheridan murmured to her as she reached him. "It seems unnecessarily complicated for a mere card game."

"Exactly," Vanessa murmured back. "I simply have no desire to work that hard for something that purports to be entertainment." Neither of her parents—and none of her friends—had liked it, so she'd never learned.

"Shh!" Thornstock hissed. "I can't think with the two of you whispering like children."

Sheridan touched her elbow. "Come, Miss Pryde. Let's go fetch you a glass of champagne from the adjoining room and leave my boorish brother to his losing streak."

"We may yet win!" Thornstock cried after them as they escaped into the other room, laughing.

They walked over to the table where a yawning footman stood at the ready to offer them champagne.

"My brother is a sore loser, I'm afraid." Sheridan gestured to the footman to pour a glass for her. "Always has been. Which is why I rarely play any sort of game with him. He doesn't understand the point of simply enjoying the game."

"And what games do *you* enjoy?"

He shrugged. "Chess. Croquet." His eyes gleamed at her. "Any kind of horse race."

"I do love a good horse race myself. We must go riding sometime."

Turning pensive, he nodded. "Sometime, yes."

After the footman handed her the filled glass, Sheridan led her over to the fireplace.

She sipped some champagne. "But getting back to your brother—for his sake, I hope he's as wealthy as I've heard . . . and not prone to bid too high on card games *or* horse races. I would hate to see his duchess beggared so early in their marriage. Judging from the little bit of time I spent talking to her tonight, I like her."

"We all do. But trust me, Olivia has nothing to fear. Thorn can't be too worried about funds, since he was willing to loan Lisbourne money."

"Lisbourne!" She glanced back toward the door and lowered her voice. "I've always heard it said that he's rich."

"Not according to Grey," Sheridan said. "I gather that years of gambling have finally caught up with him, and he's not doing well financially. Although I don't think it's widely known."

"Well, leave it to Grey to uncover such a secret. He's good at that." She shook her head. "Poor Mama. She's set on having me marry the man because she's certain he's wealthy."

Sheridan seemed to watch her closely. "But surely you would not wish such a match."

"Good heavens, no. Aside from the fact that he's over twice my age, he's very . . . he has a tendency to . . ."

"Let his eyes roam where his hands dare not?"

A relieved sigh escaped her. She'd never tried to put such things into words for a man before. "Exactly."

"Shall I call him out?" His voice held a note of steel that both shocked and thrilled her.

"For me?" Her pulse faltered at the thought until she realized he might be joking. "You wouldn't do that, and you know it."

"Are you calling me a liar?" he asked.

"I'm calling you a tease."

His gaze grew shuttered. "Well, I *am* courting you. Isn't that what a suitor would do?"

Oh. Right. Their subterfuge. She forced a smile. "A real suitor, perhaps. But not a pretend one. Still, although I know you don't mean it, I appreciate the thought. Fortunately, Lord Lisbourne hasn't done anything so far to warrant such an extravagant response . . . from a real suitor *or* a pretend one."

"That's good then. I would hate to waste a bullet on him."

Her uncle's voice came from the doorway. "I am now at your disposal, my dear girl. Even without being in the room, you brought me good luck. So we can leave if you wish."

She had half a mind to say he could play another game if he wanted. She rarely had a chance to get Sheridan to herself. But she truly was exhausted, and there was no guarantee Sheridan would stay around.

"That would be nice, Uncle, thank you. I *am* rather tired."

Lord Lisbourne appeared in the doorway next to her uncle. "I shall call on you and your mother tomorrow, Miss Pryde."

Thanks for the warning. "I'm sure Mama will be delighted to have you."

Being full of himself as usual, he didn't even seem to

register her own lack of enthusiasm. He merely nodded. "Good evening then."

"The same to you, sir."

As he walked back into the other room, engaging her uncle in conversation, Sheridan placed a hand on her elbow to stay her. "Are you *sure* you don't want me to call him out?"

"Quite sure."

"Nonetheless, tomorrow I will call on you and your mother myself. And try to time it so I arrive shortly after Lord Lisbourne."

"Now *that* I would appreciate," she said with a grateful smile. "If it's no trouble."

He stared at her a long moment before dropping his hand from her elbow with a shuttered look. "No trouble at all. You're practically a member of our family. Grey would never forgive me for letting anything happen to his favorite cousin."

Her heart sank. After kissing him, being kissed by him, dancing with him . . . laughing with him tonight, he still saw her as a little sister who needed protecting?

Not only was that disheartening, but she didn't know if she could go back to being nothing more than a friend to Sheridan. Yet how much longer could she endure the battering that his mercurial nature gave her self-confidence?

Chapter Seven

The morning after Thorn's party, Sheridan stared at the account ledgers for his estate, hoping to make the numbers resolve into something that made sense to him. Because he honestly couldn't see why his various properties' finances hadn't shown any real improvement since a year ago, when the death of his father had forced Sheridan to take them over.

He'd instituted several of the changes to his crops Grey had suggested, but so far those hadn't helped. When he'd mentioned that to Grey, his brother had said it would take time to see results. While Sheridan could understand that, surely their more abundant harvest this past autumn should have increased their income. Sheridan had even read up on ways to sell his property's viable resources, like timber and game, and had begun auctioning off items that might turn a quick profit, but while it had helped slow the bleeding, it hadn't stanched it entirely.

Damn it all to hell.

Sheridan shifted in his chair to stare out of the French doors at the courtyard garden. When he'd first seen the study, after his family had arrived from Prussia, he'd thought it badly designed. The room was long but not very wide across, a width that was reduced by the bookshelves lining either side. Since the door to the hall faced the glass doors to the garden, the only place to put a desk was off to the side of the French doors. That meant the desk chair faced away from the garden.

Over time he came to realize that the room had certain practicalities. Since the courtyard had a lot of light, which the glass doors let into the study, he could often see well enough in summer not to even need a lamp or candle until long into the evening. And if he turned in his chair, he could watch the robins and warblers come to bathe in the fountain or revel in the cool dark green of English ivy growing up the walls. These days, he spent a great deal of time seeking comfort in his little glimpse of the outdoors. It didn't substitute entirely for his morning rides, but it helped.

Today, however, it wasn't doing the trick. There was too much at stake for the gardens to soothe him. He *had* to find a way to improve the estate's income—his tenants and servants depended on him. But Uncle Armie's overspending had sunk Armitage Hall and its surrounding properties in a well so deep, Sheridan began to fear he would never be able to dig it out.

Someone at the entrance to his study cleared his throat. Sheridan looked up to see his father's man of affairs standing in the doorway.

"You sent for me, Your Grace?" William Bonham said.

"Bonham! Good, you're here. Come in, come in. I have something to tell you."

Bonham entered the room warily. "Nothing bad, I hope."

"Not any worse than what's been going on for the past decade or so."

"That's good, I suppose," Bonham said with a look of profound distress.

At least the man recognized the gravity of the situation. Sheridan stood up behind his massive desk. Like so many of the furnishings for both Armitage Hall in Lincolnshire and Armitage House here in London, it was unnecessarily extravagant and ornate. When Sheridan had the chance, he meant to refurbish the place and replace the rococo-style pieces with furniture that had clean lines and simple designs. But that would have to come much later, once he'd reversed the downward spiral of the dukedom's holdings.

He gestured to the chair in front of his desk. "Please sit. I'm a bit too restless to sit myself." After Bonham had taken a seat, Sheridan added, "I've come to a decision." He swallowed the resentment he felt whenever he thought of what he was about to do. "You were right. I must sell the best of the mounts in Uncle Armie's—*my*—stables. The sale will provide the estate with much-needed funds for the long-overdue renovations on the tenant cottages."

Sheridan paced behind the desk. "And we won't need so many mounts for riding anymore anyway." A pang hit his chest that he ignored. "Though I still say we should keep a few of the Thoroughbreds. The stud fees and prize money they bring in practically pays for their upkeep." Even if they didn't make great saddle horses.

"That's a wise course of action, Duke," Bonham said. "I know your uncle amassed a truly spectacular display of horseflesh, but having such a large stable isn't practical."

"I agree, much as it pains me to admit it." He dragged

in a heavy breath. "So you'll arrange for the auction at Tattersall's?"

"Of course. But it will take a few weeks, if that meets with your approval."

"I expected as much." Sheridan picked up a long sheet of paper from the desk and walked over to hand it to Bonham. "I've made a list of which horses are to be sold. I thought we should do two auctions, starting with the ones here in London and then later selling the ones in the country."

"If you wish. Although I still suggest—"

"That they all be sold in one big auction. I know. I remember what you said." He braced one hip against the desk. "But I've spoken to other sporting gentlemen at Father's club, and they say it can be just as efficient, maybe even more so, if the auctions are done separately."

"They're your horses, Your Grace, so of course you should handle the sales any way you see fit."

Bonham sounded offended, damn it. Sheridan had obviously been too sharp with him. "I do appreciate your advice, Bonham. You know that, right?"

"I do." An awkward silence fell between them. Bonham shifted in his chair. "I hope you and your family are well. I understand several of you were out last night with the duchess."

Sheridan bit down a sharp retort at the man's particular mention of Mother. Bonham was just being polite. "We were." Then he paused as something occurred to him. "How did you know about that?"

Bonham's cheeks reddened. "From the newspaper. There was mention of a social affair thrown by your brother at Thorncliff."

Bloody hell. "Yes, well, it was rather impromptu and casual. A relatively small crowd." So why did he feel guilty about not inviting Bonham? It hadn't even been *Sheridan's* party, blast it, and it wasn't as if Bonham had been at the charity performance.

He hadn't, had he? God, if he had, then he must be terribly insulted.

The man nodded, almost as if he'd heard Sheridan's thoughts, which was ridiculous. "Oh," Bonham said, "and the article mentioned that you and Miss Pryde are about to be wed. Congratulations, Your Grace."

The bottom dropped out of Sheridan's stomach. Who the hell had told the newspaper that lie? Vanessa would be none too happy. The courtship was supposed to be just to make Juncker jealous, not to link Sheridan and Vanessa so irrevocably that their parting of the ways down the line would damage both their names and reputations.

Bonham wasn't finished, unfortunately. "It's none of my concern, I realize, but I must say it's very brave of you to take on a wife, given your present financial difficulties—"

"You're right—it *is* none of your concern." When Bonham paled, he added, "Nonetheless, it might set your mind at ease to know that Miss Pryde has a substantial dowry." He was probably exaggerating a bit, but Bonham's concerns irritated him.

Apparently, his words *did* set Bonham's mind at ease, for the man's expression cleared. "Well, that *is* fortunate. It sounds like a wise decision indeed."

Sheridan hadn't meant to imply he might marry Vanessa, but his usual reticence about his personal life kept him from telling the fellow otherwise. "Glad that you approve," he said sarcastically.

Bonham seemed unaware of the sarcasm.

Wait. Sheridan had read the *Times* this morning, and that bit of gossip wasn't in it. "Which newspaper are you referring to, Bonham?"

"The *London Society Times*."

Sheridan groaned. That same paper had been focused on his family since their arrival in England. Actually, it had probably been printing gossip about Grey since he'd set foot on English shores twenty-five years ago.

Well, perhaps not that long, but a long bloody time all the same.

"I can send you my copy if you wish," Bonham offered when Sheridan's silence went on a bit long.

"Thank you, but no need to trouble yourself. I'm sure I can find a copy in my club's reading room."

Bonham eyed him askance. "If you don't mind my saying so, Your Grace, that's somewhere else you might trim expenses: club dues."

"Fortunately—or unfortunately, from your perspective— I don't pay dues. My father won a lifetime membership or some such. Anyway, it's free. Because if it weren't, I would leave the club without a single qualm just to save those dues."

Bonham did indeed look disappointed. Poor fellow had been working very hard to help Sheridan find some way out of the financial hole his uncle had dug for them years ago. What Bonham *should* have done was try to curb Uncle Armie's excesses when his uncle had been alive. Then again, Uncle Armie hadn't seemed to be the sort of fellow who let himself be guided by a mere man of affairs.

"Sheridan! There you are." His mother marched into the study, waving a newspaper and not seeming to notice

Bonham, who'd stood and moved to the side the moment she'd called Sheridan's name. "Have you seen the *London Society Times* yet?" She dropped the paper onto his desk. "Did you intend for them to say all this about your courtship of Vanessa?"

He forced a smile. "Mother, Bonham is here. Perhaps we could save this discussion for later." After Sheridan paid his visit to the Pryde town house to see if *Vanessa* had seen the paper. And if she had, how she was taking all this.

His mother stopped short to look about her. Sheridan could tell exactly when she spotted Bonham by her sudden blush. Was there indeed something going on between them? Or was she merely embarrassed to be talking about private matters in front of the man? With Mother, it was hard to tell.

Bonham bowed to Mother and then to Sheridan. "Actually, Your Grace, unless there's something else, I will take my leave."

"Thank you, Bonham," Sheridan said. "I do believe that's all. But I appreciate you coming such a long way for such a short meeting."

Casting a speaking look at Sheridan's mother, Bonham said, "I am always happy to visit Armitage House, Your Grace." Then he left.

As soon as he'd gone into the hall, Mother opened her mouth, but Sheridan put a finger to his lips and walked over to close the door.

She cocked her head. "What was that for? I'm sure we can expect Bonham to be discreet."

"But perhaps not the servants."

"No doubt the servants have already read the gossip. So you're being careful for nothing."

As Sheridan returned to the desk, he gestured to the

chair Bonham had vacated. "That might be the case, *if* the article is what I wish to discuss. But it isn't. Not yet, anyway."

After a quick, indrawn breath, she dropped into the chair. "So . . . um . . . what *did* you want to talk about?"

"Your conversations with Vanessa's uncle last night."

She stared at him defiantly. "I don't care what that article says. It was nothing more than a harmless flirtation."

A vise tightened around his chest. "Are you saying that the article mentioned you and Sir Noah specifically?"

Her defiance faded. "I-I thought you knew. Have you not read it?"

"Of course not." When did he have time to read gossip these days?

He picked up the paper and scanned the columns until he found the portion Bonham and Mother had mentioned.

The impromptu event, held at the Thornstock town house in Mayfair, included dancing and supper for those select few fortunate enough to be invited. The Duke of Armitage danced first with Miss Pryde, his half brother's cousin, and then later on managed to engage that same lovely woman for the supper dance. There have been rumors of late that Miss Pryde prefers the talented Mr. Juncker above everyone, but it didn't appear to be the case last evening—the famous playwright only managed *one* dance with Miss Pryde to the duke's two. Your faithful correspondent wagers we will soon hear wedding bells for Miss Pryde and the Duke of Armitage.

Sheridan grimaced. Vanessa was going to kill him. If people were assuming they were nearly engaged, she would have trouble changing that public perception so she could marry someone else. Since he was sure Juncker would never wed her anyway, that could materially damage her prospects for a betrothal with some other fellow who took her fancy.

But he still hadn't seen anything about his mother, so he read on.

> There were hints of other possible future weddings in the offing. The Dowager Duchess of Armitage was seen with Sir Noah Rayner more than once, and they looked most amiable. He, too, was successful in gaining her companionship for supper. Perhaps the fourth time is the charm for the duchess.

Anger welled up in Sheridan. "What is this . . . this arse trying to say?" He pinned his mother with a hard look. "That you were unhappy with all your previous husbands?" Like his father, for example?

It was foolish to be angry over that. His parents had never hidden the fact that their marriage had been one between friends, and romantic love hadn't entered into the equation. Much as that stuck in his craw, it was something he and his siblings considered a truth of their family.

"So is this writer correct?" he went on. "Are you romantically interested in Sir Noah? Or are you simply using him to make Bonham jealous? Or pretending to be interested in him for other reasons?"

She shot out of the chair. "I don't see how that's any of your concern."

He crossed his arms over his chest. "It's my concern if you're attempting to 'investigate' the death of Grey's father by cozying up to Sir Noah."

The pure shock on her face told him he'd made a false supposition.

Then her expression closed up with all the stubbornness he'd come to expect from his mother. "And what if I was?" She stared him down. "Weren't you doing the same thing, trying to cozy up to Miss Pryde to get closer to her mother?"

God, but Mother was certainly good at understanding how her sons thought. Despite knowing what she was after, it put him on the defensive. "I told you before, it's not as bad as it sounds."

"No point in you trying to deny it. Before Grey left town yesterday, he told me what he was planning to have you do."

That didn't sound like Grey. "Did he really?"

"Are you saying I'm lying?"

Damn. If he wasn't careful, this would degenerate into Mother making claims that he couldn't prove or disprove. "You have been known to fudge the truth occasionally. Besides, I got the impression Grey was in a hurry to leave town. So I can't see why he would visit you first."

His mother smiled a cat-in-the-cream smile. "I came upon him while I was visiting Gwyn. She was the one who gave Grey the name of a respected accoucheur in London. That's why he sought her out. Before he came here, that is."

There was no way he could dispute that. Not without talking to Gwyn. "As I told you before, I was cozying up to Vanessa because she wanted to make Juncker jealous.

That's all." When she opened her mouth as if to dispute his claims, he held his hand up. "And if you want to confirm that, you'll have to ask *her.* I've already said more than I should have."

He wasn't about to admit his mother was right about his ulterior motive for being around Vanessa. It was the sort of thing Mother might blurt out while sharing confidences with the young woman. And on some level, he knew it would hurt Vanessa deeply. He refused to do that to her. It seemed . . . wrong somehow.

As wrong as actually using her to find out what you need to know?

Inwardly he cursed. He was on a mission. His family's very lives hung in the balance. Four men were already dead. Someone had destroyed Olivia's laboratory—she could easily have died in the explosion. What if Mother or one of his brothers was next? He had to determine who was trying to kill or maim members of his family.

"Now, if you don't mind," he went on, "I have more ledgers to go over before I can pay a visit to Vanessa. She might very well be alarmed by that article in the *London Society Times.* I must reassure her that it won't cause any great damage to her plans to snag Juncker." Not to mention, he'd promised to protect her from Lisbourne. And he took that promise seriously.

His mother snorted. "If you say so."

"Is there anything else you need from me?"

She rose from the chair. "Not at the moment, no."

"Good. Then I shall see you this evening." He called out to stay her march toward the door to his study. "I hope you will keep this confidential."

"Of course. Don't I always?"

He stifled a skeptical laugh. "Not if you can avoid it."

Mother didn't seem to appreciate that, for with a sniff she exited the room. Then it was back to perusing his account ledgers once more.

Chapter Eight

Vanessa slept late and wandered down the stairs just past noon to have her breakfast. After selecting a hearty meal to see her through the afternoon's calls, she thumbed through the newspapers laid out on the table until she found her favorite, the *London Society Times*. It didn't take her long to notice an article about Thornstock's party. The more she read, the sicker she felt. Who was this writer, that he managed to be at so many private engagements? Or to have connections to people at so many private engagements?

In a panic, she turned to the footman manning the breakfast table. "Has Mama seen this paper, by any chance?"

"I don't believe so, miss. She hasn't been down to breakfast yet."

Thank heaven! Perhaps Mama really had been feeling ill when she'd left Vanessa with Uncle Noah and had come home.

But Vanessa wasn't daft enough to go check on her. Let Mama sleep. And to make sure her mother never read this issue of the gossip rag, Vanessa tucked it under her arm, grabbed a roll, and hurried up the stairs. Unfortunately, she didn't make it to her room before her mother accosted her in the hall.

Mama waved a page of newsprint at her. "What is the meaning of *this,* young lady?"

"I have no idea what you're talking about, Mama." Pleading ignorance sometimes worked.

This wasn't one of those times. "No? Then what is this?" Her mother snatched the newspaper from under Vanessa's arm.

"I'm bringing it to my room to read."

"A likely story. I wouldn't even have seen this bit of gossip if not for my friend next door, coming to congratulate me on your 'brilliant coup' last night." Mama advanced forward, swatting Vanessa with the newspaper and forcing her to back up toward her room. "So while I lay ill in my bed, you *had* to defy me, dancing with Armitage not once but twice!" She thrust the article at Vanessa. "When you could have been with Lord Lisbourne instead!"

"Lord Lisbourne was in the card room the whole evening," Vanessa protested.

"Exactly!" Her mother stabbed the article with one finger. "You could have been there, too, hanging on his arm, encouraging him, having intimate conversations. . . ."

For pity's sake, what was her mother going on and on about? How could Mama have known that the marquess was even there when Vanessa herself hadn't known until later?

Oh, no. Surely not.

Vanessa skimmed the newsprint. A few paragraphs down from the part about her and Sheridan, she found a mention of Lord Lisbourne.

Rumor has it that the card room was as lively as the ballroom. The Marquess of Lisbourne acquitted himself admirably, reportedly winning a pot early in the evening, with the heiress of Hitchings at his side.

This writer would be the death of her. "Mama, I can explain—"

Her mother sniffed. "Don't bother. I know what you're up to. And I don't like it one bit."

Vanessa tensed. Had Mama caught on to the real focus of all her hopes?

With one finger, her mother stabbed Vanessa's chest. "You're trying to make that Mr. Juncker jealous so he'll offer for you."

Relief coursed through her. Thank heaven Mama only saw things on the surface.

"Well, I won't stand for it!" her mother went on. "Next time you see Lord Lisbourne, girl, you will cozy up to him or else."

Vanessa's temper flared. She could tolerate Mama's machinations and ranting and attempts to marry Vanessa off, but she *hated* being called "girl." It smacked too much of how Sheridan insisted on regarding her. "Or else what, Mama? You will throw me out in the street? You will try to starve me as you and Papa did to Grey?"

Her mother looked startled. No surprise there. She was used to having Vanessa ignore her behavior rather than make a fuss. "That was all your father's doing. I had no part in it."

"But you didn't stop it, did you? Stand up for him against Papa?" She thrust her face in her mother's. "I am not a girl; I am a full-grown woman who knows her own mind. I am *not* going to marry Lord Lisbourne, not now, not ever. Besides, I have it on good authority that the marquess is a notorious gambler with pockets to let, to use your favorite term. So he is only nosing around me because he needs to marry a woman with a generous dowry."

Mama blanched. "That's . . . that can't be . . . It's not true." She crossed her arms over her chest. "I don't believe you. Who is this 'good authority'?"

"A very reliable one, I swear."

"If you won't say who it is, I have no way to assess the source," she said with a sniff. "So you'd best be prepared to be nice to Lord Lisbourne, because—"

Vanessa sighed. "It's Grey." By way of Sheridan, but Mama needn't hear that. "And you know Grey always comes by these bits of information honestly. You've seen him make good financial use of such things before."

Mama glanced away, the uncertainty in her face clearly demonstrating how compelling she found Vanessa's argument. "Well. Perhaps Grey is merely paving the way for his half brother to swoop in and take your dowry."

"Come now, Mama. Can't you see? It's Lord Lisbourne who wishes to take my dowry."

"I consider that unlikely."

"Fine. Then *you* can marry him." Vanessa turned and headed for her bedroom. "Oh, and by the way, he said he's calling on us today, so I'd best get dressed."

"What?" her mother screeched. "Why didn't you say so? Good Lord, I barely have time to prepare!"

The last thing Vanessa saw as she went into her room

was her mother hurrying toward her own bedchamber, calling for her maid and the housekeeper.

Precisely at three, when people from the previous night's affair could be expected to pay calls, Vanessa slipped down the stairs as silently as a cat, hoping to avoid another private meeting with her mother. Vanessa already regretted the last one. She didn't like it when she got angry and lashed out at Mama. It made her sound precisely like the child her mother made her out to be. She wanted to be in control of her temper. Papa had often gone into rages, and watching it as a child had terrified her.

Unfortunately, her mother brought out the worst in her. So Vanessa was relieved to hear from the footman that Mama was already downstairs waiting for her in the best parlor with their first caller.

Almost relieved, anyway. Because a peek inside the parlor revealed that Lord Lisbourne was their caller, and he'd clearly come "a-courting," as Vanessa's maid liked to say. As usual, he had dressed much too finely for paying calls—this time in another suit of velvet, but dark blue, with cerulean knee breeches, of all things. She supposed she should be glad he wasn't sporting a powdered wig.

And why was the marquess obsessed with velvet, anyway? He certainly liked to be seen in it. Vanessa would think it was his age making him so unfashionable, except that her uncle of nearly the same age wouldn't wear such a suit even in the grave. Surely Lord Lisbourne employed a valet who knew better than to dress him so.

Then again, she couldn't imagine the pompous marquess allowing a mere valet to tell him what to wear.

He caught sight of her in the doorway and shot to his feet. That's when Vanessa spotted what he held in his hand.

Daisies. Oh, dear. This was going to be a problem. He'd brought her a lovely bouquet of daisies and hothouse roses, and he insisted upon handing them to her instead of asking a servant to put them in water.

She held them at arm's length as if to admire them. "They're beautiful." She tried not to breathe in, but it was no use. As always for her with daisies, a fit of sneezing overtook her. "Forgive me . . . achoo! . . . Lord Lis— Achoo achoo! They're . . . I can't . . . Achoo!"

Thank goodness her mother rushed over to snatch the flowers from her. "You stop that this instant, young lady! These are lovely." She sniffed them, then glared at her daughter. "I can't imagine why you're being so silly about them."

That sparked Vanessa's temper anew. "Mama, you know why." Her reaction to daisies was so bad that they didn't even have them in their garden.

"Balderdash." Her mother looked at Lord Lisbourne, who appeared all at sea. "Pay her no mind, sir. No doubt she's coming down with a cold is all."

When he reared back from Vanessa in alarm, she had to stifle a laugh. Perhaps that was the key to ridding herself of Lord Lisbourne. She could just sneeze and cough her way to freedom.

Vanessa pulled out her handkerchief. "I do believe you're right, Mama."

Still gripping the bouquet, her mother called for a servant. After asking that they be put in a vase, she told Lord Lisbourne, "Forgive my daughter, sir. She must have picked up a chill at the theater last night."

To punctuate her mother's words, Vanessa sat down and markedly blew her nose in her handkerchief.

"Stop that, gir— daughter," Mama said as she took her own seat. "It's but the smallest of colds, since you were fine this morning."

That seemed to soothe his lordship, for he settled back onto the sofa, though he made sure to sit at the opposite end from Vanessa.

An awkward silence ensued. Her mother tried to keep up the conversation by inquiring about Lord Lisbourne's aged mother, who was nearly ninety. That proved to be a wrong turn, since the marquess went to great lengths to explain how he must stay away from any sick person to keep from giving an illness to his dear mother.

Fortunately, their butler appeared in the parlor doorway. "His Grace, the Duke of Armitage, is here to see Miss Pryde, my lady."

Her mother glared at the servant. "Tell him we are not at home."

Vanessa sprang to her feet. "Don't be rude, Mama. He will see Lord Lisbourne's phaeton and know we are home. We don't wish to insult our dearest Grey's brother." When the butler stood stoically awaiting a decision, Vanessa added, "Please show His Grace in, if you please."

Despite looking unhappy about the matter, her mother gave the faintest of nods, the butler hurried off, and Vanessa let out the breath she hadn't realized she was holding.

As he was announced, her mother and Lord Lisbourne joined her in standing. Sheridan looked particularly delicious today, his forest-hued riding coat highlighting the green of his eyes and his buckskin breeches with top boots making him appear rather casual for once.

Vanessa couldn't help but smile at him. "It was very good of you to come, sir."

Sheridan, who held both hands behind his back, bowed to her and Lord Lisbourne, then pulled out a dark bottle from behind his back and approached Mama with it. "Lady Eustace, I thought you might enjoy some perry made on my estate from our very own pears."

A surprised smile crossed her mother's face as she took it. "For me? Why, that *is* kind of you, Your Grace. Most kind indeed. I do enjoy a good cider from time to time, but I've never had the pear kind."

"I hope you enjoy it," Sheridan said politely.

He'd certainly found the quickest way to Mama's heart. Her mother did love wine and cider.

Then he turned to Vanessa and offered her a posy of lilies. "These are for you."

Her silly heart jumped. "How did you know lilies are my favorite?"

"Because I have a working nose." When she cocked her head, unsure of what he meant, he laughed. "Your scent— it's of lilies."

"Oh! Why . . . so it is."

Behind her, Lord Lisbourne snorted. Not that she cared. She couldn't believe Sheridan knew what her scent was. And bought her flowers of the same kind! How amazing that he'd noticed such a thing. She would never have expected it of Studious Sheridan. Or Saint Sheridan, for that matter. When he bowed his head low enough so that the others couldn't see, then winked at her, she had to stifle her laugh. She'd begun to notice he had a mischievous streak sometimes.

With a light heart, she went to ask the footman in the

hall to put her posy in some water. As she returned, Lord Lisbourne was saying his good-byes. Fortunately, the rules of paying calls were on her side today. Not only were callers not supposed to outstay their welcome, but if a second person came to pay a call when the first one was still there, the first was expected to leave within a few minutes of the second's arrival.

So she said all the niceties to Lord Lisbourne, barely waiting until he was out of the room before taking her seat on the sofa again. With a little thrill she noticed Sheridan chose to sit rather closer to her than the marquess had. If she had begun sneezing and coughing around *him,* would he have kept her at arm's length?

She doubted it. Sheridan didn't seem the type to worry about colds.

He smiled at Mama. "I was sorry to hear you were too ill to attend my brother's little party last night. My mother was disappointed, too."

Vanessa swallowed the urge to laugh at the unlikeliness of that.

"I understand, Lady Eustace," Sheridan went on, "that you and my mother had your debuts the same year."

That shocked Vanessa. "Is that true, Mama? Did you really have your debut so late? What were you then? Twenty-seven?"

"Twenty-six, young lady. Only a year older than you."

"Yes, but I'm not having my debut at this age."

Her mother arched one eyebrow. "And yet you aren't married. At least I didn't squander my youth without finding a husband. I had the good sense to accept the first eligible man to offer for me at my age."

"Mama!" Vanessa said, as heat rose up her neck to her

cheeks. She had to bite her tongue to keep from pointing out that for years her mother had discouraged any suitor who wasn't Grey. Because if she said what she was thinking, her mother might say something even worse.

"In any case," Mama said, "you should be able to guess why I had to marry so late. It was on account of your three aunts, my older sisters. Your grandfather wouldn't pay for a debut for the rest of us until the oldest had wed. So I had to wait until each got married before I could have my own debut."

"Oh, Mama, I didn't know."

With a sniff, her mother settled her skirts about her. "Well, now you do. Families have obligations—*parents* have obligations. And sometimes they don't allow much leeway for the children."

That was another dig at Vanessa, but she knew better than to rise to it. When things became heated with Mama, it was always better to play along than to fight. Her mother was ruthless in a fight, even with her daughter. Or perhaps especially with her daughter.

But her mother's remarks did make Vanessa wonder if Mama's own trials with trying to get married were what had made her so rabid about controlling whom Vanessa wed.

Meanwhile, Sheridan was looking from her to her mother, as if trying to assess the relationship. No doubt it was markedly different from his relationship with his own mother. They had seemed very comfortable with each other at the Thorncliff party.

Time to change the subject. "So, Mama, were you and the duchess friends back then?" Vanessa asked, now curious to know.

Her mother straightened in her chair. "Of a sort. We

went to the same balls, dinners, and parties, for the most part. But Lydia was fairly quickly wed to Grey's father. The Fletchers had an arrangement with the man, since Lydia's mother was secretly his mistress and thought that marrying her daughter to him was a good way to keep him in her—" She caught herself before saying "bed," clearly remembering a bit late whom she was talking to. "In her sphere, so to speak."

Sheridan had ice in his eyes now. "Didn't you tell me last night, Lady Eustace, that you weren't one to gossip?"

That turned her mother belligerent. "There's a difference between common knowledge and gossip."

"So this arrangement was known by many?" Sheridan asked.

"Of course. It was the worst kept secret in London."

Sheridan's brow furrowed. "And did this plan of my grandmother's to keep Grey's father in her 'sphere' work?"

"I suppose. Hard to say, since he only lived long enough to see his heir born." It finally seemed to occur to Mama that she was being most inappropriate, for she waved a hand dismissively. "Oh, why are we speaking of such dour matters? I would rather talk about your estate, Armitage. It's in Lincolnshire, correct?"

That seemed to catch him off guard. "It is indeed." Sheridan glanced at Vanessa, but she just shrugged. She had no idea where her mother was headed with this.

"I'm told that Lincolnshire is a fine place to visit," Mama said, "especially this time of year, with the harvest going on and the bull running festival approaching."

His gaze narrowed on her mother. "So you've been to my part of Lincolnshire."

"No. Why would you think such a thing?"

"Because you mentioned the bull running festival in Sanforth, near us. The festival is not well-known. In fact, I believe it's the only one left in England. A few others used to exist but those ended a couple of decades ago."

"I'm sure I must have heard about it somewhere." Once again, her mother flicked his remark away as if it were a bothersome gnat. "Anyway, I've never been to Sanforth. That much I do remember."

"I haven't either," Vanessa chimed in, "but I think I remember reading about the festival. It takes place on some saint's day—"

"St. Brice's," Sheridan said.

"Right. And isn't it just one bull that the populace chase through the town?"

Sheridan nodded, although now he was regarding her oddly. "The practice began over six hundred years ago. I'm told that outsiders keep trying to put an end to it, but the town resists that. I've actually never seen it myself."

"I just figured out where I heard about it!" Vanessa exclaimed. "It was in *The Sports and Pastimes of the People of England: Including the Rural and Domestic Recreations, May Games, Mummeries, Shows, Processions, Pageants, and Pompous Spectacles, from the Earliest Period to the Present Time.* By Mr. Strutt."

"Good God, you remember that verbose title?" Sheridan asked.

"Not exactly." She pointed to the nearby bookshelf. "I merely have very good eyesight and can read the title from here."

"Ah." Sheridan smiled at her. "You must have good eyesight indeed. I can only make out a few of the words."

"Well, I *did* read the book from cover to cover. So I was bound to recognize the title."

Her mother shook her head. "Don't let her fool you. She remembers all sorts of things like that. Makes me dizzy."

"You're missing my point, Mama. The reason you remembered about the bull running was because of me. I must have read that part to you. Or told you of it or something."

"No, indeed. Not sure how I knew about it, but it wasn't from a book. That much I'm certain."

Sheridan seemed to find that very interesting, though Vanessa couldn't for the life of her figure out why. Why did he care whether her mother had ever been to Sanforth? For that matter, why did he care about Mama having had her debut at the same time as his mother? He seemed rather fixed on figuring out Mama.

Vanessa wanted to believe it was because he needed to determine how to get around her mother's bias against him so he could marry her. But sadly she didn't think that was the reason. She just didn't know what it might be.

When the silence stretched out a bit, Mama cleared her throat. "I'm sure the people of Sanforth are glad to have you in control of the Armitage estate. From what I heard, your uncle was a profligate."

"Mama, please . . ."

"What? It's true, and he knows it." Her mother jutted out her chin. "But I'm sure the duke is doing everything in his power to improve his inheritance."

Vanessa wanted to cry. Mama was about as subtle as the newspaper. She might as well have cried out to the world that she wanted to know if Sheridan needed money.

"I'm doing my best," Sheridan said noncommittally, though a muscle worked in his jaw.

"Which is why you're here, is it not?" her mother asked in a tone she obviously thought was coy.

A groan escaped Vanessa. How was she to make this madness stop? Mama never paid her any heed in such matters.

"I don't know what you mean," Sheridan said, his tone as duke-ish as she'd ever heard him be. "I'm here to call on you and your daughter. That should be obvious."

At his cool rebuff, her mother switched tactics. "Of course. And it's very kind of you. Especially since you have far more important things to do. Like selling off pieces of your estate to my nephew. Or so I heard, anyway."

That turned Sheridan's body to stone. "For a woman who claims not to be a gossip, you certainly spread a lot of it." He leaned forward. "But I should warn you—I don't like schemers of any kind. Which means I will not let you wheedle the details of my financial situation out of me for your own amusement. And if you're hoping to shame me in front of your daughter, think again. Vanessa and I are friends, and that friendship isn't likely to be broken by you."

His words made her want to cry. *Friends?* He still saw her as merely a friend? She supposed that was better than being seen as an enemy, but she wanted a bit more from him than that. How was she to change the way he regarded her? *Could* she change that?

Then the rest of his words sank in. Oh, Lord, if he ever found out that her attempt to make Juncker jealous was really a "scheme" to gain his own hand in marriage, Sheridan would end their "friendship" without a backward glance. But she was in the thick of it now. She could hardly change horses midstream. Nor suitors, either.

The clock rang the hour in the hall, and Sheridan rose. "I do believe I've overstayed my welcome."

Judging from the stiffness of his bearing, not to mention his words, Vanessa knew he was truly insulted.

Still, he managed to show them both common courtesy, for he bowed and said to Mama, "I hope you enjoy the perry, madam." Then he turned to Vanessa with only the slightest softening in his demeanor and said, "Thank you for the conversation. Good day to you both."

And he left the room.

Vanessa was *not* going to let him leave things like that. She headed right after him, ignoring Mama crying out after her, "You come back here this minute, girl! I will *not* have you running after Armitage like a common trull."

Fortunately, Vanessa could outrun her mother any day. She caught up to him as the footman was handing him his hat and greatcoat. "Sheridan, please let me apologize for my mother. She—"

"You needn't apologize for her. I know it was none of your doing."

"But—"

"Don't worry." With a glance at the footman, he pulled her aside and lowered his voice. "I will still hold to our bargain concerning Juncker."

That shocked her so much she could barely stammer the words, "A-All right. Thank you," before he was out the door and down the steps.

A few moments later, she felt rather than saw her mother come up beside her.

"At least we know one thing now," Mama said, a hint

of self-satisfaction in her voice. "He's definitely looking to marry a fortune. Otherwise, what I said wouldn't have struck such a nerve."

Still infuriated by her mother's behavior, Vanessa faced her and said, "Fortunately, I have a rather generous dowry. So that won't be a problem at all."

"Good. If he means to pay court to you, it can only attract other, wealthier gentlemen. So I suppose I can tolerate his visits to you for a bit."

"Now we can only hope *he* can tolerate *you* in the meantime," Vanessa snapped.

Then she marched up the stairs, leaving her mother to come up with whatever tale she could to explain Vanessa's lack of availability to other callers.

But Vanessa had lied to her mother. Although she *did* have a nice dowry, she didn't want Sheridan marrying her for her money. She didn't expect him to wed her for love—she wasn't even sure she wanted love in her marriage. Having spent half her life trying to gain her mother's love—or even affection—with no apparent success, she certainly didn't mean to spend the rest of her life trying to gain a husband's love. What she wanted was a husband with whom she could share her ideas, find comfort in hard times, live a peaceful existence.

With whom she could enjoy the physical part of marriage and have children. So the last thing she wanted was Sheridan forced into wedding her to save his estate, if her dowry was even enough to accomplish that. She at least wanted him to desire her for herself.

Because if she could only get him to marry her out of duty, what would be the point of it all?

Chapter Nine

Sheridan paced the drawing room at Armitage House with his blood still boiling. He was mostly mad at himself. He should have restrained his anger, found a way of getting Lady Eustace to reveal what he was trying to learn, instead of storming out like some . . . half-cocked lad with a hot temper.

"I can't believe this has you so furious," his half sister, Gwyn, said from her perch on Mother's favorite settee. "All of this stomping about isn't like you at all."

"I'm not 'stomping about'—I'm pacing. That's what men do when they're angry. Stomping about, indeed. You make me sound like a . . . a—" *A half-cocked lad with a hot temper.* He halted in front of her. "You should have seen Lady Eustace. I tell you, that woman was laughing at me. *Laughing!* She didn't even bother to hide the fact that she'd once been in Sanforth. I wouldn't be at all surprised to learn she murdered Uncle Armie and Father with her bare hands."

"We both know that's unlikely. Probably it was that Elias fellow, doing the bidding of an employer we have not yet uncovered. Besides, according to what I gleaned from your less-than-coherent tale of your visit to the Pryde house," Gwyn said, "she might have been more confused than anything. I mean, it sounds to me as if she was trying to figure out where she'd learned of the bull running, and Vanessa was trying to help."

Sheridan shook his head. "You don't understand. Vanessa gave her mother a perfectly good reason for having heard of it, so if Lady Eustace was confused, she could have seized on that. Instead, the woman flat-out said that wasn't where she'd heard about it! Without proposing an alternative explanation. She was taunting me, I swear."

Gwyn smirked at him. "I notice you're not claiming that Vanessa was trying to cover up her mother's perfidy."

"Because that would be absurd," he said. Vanessa's very name caused a different sort of agitation in him. "The poor woman was mortified by every word out of her mother's mouth. I don't know how she can endure such a mother. Now I see why Grey hates his aunt so. She's a . . . a rude, pushy gossip who insisted on mocking me about the debts I inherited."

"Ah, now we are coming to the truth of what has set you off. You didn't like looking bad in front of Vanessa."

"What? That's ridiculous." It wasn't the least true. Couldn't be. He didn't care that much about Vanessa. Did he?

Gwyn tried to rise from the settee but fell back onto it.

"Careful," Sheridan said with concern, holding out his hand to help her up. Damn, but at seven months along Gwyn was heavy now. That child of hers must be quite a bruiser.

Then again, Gwyn's new husband had the shoulders of an ox.

Once she was on her feet, she said, "I'm hungry. Are you hungry? I shall call for some tea and cakes. And perhaps an apple. Wait, does Cook still make those heavenly apple tarts? That's what I want: tea and cake and apple tarts . . . and maybe a bit of cheese. Oh, and pickles! Yes, I shall definitely want some pickles with it."

"Eating for seven, are we?" he said dryly.

"You have no idea. I think I single-handedly devoured half of the supper Olivia laid out last night." She leveled her inquisitive gaze on him. "And speaking of last night, you and Vanessa seemed very chummy."

"I have no intention of discussing last night. You and Mother are intent on marrying me off, and I won't have it."

"Why not?" When he didn't answer right away, Gwyn searched his face. "Wait a minute. Surely you're not still mourning Helene. It's been five years now."

He stiffened. "Six. And it feels as if it were only yesterday." Or it *should* feel that way. One should not get over loving somebody so easily or quickly just because that person had died. It seemed wrong somehow. "I don't want to talk about Helene."

"Well, then." She rang for a servant and gave the footman her lengthy list of food and drink demands.

Sheridan couldn't believe it. Were women in her condition always filled with a ravenous hunger? Or was it just the ones like his sister, who presently looked as if she'd swallowed a whole ham?

Unbidden, an image of Vanessa in Gwyn's situation assailed him—of Vanessa rosy and glowing, Vanessa carrying their child in her belly, Vanessa dandling their son or daughter on her knee.

Blast it! What was wrong with him? It felt disloyal to

Helene to imagine such a thing, especially since he'd never conjured up such an image with *her*. So why was he doing so with Vanessa?

As the servant marched off to do Gwyn's bidding, she waved her hand at him. "Since you won't let me talk about Helene, continue with your tirade against Lady Eustace, that 'rude, pushy gossip.' I begin to be rather glad I never met her."

"Trust me, you should be." But oddly, the heat of his anger had cooled. "I just wish I knew what her game was. She doesn't seem to like me, yet she insisted on quizzing me about the state of the dukedom's finances."

"And Vanessa didn't join in."

"No. If anything, she was horrified by her mother's line of questioning."

Deep in thought, Gwyn lowered herself carefully onto the settee. "And you're sure Vanessa knew nothing incriminating about her mother?"

"If she did, she hid it amazingly well." He shrugged. "I have to go back tomorrow. I need to find out if her mother had been hinting at the truth or was just an awful creature in general."

"You should bring Mama with you."

"For God's sake, why?"

"They were friends once, weren't they? Or at least relations. Lady Eustace was Mama's sister-in-law for the year Mama was married to Grey's father. And Mama will have the perfect reason for going—because she wants to get to know Vanessa after meeting her at Thorn and Olivia's party."

Just what he needed—his mother and Vanessa putting their heads together about anything.

Gwyn shifted on the settee. "And what does Mama have to say about Lady Eustace's whereabouts at the two house parties, anyway? Have you asked her?"

"Of course I asked her." Sheridan sighed. "For the first party, as you know, Mother was dealing with a sick infant and husband, so she barely got to see her guests. For the second party, she was in labor. So she was not in a position to know where everyone was."

"That's putting it mildly," Gwyn muttered.

"What?"

"Not in a position . . . Never mind." She cocked her head. "I still say if you bring Mama, she can get Lady Eustace to reminisce with her about those house parties more naturally than if it's you trying to elicit information."

"I suppose." He would never admit it to Gwyn, but he disliked the idea of chatting with Vanessa with his mother anywhere nearby. Bad enough he had to do it with *her* mother monitoring the conversation.

But Gwyn did have a point. He wasn't supposed to be there for Vanessa. He was supposed to be chatting with her mother. If he could call whatever that woman did "chatting."

Perhaps he should turn this on Gwyn. She had a part to play in these investigations, too.

"So," he said, trying to sound nonchalant, "have you spoken to Lady Hornsby yet?"

Gwyn scowled. "No. But not for lack of trying. She hasn't been 'at home' a single day since we started this."

"That in itself is interesting."

"I think so, too. I was planning to try again tomorrow."

Before he could comment on that, the servants came in with a feast worthy of a king. Or rather, a very enceinte queen. Gwyn's face lit up, and she barely waited until they left before she began loading a plate with the oddest combination of ingredients he could imagine.

He dropped into the chair opposite her and took an apple tart. "Do you think I'm overreacting with this investigation?" He took a bite of tart. They really were very good. "Is it possible all the deaths were exactly what they seemed for so many years—borne of accidents or illnesses? That they have no connection to each other beyond the weird coincidence that they all involved someone close to Mother?"

"You are not overreacting in the least." Gwyn had a bite of cake, then a bite of pickle. "We already have proof that Grey's father was poisoned. For all we know, the villainess poisoned Grey, too, but he survived it. We also know that the note supposedly written by Joshua to Father, which lured Father to his death, wasn't actually in Joshua's hand. And we know that Elias, who might very well have written those notes, was hired to do all kinds of mischief that nearly got a number of us killed. Then *he* was poisoned in prison. That is clearly a pattern of villainy and not mere coincidence."

"Well, when you put it that way . . ."

She nodded sagely at him as she cut two thin slices of cake and one of pickle, then made a sort of sandwich of them.

"That looks vile," he said.

"It does, doesn't it?" She cut a bit of her "sandwich" and ate it. "But it's surprisingly delicious." She licked some crumbs from her lips. "Is Mama right? Do you really like Vanessa?"

He tensed. "Of course I like her. I always have. She's a perfectly amiable woman." Who kissed like a seductress.

"That's not what I mean, and you know it."

"Perhaps so, but that's all I'm admitting to." At least to Gwyn, anyway.

Now if only he could convince himself of it.

Over the next two days, Sheridan dutifully went to the Eustace house in Queen Square at the proper time to pay calls. Both days he tried delving into Lady Eustace's whereabouts during the house parties, but she continued to be vague and unhelpful. His questions also seemed to bewilder Vanessa. He feared he might reveal his purpose before he actually found out the truth.

So on the third day, he reluctantly followed Gwyn's suggestion and asked his mother to join him when he went to pay his call. She was gracious about agreeing to do so, which made him wish he'd asked her before. What had he been afraid of?

This time when he went, it was after five P.M., when calls from family and close friends were expected to be made. Lady Eustace might not have had anything to do with his mother in decades, but the two women were still related through Grey's father. So he supposed that made them intimates for life.

When they arrived, they discovered Sir Noah already there visiting his sister. Great. Now Sheridan had to watch his mother flirting with Vanessa's uncle. At least he had Vanessa to chat with. As they had on the previous two days, they discussed everything from gardening—she enjoyed it and was knowledgeable about hybrids—to horses—she rode a great deal—to books. Unbeknownst to him, she was a great reader, and though her choices weren't the same as his, they had a mutual enjoyment of poetry. Clearly, it was Juncker's skill as a poet that had drawn her.

The thought soured him. She was simply too fine a woman for the joking, theatrical likes of Juncker. Today she wore a cheery gown of the same hue he'd been told by Gwyn was "evening primrose." Whatever it was, the dark yellow made her blue eyes sparkle and her skin light up.

Or perhaps that was just how he saw her—sparkling and alight. Damn, he needed to be careful about that. Especially since her captivating smile turned him hard in all the wrong places.

He mustn't think about her in that way. Yet he did, blast it.

The only solution was to focus on the reason for their visit—to get Lady Eustace talking. She actually seemed surprised and pleased to have Mother pay her a call. Unfortunately, his mother seemed disinclined to reminisce much about the past with Lady Eustace. Mother also seemed to be taking her time steering the conversation in the direction he wanted. He would have done so himself, but he couldn't find an opening.

So once the two women were done with broader subjects of mutual interest, their conversation lapsed into a heavy silence. Sheridan had coached his mother in what to say or ask in order to get Lady Eustace talking about the past two house parties. But as usual, Mother never could follow a plan proposed by her children. She always had to go her own way.

"So tell me, Cora," his mother said. "Is it true that

you and Eustace mistreated my eldest son when he lived
with you?"

Sheridan stifled a curse. This went far beyond going
her own way. This was leaping off a cliff. He looked to
Vanessa for help, but she was clearly frozen in shock.
Meanwhile, Lady Eustace sat there agape, obviously horrified that Mother would be so direct. And Sir Noah raised
his gaze to the heavens as if asking the angels for help in
steering this visit into calmer waters.

"Mother," Sheridan said firmly, "I hardly think this is
the time—"

"It's the only time I have," she told Sheridan. "I don't
intend to return here again, so this is my only chance to
get an answer from this harpy about her wretched behavior
toward my firstborn."

Lady Eustace had gained her wits at last. "I don't know
what Grey has been telling you, but—"

"It took me years to get him to tell me anything,"
Mother cut in, obviously not caring that Lady Eustace's
face had turned a peculiar shade of purple. "Even then, I
had to deduce the full truth from talking to servants and
the like. But that doesn't explain why you would betray
me so. What did I ever do to you to warrant that? Grey
was only a child. He deserved better from his aunt and
uncle."

Yes, he had. And though Mother was obviously filled
with righteous anger over this, it was pain he saw written
large in her face. It tore a hole in him, reminding him of
the pain he'd seen in the faces of Helene's parents.

Family could rip your heart out sometimes.

But his mother wasn't done. She leaned forward in her
chair. "*And you were my friend.* I entrusted my ten-year-old

son to you, because I thought it was good for him to learn how to run the dukedom one day and because I thought, wrongly, that he would be cared for kindly by his uncle and my friend. But now, knowing how your husband chose to treat him—starving him, caning him, trying to steal his birthright from him—I live with guilt every day. I realize that what I did was, in theory, the best thing for his future, that I couldn't have predicted how Eustace would torment him. Still—"

Sheridan stood. "Mother, we should go."

His mother shook her head. "I'm not finished." She fixed Lady Eustace with an icy look. "How do *you* live with the guilt? What could possibly have made your husband's behavior acceptable in your eyes? How could you have condoned it?" She tapped her foot impatiently. "Well, have you no answer for me? No plausible excuse? Although I doubt such a thing exists."

Lady Eustace's mouth had dropped open, but no sound came out of it. Sir Noah rose and held out his hand to Sheridan's mother. "It's such a fine day. Perhaps we should go for a stroll in Queen Square Garden, Duchess."

"That sounds lovely," she said, but didn't take his hand. "First, I'd like a reply from your sister."

Lady Eustace stood to point her trembling finger toward the parlor door. "Get. Out. Of. My. House."

Mother rose, too, with a steely glint in her eyes. "Gladly. As soon as you answer my question."

With a sad expression, Vanessa stood. "She has no answer, I'm afraid, Duchess. Or she would have told me long ago when I first asked."

"Whose side are you on, girl?" her mother snapped.

"Grey's," Vanessa said softly. "Always. Because he had no one who cared in this house but me."

That cut right through Sheridan's heart. He'd known Grey had suffered, but the enormity of how his half brother must have felt to be alone in a house with only an infant for a friend hit him hard. Now he understood why his brother hadn't wanted to return to this place, to be in his aunt's presence again. How could he?

His mother turned to Sir Noah. "I suppose we might as well take that stroll, sir. That is probably the only answer I will ever get from your sister."

Sheridan met Vanessa's gaze. Mother was right about one thing—there was no point in trying to get anything out of Lady Eustace today. "Will you join us on our walk?" he asked Vanessa.

Grimly, she nodded. He couldn't blame her. He wanted to get away from the warring matrons as soon as possible himself. Although truth be told, he understood his mother's determination to find out the truth. What had happened to Grey, which he'd only known a small portion of until today, had been unfair and unjust. And even after having repaired her relationship with her eldest son—a relationship torn asunder by forces she hadn't even known about—Mother still ached that she couldn't prevent it.

A lump caught in Sheridan's throat. Father had died without ever knowing why Grey was so distant from them all. One more reason to do his best in finding out who had murdered Father.

The four of them left together, pausing to retrieve hats, bonnets, and greatcoats from the footman in silence, as if departing from a funeral. It *was* a funeral of sorts, he supposed. It was the death of whatever little had remained of Mother's friendship with Lady Eustace.

Once they were out on the street in the light of the oil lamps, they headed across to the pretty garden mostly used by residents of the square and their guests. Sir Noah and Sheridan's mother headed straight to the statue of Queen Anne, but Vanessa tugged at his arm to get him to go down a different path.

When they were out of earshot, she said wryly, "Wasn't *that* fun?"

"Allow me to apologize for my mother—" he began.

"Don't you dare. I admire your mother. She's fierce in defending her children, but without trampling over those who don't deserve her anger. Mother deserved it, trust me."

"You were just a baby when Grey came. How do you know what he went through?"

"The same way your mother knows. From other sources. For me, it was servants. And from reading between the lines in things my parents said or overhearing their discussions when they thought I wasn't around. I did learn some of it from Grey. First from watching his wariness whenever he was in Father's presence."

"I don't imagine they got along, given what Mother said."

"Hardly. Even though Grey went off to school at thirteen, he still came home for holidays and the weeks between terms. When I was old enough, he told me some of what he'd suffered before he went to Eton. I think he just needed someone to listen and to care about it. Once he was off to school, the punishments stopped, since he wasn't ever home long enough to sustain them, but he was unable to leave Papa's oversight for good until he was twenty-one. Before then, whenever he was home, he would take me on walks in this very garden, teach me how to ride, rescue me from trees I climbed—"

"You climbed trees?" he said incredulously.

She chuckled. "Short ones. I was quite the little hoyden until I received my first fashion doll at twelve. Then Grey had to switch to taking me shopping."

"As a big brother might."

"Yes." She had a faraway look in her eyes as if remembering the past. Then she shook it off. "He was never a cousin to me. He was my big brother in every way but legally. Although Mama wanted us to marry, neither of us even considered it." She shuddered. "I can only imagine how uncomfortable that would have been."

"No doubt." He steered them to a bench where they could both take a seat, though he made certain they could still see her uncle and his mother. "Not to change the subject, but will your mother take *my* mother's accusations out on you?" The thought of Lady Eustace doing so chilled his blood. Vanessa was blameless in this.

"Because I sided with the duchess? Probably. But Mama is primarily bark and no bite. Even back then her main crime was in looking the other way while Papa did as he pleased with Grey. Just like Papa, she wanted Grey's properties. But she never had the audacity to lift a hand to him herself."

"Are you sure she won't hurt you?"

She seemed touched by his question. "Most of her ire will be reserved for your mother. No doubt I will have to endure an hour or so of ranting, but that's nothing new."

"I'm sorry if the incident today became uncomfortable for you and your uncle."

"Honestly, it's been a long time in coming." She nodded over to where his mother and Sir Noah were now engaged in a low conversation at the foot of the statue. "As for my uncle, I think your mother is making up for whatever discomfort he experienced." They sat in silence a minute. "Did you know ahead of time that your mother was planning to confront mine with the past when you brought her with you?"

"God, no. I would have left her at home if I'd even guessed." Mother clearly had forgotten the purpose of the visit. Not that he blamed her.

"So . . ." Vanessa continued to stare across to where the others stood. "Why exactly *did* you bring her?"

Damn. Now he was treading dangerous ground. "She wished to pay a much-delayed call on you, actually, to thank you for attending Thorn's party."

Her eyebrows rose so high, they nearly reached her hairline. "I hardly think any unmarried woman in her right mind would have turned down such an invitation. Certainly I wouldn't have."

"Ah." He wasn't sure what else to say.

"The thing is . . . you've come to visit me every day since that night—"

"As a man who is courting a woman should do," he was quick to point out.

"Yes. But your part of our bargain was that you would court me to make Mr. Juncker jealous. My part—such as it is—was that I'd acknowledge you were right if he proved not to care about marriage." She stared down at her gloved hands. "Neither of us has completed our part conclusively. And I can't even do mine until you do yours, which you haven't been doing at all. I mean, how can I make him jealous when he's not around to see you courting me?"

"An excellent point." Bloody hell. He'd known he wouldn't get more than a few visits to question Lady Eustace before Vanessa started to wonder at his motives, but he needed more time. Still, she'd been very patient, and without understanding what he was up to. "I do take your meaning. How do you suggest I solve the problem?"

She met his gaze, the faint blush on her cheeks unleashing an oddly savage feeling in his chest, a fiery need to possess her. At once. In every way possible. Which was madness, of course.

"That's simple," she said. "You bring *him* as your companion next time, not your mother."

"But what reason can I give to convince him to join me in calling on you?"

"Let me think." She mused a moment. "I know! You can say you need a companion to distract Mama so you can talk to me in private and pour out your heart to me."

"That would work." It would, but he wasn't sure he liked it. Involving Juncker was unpredictable. The man might treat her ill. Or break her heart. Or lay his hands on her for wicked purposes.

No, he didn't have to worry about that. Because he refused to leave her alone with the chap.

She cast him a soft smile. "Then, if Mr. Juncker cares for me at all, he will try to take your place and pour out his heart to me himself. And I will know for certain whether he wants me as his wife."

"And if he *doesn't* take the bait, you will acknowledge that I'm right about him?"

"Yes." She stared hard at him. "I merely need to know the truth."

He could see how she would feel that way, but it annoyed him she was so fixed upon Juncker. The man was a ne'er-do-well, cocky for no reason. She didn't belong with Juncker. She belonged with—

No, that wasn't acceptable. Never mind that her sweet side intoxicated him and made him want to claim her as his own. He was not looking for a wife. She might have a generous dowry, but it would never be enough to salvage the Armitage dukedom. And right now, saving the dukedom and figuring out who was behind Father's murder had to be his whole focus.

But her arm against his felt so right, and her scent of lilies fogged his brain so much that he forgot why he mustn't marry her. Lost in the glory that was her wearing a flattering gown, he was having trouble concentrating. Now that the moon was rising, lending a romantic glow to the garden, he could too easily imagine her in his bed, those ample breasts freed of constraint, and her curls, as black and shining as his freshly polished top boots, recklessly tumbled across a pillow while he—

Sir Noah and Mother came toward them. God, he hoped darkness and his greatcoat covered his body's reaction. No man wanted his mother to see him in such a state. He could only pray his desire didn't show in his face.

But clearly both Mother and Sir Noah were too distracted to notice such things. "Vanessa," her uncle began as the pair reached them, "I am going to accompany the duchess home in my curricle. I don't think I can face your mother right now. Tell her I will call on her tomorrow."

With a scowl, Sheridan stood, then helped Vanessa up. "No need for you to trouble yourself, sir. I will see that my mother gets back to Armitage House myself. Besides, my carriage is a damned sight safer at night than an open curricle."

"I'll be fine with Sir Noah," his mother said. "And didn't you want more time to visit with Vanessa?"

Vanessa sighed. "Alas, I'm not sure either of you would be welcome inside our house just now. But if I don't go back, she will stew in her own anger until she takes it out on the servants. So it's best I return to soothe her temper."

Mother looked torn. "I'm sorry you got caught in the middle, my dear."

"I'm not sorry." Vanessa's ghost of a smile showed she meant it, too. "You spoke the truth. I can always hope she got a lesson out of it, although knowing Mama, I doubt it." She looked at Sheridan. "I should go back."

"I'll go with you," Sir Noah said. "But I'm not going in."

"You'll leave your niece to bear the brunt of her mother's anger alone?" Mother surprised Sheridan by saying.

"I suppose that would be unfair." Sir Noah sighed. "But don't expect me to like it."

Then he offered his arm to Vanessa, who glanced at Sheridan. "I'll see you tomorrow."

"I'll be there at the same time I came today," he answered. Then he watched as Sir Noah and Vanessa headed back to the Pryde abode.

He gestured to his footman waiting on the steps of the

Pryde town house, and the servant hurried off to fetch the carriage.

"You're coming here again tomorrow?" his mother said.

"Yes. I promised Vanessa I'd bring Juncker with me."

"So you and Vanessa can make him jealous."

"Exactly." But it wasn't something he was looking forward to. And he *still* hadn't found out what he wanted to know from Lady Eustace.

"That woman is not interested in Mr. Juncker, you know. She wants *you*."

He shook his head at her. "You just think she does because you can't imagine her wanting anyone other than your son."

Mother snorted. "I can tell a woman who has set her cap for someone when I see her."

"Trust me—she's not interested in me. Long before she and I grew . . . cozy, she told Grey of her interest in Juncker."

"If you say so." Mother sounded skeptical.

Time to change the subject. "What were you and Sir Noah discussing? Or dare I ask?"

"Mostly we talked about Cora. He wanted a fuller explanation of what I was accusing her of, and I wanted to know where he'd been when all of it was happening."

"Ah." Sheridan put his arm around his mother's shoulders, reminded of how small and fragile she really was, despite her fierceness. The grief of suffering three husbands' deaths would weigh anyone down. "What did he say?"

"He reminded me of something I already vaguely knew from way back when Cora and I were friends—that his estate is far up north in Cumberland, which is one reason he and his wife rarely came to London before her death.

The other was she was ill a great deal. So he didn't like to leave her."

"That all sounds perfectly reasonable."

"Unfortunately, he couldn't so easily explain Cora to me: why she's the way she is, what makes her so mean, and how she managed to raise a daughter as fine as Vanessa."

"I actually think Grey might have had something to do with that." Briefly he told her what Vanessa had said about growing up with Grey as an "older brother."

His mother sniffed. "I think she merely got lucky with Vanessa. But more and more I believe Grey is right about Cora. She has the best motive of anyone to murder my husbands, if only out of resentment toward me. I married the duke she coveted, and then after she killed him, I landed in clover again with Thorn's father. After she killed *him,* I married a man she would have seen as inconsequential and, anyway, he was out of her reach in Prussia. Until *he* became a duke, too, once again giving me what she wanted—prestige and wealth. So she had to kill him."

Sheridan stifled a smile. "And the fact that she was vile to one of your children has nothing to do with why you believe this."

Mother tipped up her chin. "It just shows she is vile in general."

"There are two problems with your theory. The first is that the Armitage dukedom hasn't had wealth in years, thanks to Uncle Armie's spending."

"But she didn't know that."

"Which leads to the second problem. Your theory doesn't explain why she would wait all those years and suddenly decide to kill Uncle Armie to bring Father back to England, thus making Father into a duke as well. Wouldn't his new status contribute to her envy?"

Mother's lips thinned into a severe line. "Well . . . I mean, we don't know for certain that your uncle Armie was murdered, do we? We've just assumed it was part of the pattern. But it might not be."

That brought Sheridan up short. She had a point. If Uncle Armie had genuinely died from drunkenly falling off his horse and breaking his neck, then their father coming back and becoming duke might have merely infuriated Lady Eustace that Mother was once again "landing in clover."

"It's something to think about, I suppose," he said as their carriage approached. "I'll mention it to the others."

The carriage halted, the footman put the step down, and Sheridan helped his mother inside. Once they were settled into their seats and on their way back to Armitage House, Mother asked, "Are you angry with me?"

"For what?"

"Letting Cora have it with both barrels. I know I was supposed to question her about the house parties, but I just saw her sitting there with her cat-in-the-cream smile, and I . . . I wanted to tear her hair out after what she did to Grey."

"How could I be angry over that? She deserved it."

"But it makes your task all the more difficult."

Mother had no idea. He'd be lucky if he could even get inside the Pryde house now. "I will work it out, never fear. At the very least I have to uphold my promise to Vanessa that I will bring Juncker to visit."

"Ah, yes. And how will you convince him to join you?"

"She and I concocted a plan. I just need to hunt him down tonight so I can set the plan in motion."

"I see. Good luck to you then. Both of you will need it."

How true that was. Worse yet, after tomorrow he'd have no more reason to see Vanessa. Either she would have caught Juncker at last, or Juncker would have made it clear once and for all that he had no interest in her.

You could court her yourself. Make her your wife and have her in your bed where you want her.

He tamped down on the instant surge of heat coursing through him. Aside from not wanting to be the consolation prize for a woman who'd lost the main object of her affections, he needed to marry an heiress with a large fortune. And Vanessa's dowry, as generous as it was by all accounts, still wasn't enough for that.

So tomorrow would have to spell the end to his time with Vanessa, no matter how much he knew he would miss it. And damn, how he would miss it.

Chapter Ten

Vanessa and her uncle returned home to discover that her mother had gone to bed and "didn't wish to be disturbed." That was one of the many tactics in Mama's arsenal for ruling her roost, and it had worked well during Vanessa's childhood. When her mother was so upset with her behavior that she wouldn't even speak to Vanessa, Vanessa had often gone to sit outside Mama's door pleading with her not to be angry and asking what she could do to make it better.

It had taken her years to realize that her mother wielded silence like a weapon to make Vanessa think the world would crash down about her ears without her mother. Mama enjoyed watching Vanessa beg. Or having Father do so, for that matter. But he'd resorted to begging less and less as the years went by, choosing instead to storm about and then leave to find recourse with one light-skirt or another.

When Mama was unhappy, everyone else must be unhappy. That was how the silent treatment worked.

Fortunately, by the time Vanessa was seventeen, she realized that ignoring her mother's silence was her best recourse. One couldn't punish someone with silence if that someone didn't take it as a punishment.

Apparently Uncle Noah had learned that lesson, too, from growing up with Mama, for Vanessa couldn't miss the look of profound relief on his face when he heard that his sister had already retired for the night.

"It's probably for the best," he said. "She'll have calmed down by morning."

Vanessa sincerely doubted that.

"And at least we can have a peaceful evening," he added.

"It's all right if you want to go, Uncle. I'll be fine."

He stood there in the foyer and stared up the staircase. "Are you sure? I can stay if you wish."

"No need. I'll have a tray in my room, and then I'll read until I fall asleep." Besides, it would give her plenty of time to prepare for every contingency tomorrow—Mama raging, Mama sullen, Mama threatening to cut off the connection Vanessa had with Grey and his family.

"All right, then." Uncle Noah bent to kiss her forehead. "Tell your mother I will call on her again tomorrow."

"I will."

"Oh, and don't count Armitage out yet. If he's the sort of fellow you richly deserve, he will come to his senses on his own. Because clearly he likes you a great deal."

"I hope you're right. Because I like *him* a great deal, too."

It was true. During their previous visits, they'd talked quite a bit. She'd expected familiarity to breed contempt. Instead, she'd found him to be more of the sort of man she wanted—responsible, thoughtful, and intelligent. She didn't care if he also needed her money. She would give it to him gladly if he helped her escape the likes of Lord Lisbourne.

After Uncle Noah left, Vanessa crept up the stairs, hoping her mother really had retired for the night and wasn't just waiting to pounce on her. But Mama had either fallen asleep or she'd drunk the larger part of that perry Sheridan had brought and had passed out. Either way, Vanessa got to have the evening to enjoy the calm before the storm. Because there would most certainly be a storm, if not tonight, then tomorrow.

True to form, her mother woke her the next morning around nine and stood over her while Vanessa was still rubbing the sleep from her eyes.

Mama crossed her arms over her chest. "There will be no more visits from that witch, do you hear me, little missy?"

"Do you mean the Duchess of Armitage?" Vanessa asked, still trying to clear the cobwebs from her mind.

Her mother snorted. "I will not do that awful creature the honor of calling her Duchess. How dare she malign me in my own home! And to think we were friends once. I must have been mad to allow her within my circles."

Vanessa had to concentrate on sitting up in bed to keep from laughing in her mother's face. Somehow she doubted that the Duchess of Armitage had ever needed help in society, even before she married Grey's father.

"And there will certainly be no more visits from Armitage," her mother went on.

Her heart sank. "But Mama, he had nothing to do with—"

"No! I will not listen to your pleading. I can see what you apparently cannot—that Armitage means to court and marry you for your dowry. If he succeeds, I will be linked to Lydia forever. I shan't have it, I tell you!" She leaned down. "And given that he probably intends to call on you again today, I have made sure you won't defy me. I have already instructed the butler to say we are not 'at home' to any visitors today. Perhaps that will make you think twice before you side with the enemies of your mother again."

Vanessa sighed. "Sheridan is not your enemy, Mama." She caught herself before she could point out that the duchess had good reason for being so angry with Mama. No sense in embroiling her in another rage-filled argument.

"I don't care *what* you think of that young man. Neither of them are ever setting foot in this house again."

Mama turned on her heel and marched for the door. She paused to glare back at Vanessa. "And the next time Lord Lisbourne comes calling, you might want to rethink your determination to refuse his advances. You're not getting any younger, *girl*."

That final jab was typical of her mother, but it struck terror in Vanessa's heart. For *years,* until Grey had married, she and he had avoided being caught together by Mama. Vanessa didn't know if she could manage that with Lisbourne for even another minute. She would *not* marry that ridiculous fellow, no matter what Mama said and no matter how many times she tried to reduce Vanessa to a child by calling her "girl."

As soon as Mama left the room, Vanessa got out of bed. Last night she'd worried about Mr. Juncker revealing to Sheridan what she'd so unwisely blurted out at the Thorncliff party. But in the bright light of day, she decided he would never tell Sheridan. Mr. Juncker saw the duke as a threat to his own romantic interest, Flora. So surely he would help Vanessa gain Sheridan as her husband, if only to remove the duke from the field.

She plotted her strategy, debating whether to send Sheridan a message asking him to meet her elsewhere or come again tomorrow. But she couldn't be sure the message would reach him in time today, nor could she be sure Mama wouldn't take the same tack again tomorrow. So Vanessa discarded those ideas.

What she needed was a different strategy. While her lady's maid, Bridget, went downstairs to fetch her some breakfast, Vanessa looked through her clothes. She wanted to dress splendidly for her two callers, but if Mama saw her well-dressed, she would guess at once that Vanessa intended to defy her. That meant Vanessa would have to dress the way she would when they weren't expecting visitors, on an average day at home.

She needed Bridget's help. Fortunately, the maid would never betray her. Indeed, she'd been Vanessa's only staunch ally in the Pryde household since Grey had moved out. The other servants feared Mama, but not Bridget, thank goodness. For years, she'd been carrying out Vanessa's plots to avoid being caught alone with Grey, which was why some of Vanessa's pin money had always gone to the woman, to supplement what Vanessa knew was a pathetically small income. Mama had never exactly been generous to her staff.

Bridget entered the room, and Vanessa sat her down. "So here's the most recent occurrence in the ridiculous drama that has become my life lately."

She told Bridget about her mother's pronouncements. The maid already knew of Vanessa's attempts to spark

Sheridan's interest by using Mr. Juncker to make Sheridan jealous. Bridget also knew the pitfalls that had opened up once Vanessa had set her scheme into motion.

"I think I have a plan for how to handle today's visit from the gentlemen." Vanessa went on. "It just needs your usual brilliant mind to make sure I haven't overlooked anything."

Bridget laughed. "Forgive me, miss, but one of these days your plans will land you in deeper trouble than a scolding from your mother."

"I know," she said, clearly taking Bridget by surprise. "I swear, if it works, I will never scheme to do anything like it again." Hopefully, she wouldn't have to. Because if it didn't work . . .

No, she wouldn't consider that possibility. It would be too awful.

"Very well," Bridget said, though she looked skeptical. "What are you plotting this time?"

"I want to waylay Sheridan and Mr. Juncker before they even reach the house."

"How do you know they'll arrive together?"

"Because Sheridan said he'd bring Mr. Juncker with him. And Sheridan is generally a man of his word."

"I see."

"They'll be intending to enter in the front after disembarking from Sheridan's carriage. So when the arrival time draws near, I'll tell the butler that if Mama asks, I'll be in the back garden. Once out there, I will hurry down the alley to the corner to hail Sheridan's carriage. Then the three of us can head across the street to the Queen Square Garden and take all the time we want to visit. That will work, won't it?"

Bridget raised her eyes heavenward. "Only if they do indeed arrive together. And it doesn't rain. And your mother doesn't anticipate your defiance of her and look out a window. She hates the cold, so she's unlikely to go outside herself, but looking is another matter entirely."

Vanessa tapped her chin. "Perhaps I should tell our butler I'm walking in Queen Square Garden in the first place."

"That will definitely rouse his suspicions . . . and thus your mother's." Bridget headed to the window to gaze out. "How about this? You go into the garden wearing that old coat and large bonnet you use when gardening this time of year. I'll wait for you in the alley, where you'll hand me your coat and bonnet. Then you can head out to do the rest of your plan and I'll wander the garden doing . . . things with the plants."

Vanessa stifled a laugh. Bridget wasn't one for the out-doors. "Yes, but what if someone actually comes outside to talk to you, thinking that you're me? I don't want to get you into any trouble."

"And I appreciate that, miss." Bridget paced in front of the window. "If anyone confronts me, I'll tell them I don't know where you are, and that you gave me the coat and bonnet. No one will question that part."

It was customary for ladies to give their old clothes to their lady's maids, but still . . . "The butler might. I'll have to be wearing it when I go down; otherwise, he'll be reluctant to let me go into the back garden at all without Mama's permission. So if he then sees you in it—"

"He never goes into the garden. He hates the outdoors almost as much as I do." Bridget halted. "But you could always give up on seeing them. Will you even want Armitage after having to scheme and plot to get him?"

"I don't know. You do have a point." Vanessa sighed. "But I've come this far. And if I don't do *something,* Mama is going to marry me off to Lisbourne. So I might as well try one more ploy and hope for the best."

"That Armitage sees the error of his ways and proposes marriage?"

"Or at least sees the error of his ways and courts me in truth."

Bridget nodded. "Well, if that's your aim, then my plan is the best."

"I agree. With any luck, Mama will never even find out what we did."

Bridget looked serious. "I hope for your sake that she doesn't."

So did Vanessa.

The first thing to go wrong was utterly unexpected. Their butler, usually a man who accepted on its face whatever she told him, questioned her about her plan to garden.

"Her Ladyship informed us that you're not to leave the house," he said firmly.

"I'm not leaving the house. I'm essentially going into the back of it."

Worry spread over his features. "Are you sure she would look at it that way?"

"I can't imagine why she wouldn't. Consider how I'm dressed. Wouldn't I dress better if I were . . . I don't know . . . sneaking out or something? I certainly wouldn't wear this awful bonnet to do so. Which reminds me, I need the coat I usually wear when gardening."

He looked a bit more accepting of the tale. "But why would you want to putter about in the garden in *this* weather, miss?"

"Gardens don't prune themselves, you know. And if we aren't 'at home' to anyone today, I might as well 'putter about' in the garden."

Good Lord, was she to be a prisoner in her home from now on?

Her agitation must have shown in her face, for he bowed. "Of course." He flicked his hand to the footman to fetch her coat, then helped her into it.

Still, she didn't so much as breathe until she was outside. So far so good. Rapidly she gave Bridget her coat and bonnet, then took the bonnet and shawl Bridget offered in exchange. With a whispered "Good luck, miss," Bridget headed back into the garden. And Vanessa headed for the top of the alley where she could watch for Sheridan's carriage.

That's when she hit the *next* snag in her plan—one that was a bit more significant. Because no carriage came past her, even though she was careful to look in either direction.

Then she spotted him. Not Sheridan. Oh, no. Mr. Juncker. Walking from the other direction. Alone. Tears stung her eyes, which she ruthlessly wiped away. She couldn't keep hoping like this. Every time she did, her hopes were dashed.

But Mr. Juncker had come all this way, so she might as well be polite. She walked up the sidewalk toward him, hugging the railing of the house and hoping no one inside was looking out at that moment. When Mr. Juncker saw her and started, she held her finger to her lips, then gestured across the street. With a sly smile, he took a detour into Queen Square Garden, where she joined him.

"Forgive me for my strange behavior, Mr. Juncker," she said without preamble, "but in a fit of pique, my mother has forbidden me from accepting any calls. Since Sheridan had already said he was bringing you here today, I wanted to make sure I could tell you in person about what happened." She hoped she sounded nonchalant when she added, "Where is Sheridan, anyway? I thought you were coming here together."

"I thought so, too, but apparently I was wrong. We had agreed he would pick me up at my lodgings in the Albany. Then he sent a note saying he'd meet me here and gave me your direction. When I realized you were only a bit more than a mile away, I walked over. I take it he hasn't yet arrived."

"No. Or if he has, he was turned away." Although she doubted that. It wouldn't be like him to try calling on her before the designated time.

Mr. Juncker gazed around at their surroundings. "This is a pretty little park, isn't it? I ought to stroll over here more often."

"You should, indeed," she said, somehow rousing herself to flirt, though she wasn't in the mood. But if Sheridan *should* happen along . . .

Oh, why was she even hoping for that? He probably had no intention of coming here ever again, after that nightmarish confrontation between their mothers. He'd said he would merely keep her from complaining further. But who could blame him for trying to put distance between him and her? Mama always managed to scare off the only suitors Vanessa *might* want.

"You should give me a tour of the square, seeing as how you know it so well," Mr. Juncker said, offering her his arm. "I hate to let all this loveliness go to waste."

As she took his arm, she caught him staring at her, and his flirtatious remark hit her. Oh, Lord, she didn't want to be doing this with no Sheridan around to see. But she couldn't be rude. "This truly is a charming garden. I come here sometimes just to read and watch the birds. There are blackbirds, sparrows, robins, blue tits, and of course pigeons." Heavens, but she was prattling on and on about nothing. He would think her quite the chatterbox. "What would London be without its pigeons?"

"And its beautiful ladies to watch them," he said.

Stifling a groan, she met his provocative grin with a frown. "There's no need to flatter me, Mr. Juncker. I know perfectly well you're merely humoring me to help me with Sheridan."

He shook his head, his gaze showing interest in more than just the garden. "Hardly. I'm continuing the flirtation we began at Thorn's party the other night."

"Even though you know I've set my cap for Sheridan."

"*Especially* because I know that. I told you before. I enjoy annoying Saint Sheridan immensely."

"Well, he's not here," she pointed out. "So I'm not certain how you mean to annoy him." Her voice grew acid. "I hope you aren't one of those fellows who boasts of his conquests to other men despite the risk of ruining the reputation of the ladies he boasts about."

He sobered. "I would never ruin a woman's reputation by boasting or anything else." His eyes gleamed at her.

"But as I said at Thorncliff, lately I've begun to explore the idea of looking for a more respectable companion."

"Like Flora, you mean."

His lips tightened. "Like you." He pulled her into a corner of the garden where an overgrown box hedge and a conveniently placed plane tree formed a sort of private nook. Then he swept her into his arms. "I find myself curious to see how a respectable lady kisses."

She stared up at him incredulously. "Here? Now?"

"Why not? Armitage isn't here, and we both suspect he isn't coming. Who knows? We might find that we suit. Besides, you must be at least a little curious to see how an unrepentant rogue kisses."

With a lift of one eyebrow, she said dryly, "I think of you more as a reprobate than a rogue, to be honest."

"That's like saying a sandwich is different from a slice of ham between two slices of bread." He lowered his head and whispered, "But if you make a distinction . . . Shall we see exactly which one I am, reprobate or rogue?"

She gazed into his ice-blue eyes and thought, *Why not?* She was unlikely to see the man she really wanted ever again, except at formal affairs. And she had to admit she was eager to compare Mr. Juncker's kisses to Sheridan's, against whose standard she would forever measure all others. Unfortunately.

That decided her. "Very well."

She tipped her head back. He took that for the invitation it was and pressed his lips to hers. It was a chaste kiss, the only kind a respectable woman should like, and it was swiftly over, besides. It didn't begin to give her enough of a demonstration for comparison.

"That didn't seem remotely the way a reprobate *or* a rogue would kiss," she said lightly.

But when she started to pull away in disappointment, he kissed her again, this time with far more passion.

It was perfect. He used the perfect amount of pressure and moistness, and he held her tightly but not too tightly. His breath was sweet, and his scent pleasing enough, if not quite as good as Sheridan's spicy one. Yet his kiss seemed practiced . . . the kind a devilish fellow like him was used to giving any woman who might allow him to kiss her. It left her cold.

She couldn't quite put her finger on why it didn't move her, why her heart didn't race and her legs feel as if they'd buckle under her any minute. Unless it was because it didn't begin to compare to Sheridan's kisses.

That made her want to weep, since Sheridan was obviously not going to—

Something wrenched Mr. Juncker from her. *Someone,* that is. She opened her eyes just in time to see Sheridan punch Mr. Juncker in the face.

"What is wrong with you?" Sheridan growled as Mr. Juncker gaped at him. "How dare you take advantage of a lady?"

Sheridan pulled back as if to hit the man again.

"He didn't take advantage of me!" she cried. When Sheridan froze, she stepped between them. "He merely stole a kiss. As a certain other gentleman did at least once before."

Pulling out his handkerchief, Mr. Juncker dabbed at his lip. "You bloodied me, Armitage!"

Sheridan dropped his hands but kept them in fists.

"And I'll do it again if that's what it takes for you to leave the lady be."

"Leave her be! But I thought—" He halted, his gaze meeting Vanessa's pleading one.

So help her, she would never forgive Mr. Juncker if he were to tell Sheridan the truth about her feelings.

Mr. Juncker rolled his eyes heavenward. "You were late. I was not. You can't blame a fellow for trying."

"Trying what?" Sheridan snapped. "To ruin her?"

"Good God, no," Mr. Juncker said with a very convincing expression of outrage. "I'm not such a fool as all that. We're practically out in public! Although I confess I didn't entirely believe your reasons for insisting I come along with you. I thought you were inventing that nonsense about me distracting her mother while you expressed your affection to Miss Pryde in private. But clearly I mistook the depth of your feelings."

"Clearly," Sheridan bit out.

Mr. Juncker bowed to Vanessa. "Forgive me, Miss Pryde, for any insult I may have inadvertently made to your person. I shall leave you in the hands of your most persistent suitor."

She swallowed. "Thank you, sir." It was an inane remark, but she honestly wasn't sure what to say. She was still trying to figure out what Sheridan was up to.

Mr. Juncker was barely out of earshot, heading for the garden gate, when Sheridan fixed her with a dark look. "He had you cornered, entirely isolated. I nearly didn't see the two of you back here. What were you thinking, letting him get you alone and vulnerable like that?"

"I was thinking you weren't coming!" She crossed her arms over her chest. "And how did you find us, anyway?"

"Not that it matters, but I rode over in the carriage, hoping to catch up to Juncker inside. As we turned at the corner, I saw the two of you go into the garden, so after my coachman let me out, I followed you in here." A muscle worked in his jaw. "Why did you ask? Were you wishing I *hadn't* found you?"

She was beginning to wish it. He acted as if she'd done something wrong. But if he believed her tale about being infatuated with Mr. Juncker, he ought to assume she was behaving true to form. "Don't change the subject. It's not *my* fault you were late."

"I suppose you're happy I was."

Oh, she could strangle him sometimes. Was he jealous? Or merely playing at being an older brother as usual? "I wasn't happy, no, not after I was forced to sneak out to see the two of you in the first place."

"What? Why?"

"Why do you think? After yesterday's debacle, Mama told the butler and footmen to refuse all visitors. She wants me never to see you or your mother again. That's why I had to find a way to slip out of the back garden and wait for your carriage at the corner. Fortunately, I happened to see Mr. Juncker walking here, despite assuming he'd be riding with you." She couldn't prevent bitterness from creeping into her tone. "I suppose dukes are too important to bother with such mundane matters as being on time."

That didn't change his stiff stance one whit. "Something came up."

"And of course, you won't say what it was." She'd eluded Mama's minions just to be chastised by him? To the devil with him. As she'd told him before, she didn't need another older brother.

But when she tried to push past him, he grabbed her by the arm. "All of that's beside the point. Do you have any idea what Juncker could have done to you if I hadn't come along just now?"

She pulled her arm free. "He wouldn't have done anything more than he did. He's a gentleman."

"How do *you* know?"

"The same way I know *you're* a gentleman."

Frustration shadowed his features. "Then we're both in trouble."

When he stepped toward her, she backed away instinctively. "Wh-why?"

"Because I find it more damned difficult by the day to be a gentleman with you."

Hope sprouted in her chest, try as she might to stamp it out. "What else would you be?"

His eyes glittered at her. "A man who spends far too many nights wanting to do this." He caught her chin and lowered his head, hesitating a second as if to give her a chance to refuse. But she was too stunned to refuse even if she wanted to. Which she didn't.

Then his mouth covered hers, and her very soul sighed. This wasn't perfect at all. There was nothing practiced about it, nothing that made her think he did it routinely. No, this was messy and passionate and all the things Mr. Juncker's kiss hadn't been.

It was purely Sheridan's. She would have to give him a new nickname—Seductive Sheridan.

Because what he was doing with his mouth was tempting, intoxicating . . . downright sinful. One hand caught her at the waist, while the hand at her chin slid behind her neck as he held her still for a series of long, luscious kisses that resonated in unexpected places—her breasts, her belly, her privates. Oh, heavens. She'd never been kissed so wildly. His mouth caressed and coaxed until she parted her lips for him so he could explore her mouth with his tongue, that ardent tongue that seemed to know her all too well.

Her blood was in a frenzy now, desperately thundering in her ears. She caught his head in her own hands to hold him where he was, but with a low moan, he broke the kiss.

His eyes glittered in the fading light of dusk. "Do you have any idea how insane it makes me to see you with Juncker?"

Those words alone made her heart thump hard and fast. "How could I? You never seem interested in anything but lecturing me or . . . sternly disapproving of whatever I do."

"Oh, trust me," he said with a hint of self-deprecation, "I sternly disapprove of this. But apparently it's not stopping me."

And with that, he pressed her against the plane tree, rested one palm on it above her head, and then leaned in to take her lips once more. This time his kiss was savage, needy, a kiss that made her want him drinking forever from her mouth. She lifted her hand to fondle his glorious ash-brown curls, following them down to his neck, which she then gripped as he'd done hers.

He laid his other hand on her waist, but not for long. Giving her another hungry kiss, he slid his hand up to finger her ribs, as if counting them. Then, to her shock, he covered her breast.

She tore her mouth from his. "Sheridan! What are you about?"

"Showing you, my sweet minx, how difficult it is for me to be a gentleman around you when all I can think about is touching and teasing you, trying to tempt you as thoroughly as you tempt me."

Good Lord, perhaps Sheridan was a poet himself. He certainly made her feel like swooning. Except that if she did, she would miss this, and she wanted to squeeze every carnal drop from his caresses. He rubbed one breast through her thin gown, making her skin feel as tight as a peach's. Then he fingered her nipple with a shocking deftness. Oh, *my*. He certainly knew what he was about. She hadn't expected that.

His breath quickened, and hers did, too, as if attempting to catch and share his rhythm. When she uttered a low moan and arched her back to push her breast more firmly into his hand, he lowered his mouth to suck her neck, hard enough that, when combined with his fondling, it sent a frisson of pleasure through her, making her lift up on tiptoe.

"You're . . . you're turning me . . . into a wanton," she gasped.

He gave a dark chuckle. "Or perhaps just unveiling the wanton you've kept buried inside." He pulled her shawl away to stare down at the swells of her breasts. "Not that I mind. You have no idea how long I've wanted to taste these." Then he buried his mouth between her breasts and began to kiss and lick them at the same time he was pushing them higher from beneath, plumping them up for his tongue.

Lord help her. She wanted to die. She wanted to fly. Mostly she wanted to throw herself into his arms and never let him go. Dared she hope that this time he was finally hers?

Chapter Eleven

Sheridan knew what he was doing was wrong, and he didn't care. Seeing her in Juncker's arms had unleashed an unholy hunger in him. He wanted to stamp out every trace of Juncker, to claim her for his own . . . even knowing such an attempt would be disastrous. Her mercurial nature, which kept him oddly entertained, would also make her a terrible duchess.

But damn, how she moved him. Her mouth, so tender and sweet. Her skin, soft as feather beds. And her bountiful breasts, which he wanted to suck so desperately that he considered somehow getting them out of her gown and corset and shift. Here. In the half light of dusk. In a public garden.

God save him. His cock felt as if it would burst the seams of his smallclothes, and his hands itched to lift her skirts. One had already begun doing so, inching them up slyly as if acting independently of his brain.

He wanted her so badly.

"Sheridan," she whispered, "we can't do such things here."

"I know," he said. "I just . . . can't seem to get enough of you."

He would do penance for saying that later, but for now he didn't care about anything but licking her silky skin, stroking and caressing her under her skirts to see if she was as hot for him as he was for her. Because if she was, then perhaps she had lost interest in Juncker. Perhaps he could step in.

Not that it mattered. Not that he cared. For him, it was only desire, nothing more. He was helping her make Juncker jealous. That was all.

Liar.

He lifted his head to kiss her throat. He wished he could take down her hair, but that was definitely unwise. Instead, he settled for tonguing the pulse that beat in her neck, while his hands roamed her body, taking shameless liberties. He memorized a curve here, a sensitive patch of skin there, finding her wildly responsive to his every touch. Between her gasps and his moans, they were making an unwise amount of noise. Perhaps they should—

"She's here, I tell you," came Lady Eustace's voice. "Look, I see them. That scoundrel!"

Sheridan straightened and released Vanessa in one fluid motion, but it was too late. The unmistakable sound of a pistol being cocked disturbed the quiet of the garden square.

"Step away from my niece, sir. Or I swear you will not live beyond this moment."

Vanessa's uncle. Bloody hell. Nothing like the sound of a gun cocking to make one's own cock stand down. Which was a small blessing, he supposed.

"Uncle Noah, you can't—" Vanessa began.

"Be quiet now, my dear," Sir Noah said in a deadly voice. "You and I will talk in a bit. Go with your mother."

"Do as he says," Sheridan ordered. "I will be along shortly."

"If he doesn't kill you first!" Vanessa cried.

Her concern for him was a balm to his wounded dignity. The dignity he had recklessly tossed aside for a taste of her.

Yet he did not regret it, fool that he was.

"Go on," Sheridan ordered.

"Listen to Armitage," Sir Noah said.

With a sigh, Sheridan faced Sir Noah.

Lady Eustace motioned to Vanessa. "Come with me, young lady. Your uncle will settle this."

When Vanessa looked as if she might refuse to go, Sheridan said, "I promise I won't be long. And there will be no dueling or any of that nonsense, if that's what worries you."

"Do you swear it?" Vanessa asked in an oddly panicked voice. As if she actually cared what happened to him.

Perhaps she did, at least a little. "I swear it."

Reluctantly, Vanessa let her mother pull her away.

As soon as they were gone, Sir Noah said in a grim tone, "You sounded rather sure of me. How do you know I won't call you out?"

"Because you and I are civilized gentlemen. We don't allow women to suffer alone for our actions."

That seemed to catch Sir Noah off guard.

But Sheridan meant it. He'd seen that happen already once in his own family, with his half sister, Gwyn. Because of the unwitting interference of her twin, Thorn, she'd nearly been publicly ruined. Sheridan knew only bits and pieces of the story, but he'd managed to put it together to determine most of it. He didn't want that for Vanessa.

"I doubt we are both bad shots," Sheridan went on, "so if I agreed to a duel, I'd either kill you or you'd kill me. If I didn't agree, I'd be branded a coward. No matter which of those occurred, I'd be leaving Mother embroiled in another huge scandal, and I won't do that. I certainly won't do it to Vanessa."

"How chivalrous of you," Sir Noah said. "Too bad you weren't so chivalrous when you were attempting to seduce her."

The baldly spoken words made Sheridan wince. He could offer no justification for what he'd done. There wasn't any. "Can we get on with this, sir? I will need to break the news of our impending wedding to Vanessa, and I'd rather do it sooner than later." In hopes that she took it better the earlier he offered.

Sir Noah's stony expression softened a fraction. "So you mean to do the right thing by my niece."

"Of course," Sheridan said. "My God, what sort of man do you take me for?"

"I didn't take you for the sort to attempt seducing young ladies in public gardens, but clearly I was wrong. I could be wrong about this, too."

Sheridan stiffened, not enjoying the dressing-down by a man he'd come to like. "I find Vanessa hard to resist, I'm afraid."

"I suppose that's just as well, since you're about to be married rather hastily," Sir Noah said. "I pray she, too, finds you hard to resist. Because if she reveals to me that you were forcing yourself on her, I *will* be calling you out, scandal or no. And there will never be a wedding between the two of you, no matter the outcome. Understood?"

"Understood. I would never force anything on Vanessa." In a weak attempt at humor, he added, "Besides, I have a funny feeling if I ever attempted it, she would cut me up and eat me for breakfast."

Sir Noah didn't utter even a hint of a laugh. "I daresay I would help her."

Good God, was the dressing-down ever going to end? Vanessa would likely be growing angrier by the moment over the fact she had to marry *him* rather than her precious Juncker.

The very thought of that made his blood curdle. This was a nightmare. In trying to impress upon her the wisdom of not being alone with Juncker, Sheridan had somehow managed to teach her the foolishness of being alone with *him*.

It was one thing to dally with her; it was quite another to ruin her life. And possibly his. He didn't even know if they would suit, although if they didn't, it was entirely his own fault. If he'd wanted her so badly, he should have courted her properly. Whether they could make a go of marriage was precisely the sort of thing one sought to discover during courtship.

Even *still* he had no regrets. He wanted to believe it was because he would finally be in a position to question Lady Eustace about the past to his heart's content. He could finally determine if she'd had anything to do with the murders.

But the truth was, he didn't care about that at present. Or rather, he cared far more about getting to have Vanessa in his bed at last. Assuming she agreed to marry him. At the moment, that was by no means certain.

"If you don't mind my asking," Sheridan ventured, "how did you even find us?"

Sir Noah snorted, then began to explain just *how* Vanessa had slipped out.

Vanessa stood peering out the window of the drawing room, trying to catch a glimpse of her uncle and Sheridan. But no matter which direction she craned her neck or how high she stood on tiptoe, they were still as well-hidden from the road as she and Sheridan had been a short while ago, even after the lamplighters had come round. If only Mama had not been alerted, they might still be there.

The thought gave her a delicious warmth in unexpected places.

"Are you listening to me, girl?" her mother asked.

Vanessa jumped. "Yes, Mama," she lied.

That launched her mother into another rant, this one about how ungrateful a child Vanessa was, and how she would rue the day she married Sheridan. But when Mama insisted he was only marrying her for her dowry, Vanessa had taken all she could.

She pivoted away from the window. "He can have every penny of my dowry if it means I get to leave this house. I don't care about my dowry. I would happily throw it into his lap. I just didn't want . . . I don't want . . ."

Oh, what was the use in saying this was the last way on Earth Vanessa had wanted to gain Sheridan? That she might have borne having him court and wed her for her dowry, but having him forced into marriage because of a bit of enjoyment seemed utterly wrong? Especially since she had provoked him into it. If this had taught Vanessa anything, it was that using manipulation to get what one wished never ended well.

No, her mother wouldn't understand Vanessa's feelings. In Mama's view of the world, a young marriageable woman should use her dowry as bait to fish out the highest quality of suitor possible. Indeed, under normal circumstances, if a duke like Sheridan were rich, he would be Mama's idea of the perfect suitor.

But Sheridan was not only supposedly lacking in funds, he was Grey's brother and the dowager duchess's son, which was adding insult to injury. There was simply no getting around that in her mother's mind. Especially after yesterday's contretemps. Not only would Sheridan be forced to marry Vanessa, but he would also be forced to convince a woman he despised to *let* Vanessa marry *him*.

That is, if he and her uncle didn't go straight to killing each other. The very possibility sent a chill straight to her heart.

"I tell you this, little missy," her mother said. "If Armitage offers, you'd better accept. You are teetering dangerously near to landing a permanent spot on the shelf, and these past few days have taxed my patience beyond all bearing." Her mother marched over to her. "So if you do refuse him, I swear I will lock you up in your room until—"

"You will do no such thing, Cora," her uncle said from the doorway. "I will not allow it."

Vanessa whirled around to find Uncle Noah standing there alone. Her heart sank. Where was Sheridan? What had happened?

Her uncle stared grimly at his sister. "I require a moment alone with my niece."

Mama opened her mouth as if to protest, then seemed to think better of it. If there was anyone in the world her mother was afraid to challenge, it was Uncle Noah. "Very well," she said. "But not too long. I shall have to make plans concerning what to do with the girl one way or the other."

That sounded ominous. Thank heaven Uncle Noah was taking charge of the situation. Although once Mama was gone, Uncle Noah's mood only seemed to grow darker.

"I have one question for you, my dear. There is no right or wrong answer, only the truth. Whatever you tell me, I want you to know I am on your side."

That too sounded rather ominous. "A-All right. What is it?"

"Did Armitage take liberties with you against your will?"

The very question perplexed her. "No, indeed. Why? Did he say he did?"

Her uncle relaxed enough to flash her a rueful smile. "He said, and I quote, 'I have a funny feeling if I ever attempted it, she would cut me up and eat me for breakfast.'"

She laughed. "How gruesome. That doesn't sound like Sheridan." Her amusement faded. "Then again, I begin to think I don't know him nearly as well as I thought."

Uncle Noah sighed. "You're in a devil of a situation, my dear."

"I know. But just because he doesn't wish to marry me—"

"What? No, he said at once that he would."

She turned away, her insides knotting up. "Then why isn't he here?"

"He is. He's waiting in the hall. I didn't want him near you until I determined how much of this situation was his fault alone."

Tears stung her eyes. Her uncle really was very kind. Not many men would have taken such care for her feelings. If Papa had been alive, he would have shot Sheridan, no matter how much she protested. Uncle Noah was at least giving them a chance.

"Thank you, Uncle, for stepping into Papa's place. As I'm sure you realize, Mama would have handled everything very badly."

"True. My sister doesn't know what to do with you, never has. She's jealous of how close you and Grey are, but she can't control him, which is why she tries to take it out on *you*. I blame myself for that. I'm sorry I didn't come to London sooner to do my duty by you."

"You had your wife to look after. I always understood that."

"That was no excuse. But I'm here now, and may God strike me down if I don't make sure you are properly married to the right man."

"May I come in?" said a voice from the doorway.

Sheridan. She swallowed hard. She couldn't tell from his usual stoic expression how he felt about this.

"Uncle, could Sheridan and I have a few moments alone?"

Her uncle looked from her to Sheridan. "All right. But I'll be in the hall. And the door will remain open."

Good Lord. She really *had* landed herself "in a delicate situation," at least as far as Uncle Noah was concerned.

"Of course," Sheridan said before she could. "We merely need to . . . settle some matters."

With an understanding nod, Uncle Noah left them together.

Sheridan dragged in a heavy breath. "I don't know if your uncle told you, but you and I must marry."

The word *must* rankled. It implied that both of them were being forced, when she felt anything but that. "I don't see why we *must*. The only people who saw us together were Mama and Uncle Noah, and it's not as if they would tell anyone." She wasn't about to reveal the cruel things her mother had said about what she'd do if Vanessa refused him.

"Did your mother not tell you *how* they found you?"

"No. I . . . never thought to ask." She'd been too worried about what would happen as a result.

"Your mother kept a watch on your garden to make sure you didn't slip out. But when she noticed you always had your back to the window and weren't doing any real gardening, she marched out and made your lady's maid tell her where you were. Of course, Bridget thought you and I and Juncker were in my carriage, since that was apparently the plan. When your mother hurried to the front and didn't see a carriage, she wasn't quite sure where to go."

This was bad, very bad.

Sheridan continued his tale in a somber tone. "Then your uncle arrived for his visit. His carriage had already passed Juncker a couple of blocks away. He'd assumed Juncker was leaving after visiting you. But your mother met him at the door and made him help her find you. So he caught up to Juncker and demanded to know where his niece was. Juncker hesitated to tell him, but not for long, as you might imagine. And *that's* how they discovered where we were."

"I see."

"No, you don't see. I said all of that to illustrate why we *must* marry. It's not just your mother and your uncle who know. It's Juncker—"

"Who won't tell anyone."

"Are you absolutely sure of that? He was willing enough to tell your mother and uncle where you were. What's to prevent him from putting the tale in one of his plays?"

"He wouldn't."

"You're that sure of it," Sheridan said. "Of him."

She wasn't. And she could read in his expression that he knew she wasn't.

"Then there's Bridget—"

"Who won't tell either," Vanessa protested.

"Come now, sweetheart. What do you think is going to happen to her now that your mother knows how she helped you?"

Vanessa began to work the sash of her gown through her fingers like a Papist working a rosary. At the very least, Mama would fire Bridget without a reference, and Bridget didn't deserve that, especially not for helping Vanessa. The only way to prevent it would be for Vanessa to marry Sheridan, in which case Bridget could come work for her directly.

"And other servants know, too," Sheridan said. "There's my coachman, your uncle's coachman, your butler, probably a couple of footmen . . . My point is if you and I don't get married—"

"—someone will leak the gossip to the press," she said dully, "and I will be ruined."

"Yes. *Now* you understand."

She could feel him watching her, feel him debating what else to say.

He stepped closer to her, keeping an eye on the open door. "Would it really be so awful for us to marry?"

"I think *you* should answer that." She crossed her arms over her chest. "You're the one who used the words must marry, not I. I don't need a man throwing himself onto a sacrificial fire for me."

"And I don't need a wife who has had her heart set on marrying another man. But neither of us has much of a choice, do we?"

Vanessa looked away. If she admitted she'd never wanted Mr. Juncker, Sheridan would throw in her face the fact that he'd caught her kissing the playwright a short while ago . . . and quite willingly, too. Or at least it probably seemed like that to him.

Even if she could explain that away and tell Sheridan the truth, he'd see her as a "scheming woman" who used Mr. Juncker to make him jealous . . . which she sort of was. Especially given that Sheridan had once told her he had no desire to marry. Ignoring what he'd expressly said so she could try to gain him as her husband definitely fell under the category of scheming. It wasn't the best way to start a marriage.

Then again, neither was lying. Or rather, shading the truth. A lot. Knowing how much he would hate it. Oh, goodness, what was she to do?

"Well?" he asked. "Do *you* see a way out of this that won't ruin you?"

A sigh escaped her. "Not one that would work." And telling him the truth wouldn't change that. She would just have to hope that in time she could seem to have transferred her affections from Mr. Juncker to Sheridan in a believable fashion.

"So," he said. "We'll be marrying, whether we like it or not."

When he put it that way she wanted to cry. She had to do *something* to make this work. "I didn't say I didn't like it. I wouldn't have returned your kisses if I hadn't . . . thought well of you." Oh, Lord, what a stupid way to put it. It sounded as if she barely knew him.

He could tell, for his jaw tautened. "I suppose that's the most I can hope for under the circumstances."

"I don't want you to feel forced into this!" she burst out. "I know how little you wished to marry. And the thought of pushing you into a situation you never wanted—"

"I took advantage of *you,* sweetheart, remember?" he said kindly, brushing a curl from her cheek. "All you did was be in the wrong place at the wrong time with the wrong man."

"You? Or Mr. Juncker?"

"All right. With the wrong *men*. What I'm saying is don't worry about me." His voice grew bitter. "Besides, I stand to gain a great deal more from the marriage than you. Your dowry will help my current . . . financial situation."

"I get to be a duchess," she pointed out. "Does that count?"

"I hope so. You're going to be something of an impoverished duchess, I'm afraid. So if you wish to bow out, I would understand entirely. Although I don't think it would be wise."

"Yes, and we must always be wise, mustn't we?" she said dryly.

"It's better than the alternative, wouldn't you say?"

"I suppose." When he frowned, she added in a teasing voice, "Yes, Saint Sheridan. Much better."

"Can I make one request then?" he bit out.

"That I not call you Saint Sheridan?"

"Exactly."

"You can make it all you want," she said lightly. "That doesn't mean I have to grant it. Besides, I've been acquiring a full set of nicknames for you. Silent Sheridan. Studious Sheridan." She gave him a saucy grin. "*Seductive* Sheridan."

When he groaned, she laughed. Perhaps this would turn out well, after all. Or at least she would have fun in the process.

And it did mean she no longer had to worry about being forced to marry Lord Lisbourne. As Sheridan had said, when it came down to it, being forced to marry *him* was better than the alternative. Far better.

Chapter Twelve

Seductive Sheridan.

Sheridan would never forgive Vanessa for that parting remark, especially given that they'd had no chance to be alone in the past week. He'd heard those words a dozen times a day and even in his sleep, along with the provocative laugh that had followed it. Vanessa certainly knew how to keep a man on his toes. All he could think was that he'd soon get to play the part of Seductive Sheridan. Was it normal to be this excited about one's wedding night?

He hoped she felt the same way. He should have told her how ridiculously pleased he was that she'd accepted his offer. Even though he knew he couldn't be the man she wanted. Even though Juncker, damn his hide, had her heart. Or perhaps just a youthful infatuation?

God, he hoped that was all it was. Particularly now that he was walking with two of his brothers and Vanessa's uncle from Armitage Hall to St. Joseph's Church in Sanforth, where he and Vanessa were to marry. The ladies had gone on ahead of them in a couple of carriages, his mother, Gwyn, Cass, and Olivia in one, with Vanessa and her mother in another, but none of the men wanted to ride to town on horseback in their finery, so rather than wait for the carriages to return, Sheridan had suggested they walk.

That suggestion was quickly embraced. It wasn't terribly far, so Sheridan had often made the walk into town. Or he'd ridden Juno there. He sighed. He missed his morning rides.

Thorn came abreast of him as Heywood and Sir Noah became engrossed in conversation behind them. "Have you told her yet?"

"Told whom what yet?" Sheridan said.

"You know whom. And you ought to know what." With a glance back to make sure the two behind them weren't in earshot, Thorn said in a low voice, "Have you told Vanessa about why you've been questioning her mother so avidly?"

"Are you out of your mind?" Sheridan hissed. "I was barely able to convince her to marry me as it was. I certainly wasn't going to bring *that* up. Besides, I haven't been able to find out anything from Lady Eustace, so I dare not tip my hand until I do."

Thorn snorted. "What makes you think you'll be able to question Lady Eustace *without* telling Vanessa?"

"Trust me," Sheridan said dryly, "it will not be a problem. All of a sudden I've become Lady Eustace's favorite person. Which is ironic, considering that until I proposed to Vanessa, her mother hated me."

"It's the special license," Thorn said, with a furtive glance back. "That always impresses the mothers."

"Apparently." But in his case, Sheridan wasn't sure if it was because Lady Eustace assumed that such an extravagance meant he wasn't as poor as she'd first feared. Or if she merely hoped the special license would ensure that the wedding would be talked about in the highest circles of society, making *her* the center of attention for months to come.

He wasn't about to disabuse her of her notions by telling her the truth: He'd bought a special license solely because it meant they could marry fairly quickly. He'd feared that one of the many people who'd known about Vanessa's tryst in the garden square might tell someone before he could make her a respectable married woman.

Sheridan wasn't taking any chances. A wedding veil covered all sins.

"This is a delicate situation," Sheridan said. "It just isn't prudent to say anything to Vanessa at this juncture. After all, I might discover that Lady Eustace hadn't been involved in any way in the death of Mother's husbands. In that case, wouldn't it be better that Vanessa never learn of my part in our investigation at all?"

Because if she did, she'd feel cheated, forced to marry a man she didn't love for the worst of reasons—his inability to keep his hands to himself while he was investigating her mother.

"She seems a reasonable sort. You should talk to her."

"Look," Sheridan said under his breath, "let me handle my own marital affairs. Besides, don't you have enough to worry about without being concerned about my own part in the investigation? Or have you already learned enough about Lady Norley's whereabouts to vouch for her?"

Just as Sheridan had thought he might, Thorn didn't like it when the shoe was on the other foot. "I . . . um . . . asked Olivia to question her mother."

I know. "And has she?"

"Not yet." A flush stained his cheeks. "It's hard to find the right time, you understand."

Sheridan smirked at his brother. "Oh, I understand very well."

"Fine. Fine!" Thorn said. "I'll stay out of it. Though I still say Vanessa could probably handle whatever you throw at her."

Sheridan wished he could be sure of that. Especially when it came to their wedding night. Damn, why couldn't he stop thinking about that?

He heard some giggling and looked over to see a group of girls dressed in white with flower crowns on their heads. One little girl stood in awe of the gentlemen passing by, wearing their finest. Sheridan tipped his hat to her, and she got shy, turning and running for her mother who was coming up the walkway. All of them bore baskets decorated with ribbons.

"What was that all about?" Thorn asked.

"This is how it is in a local village, especially if the ceremony and the bridal feast don't occur in the same place. No matter how few the wedding guests, when they leave the church the entire village turns out to cheer and throw rice. They'll follow us nearly all the way home after the wedding is over."

"If you have a special license, why aren't you simply marrying at Armitage Hall?"

"Because I need these people, and they need me. I don't want some private ceremony that they're not a part of. And Vanessa agreed."

"I'll bet her mother didn't."

"No, indeed." He glanced back to see Sir Noah approaching. "Lady Eustace would have preferred the ceremony be performed at Windsor Castle."

"He's only half joking," Sir Noah put in. "My sister would happily have kicked the king out of his lodgings if it meant Vanessa could have the wedding of the century."

"And *not* a mere 'village wedding,'" Sheridan said. "Fortunately, Vanessa and I prevailed."

"Just so you know, Armitage," Sir Noah said, "I reassured Lord Heywood that every *t* was crossed and every *i* dotted as far as legalities were concerned. I told him our respective solicitors hashed out a mutually suitable settlement for my niece, so no need to worry there."

Sheridan gaped at his little brother. "What the hell, Heywood? Did you think I didn't know well enough to have a settlement negotiated for my future wife?"

"I-I had to do one myself," Heywood said while at the same time glaring at Sir Noah, "so I thought perhaps with the wedding being so hasty—not that there's anything wrong with that—but I thought the settlement might have been . . . well . . . overlooked."

"And you thought the best time to mention it was on the way to the church?" Sheridan shook his head. "If you'd been right—and by the way, I find it terribly insulting that you thought I would have 'overlooked' such a thing—but even if you had been, what could I have done about it now? Pulled Sir Noah aside for a quick settlement discussion? Then commandeered Bonham to draw it up in the back of the church while my bride and everyone else waited?"

When Thorn laughed at that, Sheridan turned on him. "What do *you* think is so funny? You're no better, trying to give me marital advice before I even sign the church register." He included Heywood in his frown. "Both of you need to mind your own business. It's my marriage, my estate, and my soon-to-be wife. Stay out of it, understand?"

Thorn scowled at Heywood as they were walking. "See what you started?"

"Hey!" their baby brother answered. "You were the one giving him marital advice."

"At least I had the good sense not to question Sir Noah about Sheridan's settlement. You forget that our brother was trained in the art of diplomatic negotiation practically from birth. He was very good at it, as I recall."

It was Sir Noah's turn to laugh. "I must confess this is making me glad I never had a brother." He paused. "Wait, who is Bonham again?"

"Man of affairs to the last three dukes of Armitage, including my half brother there," Thorn said before turning back to Sheridan. "Bonham will be at your wedding? Does Mother know?"

Sir Noah's amusement vanished. "Why does it matter if the duchess knows?"

"It doesn't," Sheridan said, sparing a warning look for his half brother and little brother. "And yes, she knows. She's the one who insisted on inviting him, precisely *because* he's been man of affairs to the last three dukes of Armitage."

They'd reached Sanforth, but none of the brothers noticed until Sir Noah said, "Should I assume that this is the church?"

Sheridan halted, and his stomach began to churn. "Yes."

"It's larger than I expected for such a small village," Sir Noah said. "Definitely suitable enough for a duke's wedding."

Even as panic hit Sheridan, he nodded. He and Helene had never progressed this far. After weeks of pain and struggle, she'd died of consumption on what would have been their wedding day. Leaving him with a broken heart that had never fully mended.

It was yet another significant moment in his life he hadn't yet shared with Vanessa. But he would. Eventually.

The four of them entered the church and he froze. He hadn't seen the women before they left. Now he was faced with the awe-inspiring sight of Vanessa resplendent in her wedding clothes. She stood at the front talking to his mother and stealing the very breath from his throat while he took her in.

Good God in heaven, how lovely she was. Sometimes in the midst of everything that had happened, he forgot that.

But today, she was spectacular. Her gown was of a blue so pale it looked like white, except when the candles were lit, and the shimmer showed it to be blue silk. Only then did he notice the lace dripping from her long sleeves, and the train of her gown lying twisted behind her, waiting for someone to straighten it.

She and his mother seemed to be having a very intense conversation. He searched the sanctuary for Lady Eustace, then relaxed when he spotted the woman chatting with Gwyn on the opposite end of the church. His female relations had all been instructed to keep the two mothers apart at any cost. He did *not* want a repeat of what had happened a week ago between the two women.

When he hurried to the front of the church, he saw his mother putting a string of pearls around Vanessa's neck. He reached them within moments. "Mother, are those—"

"The Armitage pearls, yes." She gazed fondly at Vanessa. "I know your father would have wanted your bride to have them."

Vanessa glanced at him, and a blush spread over her cheeks.

It ignited his desire anew. He was ready to have the wedding and then go straight to the wedding night, although no one would allow that. There would be toasts to them both and wedding cake. God only knew what else the women had put together in such a short time.

He supposed that was a good thing. Though he could skip all of it, Vanessa deserved a decent wedding. She wouldn't even be marrying him at all if he hadn't practically devoured her in a public garden. Thank God that once he got Vanessa in their bedchamber, he'd be able to assuage his obsessive need for her at last. Later he could deal with the consequences of letting her too close to seeing inside him. But for tonight, he meant to enjoy every single damned minute of her in his bed.

Vanessa's hand shook as she signed the church register. To her surprise, Sheridan laid his hand over hers and bent his head to murmur, "It will be all right. I swear I will make it so."

She sincerely hoped he meant that. Because everything was done now. Final. Fait accompli. The service had only taken half an hour, yet that didn't make it any less permanent. She'd gained what she wanted, although not in the way she wanted it. That was the part that stuck in her craw. What if he grew to resent her for forcing his hand?

Except that she hadn't really. It wasn't her fault they'd become carried away by their desires that night. Was it? In any case, his hand over hers felt right. And that was the most she could hope for at present.

They left the vicar's office and returned to the sanctuary, which was now empty. Everyone else had gone outside.

Sheridan paused before they joined the guests. "Are you ready for this?"

"I've been to a village wedding before," she said, smiling up at him. "I know how they work."

"All right. Just so you're prepared."

They walked out the church doors hand in hand, and she realized that the entire village was outside, everyone jockeying for position so they could be the first to see the duke and his new bride emerge from the church.

The second she and Sheridan crossed the threshold, cheers erupted. As the two of them hurried down the path, they were showered with rice and seeds and petals of winter roses. The open carriage was waiting for them, festooned in ribbons and more winter roses.

Caught up in the enthusiasm of the onlookers, she didn't even falter when Sheridan took her by surprise and kissed her before helping her up into the landau. Amidst universal cheers they were driven away, with the crowd following them for a good distance.

Despite being tied for life to Sheridan, she felt inexplicably free . . . from her mother, her fears, her past. This was the beginning of her life apart from her family. It would be her and Sheridan from now on, with any children they might make. The thought of it was exhilarating.

When they were alone except for their coachman, she caught Sheridan staring at the side of her head. "What are you looking at?" she asked. "Do I have odd ears or something?"

"I'm just now noticing that Mother also gave you the pearl earrings that go with the strand of pearls."

She held up her arm. "And the bracelet and comb as well. The whole parure, I believe."

"Ah, yes. I should at least have noticed the comb in your hair. Although, to be fair, it's in the back, and I've mostly been looking at your front."

Self-consciously she touched the earring he was eyeing. "You don't mind, do you?"

"Of course not. You're my duchess now. You should have the family pearls. I only wish there were more jewelry to give you."

She wouldn't have believed he meant that if not for the hungry look in his eyes that surely resembled that which the wolf in the children's story had given to Red Riding Hood. Too late she remembered that Sheridan's surname was Wolfe. Oh, dear.

"Besides," he went on in a husky voice that sent a thrill through her, "you wear those pearls well. *Very* well."

Vanessa wasn't sure if she should thank him for the compliment or run for the hills before her wolfish husband could devour her.

"Never have I wished more to be in a closed carriage," he drawled.

"Oh?" she asked, determined to lighten the mood by teasing him. "Why, pray tell?"

"That should be obvious. I want—"

When her laugh interrupted him, he apparently realized she knew precisely why. And precisely what he wanted, too.

He bent his head to whisper, "Later, I want to see you wearing nothing but those pearls."

So much for knowing what he wanted. She'd had no idea that Sheridan was so . . . so wicked. All thought of teasing him vanished, replaced by a vivid image of him looking her over while she wore nothing but the Armitage pearls. Her mouth went dry and her breath quickened. She began to feel a little wicked herself.

"I believe I now understand your wish for a closed carriage," she murmured.

He groaned. "I fear this will be the longest bridal feast I've ever attended."

Unfortunately, she feared the same thing.

Chapter Thirteen

Sheridan paced, waiting for Vanessa to open the door that separated their bedchambers. Her maid, Bridget, was, of course, preparing her for her wedding night, although it wasn't technically night, since the sun was still slipping into the horizon. But given that the bridal feast only included their families, who were liable to stay up celebrating until the wee hours of the morning, he hadn't had the patience to wait them out.

So after the usual wedding traditions had been gone through, he'd whisked Vanessa away. Let his brothers and his brother-in-law drink and dance with their wives. He meant to have a different sort of entertainment.

He rubbed the unfamiliar gold band on his finger, and Thorn's words leaped into his mind: *She seems a reasonable sort. You should talk to her.*

About the murders? Tonight? There wasn't a chance in hell he'd do that. Not only did he ache to make Vanessa his wife in every sense of the word, but he didn't want to risk the possibility that telling her about the investigation might destroy the tentative camaraderie he and she shared.

And while he'd been a bit uneasy to leave Mother and

Lady Eustace in the same room together downstairs, it couldn't be helped. They would have to find a way to endure each other's occasional company eventually. They might as well start now.

Unless he discovered that Lady Eustace was a murderer. Then he'd make sure she'd be out of their lives forever. He supposed he shouldn't wish that for his new mother-in-law, given it would mean his own family would have to weather yet another scandal, but it was hard not to. The woman was awful, and he despised how she treated Vanessa.

The door creaked open, and he held his breath. But it was just Bridget.

"You may come in now, Your Grace," the lady's maid said, averting her eyes.

Good God, it wasn't as if he were naked. Yet. He still wore his shirt, trousers, and undergarments beneath his favorite banyan. He was miles away from naked at the moment. Too many miles.

Still, he resisted the urge to hurry. If he fell on Vanessa like a ravenous beast, he might frighten her. She might be a saucy wench, but she was still an innocent, and who knew how that would manifest itself? The last thing he needed on his wedding night was a woman sobbing over his unfeeling deflowering of her. So he prepared himself for anything. He might have been imagining this moment practically since he met her, but he could control himself.

Then he walked into Vanessa's bedchamber to find that Bridget had vanished, and his self-control had apparently vanished with her. How else was he supposed to behave with Vanessa wearing a linen nightdress that, for all its modest, high-collared design, was practically transparent when she stood in front of the fire?

Did she realize it? Was she doing it on purpose to inflame his desires? Because she didn't need to. His desires were pretty inflamed already.

"Are you all right?" she asked him. "You look incredibly serious."

He forced his frown away. "I'm trying hard not to ravish you. But I can see every inch of you through that gown when you stand before the fire. Not that I mind, you understand. I merely thought you'd want to know."

She half turned to stare at the fire as if accusing it of complicity with him, which told him she'd definitely not posed provocatively on purpose. He wasn't sure if that was good or bad. He wouldn't mind her being provocative. He would damned well prefer her being provocative.

Then again, something about her guileless responses stoked his need even more.

"Do you wish me to don my wrapper?" she asked.

"No, indeed." He approached her, his heart hammering in his chest. What he wished her to do was take her hair down. He'd expected to find her that way, actually. Then again, he might prefer to do that himself. "If you want, I'll remove my banyan."

She snorted. "That's hardly the same. You have practically all your clothes on underneath."

He suppressed a laugh. "Should I strip down to my shirt and smallclothes then?" *Please say yes.*

"If you wish."

That was close enough to a yes for him to count it. But

the uncertainty in her eyes made him hesitate. "You're nervous."

"Aren't you?"

"Hardly. It's not the same for a man. Any nervousness we might have pretty much vanishes whenever we see a half-dressed woman."

That got a tentative smile from her, which was exactly what he'd hoped for.

He approached her to stroke a curl away from her forehead. "We don't have to rush this, you know. We have all night."

"True," she said with a bit too much enthusiasm.

"How about this? Let's go sit and talk for a while." *Even if it kills me.* "Then we'll progress at whatever pace makes you more comfortable."

She eyed him with suspicion. "Is this some sort of test?"

That caught him off-balance. "Of what?"

"I don't know." She turned away. "Mama told me that whatever you wanted, I was to do. And that even if I didn't like it, I was to say I did, anyway."

Good God. Just what he did not want of her. "Do you generally listen to what your mother says?"

Casting him a faint smile over one shoulder, she said, "Not usually, no." Her smile faded. "But in this case, she has been married, and I have not. I have nothing with which to gauge the truth of her words."

He walked up to take her hand. "Come sit with me." He led her to a smallish settee.

"We can't both fit on that," she said.

"We can." He smirked at her. "And anyway, I thought you were supposed to be doing whatever I told you to do."

She rolled her eyes. "Fine. See for yourself."

Amused by her sudden crankiness, he sat down and pulled her onto his lap. "I told you we could fit."

Clearly fighting a smile, she shook her head. "I should have known you would never do what's expected."

"You call me 'Saint Sheridan.' Isn't that the very definition of doing what's expected?"

"If you were really Saint Sheridan," she said dryly, "you wouldn't have landed us in this mess in the first place."

He chuckled. "True." Then he sobered. "Now, I know this may be a bit embarrassing, but you must tell me exactly what your mother said was going to happen tonight."

She looked at him as if he were thickheaded. "I just told you what she said."

"That's *all?* Nothing about the actual particulars?"

"No. Why?" He could see a bit of panic in her eyes. "Don't *you* know what's going to happen? Because I don't know enough to instruct you in the matter."

He stifled another laugh. "Yes, I know what's going to happen. It's just that most mothers . . ."

She stared at him expectantly.

"Never mind. How about we try this? Once we proceed to the . . . bedding part of the evening, I won't do anything without preparing you for it first. Will that make it less nerve-racking?"

"Yes, I think so." She threw her head back. "But honestly, how should I know? I'm not even aware of what I'm supposed to do." She squirmed on his lap as if trying to find a better position.

He groaned. "Well, to start with, don't do *that* for the moment."

"Why not? Did I hurt you?" With a look of horror, she tried to leave his lap, but he wouldn't let her.

"It's fine. All I meant was that since I'm aroused, your wiggling about on top of me is making me want to lay you down on the floor and ravish you too soon."

"Oh." She settled back on his lap, but more gingerly. "I arouse you?"

"You know that you do. Otherwise, I wouldn't have 'landed us in this mess in the first place,' as you put it."

She cast him a shy smile. "I don't mind the mess so much."

That made him breathe easier. He hoped she meant she wasn't sitting there wishing he was Juncker. "If we do this right," he said, his voice gravelly from the effort of re-straining himself, "you won't mind the mess at all. With any luck, you'll end up enjoying it."

"How do you know? Have you done this before?"

"A lady isn't supposed to ask a gentleman that," he said.

Her eyebrows lifted. "A gentleman isn't supposed to *do* that, except with his wife."

"Good point." He ran his hand lightly down her still-clothed back. "Let's put it this way—I have occasionally behaved less than gentlemanlike. Certainly less than saintly."

He began unbuttoning the tiny buttons of her night-dress. There were several of them, going down to her waist. And undoing them with one hand was more diffi-cult than he expected. Especially when her breath was coming in thick, shuddery gasps that resonated well below the waistband of his trousers.

"How . . . how often is occasionally?" She stared down at what he was doing. "Have you . . . ever had a mistress?"

"No. Can't afford one."

She stiffened. "Oh, trust me, if a man wants a mistress, he can always find a way to pay for her."

As a shaft of ice pierced his heart, Sheridan halted the unbuttoning. "Do you know that from experience?"

With a sigh, she nodded.

He fought for calm. "Who was he? Juncker?"

She blinked at him. "What the devil are you talking about?"

"What the devil are *you?*"

For a moment, she just stared at him. Then a furious blush rose in her face. "I didn't mean . . . I have never been . . ." She turned irate. "Why on earth would you think I'm talking about my becoming some man's mistress? As if Mama would ever allow such a thing. As if *I* would ever consent to such a thing. Good Lord, what must you think of me?"

"No idea. I confess I'm thoroughly confused. You said you knew from personal experience about mistresses being paid. What else was I supposed to think?"

"Well, not that." At his continued look of bewilderment, she added, "I was talking about Papa. He had at least one mistress."

"How in the hell would you know that?"

She shrugged. "I did the books for him. There were bills from milliners, dressmakers, glovers, and none of the items matched anything Mama or I had purchased. It was obvious it all went to some other woman. Especially since after he died, a woman none of us knew wanted to pay her respects, but Mama refused to see her. It didn't take much to figure out who she must be."

"Ah." He lifted his hand to caress her cheek. "I know exactly what you mean. I suspect my father wasn't always faithful to my mother either. Theirs was a marriage between friends. They were not in love. We all knew that."

"They argued a lot?"

"No. Actually, they almost never argued. They just lived separate lives. Father married Mother so he could sire an heir and a spare. And probably so he could advance his position in the diplomatic corps. Being married can be an advantage there, especially when you marry a dowager duchess. Once he'd sired me and Heywood, he and Mother were polite and friendly to each other, but it never went beyond that. Father's best friend was Thorn's and Gwyn's father, so he knew that her heart would always belong to her second husband. And we knew it, too."

"Did that bother you?"

"Not really. I didn't know anything else."

She nodded. "I don't think *my* parents loved each other at all. They argued constantly. It was upsetting."

"That's understandable."

They fell silent, both probably wondering the same thing. Would *they* fight? Or live separate lives?

He shoved those lowering questions from his mind. Those didn't matter. He and she were married now, and as long as he could keep thinking of her as only his bedmate, he wouldn't have to worry about going through another heartbreak.

Time to stop talking and seduce her. "Do you mind if I take down your hair?"

She looked unaccountably bewildered. "No. But you'll have to remove the pearl comb."

"Is that a problem?"

"You said you wanted to see me wearing nothing but the pearls." A corner of her mouth lifted. "You can't have it both ways, you know. Either I'm naked with the pearls on. Or the pearls aren't on, but my hair is down."

The thought of either made him randy as hell.

At the flirtatious gleam in her eyes, he smiled. "What a little parser of rules you are. But since I hadn't even noticed that the comb was adorned with pearls, I'd rather see your hair down." He whispered in her ear, "I'll be seeing you naked eventually, anyway."

She met his gaze. "I do hope I'll be seeing *you* naked as well."

That was all it took to send him over the edge. He covered her mouth with his, kissing her so thoroughly that she couldn't possibly be left wondering about his intentions. At the same time, he slid his hand inside her unbuttoned nightdress to fondle one of her full breasts, relishing how the soft silk of her nipple tightened to a fine point as he thumbed it. When she moaned somewhere deep in her throat, it only heightened his pleasure.

His cock grew painfully hard.

He broke their kiss. He had to slow this, had to be the courteous lover he knew she would want for her first time. "You need to stand up, sweetheart."

"All right." She got off his lap, and he stood, too, not even bothering to hide his erection, though he doubted that she'd noticed it.

"Turn around," he said thickly. Once she did, he took down her hair.

Good God. Doing that wasn't likely to slow a damned thing. Her mass of shimmering, cascading curls just begged to be touched. How she—or more probably, Bridget—had managed to scrape all of this into a sedate coiffure was anybody's guess.

He'd always thought of black hair as all one shade, so he was surprised to find hers a profusion of hues from a very dark brown to soft black to jet black to almost blue. It seemed to depend on the light and how the curls turned.

Filling his hands with the lovely weight of it, he marveled at how soft and springy it was. And long, too, coming down almost to her waist.

"Are you quite finished disordering my hair?" she said irritably.

He laughed. "Why? Am I taking too much time seducing you?"

"Seducing?" She faced him. "Is that what you're doing? Because I could have sworn you were indulging in your need to find all my flaws."

"What flaws?" He cocked his head. "If you're referring to your hair, it most definitely isn't a flaw."

That uncertainty came into her eyes again. "Clearly you've never had to manage it."

"No. Thank God. Because if I had my way, it would never get managed. I would have you wear it down about your shoulders forever."

"You would have me be a slattern then?"

He shook his head. "I would have you be the enchantress

that you are. And your amazing hair is one thing that makes you so."

The sudden brightness in her face made him realize she had no idea of how intoxicating she was physically, not only to him but probably to a number of bachelors. He wondered why she wasn't vain as a peacock. She had the right to be.

"We'll see if you still think me an enchantress after I do this." And with one liquid movement, she shimmied out of her nightdress, letting it drop to the floor.

His mouth went dry as he stepped back to take in the full effect. God save him. With her hair eddying around her shoulders and trailing down her arms, she was a wonder of creation. "I don't know what *you* were trying to prove, sweetheart," he said hoarsely, "but you wearing only pearls merely proves *me* right."

He reached out to cup both her breasts, which were ample enough to fill his hands and adorned with shell-pink nipples besides. She was a veritable Venus, the pearls accentuating her creamy skin and lush figure, which was rounded in all the right places, tempting a man to tease and caress and devour. Just as Mars, the Roman God of War, had seduced the Goddess of Love, Sheridan meant to seduce his own private Venus. Nor could he wait a minute longer.

Taking her by surprise, he caught her up in his arms and carried her to the bed, where he laid her out atop the sheets, the cover having been pulled back by servants in anticipation of just this moment. But when he knelt on the bed, she pushed up on one elbow to rest her head in her hand. "Oh, no, you don't, husband. You promised I could see you naked, too. It's your turn." She held out her other hand to him, the one with the pearl bracelet. "I'll loan you the Armitage pearls, if you wish, Your Grace."

"Very funny," he said dryly. "And as I recall, I promised nothing about standing naked before you. Although I suppose I can overlook your misapprehension just this once."

Then he began to remove his clothes. He only prayed he could finish before he fell on her like a starving wolf at a feast.

Chapter Fourteen

Vanessa had never seen a man so bold. Were all men this eager to undress for a lady? Because she felt decidedly odd lying here naked before him, with the pearls weighing heavily about her neck and wrist like chains marking her as his, forever.

The way he looked at her as he shed his banyan and kicked off his shoes didn't help. His eyes, hungry and hot, ate her up. A wild thrill shot through her to think of him ravishing her, even though she wasn't sure what ravishing actually was. What if she made a fool of herself in her ignorance?

He'd removed his cravat long before he'd entered her bedchamber, tantalizing her with a glimpse of his bare throat above his mostly buttoned shirt. Now he undid the remaining buttons and tugged the shirt off, revealing his entire upper body in all its carnal glory.

Heavens, what a sight. The shoulders she'd assumed must be enhanced by his clothing were all his—as broad as she'd imagined. And his chest! Oh, Lord. The only bare chest she'd ever seen was on a marble statue of Adonis, so to view a real man's was breathtaking.

Not only did Sheridan's chest look every bit as muscular as that on the Adonis, but it had things the statue lacked. Like nipples. Who knew that women and men both had them? What's more, Sheridan's chest had *hair* around the nipples, tight curls a shade darker than the hair on his head.

She ached to touch them, both the nipples and the hair, and as if he could read her mind, he approached the bed to place her hand on his well-knit chest. At once she began to stroke it. How fine it was, velvet over stone. The longer she stroked, the faster it rose and fell with the quickening of his breath.

She excited him, did she? That was certainly encouraging. It also prompted her to sit up and spread both hands over his surprisingly responsive flesh.

As she skimmed her hands down to caress his lean stomach, he groaned. "If you're hoping to make me beg, my duchess, you're going about it the right way."

"Am I?" she said teasingly, before what he'd called her registered. *My duchess.* It had a nice ring of permanency to it. Then she noticed the swelling of something in his trousers. "Oh, dear. I *did* hurt you before."

"That's how a man looks when he's aroused." He began to undo his trouser buttons. "Here, I'll show you."

She pushed his hands away, shocked by her own impudence. "Let me do it."

He gave a guttural laugh. "Why not? I should have known you'd be a greedy miss in the bedroom."

"I'm merely curious. You should have expected that.

I've never been with a man before. Not like this, anyway." She unbuttoned his trousers, only to find herself thwarted by another set of trousers beneath it. "What's this?"

"This, sweetheart, is where a man takes charge of the undressing before he erupts . . . er . . . does something he will almost certainly regret later." He undid the underpart of his clothes and shucked both sets of trousers off, leaving himself entirely nude.

And giving her an eye-level view of his lower anatomy. Especially the thick staff of flesh thrusting out from a nest of hair between his legs. It was growing rather impressively.

"God save me, Vanessa," he said hoarsely, "if you don't stop staring at my cock, I'm liable to embarrass myself."

"Your 'cock'?" She gazed up at him, wondering how he could embarrass himself when he hadn't even so much as a flushed face. "Wait, is this like a codpiece in the theater? Only bigger? And more . . . protruding?"

"Touch it," he choked out. "I want your hands on me."

She did as he asked, slipping one finger along the length of it. That only seemed to agitate him, for he seized her hand, then closed it around his "cock." "Do it like this."

His hand over hers stroked his thing, which literally moved in her fist as if it had a mind of its own. How fascinating! But she only got to stroke it a few times—marveling at the smooth texture and dark red flush of it—before Sheridan muttered something that sounded like a curse and brushed her hands away.

Then he pushed her back upon the bed and repositioned her so she was lying with her legs parted, allowing him to kneel between them, with that thrusting flesh of his veering dangerously close to her privates.

Perhaps that was on purpose. "Oh!" Was he intending to push his hard flesh inside her? That reminded her. . . . "Mama did tell me one thing—that my deflowering would hurt."

"Not if I'm careful," he choked out. "And I promise I will be. You're safe in my hands, sweetheart."

"If you say so." Meanwhile, her mind did calculations that seemed to protest he was much too large to fit inside her. But how could that be? Women did these sorts of things all the time. Would they do it if it hurt every time?

Possibly. Lord knew women did other things for men that hurt. Like having children.

He must have seen her wariness because he leaned down to kiss her, his rigid thing trapped between her belly and his. She relaxed at once. She liked kissing him. Every time he drove his tongue into her mouth, he sent her senses reeling.

After a bit, he moved down to suck her breasts, which was even more exciting. She gripped his upper arms to keep him there, to keep feeling so unexpectedly *delicious*. She wanted him closer, needed to experience more of the sensations he was rousing, not only in her breasts but in places he wasn't even touching, like her belly and between her legs.

This bedding business clearly had advantages. No wonder there were women who did it for pay—they got pleasure *and* money out of it.

Next thing she knew, Sheridan had his hand between her legs, fondling her very privates. Her privates! She barely touched them herself, and to have him stroking and teasing them . . .

Good Lord in heaven, how wonderful! He stared

knowingly at her, though his breath was coming in staccato gasps that excited her almost as much as his fondling. Because it meant he craved the touch of her, hungered for her attentions, perhaps even needed her for more than just this.

She could only hope so. She needed him, too. Desperately. She didn't want to, but apparently she couldn't stop. So she'd best be careful. Otherwise, she'd be precisely where she'd sworn never to be—at the mercy of a person who didn't love her.

Although he certainly seemed to enjoy inflaming her desires. "You like that, do you?" he asked, a hint of triumph in his tone.

"Yes." She squirmed a bit as he continued rubbing her in the most amazing way.

His own breath grew labored. He slid one finger inside of her, and she nearly came up off the bed in her eagerness to have him caress her there.

"You're so wet for me, my sweet wife. Hot and damp and wonderful." He bent close to whisper, "I love watching you fall apart in my hands."

"Is that what I'm doing? Is that how it's done?"

He frowned. "How what's done?"

Now he had two fingers inside her, and it was quite glorious. "You know. The deflowering." Because if that was it, it hadn't hurt at all, which was a relief. Perhaps she'd been wrong about what he intended to do with his aroused "cock."

He managed a chuckle. "Oh, no, minx. We've only just begun. There's more. A great deal more." A muscle worked in his jaw, as if he were restraining himself from . . . *something*. "Let me show you."

Oh, dear. That sounded worrisome.

When she tensed, he said, "Trust me. I swear I will make this as easy for you as I can, all right?"

She nodded, though she didn't like the "as I can" part.

"If you want to pause or stop at any moment, say the word." He hovered over her, somehow both a delightful and an alarming presence. "I don't relish beginning this marriage with you afraid of me." He forced a smile. "And I'm not so terrifying as all that, am I?"

She stared into his eyes. "I never thought you so before." She tipped up her chin. "But appearances can be deceiving."

For some reason, that made him laugh, although it sounded forced. "Give me a chance, Vanessa," he murmured. "You'll find that appearances are indeed deceiving. But not in the way you think. Just hold on to me."

She did, looping her arms about his neck.

He moved his hand from between her legs so he could grab his thing and guide it into the same place he'd been putting his fingers. And as he inched his thick flesh into her, she found it wasn't as fearsome as she'd expected.

Judging from his strained expression, *he* found it more fearsome than she did.

Then he started moving. In and out in slow, silken thrusts meant to seduce. His eyes were closed, so she closed hers. That made everything better. Instead of growing anxious over what was to come, she relaxed and let the motion he'd begun take her along, like a leaf floating down a river.

Being joined to him this way felt odd—and entirely unexpected—but it was also a pleasure all its own. It made them one. Husband and wife. The fulfillment of everything she'd hoped to have from him.

Well, not quite everything, but she wouldn't think about that now.

"Better?" His voice was rough and thick, as if he fought to keep going.

Or perhaps to keep going slow? She wasn't sure. "Yes." She was growing warm down below and sort of tingly. It was rather pleasant. She even found the filled-up sensation enjoyable . . . when she wasn't finding it uncomfortable. "Mostly better, anyway."

"Put your legs around my waist and hook your ankles together," he said.

Normally she would have balked at his commanding tone, but he was in charge of this since she had absolutely no idea what she was doing. She changed her position in the way he'd ordered, and instantly the tingling became something wildly pleasurable.

"Oh!" she said, her eyes shooting open. "Oh, *my*. That is . . . quite . . . a bit better. . . ."

He chuckled. "I thought it . . . might be."

He was hers now. For good. Her husband. And they could do this together whenever they pleased. She smiled up at him, her hands stroking his curly hair.

Uttering a moan, he bent to kiss her forehead. "Ah, Vanessa. You will be my downfall. And just now I don't . . . care. As long as I can have this . . . with you."

My downfall. The words should have hurt. Instead, they made her exult. He wasn't immune to her. And that was quite a bit better than she'd anticipated.

Now he began to drive into her more quickly, his eyes like flames igniting her above as his "cock" ignited her below. He rubbed one particular spot down there with his finger, too, somehow improving the already amazing feelings sweeping through her.

"Oh, Sheridan," she moaned. "My darling husband. You are . . . *magnificent.*"

"So . . . are . . . you. . . ." he murmured.

Now she was the leaf being carried along by the river's current, faster and faster as he thrust into her more quickly. Vanessa's hands slipped down to grip his remarkably broad and muscular shoulders as she held on for dear life. Something was about to happen—she could feel it down below—and the more she strained into him, the closer it seemed to approach. Her blood rushed in her ears, the way the river rushed forward toward a precipice, and she just let it . . . come.

"My wife . . ." he managed. "My duchess . . . my *goddess* . . ."

The words pushed her over the edge, sending her falling, falling toward the churning, tumbling waters below. And when she plunged beneath the surface, her body shook, and she fell back nearly insensible as he drove hard into her and gave a hoarse cry.

It was glorious.

Sheridan lay there on his side beside his new wife and tried to arrange his senses into some semblance of order. Bloody hell, had he really called her his "goddess" there at the end? He had not expected to lose his mind quite that thoroughly.

He had not expected *her.*

Now that she was curled up against his side, eyes

closed, with the covers pulled up under her arms and a contented smile gracing her face, all he could think was how beautiful she looked, with her raven curls tumbled about her shoulders and her alabaster skin aglow.

Or perhaps he was imagining that last part, one effect of the fever in his brain that came whenever he was near her. She still wore his pearls, and that, too, stirred his cock. To be honest, everything about her did.

He chuckled at the thought of how she'd insisted upon his undressing while she watched, right in the midst of his grand seduction. That had *definitely* aroused him. To have her gaze regarding him with such fascination . . .

Good God. Every time he turned around, she said or did something to tempt him. Not to mention, catch him off guard.

Now he understood what society meant when it dubbed a woman a diamond of the first water. Because Vanessa had more facets than any finely cut gemstone, and every moment he was with her, she showed a new one. He wondered how long it would take for him to discover them all. Even now, the very way she lay showed him new curves he'd missed caressing, soft places he'd missed kissing, and a thousand other small details it would take him a lifetime to catalog.

He sat up, annoyed with himself. He was turning into the most maudlin fellow ever. She didn't have to wrap him about her finger. He was doing it for her.

She opened her eyes, a slumberous look on her face. "I need to ask a favor of you."

"What sort of favor?" he asked suspiciously. Given the way he'd been thinking of her, if she asked him for the moon, he'd probably try to kidnap it from the sky.

Worry knit her brow as she laid her hand on his chest. "Do you think you could . . . well . . . promise me you will never do with another woman what we just did together?" She cast him a quick, darting look. "That you'll take no mistresses as long as I'm alive?"

The request took him aback. Why would he need a mistress? Vanessa was more than enough for him. "No mistresses. I promise." When relief brightened her face, he added, "Will you promise the same?"

She blinked. "Certainly. I promise never to take a mistress." Then she laughed gaily, dispelling some of the tension between them.

"Very amusing, minx." He tipped her chin up with one finger. "I will get you for that later."

"Oh, I dearly hope so. Just make sure it's something wonderfully naughty. I've only just discovered I rather like being naughty. At least with you."

When his blood began to race once more, he made himself cast her a stern look. "You're avoiding the subject." Not to mention arousing him again, either unwittingly or, more likely, as wittingly as hell. "Do you promise *me* you will never take a lover? Especially not Juncker."

Her gaze grew shuttered. "No lovers. And definitely not Mr. Juncker. I promise."

She was hiding something from him, but he couldn't figure out what. She'd been chaste before now; that much he could tell. No woman could pretend to be an innocent so convincingly. She had genuinely marveled at each new aspect of having marital relations.

Still, that didn't necessarily mean she had no intention of seeking out Juncker now that she knew what to do in bed. The very thought of her in love with that puffed-up, theatrical arse, possibly seeking to be with the man, tore him up inside. And if Juncker ever tried to take advantage of her feelings . . . Sheridan would call the bastard out for sure.

Fortunately, Sheridan suspected that whatever weapon was chosen—whether pistols or swords—he would be better at it than Juncker. After all, Juncker had spent his entire life scribbling poetry and pretending to be a playwright. Sheridan, on the other hand, had been trained by his father to be prepared for anything—feast or famine, peace or revolution. And once Sheridan had seen that the family's investigation might put them all in danger, he'd added lessons in shooting to his activities.

Sometimes the only way to keep the peace was to threaten violence. As Father had always said, "Peace comes at a price paid for by the sword." And Sheridan would be more than happy to thrust a sword through Juncker's heart, if it were warranted.

His stomach growled, and he realized he hadn't eaten since breakfast. Quite possibly she hadn't either. "Are you hungry?" he asked.

"Hungry, mmm," was all she answered.

She was falling asleep! He didn't know whether to be insulted that he'd bored her or pleased he'd worn her out with his lovemaking. Then again, it had been a very long week of planning and arranging the wedding. His part had only been to meet with solicitors. It was Vanessa—and his pregnant sister, pregnant sister-in-law, not-yet-pregnant sister-in-law, and aging mother—who'd done the rest. He probably shouldn't fault Vanessa for being tired. He should be shocked she hadn't fallen asleep before he could even make her his.

Well, when she woke up, he intended to have something here to feed her at least. He could ring for a servant, but he'd rather go see what was left of the food from the bridal feast. Probably some of the colder items were still on the tables in his cavernous dining room. Besides which, he might find a bottle of champagne not yet opened.

After donning the footed silk drawers he preferred to wear under his trousers, he dressed in his remaining clothes, adding a waistcoat and coat. He probably looked a bit disheveled, but at least he'd be presentable to the ladies in the house if he should happen to run across any of them, which he sincerely hoped he did not.

He paused beside the bed to pull the covers up over her shoulders, stifling a laugh as she mumbled something about "naughty food" and "oysters champagne," and then he headed downstairs.

Immediately, he ran into Thorn, of course. He was probably lucky Heywood wasn't with him.

"Aren't you supposed to be enjoying your marital bed?" Thorn asked. He was carrying a plate piled high with food.

"I enjoyed it quite thoroughly, thanks. Vanessa's asleep now, so I thought I'd pop down to find nourishment." With a sly smile, he took Thorn's plate. "It was kind of you to gather some food for me and my new bride. We're famished."

"I got that for Mother," Thorn said.

"Mother can't eat all that," Sheridan said. "Fortunately, it's just enough for me and Vanessa."

"I thought you already put the chit to sleep with your accomplished seduction," Thorn said.

Sheridan took a bite of a chicken leg on the top of the pile. "A gentleman never speaks of such things."

"Then that's a yes."

"No!" Sheridan lifted his eyes heavenward. "Not that it's any of your concern, but I wore my wife out with my 'accomplished seduction.' You wouldn't understand. Poor Olivia has to put up with your bumbling."

"Bumbling! You're just jealous of my fine technique."

"Hardly." He bit off more chicken. "And don't call my wife a 'chit.' She's a full-grown woman, as I have thoroughly ascertained."

Sheridan heard a murmur of voices from the drawing room. When he and Vanessa had "retired," everyone had still been drinking and eating in the dining room. "What's going on?"

"We're having a meeting to assess our progress on the subject of the investigation. We weren't planning to bother you with it, given that it was your wedding night, but if you'd like to be part—"

"Of course I'd like to be part of it." Sheridan glanced around the hall and lowered his voice. "What about the other guests? Lady Eustace? Sir Noah? Lady Norley and Lady Hornsby?" He frowned. "Bonham?"

Thorn began ticking those off on his fingers. "Lady Eustace went to bed. I gather she tires easily. Sir Noah went into Sanforth, hoping to find some cardplayers at the nearest tavern, since none of us wanted to join him in a game. Bonham returned to London. Apparently he had business affairs to take care of, probably for *you*. Lady

Norley retired to read in her room, and Lady Hornsby left almost immediately after the ceremony to return to . . . wherever she's been the past week. Didn't you notice she wasn't at the bridal feast?"

"I was rather preoccupied at the time, if you'll recall. Still, it's curious, don't you think?"

"Definitely. But it's Gwyn's task to interrogate Lady Hornsby, so it's not my problem."

"Your problem is to question your mother-in-law," Sheridan said, "which I gather you haven't yet managed to do. Good luck to you."

Instead of turning defensive, Thorn smirked at him. "And now *your* problem is to question *your* mother-in-law. Good luck to you, too. I'll take Lady Norley over Lady Eustace any day." He clapped an arm about Sheridan's shoulders. "Come on. Let's go see what everyone else has found out."

As soon as they entered the drawing room, the comments began. His brothers tormented him about coming down so soon after going up with his wife. Their wives rolled their eyes and shook their heads, and in general pretended their husbands *weren't* a group of jokers and buffoons.

Mother was the only one who glared—at each of her sons in turn. "Leave him be, all of you. Sheridan and Vanessa will find their way, no thanks to you lads."

Heywood laughed. "Lads! We're grown men with wives, Mother. Besides, even Saint Sheridan can endure a few jests at his expense on his wedding night."

"'Jests' would imply that your remarks are funny," Sheridan quipped as he walked over to the brandy decanter and set down his plate just long enough to pour himself a glass. "So far, all I've heard is a lot of juvenile bluster."

That started his brothers trying to outdo each other with witty insults. It didn't last long because Sheridan's cousin Joshua, who was also a major in the Royal Marines and technically Sheridan's brother-in-law, stood in the midst of the room and cried, "Enough!"

When that quieted everyone, Joshua added, "May I remind you we have a limited amount of time to do this? Sir Noah might return at any minute, or one of the other suspect ladies come down to see what all the commotion is. We need to get on with it, but without creating too much noise. Understood?"

His family muttered something to the effect that they did.

Then Joshua turned to Sheridan. "Do you wish to wait until your wife can join us to discuss the investigation into her mother?"

Damn.

He took his time about finding a chair near a table so he didn't have to balance a plate and glass on his lap.

"Yes, Sheridan, do you?" Thorn asked smugly. "Or could it be that you haven't actually told Vanessa yet?"

"I just got married today," Sheridan ground out. "I haven't had time to tell her."

Olivia eyed him closely. "Thorn told me before we were even engaged."

"You were in love." Sheridan set the plate down on the table. "That's different."

"Not then we weren't," Thorn said. "Or at least we weren't admitting it to each other."

"Although to be fair," Olivia said, "Thorn sort of let his suspicions—his unproven suspicions—about Mama slip out. If he hadn't, I might still not know."

"That's not true," Thorn said. "I would have told you before we married, I'm sure."

She lifted an eyebrow, then turned to Sheridan. "And when I found out what he suspected Mama of doing, I did give him grief for it."

"My point entirely," Sheridan said, taking a swig of brandy. He'd need it for *this* discussion. "I'd rather have at least a couple of days of wedded bliss before I broach something liable to cause contention." He set down his glass. "Besides, it's really none of her concern." When his brothers and Joshua all groaned and their wives looked daggers at him, he said, "What? It isn't. She had naught to do with any of it. She wasn't even born until ten years afterward. I'm only protecting her from the truth about her mother."

His own mother snorted. "You're not protecting her from *that*. In some respects she already knows the truth about Cora. You're protecting Vanessa from learning why she really had to marry you. Because we all know that if not for this investigation, which you performed under cover of being her friend, you would never have ended up married to her."

"That's not true," he protested. Except he knew it was.

Then a voice came from the doorway. "What investigation is your mother talking about?"

Oh, God, no. Vanessa walked into the room wearing his banyan, which thoroughly engulfed her. With his heart hammering in his chest, he rose. "Nothing to worry you, Vanessa. Go on back to bed. I'll be there shortly."

"I'm not leaving." The coldness in her eyes froze his blood. "Not until I find out what investigation you're talking about. And what in the devil it has to do with my mother."

Chapter Fifteen

With all eyes on her, Vanessa felt exposed, vulnerable. Her only consolation was that they weren't looking at her as if they took her for a fool. Instead, they regarded her with sympathy. She had allies here, thank heaven.

Sheridan was probably not one of them.

Had it really only been scant minutes ago that she'd awakened from a blissful slumber to find him gone? That she'd come looking for him, thinking to discover him in a pantry somewhere and not surrounded by his family? It seemed forever ago.

"Someone please tell me what I missed," she said through the lump of unshed tears in her throat. She'd known he hadn't married her for love—she hadn't expected that. But she'd thought he'd been spending time making Juncker jealous because he really cared about her. Because they were "friends."

She'd been wrong. He hadn't even cared *that* much. Although it hadn't stopped him from taking her to bed, had it?

Since no one had answered, she pressed on, unable even to look at him right now. "Let me see if I have this straight. You have all been investigating something having to do with Mama. And Sheridan was the one charged with questioning her 'under cover' of being my friend. Is that right?"

For a moment, the room was utterly silent, giving her a chance to remember all the times Sheridan had seemed more interested in her mother than in her, all the strange questions he'd asked, and, worse yet, the many ways Mama had avoided answering him.

"Well?" she repeated, impatient now. "Is it?"

The room exploded with explanations, too many for her to take in. But only Sheridan approached her, inexplicably holding a plate of food and a glass of brandy, as if they were peace offerings. "Perhaps you and I should go somewhere private so I can explain, sweetheart."

She glared at him. "You have little chance of that, *darling*. I need your family here to keep you honest."

Pain glimmered in his eyes before he masked it. "Do you think I would lie to you about it?"

"You've been lying to me about it all this time, haven't you?"

"No. Just . . . omitting certain details."

"You mean, like why you have to have secret meetings without me, even though we are now married? Or do you still think of me as some brainless fribble who doesn't have the intelligence to be part of your family's schemes?"

"I damned well don't think of you as—"

"You've landed in the thick of it now," Thornstock said with a laugh.

"Stay out of this, Thorn," Sheridan snapped, "or I swear I'll break your jaw."

Vanessa caught her breath. Had she somehow missed

this violent side to Sheridan's character? She'd assumed that his striking Mr. Juncker was due to her, but now that she wasn't sure if *anything* was due to her, she had to wonder.

Thornstock snorted. "Right. Saint Sheridan is going to fight me."

"Don't put it past him," Vanessa said. "He's punched a man before. I've seen him do it."

When his family stared at her aghast, Sheridan said softly, "Only for you, sweetheart."

She ignored the frisson of pleasure that his remark sent through her. Clearly, Sheridan was better at flattery than she'd heretofore realized.

"Whom did you punch?" Lord Heywood asked his older brother.

"Juncker," Sheridan said, keeping his gaze fixed on her.

"Ohhhh," everyone said in unison, as if that explained everything.

"No doubt he deserved it," Thornstock added.

It was her turn to scowl at the man. "I thought Mr. Juncker was your friend."

Thornstock shrugged. "He is. That's how I know that sometimes he can be an arse."

"Especially around ladies," Sheridan told him.

"You are *not* going to distract me from my purpose with talk of Mr. Juncker!" Vanessa scanned the room. "Will someone who is not my husband please tell me what's going on? Obviously everyone else's wife has been included in the discussion. Why not me?"

"Why not you, indeed." With a kind smile, the dowager duchess rose and walked over to take her hand. "Come sit by me, my dear, and we will answer all your questions."

As she led Vanessa toward the chair beside hers, she paused to relieve Sheridan of his plate. "I believe the food was meant for me, son." Taking the glass, she handed it to Vanessa. "And heaven knows your wife can probably use some brandy to get through *this* discussion."

If Vanessa hadn't been so angry at Sheridan, she might have been amused by his astonished expression as his mother walked off with his food, his drink, and his wife. But Vanessa wasn't in the mood to be amused just now. Staring rather defiantly at Sheridan, she took a large gulp of brandy.

It was like swallowing fire. When she had a fit of coughing, the dowager duchess handed her a handkerchief.

"Oh, my word," Vanessa said when she could speak again. "Why would anyone drink that vile stuff?"

Olivia said, "It's actually quite delicious once you get used to it." When Sheridan looked surprised by that, coming from Olivia, she added defensively, "Well, it is. But in my experience, it's better if you sip it."

Sheridan muttered something under his breath, but Vanessa pointedly ignored him. This time she took a small sip and discovered that Olivia was right. A sip provided just enough heat without overwhelming her.

The dowager duchess patted her hand. "If it makes you feel any better, my dear, most of what you're about to hear wasn't even told to *me* until a month ago. What do you want to know first?"

After one more sip, Vanessa put the glass down on a nearby side table. "Eventually, I want to hear what part Mama plays in all of this. But it sounds as if this is a bigger story than that, so perhaps someone should start at the beginning." When Sheridan opened his mouth, she said, "But not you."

Her husband sat back with a curse and crossed his arms over his chest. The baleful look he gave her held fair warning that she'd have to deal with him soon. But first she needed to get the story straight in her head.

Everyone but Sheridan looked to Major Wolfe, and he sighed. "I suppose I am the most objective observer. Besides, there are things I need to report on to all of you anyway, so I might as well be the one to start."

Report on? When they'd used the term *investigation,* they hadn't been exaggerating.

Absently Major Wolfe rubbed his knee. "Over the past year, Miss . . . er . . . sorry . . ."

"Please call me *Vanessa,*" she put in. "I consider all of you my family, even if my husband doesn't seem to think I am."

Now Sheridan was positively glowering at her.

"Very well," the major said. "Feel free to call me Joshua. Everyone else does."

"Thank you," Vanessa said.

"In any case, we have come to realize that the dowager duchess's three husbands were quite possibly murdered."

She thought surely she'd misheard the man. "Murdered?" she said, just to clarify. "Three dukes? Surely someone would have noticed that."

"The deaths were disguised as illness or accidents." The major cast Sheridan a quick look. "Indeed, it was your husband who first noticed the inconsistencies."

"After our uncle *and* our father died within months of

each other in suspicious accidents," Heywood added helpfully.

Joshua nodded. "To be honest, we all thought Sheridan was daft at first. Then mysterious things kept happening—"

"Like a fellow named Elias trying to sabotage Thorn's carriage," Lady Gwyn said. "While me and Thorn and Mama and Joshua were traveling to London in it! Then there was the discovery that Grey's father didn't die of an ague, but was poisoned by arsenic decades ago." She smiled over at Olivia. "Olivia actually discovered that."

"No thanks to Elias," Olivia said, "who blew up my laboratory the first time to keep me from discovering it."

When a chill spread through Vanessa, she began to think she'd put the brandy down prematurely. She couldn't believe what she was hearing! "The *first* time? And who's Elias?"

"A villain for hire, we think," Olivia said with surprising nonchalance. "He was poisoned in prison before he could tell us anything." She laid her hand on Thornstock's knee. "But that was after Thorn whisked me away to the country and bought me a whole new laboratory so I could do my experiments again."

Good Lord. Explosions and arsenic poisonings and experiments and manufactured "accidents." What else was this family dealing with? Sheridan's treatment of her seemed inconsequential by comparison.

She thrust out her chin. No, she would *not* let him get away with it so easily. *You lied to him about your feelings for Mr. Juncker. You wouldn't have ended up married to him if you'd told him the truth.*

Shoving that uneasy thought into a dark place in her

mind, she picked up the glass of brandy and took another warming sip.

"I know this is a great deal to take in all at once," the major said, having obviously noticed her brandy consumption. "But you can see why we've been trying to investigate it."

"On our own," Lady Gwyn said, "since none of us knows whom to trust outside the family."

"Although we've narrowed our suspects to three possible villains," Joshua said.

"You mean *villainesses,* don't you?" Sheridan's gaze fixed upon her now.

It took Vanessa a moment to comprehend why. Then she scowled at Sheridan. "You think *Mama* had something to do with this?"

"Grey certainly thought so." Sheridan dragged in a deep breath. "*He* was supposed to be the one to question your mother. But given your mother's dislike of him and with Beatrice so close to having her child delivered, he wanted to be with her, so—"

"He asked *you* to do it," Vanessa finished for him. Her heart sank. If Mama proved to be a murderer, how could she bear it? Granted, her mother wasn't the easiest person to live with, but Vanessa didn't want to see her jailed, or worse yet, hanged. She could see why Grey would think Mama capable of it, but he was wrong. He had to be wrong.

Something else occurred to her. If Grey hadn't asked Sheridan to do the questioning of her mother, Vanessa wouldn't be married to Sheridan at all. Although at the moment, she wasn't sure her cousin did her any favors. "Wait," she said as the word *villainesses* sank in, "you suspect *three* women?" Clinging to the possibility that it was one of the others, she met Joshua's gaze. "Mama and who else?"

Olivia said tartly, "My mother and Lady Hornsby."

Good Lord. All were respected women of rank. "I assume you don't suspect them of colluding with each other to do this."

"No, of course not," Joshua said. "Although they did have their coming outs together. Along with the dowager duchess." He paused. "And yes, we eliminated my mother-in-law first. For one murder she was in labor, and for Uncle Armie's she wasn't even in the country. Although we believe that the individual who committed the first two murders probably hired someone to commit the second two—perhaps Elias—we don't think anyone could have arranged that from afar. The dowager duchess's family was in Berlin at the time, at too great a distance to do so."

Vanessa tried to think through what he was saying, but she couldn't make sense of it. "Why on earth would this . . . 'villainess' wait decades to again murder someone—or have him murdered, for that matter?"

Joshua shrugged. "We think Uncle Armie was murdered to bring Sheridan's father and mother back to England so that Sheridan's father could be murdered."

That sort of made sense. Except for one thing. "Yes, but why *then?* There had to be a reason your uncle Armie wasn't murdered ten or twenty years ago instead of last year."

"Well," Joshua said, "his death wouldn't necessarily have brought Sheridan's father back unless Uncle Armie had already inherited the title. If Sheridan's grandfather had still been alive, it might not have made as much difference. And Uncle Armie's wife dying could also have set everything in motion, since there was always a chance she might bear *him* the heir."

"Yes, but that was ten years before Uncle Armie was murdered," Sheridan put in. "Admit it, Joshua, that's the one flaw in our tidy assumptions. Why did the killer wait so long? She had to have had a reason."

At the word *She,* Vanessa stared at Sheridan. "And I still don't see why you're suspecting women in the first place. I mean, wouldn't it make more sense to suspect men? Surely men commit more crimes than women."

Joshua nodded. "True. But whoever committed the first two murders had to have access to Grey's father and Thorn's father. There were house parties going on for both murders, and the only guests who were present for both were those three women."

Vanessa frowned. "I don't understand. Why do you assume the killer was a guest?"

"The servants were all attached to the houses where the parties were," Thorn said. "They wouldn't have been at both parties."

"Unless they were personal servants," Vanessa said. "I'm sure Lady Hornsby travels with a lady's maid and a couple of footmen, don't you think? I know Mama generally insists on having our family physician travel with us. She has all sorts of ailments, you know. The only reason she didn't bring him this time was he wasn't in town for her to ask him."

The dowager duchess leaned forward. "Lady Norley said she always brings her lady's maid as well. Did any of you consider the personal servants?"

The men looked at each other.

Vanessa shook her head. "You didn't, did you? Men. They never consider the domestic staff."

Joshua straightened, clearly annoyed at having this oversight shown to him. "You have a point. But we can't be sure those same servants were working for their employers during both parties. Besides, we have to rule each woman out before we can even look into their servants."

"True," Thorn said.

Joshua went on. "And perhaps now that Vanessa is caught up on everything, we can proceed to covering more recent events. Sheridan, did you learn anything from Lady Eustace?"

When he glanced at her warily, Vanessa merely tapped her fingers on one silk-clad knee and tried to ignore him. She did wish women had wrappers like these banyans. They were much less revealing. But she also wished this particular banyan didn't smell so temptingly of her husband's favorite spicy cologne. It reminded her of how tenderly he'd deflowered her.

Blasted man. Every time she wanted to stay angry at him, she remembered some . . . some nice thing he'd done. Perversely, that made her glare at him. "I suppose you got Mama to admit to murder while I wasn't around."

"Hardly," Sheridan grumbled. "I can't even get her to talk about those two house parties."

"That's because you're going about it all wrong," Vanessa said. "Mama only lapses into memory if the memory reflects particularly well on her. You need to appeal to Mama's belief that everything is about her. Better yet, you should let *me* question her."

Sheridan narrowed his gaze on her. "Not a chance. She's your mother. How could we trust you to be objective?"

She sniffed. "I can be plenty objective about Mama, which you would learn if you'd just let me wheedle the truth out of her."

Olivia straightened in her chair. "If Vanessa can question her mother, I don't see why I can't question mine."

Joshua cast her a stern look. "Does that mean Thorn hasn't questioned your mother yet?"

"Well, no." Olivia shot her husband an apologetic glance. "But he and I both will make sure to find out from her what we can. She's really quite reasonable once you get to know her."

"She is, actually," Thorn said. "Putting aside her attempt to blackmail me into marriage nine years ago, that is."

"Thorn!" Olivia protested.

"I deserved it, sweeting. It's fine."

"Hmph." Olivia turned to the group. "Grant you, Mama will do almost anything to protect her family, but I can't see her killing anyone with no purpose, and I wasn't even born when the first two murders happened, so she would have had no reason. Whereas Vanessa's mother . . ." She trailed off, as if realizing she was about to say something rather condescending. Vanessa didn't mind, having learned, in the short time she'd known Olivia, that the woman was generally blunt.

"Look," Vanessa said, sweeping her gaze about the room, "I know Mama can be difficult, even cruel. Certainly she was horrible to Grey. But to murder two people and arrange the murders of two more? The impracticality of it alone rules out Mama. Why, she couldn't even manage my debut ball by herself—she had to get Grey to help her. Trust me, my mother could never be a master criminal of the sort you're describing. That would require far too much effort."

The dowager duchess nodded. "That is more in line with the Cora *I* used to know. Her wickedness was always borne of weakness." She turned grim. "She preys on children who can't defend themselves and her own daughter who only wants her love. But murder three powerful dukes and a newly minted one? I'd be shocked to find out she would risk it. And for what? Why would she keep killing dukes, anyway?"

"Because she was hoping to have her husband inherit the dukedom?" Joshua said.

"That only works for the first murder." Sheridan frowned. "Although we honestly don't know if she poisoned baby Grey as well. He was sick at the same time as his father."

"But if Mama had given him arsenic," Vanessa pointed out, "wouldn't he have died? I can't imagine an infant surviving such a poisoning. Even if he had, even if Mama was responsible for the former Greycourt's death, what reason did she have for killing Thorn and Gwyn's father?"

"To be honest," Joshua said, "we're still a bit fuzzy on the motive or motives for the two earlier murders. The only thing we seem to agree on is that it involves the dowager duchess." Everyone looked at him in outrage. "Not as a suspect, mind you, but as a victim in some way."

"There's at least a motive for Lady Eustace to have murdered Grey's father," Olivia said. "But my mother has no motive for any of the murders. Access without a motive doesn't prove much unless you can put the arsenic in her hand."

The dowager duchess looked at Olivia. "And the second

murder—if it was one—was made to look like a carriage accident. I cannot see your mother sabotaging a carriage. Can you?"

"Of course not," Olivia said. "She wouldn't even know how."

"Are you saying the villainess must be Lady Hornsby?" Joshua glanced at Olivia. "Or one of the personal servants of the three women?"

"I wouldn't put it past Lady Hornsby," Gwyn grumbled. "She keeps avoiding me. It's almost as if she knows what I'm after."

"She did leave the wedding before I could even so much as speak with her," the dowager duchess said. "Although it's not unusual for her to leave events early. She has quite a busy social life."

After another quick sip of brandy, Vanessa jumped in again. "And what would be *her* motive?"

"She wanted my first husband," the dowager duchess said. "And our marriage thwarted her in that."

"She was also rumored to have been meeting our father behind your back," Thorn said quietly.

"I told you," the dowager duchess said, "that is ridiculous."

Vanessa took another, bigger sip of her brandy. Olivia was right. It was rather delicious when one sipped it.

"You also told us that Lady Hornsby's husband died of an ague," Olivia said. "Like your first husband? Is it possible she poisoned her own husband?"

"I suppose it's possible but it's highly unlikely," the dowager duchess said. "And if it were done so she could gain Thorn and Gwyn's father, then why not kill me instead? Why kill my second husband? It makes no sense."

"It really doesn't," Gwyn said. "She has no good motive. The only person she *might* have had a reason to kill was her late husband."

Sheridan nodded. "And he was old, so she could have just waited until he died."

"Or perhaps she has a maniacal dislike of men and merely sought to eliminate them for herself and her closest friend where possible," Thorn said.

Vanessa found Thorn's remark so ridiculous that she sipped more brandy. As she did, she noticed Sheridan wearing a skeptical expression. At least she wasn't the only one who thought Thorn's statement was absurd.

"Let's leave motive aside for the moment," Joshua said. "We simply don't know enough yet to determine what that might be. First we need to establish whether they had anything to do with the murders. We suspect that Sheridan's father was lured to the home my sister and I used to share so he could be pushed off that bridge, possibly by Elias. I showed a forgery expert both the note used to summon the duke and the letter Elias wrote to Lady Norley. The expert said they *might* have been written by the same person, but he couldn't swear by it."

"Speaking of Elias," Thornstock said, "do we have any idea who poisoned him in prison?"

"Unfortunately, no," Joshua said. "I questioned every guard and every individual who worked in the kitchen. Either they don't know or they're not saying. The prisons are notoriously corrupt, so those who work in them are more afraid of their superiors than of someone like me, who is merely with the marines and not an official employee of the courts. In time I could perhaps learn the answer—with more thorough research into each individual's connections—but at the moment that line of pursuit will have to be tabled. However . . ."

Joshua walked over to where a stack of papers sat atop a writing table. "I fortunately had the forethought to have a sketch made of Elias at the morgue. Gwyn drew up copies for all of us."

"They don't look like buildings, do they?" Thorn quipped. Apparently Gwyn had a love for anything involving architecture.

"Very amusing," Gwyn drawled. "You're merely jealous that I know how to sketch whereas your only talent is . . ." When Thorn stiffened, she paused. "Being insufferable."

Joshua rolled his eyes. "In any case, only Thorn, Olivia, Gwyn, and I have even seen the fellow, so one of you might recognize him from another context. I also figured that Sheridan could show them around in Sanforth to see if anyone recognized the lad. Because if Elias had been close by at all—"

"Then he might have been the one to kill both men," Heywood said.

"Exactly," Joshua said.

"I don't know," Thornstock put in. "Elias didn't strike me as the sort of fellow to commit murder at anyone's bidding. He was careful not to blow up the laboratory until he was certain Olivia wasn't in it."

"Ah, but she's a woman," Joshua pointed out. "He might have felt differently about killing two aging dukes. Especially if he was being paid well to do so."

"True," Sheridan said. "And I agree that the sketch should be shown around town. But I can't be the one to do it. Someone else will have to."

"Planning on an extended honeymoon, are you?" Thorn asked.

"Are you?" Vanessa repeated. She was finding this whole discussion fascinating. Or perhaps it was merely the brandy.

"Unfortunately, no." Sheridan was avoiding *her* gaze now. "I'm meeting with Bonham in London to discuss some questions I have concerning the books for the estate. I need to go over the accounts before my meeting, so Vanessa and I and her mother leave in the morning."

"We do?" Vanessa asked. No one had consulted *her* about the matter. That made her take yet another sip of the brandy. It truly *was* quite warming.

"Perfect!" Gwyn said. "You can question Lady Eustace on the way."

"I'll try," Sheridan said. "But she's not that forth-coming."

"That's true," Vanessa said. "Not at'all."

Joshua walked over to pour a glass of brandy himself.

"I thought you only drank rum," Thorn said.

"I prefer rum, but any port in a storm, as we seafaring fellows like to say." Joshua took a long swallow of the liquor.

"He should be careful," Vanessa whispered to the dowager duchess, but it came out rather loud. "It's best if you sip it."

Joshua chuckled, but Sheridan stalked over to pick up Vanessa's nearly empty glass. "How many 'sips' of this have you had?"

Vanessa tipped up her chin. "As many as I want, thank you very much."

"You see what you started?" Sheridan told his mother.

"What *I* started! You're the one who misled her about your intentions."

"Yes," Vanessa said, slurring the word a little. "Exactly. You misled her . . . me . . ." She waved her hand at his mother. "What she said."

"Shall I go on?" Joshua asked.

"Certainly," the dowager duchess said. "But I think I'll take Vanessa upstairs to bed. It's late, and I'm sure she's quite tired."

"Is that what we're calling it now?" Gwyn murmured to Thorn.

Sheridan glared at them both. When the dowager duchess helped Vanessa to a stand, he started to follow the two women. "I'll go with you."

"No, indeed," his mother said. "You need to be here for this discussion. I, on the other hand, do not. I'll just make sure Vanessa is settled into bed, and I'll return."

"All right," he said warily.

The last thing Vanessa saw before she was led away by the dowager duchess was Sheridan staring after her with concern on his face. It helped to assuage a tiny bit of her hurt feelings.

She and his mother, who kept her arm about Vanessa's waist, climbed the stairs in silence. As soon as they entered Vanessa's bedchamber, however, her mother-in-law released her to pull back the bed coverlet. Vanessa swayed a bit, but mostly she just wanted desperately to sleep.

The dowager duchess's sharp intake of breath as she stared down at the bed seemed to preclude that happening. "Oh, dear, I'll have to find your maid. Where is Bridget, my dear?"

"Upstairs, I think? I dismissed her for the evening."

Vanessa frowned. "Didn't expect my husband to have a family meeting on our wedding night."

Her mother-in-law smiled. "And we're all sorry about that. We didn't expect him to do so, either. But I gather he came down to get food and encountered Thorn. You know men and their appetites." She walked over to unknot the belt of Sheridan's banyan, which Vanessa still wore. "I'll have to call for your maid. There's blood on the sheet—I'm sure you don't want to sleep on that."

"Blood?" Vanessa closed her eyes. They were so heavy.

"Your virgin's blood, dear girl," her mother-in-law said as she came behind her to slip the banyan off her shoulders.

"Oh. Right. Bridget told me 'bout that." She'd also said if there wasn't any blood, there would be a Great To-do. "That's . . . good, right?"

"It's fine. But it means we do need these sheets changed. Wait here a moment. Don't move. I'll be right back." The dowager duchess left to go out into the hall.

Vanessa was so tired. And the bed was *right there*. Why couldn't she get into it again? Something about blood? P'raps she was confused. She honestly couldn't remember.

She just climbed into bed, put her head on the pillow, and promptly fell asleep.

Chapter Sixteen

As soon as Vanessa and Mother had gone, Joshua had suggested they might all want some refreshment. He'd called for a servant, who'd gone off to fetch tea, wine, and ale, along with some cut-up oranges and apples. Sheridan and the rest of the family had made small talk while that was set up.

But now that the servants had left, Joshua took one last gulp of brandy and set down his glass. "Where were we?"

Sheridan settled back in his chair, glass of wine in his hand. "You were giving us your report. And suggesting that I question the good citizens of Sanforth."

"If you'll be gone, I can do it," Heywood said.

"Will Cass be all right with that?" Joshua asked.

"Of course," Heywood said. "The only reason she's not here at present is . . . well, she sleeps a great deal."

"Of course she does," Joshua said. "She's due any day. Am I right?"

Heywood chuckled. "You are indeed."

It struck Sheridan that Vanessa might end up carrying *his* child soon. The thought of it gave him such pleasure he couldn't even concentrate on what the others were saying. Of course, if she was so furious over his subterfuge that she refused to let him bed her again . . .

No, that wouldn't happen. She had enjoyed their love-making. He was certain of it. She might be angry right now, but eventually she would see that what he'd done was for a good purpose.

Lying to her. Misleading her. She won't see it the way you do.

"Gwyn?" Joshua said. "Why don't you tell us what you've discovered about Lady Hornsby?"

Gwyn stirred more sugar into her tea. "I already told you."

"Yes, but why don't you tell the people in the room who are *not* married to you."

"Oh. Of course." She sighed. "I haven't learned much, I'm afraid. I couldn't get her alone, even at the wedding. She was decidedly uninterested in talking about anything but how perfect the ceremony was and how beautiful Vanessa looked."

"My wife did look beautiful," Sheridan said. "She always does." When the others laughed, he said, "Well, it's true."

"And you aren't smitten in the least," Thorn said dryly.

Sheridan wasn't smitten, damn it. He dared not be. That would be like laying his heart out on a table and waiting for life to slam it with a mallet.

Gwyn grinned. "*Anyway,* I plan to pay Lady Hornsby a call as soon as Joshua and I return to London, which won't be long after Sheridan. With any luck, the countess won't be gallivanting around the country somewhere. And you never know—she might have something to say about the other ladies that will prove useful."

"One can always hope." Joshua scanned the room.

"Anything else to add? Because I don't know about the rest of you, but I've covered everything I can think of."

"Excellent!" Thorn said. "There's still ham, bread, and cheese in the dining room. And tarts."

Olivia's eyes lit up. "Apple tarts?"

"What else?" Gwyn rose and waddled toward the door. "As long as there are also pickles, I am joining you."

Heywood shook his head. "Thank God Cass doesn't indulge in that grotesque combination or I would never make it through a meal."

"You get used to it," Joshua said.

When he started to follow his wife, cane in hand, Sheridan stopped him. "Could I speak to you alone a moment?"

"I'll be there shortly, dearling!" he called after Gwyn. Then he turned to Sheridan, all business now. "Is this about your new wife?"

"Actually, no. It's about William Bonham. I can't figure out if Mother invites him to things because he's courting her or she's just trying to be nice or what. But I would like you to investigate him."

Joshua blinked. "He's worked for your family for a good long while, from what I understand."

"Yes, ever since Uncle Armie first inherited fifteen years ago. Father didn't use him for too many matters—most of what he needed done had to be handled in Berlin, so I just want to be sure Bonham has no skeletons in his closet. Especially if he and Mother are involved with each other."

"I see what you mean. Although I might remind you that it's always hard to watch your mother being courted if you've only ever seen her with your father."

Joshua had a point. And except for Thorn, who thought

everyone was beneath their mother, the others didn't seem nearly as bothered as Sheridan by the . . . By the what? Friendship? Courtship? Sheridan didn't like not knowing what it was. "You're probably right. Mother does deserve a bit of happiness, too. I'm just not entirely certain she could find it with Bonham."

"Then do you also want me to look into Sir Noah?" Joshua asked. "He, too, seems to be showing an interest in her, judging from how he and Bonham took turns glaring at each other during the ceremony earlier."

"I noticed. And it probably wouldn't hurt to find out more about the man. You might want to ask Grey about him, too. I've never heard him so much as mention Sir Noah." Sheridan sighed. "We may have to do this sort of thing for a while. Mother seems to be attracting every widower around. I had no idea there were so many eligible widowed bachelors."

"As long as it's just the two," Joshua said with a laugh, "I can handle looking into their backgrounds. But try not to hunt up any more."

"Trust me, I didn't hunt up the two we have. Men are drawn to Mother like bears to honey. Always were, from what I understand."

"It's not surprising. Your mother is a kind soul. Men notice that above all things." Joshua got a fond look in his eyes. "I certainly noticed it in your sister."

"Gwyn? Kind?"

"You're her brother, and brothers don't always see their sisters in the same way as their sisters' husbands. Speaking of which, if we're done . . ."

Sheridan nodded, and they parted at the door, with Sheridan heading upstairs and Joshua going into the dining room. Sheridan's stomach rumbled, but he didn't care. He'd had enough of his siblings and their spouses for one night. He wanted his wife.

He thought about what Joshua had said. Vanessa *could* be kind sometimes. But she could also be fiery and engaging and full of surprises. Any one of those things might endear her to him, but all of them combined made her irresistible. That thought had him quickening his steps.

Besides, he wasn't sure he wanted to leave Vanessa alone with his mother for too long after what had happened. No telling what sort of secrets Mother might reveal. And he meant to tell his secrets to Vanessa himself.

When he reached the hall that led to the master bedchambers, he saw his mother slipping out of his wife's room. She came toward him as if to waylay him.

"You need to fetch Vanessa's maid." She paused. "Actually, any maid will do. The sheets on the bed should be changed."

"Why?"

"There's blood on them, of course."

"Of course? I assure you that I would never hurt . . ." He trailed off as he made the connection. "Oh. Right. I . . . er . . . guess I didn't notice the blood."

"Hardly surprising, given what the two of you were doing together."

He could feel heat rise in his face. "I promise I did nothing any other man wouldn't have done on his wedding night."

"I realize that. And if you'd actually hurt her during the act, I'm sure she wouldn't be smiling in her sleep the way she was when I left."

He lifted his eyes heavenward. "I can't believe we're actually talking about this."

"I'm merely trying to be helpful. Anyway, she's lying in her own blood right now and needs to be moved. So call a footman, too. Unfortunately, she was so tired that she crawled into bed before I could fetch anyone. You really need to increase your staff now that you're married."

Lifting an eyebrow, he muttered, "Tired? Or tipsy on the brandy you forced on her?"

"Tipsy? On one glass?" his mother said. "Don't be absurd. And I didn't force it on her, although I'll admit I probably shouldn't have given it to her when I knew she hadn't eaten much and was exhausted to boot. But she'll be fine in the morning. Before that, however, you should fetch a footman to move her."

"No footman is going to carry my wife anywhere," Sheridan snapped. "I'll do it myself. And while I do, you can fetch the maid."

"All right." She said it cheerily as if that was what she'd intended all along, and then hurried off toward the servants' stairs.

Good God, he wished now he hadn't sold the dowager house to Grey for a tidy sum—which had gone right back into keeping the estate afloat. Perhaps Grey would rent it to him for a song. Because having Mother underfoot, despite the massive size of the house, was going to be trying. Although he supposed it would be nice for Vanessa to have a female friend other than Bridget in the house. Vanessa and his mother did seem to like each other, after all.

That reminded him—he had to move Vanessa. He walked into his wife's bedchamber. Sure enough, Vanessa lay on the bed, his banyan now tossed unceremoniously over a chair. He almost hated to disturb her, but Mother was right; she'd be more comfortable in a clean bed.

His own.

A surge of possessiveness made him walk to her bed and pick her up as carefully as he could in an attempt not to wake her. Now that he had her in his arms, he could see the shadows under her eyes. She'd been running full tilt since they'd agreed to marry. That, coupled with their lovemaking and the emotions that hearing about the investigation had probably roused, must have exhausted her.

And callous husband that he was, having her in his arms was rousing his need again. Which was entirely unacceptable.

As he reached the adjoining door, he shifted her so he could turn the knob. She muttered something unintelligible and snuggled against his neck. That only aroused him more, damn it. Because she looked even more enchanting than before, if such a thing were even possible. With her hair tumbling over his arm, her long eyelashes looking like the black fringe on a lady's shawl, and her nipples forming points against her linen nightdress as he carried her into his colder room, he wanted nothing more than to bed her yet again.

He scowled at himself. With her breath warm against his skin, she was a hothouse rose, and he was behaving like the wicked seducer who wanted to pluck all her petals.

"Let me," his mother said from behind him and hurried over to pull down the covers for him.

After laying Vanessa on his bed, he turned to draw the covers up over her.

When he stood staring at her a moment longer, his

mother said, "She's sleeping now. You should leave her alone tonight."

"Thank you for the advice," he said tightly. "But she's my wife, and I can handle matters from here."

That didn't send his mother packing, however. "Have you told her anything about Helene?"

With a groan, he darted a look at Vanessa, but she seemed to be deeply asleep, curled up under the covers as if she hadn't a care in the world. Still, he wasn't taking any chances. He pulled his mother over near the open adjoining door. Inside the other bedchamber, a couple of maids were busily changing the sheets, flashing each other knowing looks over the bloodstain.

It was one of the things he hated most about being a duke. One's entire household gossiped about one and felt invested in one's success. He always felt that any failure dragged not just him but everyone else in his orbit down with him.

He pulled the door to for a moment. "Not that it's any of your business, Mother, but no, I haven't mentioned Helene yet. I will, however, when the time seems right."

"If I were you, I'd make it sooner rather than later. You don't want her hearing about Helene from one of your brothers—or, God forbid, Gwyn." She started to push open the door into the other room, then paused. "You should have told her what you were about with her mother, you know, if not while you were doing it, then in the past week, after you became betrothed."

He ran a hand through his hair before lowering his voice, so as not to wake Vanessa. "I didn't tell her the truth because I didn't want to risk having her alert her mother if Lady Eustace happened to be guilty."

His mother snorted. "You didn't tell her the truth because you were afraid she wouldn't marry you if you did." Mother then walked into the other room and closed the door behind her.

He wanted to call her back, to deny her words, to insist that he and Vanessa had been forced into marrying because of his reckless physical attraction to her. But he couldn't. Because his mother was right. Somewhere in the depths of his soul he'd had a longing for Vanessa that had been damned near impossible to ignore.

If he didn't watch himself, he would end up just as captivated by her as he'd been by Helene. And *that* way lay pain and ruin.

Chapter Seventeen

The sound of curtains being opened and the sunlight streaming through the large, many-paned window to hit Vanessa's closed eyes woke her in a hurry. Where was she? Her bedchamber in their town house had no window as large as that.

Wait, this wasn't her bedchamber.

Bridget hurried over to the side table nearest her mistress and placed on it a tray containing toast and tea and everything that came with those. "Forgive me for waking you, miss—I-I mean, Your Grace—but His Grace said he means to leave for London in an hour, so I thought you might need the time to get ready."

That sent Vanessa bolting up straight in bed. "You needn't get all formal with me, Bridget. I may be a duchess by marriage, but I'm still the same mistress you have come to know and fear."

Just as Vanessa knew it would, that elicited a laugh from Bridget. "All the same, mistress, I think I'd best use your proper title when we're around others."

"Probably. Especially Mother. Sadly, she is going to

have a fine time lording it over everyone. And bemoaning how I had to marry a poor duke."

"That's more than likely."

"Where's my husband, anyway? Isn't this *his* bed-chamber?"

Vanessa had seen it earlier in the week when they'd given her a tour of Armitage Hall, and it was every bit as nicely appointed as the rest of the house. It was just a pity that the curtains needed mending and the bed drapings replaced and sundry other items taken care of.

"His Grace dressed while you were sleeping. You didn't even move!" Bridget poured Vanessa her tea and doctored it with plenty of cream and a tiny bit of sugar. "You must have been exhausted. And his valet is very quiet."

Vanessa took a big swallow of tea. "Is everyone waiting on me to be ready?"

"Not quite. The trunks are already loaded onto the servants' carriage, but your carriage is being searched rather thoroughly by two or three burly footmen. Perhaps His Grace's carriage is prone to breaking down?"

More likely, His Grace's carriage was prone to being damaged in an attempt to kill him . . . and her and Mama, since they would be with him in his carriage. That sobered her at once. Whatever was happening to the dowager duchess's family was liable to affect her, too, by association. She hadn't thought of that last night when they'd been relating the story of all the mishaps and murders.

Bridget examined the pocket watch Vanessa had bought her one year. "Now you have fifty minutes to get ready, mistress. Give or take a few."

"Oh, all right." Grabbing a slice of buttered toast, she

munched it as she went into her bedchamber and Bridget came behind her with the tray.

Unsurprisingly, her clothes were already laid out on the bed. She'd never had to complain about Bridget. Her lady's maid was always prepared for any contingency.

With ten minutes to spare, she marched down the stairs, tugging on her gloves of Princess Elizabeth blue and tying her bonnet of the same blue, trimmed with scarlet. This was her favorite ensemble of the trousseau Grey had insisted on buying her as a wedding present: a simple Princess Elizabeth blue carriage dress, a pelisse of scarlet wool lined with white fur, a white fur muff, and the bonnet and gloves that went with it.

As she walked out the door, Sheridan looked up from speaking with one of the footmen, and the admiration in his eyes was unmistakable. It warmed her far more than her fur-lined wool pelisse. Especially when he helped her into the carriage, refusing to release her hand until he had a chance to kiss it.

She swallowed hard. She hoped his behavior was an indication that not all was amiss between them. But she wasn't ready to forgive him quite yet. Before that happened, she needed him to answer some questions.

Before she could broach even one, her new husband shifted his stance so he could gaze up the steps and said, "Your mother is late."

Vanessa nodded. "That's typical of her, I'm afraid. We shall simply have to hope there won't be too many times we have to travel with her."

He consulted his watch with a frown. "I trust you slept

well?" he said, then turned his gaze to her and banished his frown. "You certainly look well this morning."

"Why, thank you. I did indeed sleep well." She straightened her pelisse. "Your bed is very comfortable."

He leaned in the open carriage door. "And seeing you in it made me very happy," he said in a low rumble that had her squirming on the seat, remembering their lovely romp in *her* bed earlier last night. Though she did wonder why he hadn't made any advances while she was in his.

"Thank you for putting me to bed," she told him.

"You have my mother to thank for that more than me. I hadn't even noticed that you'd been lying in your own blood."

"To be honest, neither had I. Still, I vaguely remember you moving me to *your* bed."

He eyed her closely. "I thought you weren't awake."

"I wasn't, really. I just roused enough to realize someone was carrying me who smelled like you." She cast him a rueful look. "You wear a very distinctive scent."

"Ah."

"And I'm sorry I got foxed. I don't usually drink spirits at all."

He chuckled. "I could tell."

"I was just upset that—"

"I know. You had a right to be. And I'm sure you have more questions. But we must discuss those in private tonight at the inn where we're staying in Cambridge." He nodded to where her mother was descending the steps, scolding some poor servant as she came.

Vanessa sighed, wishing she had more time. But she did want to know one thing before they set off, something she thought—or rather hoped—she might have dreamed. "Who is Helene?"

The stricken look on his face told her she hadn't dreamed it. "We'll . . . discuss her tonight as well."

"She's not your mistress, is she?"

"God, no." He lowered his voice. "I told you. I've never had one."

"One what?" Mama asked as she reached him.

When Sheridan stiffened, Vanessa said, "A pet. I was telling him we should get a poodle."

He lifted an eyebrow at her as he helped her mother into the carriage. "And I told your daughter that if we do get a dog—which I'm not averse to—it won't be a poodle."

Her mother settled into the seat beside Vanessa, facing forward as was proper for women traveling with men in a carriage. "I can't imagine why you'd want one of those filthy creatures in your house, Duke. I never allowed one in mine."

Sheridan exchanged a sympathetic glance with Vanessa as he took the seat directly opposite her. "A dog, Lady Eustace? Or a poodle?"

"Both." Mama shook her head. "If you acquire any dog, you will soon find them too troublesome to endure."

Vanessa ignored her mother. "What breed would you prefer, Sheridan?"

"A setter. I like setters. Growing up, we had two as pets."

"Oh, I forgot about that." Vanessa ventured a smile. "Grey told me he had to leave his setters behind. It follows that the rest of you inherited them."

Sheridan nodded. "They died five or so years after he left. But they were my constant companions until then."

"Did you ever get another?"

"No. My mother mostly agreed with yours on the subject of dogs being filthy creatures. Which is why she had a cat. They clean themselves."

"Oh, I *love* cats!" Vanessa had always wanted one of those, too. But Mama had forbidden even that. No pets for her.

Now that she was married, however, she could acquire whichever pets she wanted. That hadn't occurred to her until just now. Then again, she would have to consult with Sheridan first, which was only slightly better than having to pass every decision through her father, her mother, or a trustee. Truly, even when women got what they wanted, they didn't get everything they wanted.

The conversation lapsed at that moment. With Sheridan watching them both as if trying to figure out how to begin his interrogation of Mama, Vanessa turned to looking out of the carriage window at the lovely scenery. She knew they were supposed to get her mother to tell them where she was during the house parties, but Vanessa's heart wasn't in it.

Last night, she should have asked her questions. Perhaps when she'd felt his eyes on her, as if he was wondering if he should wake her. But she hadn't been in the mood. She'd been tired, not to mention weary of discussing what he'd kept from her. Between the possibility that Mama had been a murderer and that Sheridan might have to be the one to trap her into confessing, Vanessa had needed time just to think of what to say to him about the enormous secret he'd been hiding from her. And to ask what else he might be keeping from her.

Eventually, she would have to ask her questions, if only

to put her fears to rest. But with Mama in the carriage now, she would be forced to delay her questioning. Her mother had a way of turning every conversation around to herself, anyway.

"I don't understand why we had to leave the country in such a hurry," Mama said in her most peevish voice. "Armitage Hall was a very striking residence. I'm sure it will be even more appealing once improvements are made to it."

"The only improvements I'll be making at present will be to my tenant cottages," Sheridan said curtly. "My tenants . . . *our* tenants have waited a long while for their landlord to do much-needed repairs."

"I suppose you will use my daughter's dowry for that." Mama sniffed. "Although one would think you would first wish to improve your own house rather than wasting money on—"

"I agree with my husband," Vanessa cut in. "Tenants are the backbone of an estate, and thus they deserve our care." Realizing she sounded curt, Vanessa added, "Besides, Mama, you wouldn't enjoy having only a village as small as Sanforth to provide amusements for you. Sadly, St. Brice's Day is past, so you can't even see the running of the bull."

Sheridan smiled warmly at Vanessa. "*I* haven't yet seen the running of the bull, and I live there. Then again, last year I was in mourning and couldn't really attend such things, and this year I was in London."

Vanessa ventured a smile of her own before turning to deal with her mother. "Which is where you generally prefer to be, Mama. I can't imagine why you would want to stay in the boring old country."

Sheridan obviously caught the sarcasm in her words, for he tightened his lips as if trying not to laugh. The only reason Mama had been whisked away from Armitage Hall was to prevent her from renewing her fight with the dowager duchess.

Fortunately, her mother hadn't figured that out. "You do have a point, my dear. Although it will be hard to be in town without you." Mama drew out her handkerchief to dab at her perfectly dry eyes. "I shall miss you so. While London does, of necessity, have more choices for entertainment, what good is it if I must attend them alone? Now that you are married, the three of us should go to some of them."

Lord help her. The last thing she wanted was her mother treating Vanessa's marriage as a club she could join.

Just as Vanessa was frantically hunting for something to discourage Mama, Sheridan winked at her. "Unfortunately, Vanessa and I can't stay long in town. A few days at most."

How clever of him to have stepped in so readily. He was proving to be a good husband in some things, and apparently more than capable of handling her mother. Which was an art in itself.

"After I've met with Bonham," Sheridan went on, "we'll be returning to Armitage Hall to begin on those improvements I mentioned. I'm afraid you will have to rely on some of your friends to accompany you to places. Or your brother."

"Noah? I suppose he might be willing. He said he means to stay with your family at the estate until they depart for town tomorrow. And speaking of your estate,

I trust you mean to improve your stables, too. Why, there weren't even enough good saddle horses for riding." She shot Sheridan a coy look. "You shall have to remedy that at once, Duke."

The pained expression that crossed his face was hard to miss, though he masked it quickly. "I hope I can manage that soon." He eyed Mama with interest now. "Do you ride, Lady Eustace?"

Her mother gave a girlish laugh. "Well, of course. In my youth, I was quite a good rider."

He nodded. "I thought my mother had mentioned that. She spoke of how fine your seat was when you were at the house party at Carymont for Grey's christening, all those years ago."

"Did she? That was kind of her." Mama's use of the word *kind* dripped with disdain. "But she must have forgotten she only saw me ride the first day, when we all went out for a tour of the estate. A hare darted out and spooked my horse, which threw me."

Her mother used her hands to describe the event, her handkerchief fluttering with every movement. "My leg hit a rock and was in such a state I couldn't even move it for the rest of the visit! I spent all of my remaining time near the fire with my leg propped on a cushion. Well, all my time until the tragedy, that is."

Sheridan's gaze shot to Vanessa, and an unspoken message passed between them. Her mother couldn't have been the one to poison Grey's father. Granted, they would have to confirm her mother's story with servants at Carymont and perhaps with the dowager duchess, who ought to have remembered that. But Mama seemed blissfully unaware that she had just removed herself from the list of people who'd possibly killed Grey's father.

Relief swamped Vanessa. Oh, thank heaven it wasn't Mama! Her mother might exasperate her, but Vanessa didn't want to lose her. Besides, if Mama had proved to be a murderer, Vanessa would never have been able to look Grey in the face again.

On the other hand, Mama being exonerated meant that she and Sheridan had married for naught. What if he resented that? What if he regretted taking up with her at all? If he hadn't accepted Grey's request to question Mama, Sheridan wouldn't have been in a position to flirt with her or kiss her or . . .

"My wife . . . my duchess . . . my goddess . . ."

Surely those words hadn't been a complete lie, had they? He must have felt some small affection for her in order to have initiated her into marital relations with such loving care.

How she wished she'd already asked him the question she needed an answer to. Because now she had a whole day ahead of her to dwell on it before she could actually ask him. And with Mama around, it would be a long enough day as it was.

By the time they reached Cambridge, Sheridan was growing restless. Just to be sure Lady Eustace hadn't been involved in the murders, he'd asked her what the second house party had been like. She'd described an exciting round of amateur theatricals, held to amuse her friend Lydia during her confinement. When asked about servants, she'd scoffed at him. Who cared what servants were there?

He and his family cared. But that was a question he'd have to leave to Vanessa to pose. He didn't want to show his hand, and his wife could question her mother more naturally.

Still, he was fairly certain Lady Eustace hadn't committed any of the murders. Vanessa was right—her mother might be cruel, but she didn't have the ambition for such an elaborate scheme of villainy. And she really didn't have a motive for it, either.

Once at the inn, Lady Eustace was more than ready to retire, after asking that a tray be brought to her room, courtesy of His Grace, of course.

Sheridan would have paid for fifty trays if it meant he didn't have to spend one more minute in the woman's presence. Of course, now he had to face his new wife and explain why he'd deceived her . . . if he could even do so to her satisfaction. He wasn't sure he could.

But he had to try. Just watching her remove her red pelisse to expose a gown of diaphanous muslin thin enough to glide over the curves of her body made him want to tear it off of her so he could feast on all her silky places. He meant to have her again tonight, assuming she wanted the same thing. Somehow he had to convince her they could make a very good pair, despite their rocky beginnings.

Fortunately, his credit was still good at this inn in Cambridge—their lodgings were well-appointed, with fireplaces in both rooms of the suite for him and Vanessa. One was a bedchamber with a large tester bed and plenty of space for the two small trunks they'd brought containing the items they'd need for traveling. The other was a sort of sitting room, which not only had a settee with a side table but also contained a dining table with four sturdy, old-fashioned chairs.

Shortly after their arrival, their dinner was brought up—a hearty ragout of mutton, mushrooms, potatoes, and carrots paired with a bottle of Madeira. But once they sat down to eat, he noticed that Vanessa only picked at the food and didn't drink the wine at all.

"Aren't you hungry?" he asked. "You hardly ate anything at lunch."

"I need to ask you something." She lifted her gaze to his. "And I want you to tell me the truth no matter how much you think it might pain me."

Damn. That did not sound good. "All right."

"If not for needing to question Mama for your family's investigation, would you ever have offered to make Mr. Juncker jealous by courting me?"

Leave it to Vanessa to go right to the heart of their situation.

Despite what she'd said, he debated lying. But it was time to stop avoiding the truth with her. "No, I wouldn't have."

Her expression was hard to read. Was she hurt? Upset? Relieved? He couldn't tell. Then he noticed how she was rubbing the handle of her fork, back and forth, over and over, as if she were trying to keep from showing him how she felt.

That did something to his insides. "But that doesn't mean I'm unhappy at how things turned out, at having you become my bride. I'm not unhappy in the least. And surely you can tell I'm attracted to you."

She looked right through him. "Just not enough that you would have courted me on your own."

He stiffened. "Probably not."

"You could have gone another way entirely with your plan, you know, and revealed to me what you were after from Mama. I would have helped you get the truth out of her, and the whole courtship thing would have been something we did for the sake of keeping Mama's suspicions at bay."

He scoffed at that. "You're saying you would have helped me determine whether your mother was guilty of murder?"

"I swear I would have done whatever you needed, if only to prove that Mama wasn't capable of it."

"And how could I have been sure you wouldn't tell her our suspicions?"

Vanessa winced. "I suppose you couldn't have. But I daresay Grey should have known. Grey should have asked for my help directly. I would have helped him if *he'd* asked for sure." Now Sheridan could hear the hint of betrayal in her voice. That seemed to be at the root of her distress. "But no one asked me. Instead—"

"I know. Grey just handed the whole thing over to me." Grey, her big brother. The one she loved dearly. No wonder she felt betrayed. "And I stepped in and took care of it myself."

"While letting me think you wanted to protect me from Mr. Juncker."

That roused his temper. "I *did* want to protect you from Juncker. It was clear you were besotted, and he was only interested in dallying with you."

"It was clear, was it?" she said coldly.

He chose to ignore that odd reaction. "I realize I let the subterfuge go on far too long. My mother says I should have told you in the week before we married, that I should have given you a chance . . ."

"To refuse to marry you?" She took a small sip of her wine. "Perhaps I would have taken that chance, but mostly because I would never wish to wed any man who felt forced into it, either for the money or any other reason."

He wasn't sure why, but that angered him. "Let's get one thing straight. I didn't marry you for the money. I married you because I had . . . acted on my physical urges and thus put you in a difficult position." He rose to pace the room. "I know what a gentleman should do when he destroys a woman's reputation, however unintentionally, and I am a gentleman at heart." He paused to stare down at her. "Perhaps I should amend that. I'm a gentleman except when I'm around you. Then I lose all reason."

God, he shouldn't have admitted that, especially to her. Already her expression had softened. Why, he didn't know. She was in love with Juncker, wasn't she?

He was about to ask her when she said, "You don't need my dowry?"

Vanessa was blunt—he'd give her that. "I didn't say that. It will help matters, to be sure. Unfortunately, I need a great deal more money than most women's dowries could probably offer."

"And certainly not mine."

"Vanessa, I wasn't—"

"It's all right. I understand."

"It's not what you think."

"What isn't? That you were forced to marry me? That in time you will come to resent that?"

"Absolutely not," Sheridan said firmly. "My attraction to you is enough for me."

"Right now." She sighed. "But who knows if it will be enough for you later? Eventually my looks will fade."

"You don't understand. I wasn't lying when I said I would choose not to marry if I could."

She took a couple of deep breaths. "Because of Helene?"

He debated whether to admit that. But he'd promised her the truth. And she deserved to hear it. "Yes," he said softly. "Because of Helene."

Chapter Eighteen

Vanessa wasn't sure she should have started this, since every word was a dagger through her heart. But they were married now. They should have no secrets between them. She refused to have a marriage like Mama's, where Papa did as he pleased while Mama grew increasingly unhappy and bitter. She wasn't certain which had come first—Mama's unhappiness, which drove Papa to have mistresses. Or Papa having mistresses, which drove Mama to become unhappy.

It didn't really matter, since the end result had been the same—her parents were miserable and had been since before she was born. She didn't want that for herself. Even if she could only have a marriage between friends, it was better than what her parents' marriage had become—a marriage between enemies.

"Tell me about Helene," she said, forcing herself not to show her pain. Until yesterday, she had never guessed he might have had another woman in his life. If she'd known that, she might not have tried so hard to gain him as her husband. "Did she end up married to someone else? Or did you have to leave her behind in Prussia?"

He gave a harsh laugh. "You could say that. I left her behind in a Berlin grave."

Now *that* she wasn't expecting. "Oh! Oh, Sheridan, I'm so sorry. Was she . . . Were you . . . *married* to her?"

"No. Merely engaged." He walked back to his chair and sat down to pour himself a glass of Madeira. "We met during her debut."

When he fell silent, she said once more, "Tell me about her."

He sipped some Madeira. "She was very pretty."

"You don't need to fudge the details on my account." Even if it killed her to hear them.

"All right. Beautiful, then, but in a different way from you. She was tall and thin and had translucent skin. Little did I know that her thinness and skin were because she was in the early stages of consumption."

"Good Lord." Vanessa's heart went out to him. "That must have been awful, I know. Consumption is an ugly, horrible way to die. Anyone who loves a consumptive has to watch as their beloved wastes away before their very eyes."

He shot her a questioning look. "You sound as if you're familiar with it."

"Uncle Noah's wife died of consumption," she explained. "I think that's one reason he's finally ready to marry again. Being married to a consumptive means losing them bit by bit, until by the end you hardly see the person you knew."

"That's an accurate assessment." He traced the rim of his glass. "Of course, I didn't realize Helene was ill when I was courting her. I don't think even her parents knew at that point. She'd always been thin, and she'd grown tall long before I met her."

"You were in love with her," she said, tamping down her pain at the thought. She mustn't let it show. She was *not* going to be one of those women who pined for a man who didn't love her, could *never* love her.

"I was as in love as a man of twenty-three can be." He cast her a rueful smile. "I didn't know what love is, to be honest. She was attractive and elegant, the sort of woman who would have been perfect as a diplomat's wife."

"Or a duke's," she put in.

"I don't know about that. She wouldn't have wanted to move here, I imagine, even if she hadn't become ill. When Uncle Armie died, Father was determined that I return with the family so he could prepare me for inheriting the title and estate from him. If I'd had Helene as my wife, if she'd lived, I might have fought harder against coming here. But without her, there was honestly no point to staying in Prussia."

And if he'd succeeded in staying there, Vanessa would never have known him. It was horrible and selfish of her, but she couldn't regret that Helene had died. She only wished the woman hadn't apparently taken Sheridan's heart into the grave with her.

Sheridan sighed. "But, as they say, 'If wishes were horses, then beggars would ride,' and all that. She didn't become my wife and she didn't come here with me or live there with me, and that was that." He met Vanessa's gaze. "It's all in the past now."

"Hardly. I can tell from the way you're clutching that wineglass that it's not 'all in the past.'"

"I suppose you want the details of my ill-fated romance with Helene." He stared down at the glass in his hand. "You insist on dragging the whole of it out of me."

She reached over to clasp his free hand. "I insist on knowing why it has kept you from marrying. Why you would not have married *me* if it hadn't been for our being caught together in the garden."

"You do deserve to know that." He sipped some wine, then set the glass down and gently withdrew his other hand from hers.

Swallowing hard, she put her hands in her lap and tried not to show how his withdrawal bothered her. But she needed to know the rest, to know what—or who—she was up against.

"I courted Helene for the whole Berlin season," he said in a measured voice, as if he were controlling his emotions. "She and I had little in common. But we both loved music, especially Mozart, whom I had seen play when I was nine."

"Mozart wrote wonderful music for dancing."

"He did indeed. Of course, by the time Helene had heard of him, he'd already been dead for ten years or more."

Vanessa didn't think it wise to point out that Helene might have only "loved" Mozart's music because Sheridan did. She didn't want Sheridan thinking she was being petty. But she did know plenty of young ladies who routinely changed their likes and dislikes to suit a man they wanted.

He set his wineglass on the table between them. "In any case, we discovered we were well-suited temperamentally, both being of a rather taciturn nature." A muscle worked in his jaw. "I offered for her, and she accepted. But her family wanted a long engagement, so we agreed to wait a year to marry."

"A *year!*" she exclaimed. "That is long indeed."

One corner of his lips quirked up. "Considerably longer than a week, to be sure."

"True. Though, to be fair, you and I have known each other for a year and a half. We just weren't betrothed but a week."

He gazed at her with an odd expression, then abruptly rose to go stoke the fire. "Anyway, I think Helene's parents were concerned that as a diplomat, I might take her away from Prussia for my postings. And perhaps they would have been right."

Returning to the table, he took another sip of his wine. "Neither of us was pleased about waiting so long, as you might imagine, especially Helene, who wanted us to elope. I refused, thinking of the damage it would do to my diplomatic career. I came to regret that decision, because by the time the year was up she was dead."

"That must have been awful for you," Vanessa said. "And her family, of course."

He nodded, as if to acknowledge the veracity of her statement. "As she grew more ill, she told me I should end our betrothal. But that felt . . . wrong somehow. Eventually, Mother prevailed upon me not to visit her, for fear that I might catch the disease myself."

"But you went anyway."

He started. "I did indeed. How did you know?"

"Because you're a good man, a responsible man. And that's what such a man does." She smoothed her skirts. "Especially a man in love, who has already committed himself to a woman."

"Yet I wasn't there at the end," he said in a hard voice. "She died alone in her bed at night. And I—"

"Felt guilty." She reached across to cover his hand with hers again. "But you shouldn't. Many people die alone simply because none of us know when the moment of death will be." She caught her breath. "Papa died alone. And despite all the awful things he'd done, I still wished I could have been there to say good-bye."

He gripped her hand. "Now you understand why my family and I feel compelled to solve our fathers' murders. Especially *my* father's, since he was essentially father to us all. He died alone, too, with only his murderer as companion."

A lump stuck in her throat. That explained so much about his and his siblings' obsession. She remembered Sheridan's father, a nice man, if a tad reserved. Much like his son, actually.

Sheridan stared down at her hand in his. "I'm telling you all this now by way of warning you that I've lost much because of the deaths of those I love. You asked me why I would have chosen to remain a bachelor if I could have. The truth is . . . I just can't go through that pain again."

"You're expecting me to die soon, too, are you?" she quipped.

His gaze shot to hers. "Don't even joke about that." He reached up with his other hand to stroke her cheek. "Losing Helene and then Father hurt so very much that I have no desire to repeat the experience. I would rather have the sort of marriage my parents had than suffer through such agony again."

"In other words, you don't intend to let yourself love me or let me see the real you."

He tensed, then nodded.

"What if our marriage becomes something more like

what Grey's parents had, or, worse yet, the sort of marriage *my* parents had? Not allowing yourself to love doesn't guarantee a life free of pain."

Releasing her hand, he sat back in the chair. "But it eliminates a primary source of pain, doesn't it?"

"You'll deprive yourself of one of life's greatest joys out of a determination not to experience the pain love can also bring? That's like refusing to ride because you fear falling off."

He cast her a stony stare. "You can't understand. You've never lost someone who was the center of your world."

She couldn't argue with that. It was true. She took another tack. "And when we have children? Or are we having children?"

"I would like to, yes," he said warily.

She leaned forward to fix him with an earnest look. "Will you try not to love your children, too, so you don't suffer pain if one of them dies? Parents do outlive their children sometimes, you know."

He rose from the table, his lips set in a thin line. "Of course I will love our children."

"Just not their mother."

He whirled on her, his eyes blazing. "And what of you and how you feel about me? You're in love with Juncker. That probably precludes your ever being in love with *me,* doesn't it?"

Oh, but he knew how to turn the knife, didn't he? She stood to face him. "I never said I was in love with Mr. Juncker."

"You didn't have to. It was painfully obvious when I caught him kissing you and you not stopping it."

She should tell him that she didn't give a fig for Mr.

Juncker. That she never had. But then Sheridan might figure out that the only object of her affections had always been *him*. And not only would he be convinced she'd somehow manipulated the situation so he would have to marry her, but she would look like a pathetic fool for wanting a man who could never love her. She had too much pride for that.

"To use your own words," Sheridan said in a hollow voice, "'Tell me the truth no matter how much you think it might pain me.' *Are* you in love with Juncker?"

He would find any answer she gave to that unsatisfying. It was time she turn their discussion to something both of them would find more satisfying.

She walked up to clasp his head and kiss him soundly on the mouth. When she drew back, she said in a low voice, "I don't want to talk about Mr. Juncker or Helene or even the murders." She untied his cravat and tossed it aside. "I don't want to talk at all." She tugged on his coat, and he obligingly shucked it off. "This might be the closest thing we'll have to a honeymoon, and we're alone." She began to unbutton his waistcoat. "I'd much rather do something more . . . enjoyable."

Seizing his hand, she placed it on her breast. He just stared at her, as if he couldn't believe she was being so brazen. She couldn't believe it herself. But how else was she to take his mind off of Mr. Juncker except by seducing him? She wasn't quite sure how to go about it, but she would work it out as she went along.

She kissed him again, this time lingering over his mouth. And he stayed frozen for about half a second. Then he shrugged off his waistcoat and slung his arm about her waist to pull her hard against him for a kiss as darkly needy as it was delicious.

"Damn it, Vanessa," he whispered against her lips. "You are . . . making this bloody hard."

She certainly hoped so. Because she had no intention of being wed to the saint everyone took him for. What she wanted was the sinner, the part he only showed her. Sinful Sheridan was at least capable of love. "I think"—she whispered back—"*you* are the one making *this* hard." And she put her hand on his trousers, right where a bulge was forming most pleasingly.

With a groan, he grabbed her hand and held it more firmly against that evidence of his arousal. Then as he moved it up and down, he turned to kissing his way down her neck to the low scoop of her bodice. "Turn around, my temptress," he said in a rough voice that sent shivers along her senses.

She did as he bade, her pulse quickening in anticipation.

Swiftly, he undid the fastenings of her gown, then untied her corset and shoved it all off, leaving her in her shift and stockings. As he circled back around in front of her, she untied her shift. Before she could remove it, he pulled the opening apart and loosened the tie so he could bring the front down far enough to bare her breasts. "I never tire of these," he growled.

Taking her by surprise, he lifted her onto the table, then pulled his chair around so he could sit down and feast upon her breasts. There was something so . . . carnal about having him sucking and licking and teasing her nipples while sitting casually at the table. "I like having you . . .

feed on me," she said with a little laugh as she buried her fingers in his silky curls.

"I like having you for dinner," he murmured against one breast. "You smell good. You taste good. You make me so . . . very . . . hungry. . . ."

The husky way he said it shot a thrill through her. "You are . . . a flatterer."

Perhaps the way to a man's heart truly *was* through his stomach. The thought made her giggle, and he paused to stare up at her with a raised eyebrow. Not wanting to explain, she said, "When will you take these off?" and tugged at his trousers' waistband.

At once he sat back and pulled off his boots. "Touch yourself," he said.

"Wh-What? Where?"

"Your breasts. Touch them. Don't you ever touch yourself?"

"Only to bathe. Why?"

He groaned as he stood to unfasten his trousers. "Pretend you're bathing. Better yet, pretend I'm bathing you."

"Ohhh." Why did the very idea make her all trembly?

Feeling a bit self-conscious, she began to rub her breasts. It felt so-o-o *naughty*, especially since he still wore half his clothes.

But not for long. As she fondled her bosom shamelessly through the opening of her shift, he continued undressing, his gaze eating her up. "You're a feast for a man's eyes, my wanton wife."

She surveyed his now-bared chest with its impressive muscles, then his undertrousers, or whatever they were called, which were bulging impressively. "As are you, my wanton husband."

Only when he was completely naked did he resume his seat in front of her. Spreading her legs, he said in a harsh rasp, "And I do believe I'm ready for dessert." He pulled her shift up just enough so he could thrust his head beneath it.

Then he kissed her right on her privates, a spot she'd never imagined anyone wanting to kiss. As she caught his head to her, he began to stroke her down there with his tongue. At first it tickled, but the more he used his tongue in long, hot caresses, the more it stirred her already heightened senses. And it was . . . *marvelous*. He made her quiver on the inside, he made her quiver on the outside, he made her quiver everywhere a woman could.

Oh. *Heavens*. How amazing! The man was clearly a master of the bedchamber.

As she squirmed beneath the rasps of his tongue, his thumbs stroked small circles on the inside of her upper thighs, which had suddenly become quite sensitive.

"This . . . seems very . . . wicked," she choked out.

He paused long enough to ask, with a ghost of a smile, "Do you mind being wicked?"

"With you? No."

"Good," he ground out, then returned to teasing her down there with his lips and tongue and teeth until she thought she might explode out of her skin.

"Sheridan . . . I want . . . I want . . ."

"What do you want, my wicked wife?"

"You . . . inside me. . . ."

He tormented her a bit more with his clever tongue, then asked, "Are you *sure* that's what you want?"

"Oh, yes . . . *please* . . ."

"Very well," he said, and wiped his mouth on her shift.

Then he pulled her off the table and onto him, so she was straddling his thighs, with her knees resting on either side of his narrow hips on the seat of the wide chair.

"What are you doing?" she asked.

"If you want me inside you, then mount me."

She blinked, at first not understanding. Then it dawned on her. He wanted to do what they'd done last night, only in reverse. How very . . . intriguing.

And this way, she would have all that male glory in front of her while she "mounted" him.

"Well?" he asked, with one eyebrow quirked up and his lips smirking.

"That sounds like something I might enjoy."

"Might? I will make sure you do." He grabbed the hem of her shift, which was already bunched about her hips. "But first, let's get rid of this." And with a quick motion of his hands, he dispensed with her shift. "That's better," he said, his eyes gleaming.

"You like seeing me naked, don't you?" she said, preening a bit.

"You're still wearing stockings."

"Shall I take those off, too?"

"God, no." He smoothed his hands up her thighs to her garters. "I like you in stockings."

"You like seeing me *almost* naked," she teased. "In pearls. Or stockings."

"Oh, yes." He gazed at her breasts. "I certainly do."

"And I like seeing you . . . beneath me."

"Witch," he said, and smiled. "Now it's time you see me, feel me . . . inside of you."

Sheridan had never imagined a picture as erotic as Vanessa perched naked atop him in stockings, which somehow made the image even more erotic. His duchess proved a quick study, too. All he had to do was give her a few instructions and guide her down his rigid cock to have her encasing it in pure, delectable heat.

God save him, he could die happy with her like this, on top of him, around him. Filling his senses with her delicious taste, musky scent, and her sweet, sweet doe-eyed wonder at having learned something new about bedsport.

"Now you have to . . . move, my wanton goddess," he choked out. "Up and down. The way I moved in you . . . last night."

"Ohhh. Of course," she said, her breath quickening. "Makes sense."

She did as he asked, and he nearly erupted right then and there. She was like hot satin, sparking flames, setting him ablaze. He filled his hands with her bountiful breasts—he did love how buxom she was—and thrust up into her, now impatient for her to move faster.

But she didn't take the hint. And when he saw the teasing smile on her lips, he knew she was doing it on purpose just to torture him.

"You're . . . enjoying this . . . aren't you, minx?" he rasped.

"A little." Squirming atop him, she broadened her smile. "Mostly, I am . . . figuring out . . . what you like."

"I like faster," he growled. That was what he got for letting *her* set the pace.

She gave a throaty laugh and increased her rhythm. Shimmying and twisting, she rode him as if he were a Thoroughbred, seeming to be searching for the best way to find her own pleasure and ignite his. He let her have whatever she wanted. Because he wanted what she wanted.

And because the fact that she enjoyed lovemaking relieved him. He'd been told plenty of respectable ladies did not. But she was a natural-born wanton, driving him slowly insane.

"Oh, Sheridan . . ." she whispered, as she spread her hands over his chest and even thumbed his nipples, giving him a taste of what it must feel like when he did it to her . . . or she did it to herself.

The memory of how she'd looked while touching herself inflamed him even more. She was moving quicker on his cock now, and his hips took over, pumping up into her hard as he gripped her arms and stampeded toward his own release. "Ah . . . my sweet duchess . . . you're mine now . . . always. Mine."

"Yours . . ." she breathed. "Forever."

The words were a vow. They ought to alarm him. Instead, they roused a fierce possessiveness as he neared his release. He felt her tightening around his cock seconds before she uttered an inarticulate cry and he exploded inside her.

As she slumped against him, his seed still spilling into her, and her mass of curls spilling over him, he uttered his own vow. "You're mine. Under the covers. Over the covers. Everywhere."

"Yes." She nuzzled his neck. "Oh, yes, my darling."

Only later did he realize, after carrying her to bed, that she'd never answered his question about Juncker. Instead, she had tried—successfully—to seduce him. Only later did he wonder, as he threw his arm over his still naked and already sleeping wife, if she'd thought of Juncker while she was making love to him.

God, what if she had? What if Juncker had her heart while Sheridan only had her body? He had to know. But asking her about Juncker again was liable to get him nowhere. She'd already evaded the question of how she felt about the bastard once. Nor did he have the right to ask her, when the memory of Helene still haunted him.

Or rather, the memory of the pain of losing her. After six years, he could barely remember Helene herself. That bothered him. Shouldn't the woman he'd once been in love with have earned more of a place in his heart than this . . . this faint echo of her presence?

For God's sake, his own mother had lionized Thorn's father. Her former love had stood between her and Sheridan's own father. That was why Mother and Father had never been in love with each other, never even had a chance to be in love with each other . . . because she'd still been clinging to the memory of the man she'd been married to for merely a year. Even after twenty-nine years, that had never changed.

Yet he couldn't even mourn Helene for more than six years.

You'll deprive yourself of one of life's greatest joys out of a determination not to experience the pain love can also bring? That's like refusing to ride because you fear falling off.

He laid back to stare up at the ceiling. How could Vanessa have the audacity to spout her opinions about love when she didn't love him either? She certainly hadn't said she loved him. Did she really expect him to take that leap when she wouldn't take it herself?

Unless she'd already taken it with Juncker.

And if she had? Then he would have to find some way to tear her from the fellow. Because he refused to be cuckolded—even just in spirit—by that . . . arrogant arse.

As soon as they reached London tomorrow, he would find Juncker and determine exactly how much there had been between the faux playwright and Vanessa. Because Vanessa was his now. He'd meant that when he said it. And no damned poet was going to take her away from him, in spirit or anything else.

Having made that promise to himself, he was finally able to drift off to sleep.

Chapter Nineteen

They reached London midafternoon the next day. Sheridan had never been so glad to see the city and rid himself of his new mother-in-law. He'd spent the entire journey watching his wife skillfully manage her mother, and he honestly wondered how she did it without wanting to strangle the woman.

Lady Eustace was a pest, plain and simple. First she was cold, then she was hot, then she needed air, then the air made her cold. The sequence was repeated ad nauseam until he informed his wife that *he* needed air and intended to get it by riding on the perch with his coachman. When she cast him an apologetic look, he felt guilty about his defection but not enough to offer to stay.

Besides, riding with Vanessa was a torment all its own. Despite the fact that she wore some all-encompassing, dark-green redingote that fastened up to her chin, he could still remember what sweet temptations lay beneath it. He resisted the urge to relive last night's enjoyments. The last thing he wanted was for his mother-in-law to realize what he had in mind for her daughter. One more reason to sit atop the perch with his coachman, no matter how odd the man probably thought it.

Once they'd left Lady Eustace at her town house and were heading the short distance to Sheridan's massive, money-eating London manor, Vanessa seemed to revive, at least enough to flash him a cheery smile. "The staff are expecting us, aren't they?"

"They are." Fortunately, he'd introduced her to them before the wedding and had watched as she charmed them all with a compliment here and a question for an opinion there. "I do have to pay one call before dinner."

Her face fell. "It can't wait until tomorrow?"

"I'm afraid not. But it won't take long, I don't think." He lied for all he was worth. "Just a minor business matter I was supposed to handle before I left for Lincolnshire. I'll be back by dinner, I promise."

She nodded, though her cheeriness seemed to fade some. "I wanted to have our 'at home' day tomorrow. Will you still be able to join me then?"

"Of course."

Gwyn had already warned him that newly married couples were expected to have a day at home where they could accept callers eager to express their congratulations.

Seeing her fight to hide her disappointment, he shifted from his seat across from her to sit next to her instead and take her hand. "I swear I won't be gone long."

He hoped not, anyway. He knew where Juncker lived, and if the arse wasn't there, he knew to look for him in Covent Garden, though finding the fellow there would take far longer. When she gave him a tremulous smile, he couldn't resist kissing her. What he'd intended as a quick kiss to soothe her fears rapidly turned into something more passionate.

The coach stopping before Armitage House jarred them both out of their shared pleasure.

She gave him a slumberous look he recognized only too well from when he'd awakened her this morning. "Shall I wait for you wearing only the Armitage pearls?" she said in a low voice that reverberated through every inch of his randy body.

For a moment, he considered having the coachman take a turn about Hyde Park while he seduced his wife.

But no, he had to do this first. Otherwise, he'd always be wondering who she was really thinking about when they made love. "I think that would shock my staff at dinner, don't you?" he quipped.

She laughed gaily as the footman opened the door and put down the step. Sheridan jumped out and helped her down, then as she climbed the steps, he told his coachman to take him to the Albany.

Thankfully, Juncker was in his rooms, or so a member of the staff told him. Forgoing the man's offer to fetch Juncker downstairs, Sheridan went upstairs alone, not wanting anyone to warn Juncker he was coming. It had finally occurred to Sheridan that the last time they'd seen each other, Sheridan had punched him. The man might not be that eager to meet with him.

Sure enough, when Juncker opened the door at Sheridan's knock, the man scowled at him. "What are you doing here?"

"I've come to talk to you about my wife."

Juncker had the door open only partway and wasn't

budging to let Sheridan inside. "You've got it backward. You should talk to your wife about me."

"I tried. She wouldn't tell me a damned thing."

Juncker looked him over, then sighed. "Come in then, if you must."

As Juncker walked away, Sheridan pushed the door open to enter the man's rooms. They were much finer than Sheridan would have expected a poet's to be. "My brother must pay you well to pose as writer of his plays."

"You know about that?"

"Olivia blurted it out accidentally."

Juncker chuckled. "That sounds like her." He didn't seem upset, which surprised Sheridan. And when Juncker then walked over to pour himself a brandy and asked Sheridan if he wanted one, the man surprised him even more.

"This is not a social call," Sheridan bit out.

Juncker lifted his glass. "Suit yourself." He sipped some before narrowing his gaze on Sheridan. "You're not planning to punch me again, are you?"

"That depends on what you tell me about your involvement with my wife."

Vanessa paced her bedchamber. Where in creation was Sheridan? She'd asked the staff when dinner was generally served, and they had said seven P.M. It was six-forty-five and no sign of Sheridan. So much for his promise to be home shortly.

It made her nervous. This was the first meal she was in charge of in her new home—well, her new London home—and she didn't want to ruin it. Sheridan struck her as the sort of man to expect things to be timely and orderly.

Except for in the bedchamber. No, she wouldn't think of that. It would just start her worrying again.

The connecting door opened, and her husband stepped in. "There you are. I thought you'd be down in the drawing room having a glass of wine."

She let out the breath she hadn't realized she was holding. She pointed to his bedchamber. "You just have time to change for dinner. The staff told me—"

"Don't fret. As soon as I came in, I told them to delay it an hour."

"All right." She thought about telling him that meals in progress didn't keep well when delayed but figured he probably wouldn't understand. He was a man, after all. "Did your meeting go well?"

"Quite well, actually." He was watching her particularly closely, for some reason.

Oh, dear, did she have something in her teeth? She shouldn't have eaten that pear after arriving. Perhaps there was a piece of peel in her teeth. Now, how was she to give a reason for needing to look in the mirror despite being fully dressed?

"So," he went on, "I have a question for you. It's the same one you refused to answer yesterday: Are you in love with Juncker?"

That brought her up short. Why on earth was he asking that *now?* Apparently her seduction of him last night had only bought her a day. And she was tired of avoiding the issue. "No, I am not. I never was."

He stared at her. "That's not what Juncker said."

"Wait a minute—you *talked* to Mr. Juncker about this? When?"

He hesitated to answer, and that told her a great deal.

"You talked to him this afternoon, didn't you?" She stalked across the room toward him. "*He* was your meeting!"

He scowled. "I had to know, damn it. Since you wouldn't tell me . . ."

She planted her hands on her hips. "And he said I was in love with him? Why, that . . . that scoundrel! He lied."

"Did he?" Sheridan said, his expression impossible to read.

"He most certainly did!" She paced around Sheridan. "But why would he lie? What could it possibly gain him? He knows I don't care about him, so it couldn't be anything like that. Besides which, he swore to keep my secret. Dirty traitor."

"What secret?" Sheridan asked in a hard voice.

Oh, dear. She shouldn't have said *that*. Sheridan had her so flustered that she didn't know which way was up.

Well, there was no help for it now. She had to tell him, if only to counter Juncker's lie. "The secret that . . . I only ever wanted you. That I was never interested in Mr. Juncker. I merely used him to make you jealous." She tipped up her chin. "And it worked, too, didn't it? Or at least a little."

"What made you assume it would work in the first place?" Sheridan asked, again using that voice that told her nothing of what he was thinking.

She swallowed hard, hating that he was making her expose herself. "Because I had the sense that you found me as appealing as I . . . found you. But then I couldn't ever get you to notice me. You seemed determined to treat me like Grey's little sister, which made no sense. I couldn't figure out if you felt the same way as I did. I was a woman, full-grown, wanting you to see me for who I really was."

"So you decided to use Juncker to make me jealous? Why him, of all people, if you had no feelings for him?"

Good Lord, this was difficult. "I didn't exactly plan that. I barely even knew who he was. But around the time of your father's demise, Grey guessed I was interested in someone, and I didn't dare tell him it was you. I knew he would reveal it to you if I did, and I feared you would find my interest in you suspect. You know—you'd see me as the silly young woman enamored of a duke. That's why I told Grey it was some poet. I'd been reading Mr. Juncker's poetry, and it seemed logical."

She sighed. "Except that the whole thing got terribly out of hand. Mr. Juncker somehow got wind of my interest in a poet and started behaving differently toward me. Until then, I had barely had any association with him, and suddenly he was flirting with me and pretending he knew me. So I gave him womanly advice, knowing it would put him off. But I think he then assumed he could use me to annoy you and Thornstock."

"He was right," Sheridan muttered.

"What?"

"Nothing," Sheridan said. "That's all it was. A scheme gone terribly awry."

"I suppose you could call it that." She turned away from him. "And we both know how much you hate schemes. And schemers."

"I do, that's true," he said softly. "But I could never hate you."

Her heart hurt, and his words only soothed the hurt a little. "I know you will never believe this, but Mr. Juncker lied about my interest in him. I *never* told him such a thing."

"I know." He came up close to put his arms about her waist.

"You believe me?"

"Yes. And I believe him. He did lie to me . . . at first. As you said, Juncker enjoys annoying Thorn and all his friends and relations. He's a prankster, that one. But when I looked at him as if I might throttle him, he quickly admitted the lie." He lifted an eyebrow. "Mr. Juncker has a strong tendency toward self-preservation."

Breaking free of his hold, Vanessa turned on him. "Are you telling me, that when you came in here just now, you *knew* I'd never had an interest in him?"

"I did," he said, though he suddenly looked wary. "But I had to hear it from you. I don't trust Juncker."

"Yet you believed him at first." She bore down on him. "When he said I was in love with him."

Sheridan held his hands up. "Not entirely, sweetheart, I swear. Before he even admitted the lie, I began to consider a few things—like the fact that you only started talking about Juncker when I was paying more attention to your mother than to you. And the fact that you flirted with me long before Grey mentioned Juncker in connection with you."

"That wasn't enough to convince you?"

"Well, you did change the subject last night when I asked about Juncker. You seduced me to take my mind off of him. And honestly, you didn't give me many other signs that Juncker might be wrong."

"Many other signs. Truly?" That really annoyed her. "I agreed to marry you."

"Only because we ended up caught in each other's arms." He cocked his head. "And that happened because you were letting Juncker kiss you with great enthusiasm. Or have you forgotten that?"

"I haven't." She crossed her arms over her chest. "Have *you* forgotten that you didn't show up for the visit you promised? That you left me to Mr. Juncker after saying you would accompany him? I assumed I had lost you. If I'd ever had you. I kept trying and trying to get your attention, and after our kiss at the theater, you didn't so much as give me a buss on the cheek. So yes, when Mr. Juncker asked to kiss me, I agreed. I figured why not? If I couldn't have you, what difference did it make?"

"I'm sorry." He seemed to look at her through new eyes. "I had no idea you were chasing me all that time."

"And if you *had* known it, would you have spent time with me?"

He dragged his fingers through his hair. "Perhaps. I'm not sure."

"Meanwhile, after we married, I eagerly shared your bed. Twice. And the second time was after I'd found out you'd only been showing me attention because you needed to interrogate my mother. That was well before you went to visit Juncker and believed his nonsense. How much more proof did you need that I cared about you?"

He caught her by the waist. "You're right. I should have trusted you. I was just—"

"Jealous?"

"Yes." He bent his head to kiss her temple. "It made me insane thinking he might have your heart."

"It's fine that your late fiancée has yours," she whispered, "but it's not all right that I might have chosen a different man before you?"

"Vanessa . . ." he said in that placating voice she hated.

"I have always wanted you, Sheridan Wolfe. Not because you're a duke, and not because you're Grey's brother, although that's certainly a consideration. But because you are you. And if that's not enough for you—"

"It is, my sweet duchess. I swear it. I'm happy we're married. I know that's hard for you to believe, but it's the truth."

He took her into his arms and began to kiss her.

She tore her lips from his, not quite ready to forgive him. "The servants are expecting us to eat dinner at the appointed time."

"Are they?" he murmured and continued trying to kiss her.

"Sheridan! I just got dressed!"

"I'll help you get dressed again," he said in a husky voice. "But I desperately want to make love to my wife."

To be honest, she desperately wanted the same thing. "All right," she whispered against his lips.

With a laugh, he backed her toward her bed and she let him. She had no self-control at all when it came to Sheridan.

He still hadn't said he loved her, but then she hadn't said she loved him either.

Did she love him? She very much feared that she did. He was the only man she'd ever really wanted, and it had taken her years to find him. He was the only one who stood up for her, who shared her love of books and understood her love of gardening. The only one who made her blood roar and her heart leap. But he'd already told her once he had no intention of being in love again, and she didn't know how she'd bear it if he said those same words once she'd bared her heart to him.

She would just have to show him how she felt and hope that one day he would share her feelings.

Chapter Twenty

Two days later, Sheridan sat in his study in the London manor house, poring over the estate accounts in preparation for the dreaded meeting with Bonham that afternoon. He'd put it off longer than he should have.

Yesterday, the rest of his family had returned to London, including his mother, who would still be living with them for the time being. But she probably wouldn't be around much. She planned on heading off to Carymont tomorrow to see how Beatrice and Grey were doing, since Beatrice still hadn't had her baby. No doubt she'd be visiting the others frequently.

He didn't mind that in the least. Having one's mother around while one was adjusting to married life was very trying. But as soon as Mother left—and the meeting with Bonham was over, he could enjoy spending time with Vanessa. He might actually have a chance to do something with her other than swiving. Not that he minded the swiving. Leaning back in his chair, he smiled to himself.

"What are you smiling so secretively about, my darling?" Vanessa asked as she bustled into his study.

"I was merely thinking about last night. And the night before that. Oh, yes, and the night before that. And the—"

"I know what you're trying to do, Sheridan Wolfe, and you will not seduce me into telling Bonham you're indisposed or anything like that. When he comes this afternoon, you'll need to be prepared."

"Damn. Unbeknownst to me, I married a nagging woman," he said in mock alarm. "Ah, well, I suppose I'm stuck with you now."

"Very amusing." With a lift of her impervious and very lovely eyebrow, she came around to his side of the desk to look out the window at the courtyard garden. "I can see why you said you liked your study. The garden behind you gives you a nice glimpse of the outdoors."

"It does, indeed," he said, turning in his chair to look out at it himself.

"That will be the first thing I tackle as lady of the house. Your little garden there could clearly use a bit of care, and I will enjoy getting it under good management."

Sheridan pulled her closer. "I can think of other things you could get 'under good management.'"

She laughed. "You are insatiable, sir. And this is neither the time nor the place for it."

"I don't know about that," he said, smoothing one hand over her hip to her thighs.

Rolling her eyes at him, she turned to gaze down at his desk. "So these are the account books?"

That reminder ruined his mood. "They are, indeed." He dropped his hand from her lovely body. "I realize everyone keeps their accounts differently, but I can't make heads nor tails of Bonham's system. Every time I think

I've figured it out, something else comes up to tell me I have not."

She picked one of the books up and looked at it. "Well, no wonder. It makes no sense."

"Don't tell me the numbers swim before your eyes, too."

"No." She eyed him oddly. "What do you mean?"

God rot it, he shouldn't have said that. "It's nothing."

"It's not nothing. Some people have trouble with numbers. My great-uncle used to have a terrible time. Then my great-aunt would complain of how he drove her mad whenever he had to meet with his estate manager." She pointed to a figure. "What is this?"

"It's seven hundred and twenty-six pounds."

"No, my dear. It's seven hundred and sixty-two pounds."

He looked at it again. "You're right. I can see it now, but I'd swear it was—"

"Here, let's try another one." This time she took a ruler and laid it underneath a figure. "What's this one?"

"That's five thousand and twenty-five pounds."

"Look at it again."

He scowled. "What's the use? Every time I look at a number, I can't trust what I see."

"That's just a simple matter of having someone look at the numbers for you. Honestly, you shouldn't even be bothering with this. You have a man of affairs. It's his job."

"My father always said any man of property ought to be able to look at the account ledgers and tell whether someone was cheating him or he could be doing some aspect of estate management more efficiently."

"I suppose your father had a point, but I don't see why

you should have to take it this far." She raised an eyebrow. "Besides, for how long did your father manage an estate?"

That brought Sheridan up short. "Six months or so. I always assumed my grandfather had passed down his own rules of estate management, but if he had, he would have passed them down to Uncle Armie, not my father."

"So your father really had very little experience at all."

"I don't suppose he had." He'd never thought of it like that.

"Your Uncle Armie was the other person you and your siblings think was murdered?"

"Yes. He's the one who ran the estate into the ground."

"Are you sure of that?"

Sheridan sat back in his chair. "I am. Before I inherited, Father knew it, the tenants knew it, and Bonham knew it. If I could just figure out Bonham's system, *I* would know it. He has tried time and again to explain it to me, but apparently my issue with numbers keeps me from being able to make sense of it."

"Hmm." She looked skeptical. "If you want, I could read over the ledgers for you, and see if *I* can figure it out. I'm good with numbers, and I used to do the books for Papa."

"Forgive me, sweetheart, but that's not a ringing endorsement, given that your parents struggled under your father's management."

She set her hands on her lovely hips. "That was because of Papa's mistresses and Mama's overspending."

"Uncle Armie had plenty of mistresses himself, and overspending was how he operated."

With fire in her eyes, Vanessa rested one hip on the desk. "Yes, but he had a duke's income behind him—

plenty of tenants and other investments. Whereas Papa, as a second son, only had our country house in Suffolk left to him by his mother. He had no tenants. He couldn't afford either overspending or mistresses, but that didn't stop him. Why do you think he tried to steal Grey's unentailed properties?"

She did have a point there.

"And believe me," she went on, "I did my best to make the argument that we would have plenty to live on if he would stop spending so much on 'Mama.' We both knew he wasn't spending all of it on Mama and me, but he pretended otherwise, and I let him. No one stood up to Papa, least of all me."

"Grey did," Sheridan said softly.

"And he suffered for it, as you know." She thrust out her chin. "What little we were left to live on was only available because I . . . hid assets to keep us from debtors' prison. It's possible Mr. Bonham did something similar to keep the dukedom afloat. He *has* been with the Armitage dukes for decades, after all."

"Surely he would have said something about it to me if he had."

She shrugged. "Perhaps he's waiting to see if he can trust you, whether you're going to be able to handle the extra funds if he reveals them to you."

Sheridan doubted that, but he could tell she was hopeful. A month ago, he would have assumed that her hope stemmed from a desire for money. Now he knew she simply wanted to help him, which was very sweet, but probably a lost cause.

"What do you have to lose if I look at the books?" she asked. "Are you doubting my intelligence again?"

"Again? When have I ever doubted your intelligence?"

"When you thought me a frivolous ninny."

"I have long since been disabused of that notion, if I ever really believed it."

That was the right thing to say, for she softened her stance. "So you'll let me go over them."

"If you want to so badly, absolutely. But you'll have to explain to me whatever you find, so I can articulate it for him."

"Of course. Let me just glance over this one first to see if I can tell what system he uses."

"He says it's double-entry."

She shook her head. "It doesn't look like double-entry to me."

Suddenly Gwyn burst into the room. "Where's Mama?"

Sheridan stared at her. "I have no idea. Why?"

"I'm hoping she knows what has happened to Lady Hornsby. The countess isn't in London or at her estate, according to her servants, who are being decidedly un-communicative about where she actually *is*." Gwyn dropped into a chair across from his desk. "Do you think she got wind of our investigation and left London for parts unknown?"

"I suppose anything is possible at this point," Sheridan said. "You should send your husband to investigate."

"I can't. Joshua left London last night in furtherance of something he is investigating for you, he told me, though he wouldn't say what."

Sheridan chuckled. "That's because your husband knows that once he tells you, it will be broadcast far and wide."

"Hardly. I've kept Thorn's secret all this time. I'll bet you don't even know what it is."

"I'll bet I do," Sheridan countered. "But I swore I wouldn't tell a soul, and you, dear girl, nearly told it yesterday."

"What secret did she almost tell?" Vanessa asked. "My heavens, your family has a great many secrets."

"I'll tell you later," Sheridan said to Vanessa in an undertone. He could always reveal how Olivia and Thorn had met. That was a juicy secret indeed. Although at the rate Gwyn and Olivia were going, the secret of Thorn's identity as a playwright could be out next week.

His mother walked in.

"Good God," he exclaimed. "Why are the lot of you congregating in my study? Don't you have rooms—or in your case, Gwyn, a *home*—of your own?"

Mother pouted. "I learned that Gwyn was here, that's all. I wanted to see if she'd heard whether Grey and Bea's baby had been born yet."

"No, it hasn't," Vanessa said even as she looked over the account book. "They're still waiting."

Sheridan cast her a surprised look. "How do *you* know?"

"Bridget heard it from a servant in Grey's household. She's on very good terms with his staff."

"That doesn't surprise me," Sheridan muttered. "Your lady's maid is quite the resourceful female."

Ignoring him, Gwyn turned to their mother. "I have lost Lady Hornsby, Mama, and no one can tell me where she is."

"Oh! I did mean to mention to you that she owns a romantic little cottage near Richmond Park. I'd forgotten all about it. It's where she retires to if she's having a tryst with a married lover. Here, I'll write down the direction." She walked over to Sheridan's desk and took out a pencil and some paper. When she realized both of her children were staring at her, she said, "What? I went there to keep her company once when her . . . er . . . current lover was delayed up north."

"I think you're right, Vanessa." Gwyn stood and walked over to take the piece of paper from their mother's hand. "We *do* have a lot of secrets. And I guess I know what I'll be doing the rest of the morning."

Sheridan scowled. "You're not riding out to Richmond Park alone, are you?"

"I'll take a footman," Gwyn said breezily.

"You damned well will not." Sheridan shot to his feet. "You'll take me, and I'll carry my pistol just in case. Joshua would never forgive me if I let his very pregnant wife go with only a servant to an adulterer's nest. Anything could happen."

"Ooh, yes," Gwyn said sarcastically. "I might see some marquess—or judge—naked."

"And if you did," Sheridan said, "you might not live to tell the tale. So I'll bring this just to be safe." He opened a desk drawer and removed his pistol case, then turned to Vanessa.

Before he could even say anything, however, she said, "Go, go. I'm just planning to sit here looking over these account books. And if you don't arrive home before Mr. Bonham gets here, I'll make your apologies."

"Thank you, sweetheart." He bent to kiss her, then headed for the door. "Mother? Are you coming?"

"No, dear," she said. "I'm traveling again tomorrow, so the last thing I want is to spend an hour each way to Richmond Park in a coach."

"Very well. We shouldn't be too long. With any luck we'll be back long before Bonham arrives."

Vanessa had already only been half paying attention to the conversation, so when Sheridan and Gwyn left, she was quite absorbed in the account books. They made no sense. Sheridan might be blaming himself for the problem, but that was only because he was wary of how he saw numbers.

She, on the other hand, saw numbers perfectly fine, and these made no sense. They didn't add up in the least. She needed an orderly way to look at everything because she didn't have enough time to figure it out before Mr. Bonham arrived.

"My dear," a soft voice said, and Vanessa nearly jumped out of her skin.

Then she realized that the dowager duchess hadn't actually left. "Forgive me, Duchess," she said with a smile. "Sheridan's talk of adulterers' nests and pistols and such has made me a bit skittish."

"We all are these days. And please, call me Mother. All the other wives do."

"I'd be honored," Vanessa said.

"Anyway, I won't keep you long, but I did wish to ask you one thing before I return upstairs."

Vanessa sat back warily. "And what would that be?"

"Did my rapscallion son tell you about Helene?"

"He did. He explained that it was a very difficult time for him."

"It was, indeed."

Vanessa swallowed. "I gather she was a wonderful person."

Her mother-in-law snorted. "Not quite as wonderful as my son considered her to be. Personally, I found her flighty and frivolous . . . until her tragic condition imbued her with a certain nobility of manner."

A sigh escaped Vanessa. "I'm afraid all that remains of her character in Sheridan's memory is that 'nobility of manner.'"

"Don't misunderstand me. Her death *was* a tragedy. I knew her parents, and they were lovely people. They didn't deserve to lose a daughter so young. If it had been Gwyn . . ." She shook her head. "I would never have been the same."

"I can well understand that."

"The problem is Sheridan is much like his father. Once he takes to a person, he is loyal to a fault. Maurice married me because I was the wife of his friend and I needed a husband, so loyal friend that he was, he wed me. That quality is wonderful in a lord of the manor. I can always be sure that Sheridan's servants, tenants, and other staff will never go without, not if he can help it. He will fight tooth and nail to make sure that anyone he cares about is provided for."

"I've noticed that about him. He seems very dedicated."

Her mother-in-law sighed. "But somehow, when it comes to Helene, that quality has become twisted in his head. He feels if he admits he no longer loves her the way he used to, then he's somehow being disloyal to her."

"I think you're right about that." It made her heart sink even more. "To be honest, he married me out of a sense of duty, which isn't much different from loyalty. In his mind, he'd ruined my reputation, so he had to fix that. But I wasn't terribly concerned about that. I just wanted him— *want* him—to love me. What if he never can?"

Her mother-in-law came around the desk to put her arm about Vanessa's shoulders. "I think he already does love you. He merely doesn't want to admit it to himself, stubborn devil. He's kept the torch lit over her grave for so long that he doesn't know how to put it out. I fear it will take something very powerful to change that state of affairs. We shall merely have to hope it comes along before you've been married thirty years, as I was to his father."

"Thirty years! I don't want to wait thirty years to see myself loved by the man *I* love."

"I was only joking, my dear." The dowager duchess walked toward the door, then muttered, "Mostly, anyway."

Vanessa groaned. She certainly hoped her mother-in-law was joking. And how could the man be so good at noticing her feelings but be so blind to what his own feelings were?

Unless he didn't feel as deeply as Vanessa did. He'd been forced into marriage, after all.

I think he already does love you.

Oh, she hoped that was true. She would cling to that possibility as long as she could. In the meantime, there was one way of endearing him to her, and that involved solving the issue of whether Bonham's bookkeeping could be trusted.

With that, she settled down to work.

Chapter Twenty-One

Two hours later, Sheridan and Gwyn left Lady Hornsby's and headed for his coach. "That was an utter waste of time," Sheridan grumbled.

"I told you and the rest of them it wasn't her. She might enjoy seducing young—and old—men more than she should, and she might be a bit saucy in her language, but at heart she's a decent sort and very kind."

"Except for the periodic cuckolding of other people's husbands."

Gwyn sighed. "True. Except for that."

He helped his half sister into the coach and climbed in after her. "I still can't believe the countess has been having an affair with Lisbourne all this time." He shuddered. "Vanessa has no idea what a close call she had."

"I doubt Lady Hornsby would have stood for seeing Lisbourne marry a much younger woman, anyway, at least not while she and Lisbourne were having an affair. And there's no telling—perhaps in time *she* and Lisbourne will marry. He has an heir already, and it's not as if she could have children, anyway. Hornsby left her well off, and Lisbourne needs money. It could be a match made in heaven."

"If you say so." Privately he was skeptical. "But you think she was telling the truth about the house party?"

"The first one? Undoubtedly. Hornsby wasn't the best husband, from what Mama has said, so it makes sense she would have gone off to her little love nest with her first lover—of many—as soon as possible. We'll have to compare notes with Mama, but I think it's believable."

"Lady Hornsby's explanation of what she was doing during the second house party seems a bit more believable to me. I can easily see how she would be reluctant to attend a house party when gossip was circling around society that she was mistress to Thorn's father. Assuming that she and Mother were still good friends—and we have no reason to believe otherwise—she would have stayed away out of courtesy to Mother."

"But why was she listed as a guest at the party?"

"Those lists were invitation lists," Sheridan pointed out. "Did you keep a list of the people who attended your ball a few weeks back? I daresay you only kept a record of whom you invited."

Gwyn frowned. "True. I hadn't thought of that. I wonder if Mother would remember if Lady Hornsby was at the house party. If she remembered one way or the other, though, wouldn't she have told us?"

"Not if she was in labor during the whole party."

"Oh, right. I forgot she was in labor."

"I don't know how you could forget that," Sheridan teased her. "She was in labor with you and Thorn."

Gwyn made a face at him, and he laughed.

Then both sat quietly for a bit. Finally, Sheridan said, "I guess this means we'll have to look into servants and other staff now. Because you and I both know Lady Norley isn't some master criminal. I could believe it of Lady Hornsby perhaps and definitely of Lady Eustace, but Lady Norley is a likable lady who puts up with her arse of a husband because she loves her stepdaughter."

Gwyn nodded. "That about sums her up." She nudged his knee. "Meanwhile, how is married life treating *you?*"

"Pretty well, under the circumstances."

"You did finally tell Vanessa about Helene, didn't you?"

"I did."

"And you told Vanessa you're in love with *her* now, right?"

He stiffened. "I'm not in love with Vanessa. I have great affection for her, and I certainly have a healthy desire for her, but love? I don't *want* to be in love with her. The last time I was in love, it nearly destroyed me."

"Yet here you are, completely whole again." Gwyn shook her head. "Nobody *wants* to be in love. Why would anyone choose an emotion capable of ripping one's heart to pieces?"

"Exactly what I was saying."

"You're missing my point. You don't choose love; love chooses *you*. You have no say or recourse, and when it happens, resistance is pointless."

"That sounds alarming." It also sounded close to how he'd felt with Helene years ago. Actually, it was closer to how he felt with Vanessa *now*. Bloody hell.

Gwyn tried to stifle a yawn but wasn't successful.

"You're tired," Sheridan said. "Why don't you nap a bit on the way back?"

"Thank you. I believe I will." She patted his hand, then

put her head against the squabs and promptly went to sleep.

Gazing at her, he wondered if Vanessa would be so tired once she was enceinte. Would she eat strange foods? Would she even be happy to carry his child?

Will you try not to love your children, too, so you don't suffer pain if one of them dies?

He grimaced, remembering what Vanessa had said about children. He should stop dwelling on that and turn his thoughts to figuring out where to go next in their investigation.

Unfortunately, by the time he and Gwyn reached her town house, he hadn't come up with much of a plan. To his surprise, Joshua was apparently waiting for them to arrive, because before Sheridan's footman could open the carriage door Joshua appeared at the bottom of the steps, cane in hand. "Hold up, Sheridan. I need to speak to you before you leave."

Sheridan leaned out of the carriage window. "I'm meeting with Bonham in half an hour to go over the books, so this had better be important."

"It's damned important. Where are you meeting with Bonham?"

"At my house. Why?"

"Because this concerns him. And I should go with you." Joshua glanced in the carriage and said, "You shouldn't go, sweeting."

"I want to hear what you found out. I'm part of this, too, you know."

Joshua hesitated, but he probably knew better than to argue with Gwyn when she'd dug in her heels. "All right.

But once we reach Sheridan's, I'm sending you back home."

That certainly sounded worrisome.

Joshua got in and took a seat beside his wife. As soon as they were off, he said, "I haven't left town to confirm the details of Sir Noah's past, but I did speak to a number of gentlemen who know him and will readily vouch for him. So I think we can rule him out."

"Thank God," Sheridan said. "I wasn't looking forward to telling Vanessa I suspected her uncle of anything. Bad enough I suspected her mother. Who, by the way, is now excluded as a possibility."

"I'm not surprised," Joshua said. "I did as you asked regarding Bonham. Fortunately, once I discovered his previous identity, everything was fairly easy to investigate."

Alarm caught Sheridan by the throat. "What previous identity?"

"Before your man of affairs was William Bonham, he was Henry Davenport."

"Wait, that surname sounds familiar," Sheridan said.

"You may have uncovered it accidentally in the course of questioning Lady Eustace," Joshua said. "Did she ever mention a young man who killed himself when your mother refused to marry him?"

Sheridan felt as if a fist of ice closed around his heart. "Matthew Davenport. Yes. Died for love."

"That was Bonham's—Henry Davenport's—older brother."

"Dear heaven," Gwyn whispered.

"As you might imagine, it's no coincidence," Joshua said. "After Matthew killed himself, his family fell on hard times. The scandal ruined Henry's father, who was a barrister. He lost all his clients and his reputation. Eventually he and Henry's mother ended up in debtors' prison, where both died, leaving sixteen-year-old Henry to fend for himself. So the very clever Henry changed who he was in order to survive. Since he knew a good bit about the law, thanks to his father, he took the name of an obscure member of his mother's family, long deceased, and somehow got a place as a clerk in a solicitor's office."

"I did know Bonham had a background in law," Sheridan said. "That must be why Father sometimes referred to him as his solicitor."

"Probably. The solicitor Bonham worked for was so impressed with his work as a law clerk that the man often took Bonham on trips made on behalf of their clients." Joshua's expression turned grim. "Guess who one of the solicitor's more important clients, a wealthy banker, was a friend to."

"Good God," Sheridan said, his heart pounding. "Grey's father."

"Precisely. I daresay Bonham was shocked to hear that the house party he was attending with his employer was hosted by none other than Lydia Fletcher Pryde, the new Duchess of Greycourt, whom he probably saw as ruining his family."

"I don't understand." Gwyn stared at her husband. "If he blamed Mama and wanted revenge on her, why kill her husband? Why not just kill *her?*"

"We'll never know for sure, unless he admits it," Joshua said, "but I suspect he intended to do so. Instead, the poison somehow ended up in the duke's food or drink. And afterward, when he saw how little your mother mourned her husband's death, that probably only reinforced Bonham's image of her as a deadly siren, who used her beauty and charm to prey on his brother and other hapless men."

"That's not fair!" Gwyn cried. "By all accounts, Grey's father was a despicable man who essentially married her so he and Mama's mother could continue their affair without its being easily noticed by people in society. Apparently our maternal grandfather didn't care who our grandmother chose to bed, as long as she was discreet."

"You knew about that?" Sheridan said. "I only heard of it recently, when Lady Eustace told me. I confess I was so shocked, I didn't quite believe her."

"I don't know if it's true, but I learned of it from Grey, who learned of it from his uncle, who'd thrown it in his face on occasion."

"I never knew any of it," Joshua said. "And I daresay Bonham didn't either. Your poor mother. No wonder she married again so swiftly. What was it, a year later?"

"Two years." Gwyn thrust out her chin. "And she married *our* father for love."

"Still, two years is quick in some people's minds, and Bonham would have seen the hasty wedding as evidence of her conniving nature, since he was already predisposed to hate your mother. I'm sure he plotted the best way to get his vengeance on her. So he got his employer invited to that same affair or drummed up an excuse for needing to bring a document to be signed himself or some such. Once there, I suspect he couldn't bring himself to kill a woman in labor. But perhaps he thought that killing the man she loved might lead to her dying in labor."

Gwyn scowled. "The man is a monster."

"Who lost his entire family at sixteen, Gwyn," Sheridan

said. "I'm not excusing him for it, but having lost Helene to illness, I can only imagine how he felt losing a brother to suicide and his parents to illness. He had to blame it on someone. And he picked our mother to blame it on, because she rejected his brother. In his mind, she had set the chain of events in motion."

Joshua snorted. "We don't know your mother's side of the story yet, Sheridan. She may not have been as cruel to his brother as Bonham thinks."

Gwyn nodded. "I suppose once Mama married Papa, and he took the family to Prussia, Bonham could do nothing more. Following them there would have been difficult, I'm sure."

"Yes," Joshua said. "Clearly he gave up his plans for vengeance, at least temporarily. He got his law degree and acquired some wealthy clients. He even got married. Somehow he finagled his way into becoming your grandfather's man of affairs."

"There's no 'somehow' about it," Sheridan said. "Bonham has a reputation for being brilliant, having a talent for not only the law but accounting. Father said that my grandfather often sung his praises in his letters."

"That's a good point," Joshua said. "Everyone I talked to who knew him said he was gifted with both numbers and contracts, the best solicitor they'd ever used. No one would have guessed him to be a double murderer."

"Not just a double murderer," Sheridan said grimly. "He killed my uncle and my father, too." He mused a moment. "The only thing I can't figure out is why, after serving my grandfather and uncle for years, he suddenly decided to kill Uncle Armie to bring Father and the rest of the family back to England so he could kill Father, too. Why decide to do it nearly thirty years later?"

Gwyn furrowed her brow in thought. "Bonham's wife died shortly before Uncle Armie did. I remember because Bonham was still in mourning when we met him. And Mama said his wife never bore him any children."

"So it must have really stuck in his craw that Mother had five," Sheridan said, "two of them dukes at the time. That she was living a relatively happy, full life in spite of all his attempts to ruin it."

"Is that why he's been acting as if he's courting your mother?" Joshua settled back against the squabs. "He could have murdered her ten times over by now. So has he given up on revenge and decided to try marrying your mother instead?"

As awareness dawned, Sheridan groaned. "That might be his eventual plan—as her husband he would have complete control over her—but I don't think he was necessarily trying to bring Father back to England when he killed Uncle Armie. I think Uncle Armie discovered what Father discovered later and what got them both killed."

Sheridan tensed up. "The brilliant William Bonham is embezzling money from the dukedom and quite possibly has been doing so for the past couple of decades. He has apparently decided he might as well get rich off of his revenge."

Joshua swore under his breath. "You have proof of that?"

"Not yet. But Vanessa suspected something was wrong when she looked over the account ledgers this morning—" Sheridan let out an oath, then pulled out his pocket watch. "Damn. It's nearly four. That's when Bonham and I agreed to meet." His blood roared in his ears. "I left Vanessa looking over the books. And Mother is home as well."

Sliding open the front panel, he called up to his coachman. "Make haste, Harry! We've got to get back to Armitage House at once."

Immediately, the coachman increased his speed.

"When we get there," Joshua said, "I want you to stay in the coach, Gwyn."

"Not on your life! I can help."

"You're carrying our child," Joshua said hoarsely. "I don't want you anywhere near that unpredictable bastard."

"I don't have to be near him to be a help. I can at least keep Mama preoccupied."

Sheridan nodded. "That could be useful."

"What if he decides to finally try killing your mother?" Joshua bit out. He took Gwyn's hand in his. "If you get in his way, sweeting—"

"I won't." Gwyn set her shoulders. "You won't even know I'm in the house."

Joshua looked as if he might argue, but Gwyn was clearly set upon resisting. "Fine," he said. He looked at Sheridan. "We'll need a plan."

"We will indeed." Sheridan's heart beat the frenzied pace of a soldier heading into battle. "Are you armed? Because I have my pistol case with me, and you can use one of my pistols. They're both loaded. We didn't know what we might encounter at Lady Hornsby's."

With a gleam in his eyes, Joshua opened his greatcoat to show two pockets, each containing a pistol. "I thought we might need these."

"And his cane becomes a sword," Gwyn said helpfully.

"Actually, this is the cane that has a smaller pistol in

the handle," her husband corrected her. "But I do have a blade in my boot."

"Good God, you're a walking arsenal!" Sheridan said. "Though I'm glad of it. Even now Vanessa might be alone with that . . . maniac."

"She'll be all right." Gwyn reached over to squeeze his hand. "She's quick-witted and resourceful. And Bonham has no reason to suspect we've figured out his game, anyway."

"He might gain one if Vanessa confronts him about the embezzlement," Sheridan said.

"Assuming that she's unraveled it," Joshua said. "If she has, she surely won't even let the scoundrel in."

"But if she does for some reason, she'll have to convince him she knows nothing of it, or she might be dead before we can reach her. He'll have nothing to lose."

No one argued with that. Who could? They knew he was right. Sheridan had left her alone with those ledgers . . . with Bonham on the way. And without telling her he loved her.

Of course he loved her. His feelings for Helene had been a pale imitation compared to the soul-abiding love he had for Vanessa. Otherwise, he wouldn't have this gut-twisting fear for her in his chest. She was his life, his heart. And all he wanted was the chance to tell her. Because if he lost her before he could do so . . .

No, he wouldn't let that happen.

Hold on, sweetheart, we're coming. I'm coming. Just stay alive until we get there.

Vanessa was rather pleased with herself. She'd taken a sheet of the ledger and redone it properly on a piece of clean paper. Her calculations showed she was right. Mr. Bonham's numbers didn't match up. It was a small amount, but if he'd been doing it for years it would add up to a great deal of missing money. And she knew exactly whose pockets it was going into, although it would take months to redo the ledgers to find out exactly how much he'd stolen.

No wonder the dukedom was struggling. Sheridan had been right to question Mr. Bonham's figures. Even not being able to see the numbers right, he'd deduced that something didn't make sense, and that was impressive.

How had Mr. Bonham managed to do it for so long without being caught? Perhaps he hadn't embezzled anything during the days of Sheridan's grandfather. Then, once Uncle Armie took over—a man who, by all accounts, wasn't terribly interested in such matters—Mr. Bonham had been better able to siphon off funds. He could have drained away the money and deemed it overspending on Uncle Armie's part.

A frisson of fear swept her. Sheridan and his siblings were nearly certain that Uncle Armie had been murdered. What if Mr. Bonham had let his greed govern his actions and had become more blatant in his stealing? Perhaps even the negligent Uncle Armie had noticed something was wrong. If he'd threatened Mr. Bonham with the possibility of firing him or having him arrested . . .

She shivered. That would mean Mr. Bonham had murdered Uncle Armie. And Sheridan had said his father was adamant about Sheridan learning to examine the books on his own. Perhaps Sheridan's father had suspected Mr. Bonham of embezzlement, too. Perhaps Mr. Bonham had murdered *him* for the same reason.

Then when Sheridan had come along, clearly having issues with seeing numbers correctly, Mr. Bonham had probably decided not to worry about being caught, thinking that Sheridan would never notice his small, purposeful errors.

Arrogant scoundrel! She'd been told Mr. Bonham was a man of some wealth. Now she wondered if he'd just been stealing from the Armitage dukedom or from others of his clients as well.

Their butler appeared in the doorway to the study. "Your Grace, Mr. Bonham is here. He has an appointment with the duke. Shall I show him in?"

"Has the duke not returned?" she asked.

"Not yet, no."

"Does Mr. Bonham know that?"

"I don't believe so. I certainly didn't tell him."

"Very judicious of you." She debated what to do. But she didn't want Mr. Bonham anywhere near her without Sheridan there. Especially now that she knew he couldn't be trusted. "Why don't you tell him to wait, Phipps? Say that my husband is busy doing something else and will be with him shortly."

"Very good, Your Grace."

As soon as the butler left, she went back to perusing the ledger. She should probably find another ledger from an earlier time. She stood and went to the bookshelf where Sheridan kept them to see if she could find one. It would help determine if—

"Where is His Grace?" a hard voice asked.

She jumped. "Good heavens, you startled me, Mr. Bonham," she said, her heart pounding in her ears. She took a second to compose herself before turning to face him with what she hoped was a duchess's imperious manner. "Phipps must have misunderstood when I told him to have you wait."

"He stuck me in a parlor and left. The duke is never late for our appointments, so where is he?"

"That's none of your concern," she said, copying Mama's tone of aristocratic condescension. "He'll be here shortly, I'm sure. Perhaps you would prefer to wait in the parlor until he arrives."

Ignoring her tone, he entered the room. "What are you doing with the duke's ledgers?"

"I'm tidying up, of course," she said. "He had a number of them strewn on his desk, and he asked me to put them away."

Mr. Bonham looked a bit suspicious still. "Can't imagine why he'd need more than the current ledger."

"I can't either," she said blithely. "Not that I would know anything about bookkeeping. It's all Greek to me."

"Is it?" He edged nearer the desk.

That was when she realized that her piece of paper, where she'd worked out what the true numbers were supposed to be, lay right there in plain sight.

But he hadn't seemed to have noticed it yet. She walked back over to the desk as nonchalantly as she could manage. "I'm sure my husband will be here any minute. Would you like some refreshment? Tea? Coffee?"

Meanwhile, she slid the sheet of paper beneath the ledger, trying to be unobtrusive.

Apparently not unobtrusive enough, for Mr. Bonham loomed up next to the desk and said, "What's that you're hiding?"

"Hiding! Why would I be hiding anything?"

"That's an excellent question," he snapped. "Why would you?" And before she could even react, he slid the piece of paper out from under the ledger and into his hand.

He perused it carefully. Then he met her gaze. "The duke knows. Or at least suspects."

"Knows what? Suspects what?" she said, fighting to appear flighty.

"You can stop pretending to be stupid now, Duchess. I am no fool. And I want to know everything you and the duke have figured out about my accounting practices."

Chapter Twenty-Two

As soon as Sheridan's coach pulled up in front of Armitage House, they spotted Bonham's phaeton parked there and his groom sitting on a step awaiting his master. At the sight, Sheridan's blood turned to ice.

Not bothering to wait for Joshua and Gwyn, as soon as the coach stopped, Sheridan leapt out and ran up the steps. When he entered, his butler said, "Oh, there you are, Your Grace. Mr. Bonham is awaiting you."

"Awaiting me where?"

"In the parlor, of course. Since you hadn't arrived yet, the duchess told me to put him there until you did."

"Thank God," Sheridan muttered and strode to the parlor they used for tradesmen and the like.

But it was empty.

Sheridan hurried back to the entryway. "He's not there."

"But . . . but that's where I left him," Phipps said.

"Apparently he didn't stay put."

Gwyn and Joshua entered, and Sheridan explained the situation.

"So he's quite possibly alone with Vanessa," Gwyn said.

"Yes."

Sheridan turned for the hallway, but before he could march down it to his study, Joshua grabbed his arm. "We have to be smart about this. Remember the plan. We have no reason to believe that Bonham suspects anything. He's been with all of us socially many a time. We might still find him chatting with Vanessa."

"That's what worries me. I told you, she thinks he's simply a bad accountant. At worse, she suspects him of being an embezzler."

"If she has even considered the possibility that he's embezzling, she will hide her opinions. You need to learn to trust your wife, Sheridan. She has good instincts."

Even knowing his brother-in-law was right, Sheridan could hardly keep from barreling down the hall and into his study with guns blazing. "It's not her I distrust. Bonham didn't get this far along—fooling everyone he came into contact with and killing those who caught on— without being both perceptive and deceptive. It has proved a deadly combination."

Worry knit Gwyn's brow. "I'll go stay with Mama." She turned to Phipps. "Where is my mother just now?"

Phipps was eyeing the two men with blatant curiosity. "The last time I saw her, my lady, she was in the music room."

"Thank you, Phipps," Gwyn said and headed for the stairs.

Perhaps Joshua was right, and everything would be

fine. So why did Sheridan have this instinct telling him Vanessa's life was at stake?

Joshua turned to Sheridan. "Ready?"

Sheridan checked the loaded pistol tucked into the fall of his trousers, and the other in the tail pocket of his coat. "Ready."

"Give me a few minutes to get into position."

With a terse nod, Sheridan watched as Joshua headed for the closest door leading out into the courtyard garden. He waited as long as he could bear it, then walked down the hall to his study. The door was closed, damn it.

Pasting a look of nonchalance to his face, he carefully lifted the door handle and opened the door.

He walked in to find Bonham holding Vanessa's arm and they both stood behind the desk, looking down at something. The minute the arse saw Sheridan, he thrust a pistol to Vanessa's head. "Your wife already took me for a fool. So I suggest you do not."

Sheridan's heart damned near stopped right there. "I wouldn't dream of it," he said hoarsely. He stared into Vanessa's frightened eyes and gave her a speaking look he hoped she understood.

I won't let him hurt you. I'd rather die first. I love you.

God, how he wished he'd said the words sooner.

"Pull the door to," Bonham said. "I don't want some servant witnessing our conversation."

Sheridan did as Bonham said, although he itched to throw himself across the desk and get his hands around Bonham's throat instead. But Bonham's position meant he could shoot Vanessa with deadly accuracy, while Sheridan risked hitting her if he fired a shot. Given the bodies the man had left behind him, Bonham wouldn't hesitate to do it, either. Sheridan couldn't endanger her. *Wouldn't* endanger her.

That was why when Sheridan saw Joshua appear through the glass of the French doors behind Bonham, it was not a relief. "What do you want?" Sheridan said. "I won't let you take her." He shook his head as if to emphasize the words, and Joshua nodded to show he understood Sheridan's signal that it wasn't safe to shoot Bonham. Yet.

"You have no choice," Bonham said. "She'll be fine as long as you don't follow us. As soon as I get clean away, I'll release her. You have my word."

"The word of a thief. What good is that?"

"I knew it!" Bonham hissed. "Your wife denied the possibility that you had caught on to my financial indiscretions, but once I saw her notes, I knew she was lying."

"I didn't catch on to anything," Sheridan said. "Vanessa did. She's a clever sort, my wife."

"She'll be a *dead* clever sort if you don't let us leave. Now!" He started dragging her around the desk, while Sheridan's heart dropped into his stomach.

"You're not leaving here with her," Sheridan said, thrusting his hand in his fall to seize his pistol handle. Best to be prepared for anything. "Take me instead. That will make it more likely that you escape. And it will drive a stake through Mother's heart. That's what you want, isn't it? To hurt my mother the way she hurt your family?"

As Vanessa's eyes widened, Bonham scowled. "What do *you* know about it? You've never suffered a day in your life."

"No? I lost my father and my uncle all in the same year, thanks to you. So I know quite a bit about suffering."

Someone burst through the study door behind Sheridan. "William!" a voice cried. "What on earth are you doing?"

It was Mother, damn it. "Get out of here," Sheridan said, never taking his eyes off Bonham. "I'll handle this."

"I'm not leaving," she said stoutly. "Not until you tell me what's going on."

Sheridan debated how much to reveal. But she might know something the rest of them didn't, something to help save Vanessa. "Bonham killed your husbands," Sheridan said. "And Uncle Armie and Elias."

"Don't be ridiculous," Mother said. "He would never . . . He couldn't . . ." She trailed off as she realized Bonham hadn't defended himself.

"He's not the man you think he is," Sheridan said. "You would have known him as Henry Davenport."

"*Matthew's* brother?" she whispered.

"Yes. So you knew Henry, too, did you?" Sheridan asked.

"I never met him, no, but I heard Matthew speak of him. Matthew said he was quite clever."

Bonham scowled at Sheridan. "How did you find out my real name?"

"I didn't. My brother-in-law did. Once he realized you'd made yourself over, the rest was easy. You didn't hide your tracks nearly as well as you thought."

Bonham fixed Sheridan's mother with a stare that would freeze blood. "Thanks to you, I lost everything, you know. Matthew killed himself, and my entire family was ruined, all because you thought him beneath you."

"That's not true!" Mother protested. "I would happily have married Matthew if I could have! But Mama had already convinced Papa to betroth me to Grey's father in exchange for forgiveness of certain debts. They told me if I didn't marry the duke, Papa would go to debtors' prison. I was young, and I . . . didn't understand I had a choice."

"Liar!" Bonham spat, his face contorted with rage. "You broke Matthew's heart. You told him you didn't want him."

Mother glared at him. "By the time Matthew proposed, I was already betrothed! And my fiancé threatened to kill Matthew if I so much as breathed a word about the circumstances of our impending marriage." Her breath caught in her throat. "It didn't matter. Matthew died anyway."

"He didn't *die*. He killed himself, you . . . you harpy! You might as well have tied the rope around his throat yourself." Bonham's pistol hand shook.

Sheridan's blood ran cold. If that arse harmed Vanessa— "See here, Bonham, whatever your conflicts with my mother, my wife has done nothing to you. She doesn't deserve to die. Take me instead."

"The hell I will." Bonham glanced from Sheridan to his mother. "If I take anyone in exchange, it will be the dowager duchess."

God, the man's hatred of Mother went beyond all bounds.

"I don't understand, Will— I mean, Henry," Mother said. "How could you pretend to be my friend this past year or more when secretly you despised me so?"

Sheridan wondered that himself. Perhaps Mother, as Bonham's "friend," could convince the arse to let Vanessa go.

If only the bastard would move his damned pistol. Sheridan was more than ready to shoot.

Gwyn burst into the room. "Mother!" she cried, trying to tug their mother from the room. "Come, we must go. Let Sheridan take care of this."

"So," Sheridan said to Bonham, "there's four of us here now. Do you plan to kill us all? Because I swear that if you shoot Vanessa, you're a dead man." He stepped closer to the desk. "I will throttle you before you can even reload."

Having seen Sheridan on the move—and his wife in the room—Joshua loomed up closer to the French doors, making sure not to be directly behind Bonham in case Sheridan got off a shot.

Gwyn at least knew to ignore the sight of her husband where he wasn't supposed to be, but their mother was startled and clapped her hand over her mouth to keep from crying out. As Bonham had said, he was no fool. When he saw her reaction, he turned toward the glass doors, and the pistol left Vanessa's head for a few precious seconds.

Sheridan knew that might be the only chance he got, and apparently Vanessa read his intention, because in that moment, she twisted away from Bonham and his pistol. And Sheridan took his chance and shot.

The bullet went clean into Bonham's head.

Then everything happened at once. Bonham crumpled to the floor. Joshua burst through the French doors and used his cane to sweep Bonham's still-loaded pistol away from the man before bending to check Bonham's pulse. And Vanessa threw herself at Sheridan.

"Oh, darling, I'm so sorry," she whispered. "I didn't

realize he had sneaked in until it was too late to hide my notes, and he'd—"

"It's fine, sweetheart. Nothing is your fault. You did well, and it's over now. Finally, it's over." He grabbed her by the shoulders and ran his gaze over her. "He didn't hurt you, did he? You're all right?"

"Of course I'm all right." She cast him a tremulous smile. "I'm with you, aren't I?"

"You will always be with me, if I have anything to say about it."

Joshua came up to them and murmured, "He's dead. I'll send for Fitzgerald. I'll explain everything to him. You might want to take Vanessa out of here, though." He glanced behind them. "It looks like Gwyn has already whisked your mother away."

With a nod, Sheridan looked over to find Vanessa staring back at Bonham with horror on her face. "Come, sweetheart, let's go outside."

In the courtyard, she could see the winter roses and the ivy and all the things that made her happy. And he could keep an eye out for when Lucius Fitzgerald, under-secretary to the War Secretary, arrived and needed to speak to him. Thank God for Joshua and his connections in government.

As soon as they were out there, he caught her to him and kissed her forehead and cheeks and every part of her face dear to him, which was pretty much every part of her face. "I love you, my sweet, brave duchess. I should have said it before I had to face the possibility of losing you, but—"

"You love me?" she said, her eyes alight. "You mean that?"

He smiled. "Cross my heart and hope not to die. At least not until we're old and gray."

"Then I suppose I can admit I love you, too, with all my heart and mind and body." She kissed him just long enough to have him craving her again.

But when he tried to deepen the kiss, she pulled away. "What about Helene?" she asked hesitantly.

"What about her?"

"You said you didn't want to love again. Because of her."

"To quote my brilliant sister, 'You don't choose love; love chooses *you*. You have no say or recourse, and when it happens, resistance is pointless.' I've been fighting hard to resist you, with absolutely no success."

He tipped up her chin, emotion clogging his throat. "In the past few days I've learned that the past shouldn't eclipse the future or one ends up like Bonham—stuck, which is a dangerous place to be. I've been stuck in the past for far too long. I loved Helene once, true, but I've finally put her back where she belongs. You're my present and my future, the woman I want to have children with, the woman I love. You're my rising sun and my harvest moon. You're everything I need, and nothing I have ever had. Until now."

Her flirtatious smile snagged his heart. He'd thought he might never see it again.

But before he could kiss her, she straightened his cravat in a very wifely way. "It appears I was telling the truth, after all, when I informed Grey a year ago of my interest in a poet. You are more poet than I realized, my love."

"That only proves how you underestimate me." He

cocked up one eyebrow. "I am not merely a duke under the covers, you know."

"No, indeed. You're also an excellent shot and a fine lover. Although I haven't had enough experience in the latter to be sure. Perhaps we could use a bit more practice later, after Mr. Fitzgerald has come and gone?"

His blood heated just at the thought. "You know what they all say, my dear wife. Practice makes perfect."

Epilogue

December 1809

Vanessa didn't know if she would survive the Christmas house party at Armitage Hall. According to Sheridan, it had been *years* since anyone had contemplated such a gathering. For Vanessa, having never hosted one so large or even attended one with forty guests, the sheer size of it was overwhelming.

While most of them were family, she and Sheridan had chosen a few of the dowager duchess's close friends to cheer her up after her shock at discovering that Mr. Bonham had been systematically picking off the people she loved (and some she didn't). Vanessa's tactic must have worked because the dowager duchess had been eager to help, and more than eager to chat with the guests.

The Enceinte Trio, as Vanessa had privately been calling the three pregnant women in the family, had initially vowed to help, too. Then Beatrice's baby had been born three weeks ago, and Gwyn's *twins* had been born last week, and that only left Cass, who, fortunately, wasn't due until sometime next year. Vanessa's sister-in-law Cass had a talent for arranging and organizing, so Vanessa had been relying on her quite a bit. Besides which, Cass and Heywood lived right up the road, so she and Vanessa were rapidly becoming friends.

Cass came up to where Vanessa sat at a table in the drawing room, putting together kissing boughs. She wanted lots of them, one for every hall and public room in the manor. "Lady Hornsby wants to be in a bedchamber that adjoins Lord Lisbourne's. Are you fine with that? Also, our mother-in-law has put your uncle in the room adjoining hers, if that's all right." Cass arched an eyebrow. "At the rate we're going, your party may end up in all the gossip rags."

"I don't care. And it doesn't matter to me who adjoins whom, as long as they don't ask me to change the sheets when they leave, if you know what I mean."

A laugh burst out of Cass. "You are quite an outrageous lady, aren't you?"

"I try. Why do you think Saint Sheridan married me? He needs someone to poke holes in his halo on occasion." Vanessa paused in her work to examine her map of the house. "Now I have to move other people around. Did your aunt and your cousin come? I was planning to put Lady Hornsby in this darling little suite in the east wing, but with her changing rooms it would be perfect for *them,* although I would swear it hadn't been cleaned in years, until yesterday."

"No, they couldn't attend." Cass shook her head. "Kitty is throwing a party of her own in London, and I shudder to think how it will turn out. She's not . . . adept at these things like you and I."

"We're here!" a cheery voice sounded behind her.

"Unfashionably early, of course, but we thought we could help."

Vanessa jumped up and whirled around. "Gwyn! No one told me you were coming. You just had twins—what are you doing traveling? And Beatrice! You're here!" She threw her arms about them both. "I can't believe you came!" Then she pulled back to frown at them. "You shouldn't have come. Are you certain you're both up to it?"

"Do you really think we would miss your big affair?" Beatrice said. "Not on your life. Besides, our husbands have been driving us mad worrying about our health. I am tired of drinking possets. I can't wait to have some of the estate perry you brew up so well."

"I don't brew it up," Vanessa said dryly, "although from the way Sheridan extols its virtues, you'd think he squeezed the pears himself."

"What's wrong with a good posset?" Cass said. "I like possets myself. We received a posset set for our wedding, and our cook uses it quite a bit."

"If I want medicine, I'll take medicine," Gwyn said, "and if I want an alcoholic beverage or dessert, I'll drink some wine or eat a syllabub. I do not want my medicine and beverages combined."

"And while I don't have Gwyn's objection to them, I don't want a posset every day, twice a day, trust me." Beatrice took a deep breath. "It's so lovely to be home again. Or as close to home as I've been in a while. Have you decided what to do about the dower house? Grey is happy to do whatever you and Sheridan need."

"I think the dowager duchess is actually going to live there." Vanessa smiled. "Which is wonderful because that means she'll be nearby. Of course, my uncle might end up having a say in that. . . ."

"That would be wonderful. I like your uncle." Gwyn scanned the drawing room. "Where's Olivia?"

Vanessa laughed. "She's probably off somewhere trying to turn perry into wine or using ink and sulfuric acid to melt iron. Heaven only knows. That woman loves doing her experiments, and since she and Thorn arrived yesterday, she's probably already in the midst of one."

"Well," Gwyn said confidentially, "we brought her a gift."

"What sort of gift?" Cass asked.

"You'll find out when Joshua and I give it to her," Gwyn said. "What's this you're working on? Can we help?"

"I would certainly welcome help from all of you," Vanessa said. "I've been making kissing boughs for all the halls and parlors and the dining room and the breakfast room. I still have about ten left to put together."

"Good Lord, that's a great many kissing boughs." Beatrice took a seat beside Vanessa and picked up a piece of ribbon. "But I do enjoy making them."

"It sounds like fun." Gwyn took a seat on the other side of the table next to where Cass had been working earlier. "But I've never done one, so you'll have to show me how. And where are the men, anyway? I wish to see my brothers, the scamps who haven't written me a single letter since last I saw them."

"They're staying out of the way," Vanessa said, "like the clever men know to do."

The women all laughed.

"They should be coming in any minute now," Cass

said and joined them at the table. "They're off shooting partridges. They do love their guns."

"And their partridges," Beatrice said. "Or at least Joshua always did. You have no idea how many partridges I have picked shot out of for my brother. That is definitely one advantage to marrying a duke."

"Fortunately," Gwyn said, "I do *not* have to pick shot out of partridges for Joshua. My husband knows better than to ask."

"I would hate picking shot out of anything," Vanessa said hoarsely. "It was bad enough just to witness Mr. Bonham being shot with a pistol."

Gwyn put an arm around her and squeezed. "I completely understand since I witnessed that dreadful fellow Lionel being shot, too." She grimaced. "Although honestly I would have preferred shooting him myself after what he put me through."

"Not to mention what he put my brother through," Beatrice said. "Getting back to Mr. Bonham, how is our mother-in-law faring? At some point, we all thought she might marry the arse."

"Beatrice!" Cass said, shocked at her use of the word *arse.*

"What? Don't tell me you haven't wanted to use that word in reference to him at least once in the past month."

"Well . . ." Cass said.

"The dowager duchess has been rather quiet about the whole matter," Vanessa said, to avoid any more talk about cursing, "but not to any worrisome degree. I think he brought up a great many old memories about her first love and her first terrible marriage. Sorry, Beatrice. I know the man was still Grey's father."

"I don't mind, and I doubt Grey would either. If Mr.

Bonham hadn't poisoned his father, none of the rest of us would probably have ever met."

"Or been born." Gwyn frowned. "Oh, let's not talk about that."

"I do hope that the money he stole will go back to his clients," Beatrice said. "From what I read in the papers, he wasn't just embezzling from the Armitage family."

"Unfortunately, that has proved to be correct," Vanessa said as she worked. "And in a couple of cases, he actually forged the client's signature, so if he'd lived, he would have been hanged for his crimes anyway, and that is before his murders are even considered."

"Joshua told me that those murders," Gwyn said, "if taken singly, probably couldn't have been proven sufficiently to see him punished for them, but considered together would have almost certainly resulted in a conviction. How clever of Sheridan to have recognized the 'accidents' as murders in the first place. If not for him . . ."

"That leech would still be trying to destroy the family," Vanessa said. "I hope you all will give credit where credit is due."

"I'll be the first to do so," Beatrice said. "But is Sheridan safe now? I assumed no one would prosecute him for Mr. Bonham's death, but I wasn't sure. I tried to find out if they had from Joshua, but he didn't want to talk about it while I was enceinte, and he's the worst letter writer in the history of letter writing, especially when it comes to writing his sister."

"The magistrate deemed it a justifiable homicide," Vanessa said, "since Sheridan was protecting me from almost certain death."

She would never forget the look of terror in his eyes

that night when he'd first seen her in Mr. Bonham's clutches. His expression had held such stark determination to save her that she'd known he would do whatever he must to rescue her from harm. Remembering that expression on his face still warmed her heart.

"As for the money," she went on, "that's all tied up in legal issues, but if there is a settlement in the civil case against Mr. Bonham's estate, then we may see some financial relief from it, especially since he has no family to inherit. I'm systematically going through the accounts right now to determine where the worst losses are for use in the civil case." She tied a piece of wire on the end of a mistletoe branch. "Fortunately, Sheridan is convinced that without Mr. Bonham misleading the family, doctoring the books to cover his perfidy, and stealing our money, we can recoup even without a settlement, and I share his optimism."

Cass surveyed them all. "Do you think Mr. Bonham was really trying to court the dowager duchess? I mean, if there was no one to inherit his ill-gotten gains, why keep on fighting?"

"You weren't there, Cass." Vanessa shuddered, remembering Mr. Bonham's vile words to the dowager duchess. "I think if he could have killed her right there, he would have. He wanted to destroy her and all of her descendants. And if it had taken sucking the financial marrow out of the Armitage family, he would have done so."

"Then thank heaven he's gone," Gwyn said brightly. "And I do not wish to give him any power beyond the grave by discussing this one minute more. Agreed?"

"Agreed," Vanessa said wholeheartedly. "Now, I must hear about the babies. Did you bring them all? Did you bring any?"

"They're all with us," Gwyn said, tying a ribbon into a bow about a sprig of cedar, "mostly because both Beatrice and I are doing our own breastfeeding."

"There will be no wet nurse for little Maurice," Beatrice said stoutly.

"Nor for little Isabel and Andrew," Gwyn said. "Even if it kills me to feed two of them. And it just might."

"They won't be any trouble, though," Beatrice said. "We brought our nursemaids."

"I appreciate that," Vanessa said. "And that's why we opened up and thoroughly cleaned the nursery, just in case."

Olivia marched into the drawing room at that moment. "Vanessa, do you have any aqua regia?" When the group burst into laughter, she paused. "Oh, everyone is here. How lovely!"

"I told you she'd be doing an experiment," Vanessa said to the others before turning to Olivia. "And what do you mean to do with aqua regia, if I had some, which I don't?"

"I mean to dissolve gold. Mama doesn't believe it's possible."

"Do you *have* gold you can spare to dissolve?"

"No, but Mama has a broken chain I could use." Olivia sighed. "Although actually, it's probably not wise to do it without laboratory equipment. You don't have any flasks and such here, do you?"

When that last was said with a hopeful intonation, Vanessa shook her head, trying to contain her amusement. "The only flasks you'll find on the estate are the ones the men have, filled with brandy and taken for their shooting expedition."

"How much would you wager that both the flasks *and*

the game bags will be brought back empty?" Beatrice said, nudging Gwyn.

"*My* husband will bring back a full game bag, I assure you," Cass said.

"Well, we all know that Thorn won't have shot anything," Olivia said and took a seat at the table on the other side of Vanessa, "and he does love a bit of brandy, so I'll wager one broken gold chain that my husband is the most likely to bring back an empty flask and an empty game bag."

"I'll wager one of the twins that Sheridan brings back a full game bag," Gwyn said.

They gaped at her.

"I'm *joking*. Well, mostly. Those two don't even sleep at the same time. And have you ever tried breastfeeding two babes at once? It's not easy, I'll tell you that."

"Is my wife complaining about breastfeeding again?" Joshua said from the doorway.

"Always," Gwyn said as her husband walked over to kiss her head. "So should we give Olivia her present now?"

"Wait until Thorn is here."

As if the words had magically conjured him up, Thorn said from the doorway, "Do I hear my name being taken in vain?"

The room instantly filled with men in greatcoats stamping to get blood back into their cold feet and jockeying for position by the fire. Thank goodness Vanessa hadn't let the servants roll out the good carpet until *after* the men finished their shooting.

Grey entered in the midst of everything. "Sheridan, where do you keep your brandy?"

"Here, have some of mine," Thorn said and handed his flask to Grey.

"I guess I am the proud owner of a broken chain," Gwyn told Olivia.

"Grey hasn't drunk from it yet," Olivia said.

Sure enough, he opened it and tipped it back, then scowled at Thorn. "It's empty."

"I know," Thorn said, smirking at his older brother, who threw the flask at him.

Thorn ducked, and the flask hit Sheridan in the back.

"What the hell?" Sheridan cried and tossed the flask back at Thorn, who ducked again.

The flask hit the table, dislodging a half-completed kissing bough. Just then, the dowager duchess came in and cried, "Boys, boys!! Behave yourselves!"

Her sons stopped and then burst into laughter. Meanwhile, their wives just rolled their eyes. Gwyn gave Joshua a look, and he nodded. So she rose and tapped on the table with the flask until she had everyone's attention. "My husband and I have something to give Olivia."

Thorn looked at Olivia, who shrugged.

"It's not Christmas yet," Sheridan said.

"Then we'll call it an early Christmas present," Gwyn said. "Joshua? Do you want to do the honors?"

Now they could see he was carrying something in his left hand. It looked like a newspaper. "This is a very special copy of *The Chronicle of the Arts and Sciences*."

Thorn caught on first and began to grin. But as Joshua came over to give it to her, Olivia looked bewildered. "Why, thank you," she said and put it in her lap. "I do enjoy that paper."

"Dearling," Thorn said, "open it to the science section and read it."

When she did so, she gasped. "They took it! They took

my article!" She jumped up to hug Joshua. "Oh, thank you, thank you!" She ran around the table to hug Gwyn.

"Well?" Sheridan said, exchanging a fond look with Vanessa. "At least tell us the title."

She held the paper in front of her and read aloud. "'The Use of Hydrogen Sulfide and Hydrochloric Acid Forensically to Detect the Presence of Arsenic in a Corpse.' By the Duchess of Thornstock." Then, in typical Olivia fashion, she beamed at everyone. "Thank you, everyone, for helping bring me to this moment."

Everyone clapped and cheered at her success, which brought tears to Vanessa's eyes. The family had been through so much, and yet they could still care so deeply for each other . . . and each other's spouses.

Olivia walked over to tug on Thorn's coat sleeve. "Now tell them *your* news."

"Nonsense," Thorn said, in an uncharacteristic gesture of humility. "It's your moment."

"Then I will tell them," Olivia said. "Thorn has written a play. It's a very clever, very witty tale of two warring playwrights. And it will be produced under his own name."

"So," Vanessa called out, "you're not publishing under Juncker's name anymore?" She and Sheridan had scarcely been married a week when her husband had told her about Juncker's and Thorn's "arrangement."

"How did you know—" Thorn scowled at Sheridan. "You told her."

"Only because I realized that everyone else already knows," Sheridan said.

"Mother?" Thorn asked.

"Sorry, son, but all it took was me seeing one play to know you wrote it," she said.

"Grey?" Thorn asked.

Grey laughed. "Did you really think Beatrice and I didn't notice your behavior that day we discussed 'Juncker's' plays in the carriage?"

"And you already know that *I* knew," Gwyn said. "Which means Joshua knows."

"Good Lord," Thorn said, shoving his fingers through his hair. "Juncker is going to kill me."

"You pay him," Joshua said. "He shouldn't care."

"Exactly. I am his main source of income. And he really likes being the author of the Felix plays."

"I suspect he'll recover," Olivia said with a laugh. "Last time I talked to him, he was working on something new. Besides, we're your family. We'll keep your secret."

When Thorn eyed her askance, everyone else laughed.

"Where *is* Juncker, anyway?" Vanessa asked. "He was invited."

"Oh, I forgot to tell you," Sheridan said. "He couldn't come until closer to Christmas."

Vanessa narrowed her gaze on her husband.

Sheridan lifted his hands. "I swear! He won't be here until next week."

Grey approached to stare down at the table. "What *is* all this, anyway?"

"We're making kissing boughs," Olivia said as she returned to take her seat at the table. "Vanessa wants them everywhere."

"Good idea," Thorn said, and came over to sit next to his wife. "I'm all for the kissing boughs. So how does this work?"

"*You're* going to make a kissing bough," Vanessa's mother-in-law said skeptically.

"Why not?"

The other men looked at each other. Grey said, "Why not, indeed?"

Then they all crowded in around the table with their wives and started picking up sprigs and wire and ribbon. They were short a chair, so Vanessa rose and said, "I have some hostess matters I must take care of anyway."

Besides, she could feel the tears gathering in her eyes, and she didn't want to embarrass herself in front of the others. She hurried from the room but didn't get very far down the hall before Sheridan came out after her.

"Vanessa, are you all right?" he asked when he caught her blotting her eyes with her handkerchief.

"I'm fine," she managed to get out through her tears. She came back to where he was standing just outside the drawing room. She looked inside. "It's just so beautiful. I've never had a family like this."

"And now you do," he said, smiling as he took her hand in his.

She blotted her eyes some more. "You don't mind having to endure Mama for my sake?"

"Not a bit. You're worth it."

They stood a moment, absorbing the scene.

"You were right, you know," he went on. "Depriving oneself of love to avoid pain is indeed like refusing to ride for fear of falling off. Some things are just worth whatever pain or discomfort they give. Because what they offer is better than we can imagine."

And as he slipped his arm about her waist, she smiled at her new family.

Definitely better.

Be sure not to miss Juncker's story in
"When We Finally Kiss Goodnight,"
Sabrina Jeffries's novella, included in . . .

A YULETIDE KISS

Three holiday novellas by
New York Times *bestselling authors*

Sabrina Jeffries

Madeline Hunter

Mary Jo Putney

On sale in the fall of 2021

Connect with U s

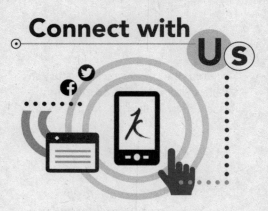

Visit us online at
KensingtonBooks.com
to read more from your favorite authors, see books
by series, view reading group guides, and more.

for sneak peeks, chances to win books and prize packs,
and to share your thoughts with other readers.

facebook.com/kensingtonpublishing
twitter.com/kensingtonbooks

Tell us what you think!

To share your thoughts, submit a review,
or sign up for our eNewsletters, please visit:
KensingtonBooks.com/TellUs.